Justicar Jhee and the House of Sorrows

-The Justicar Jhee Mysteries Book 3-

by Trevol Swift

To my secret weapon Adam.
To all my family's past and present service members. Thank you.

Join the Swiftnesse Community

Join the Swiftnesse Readers' Club to get a free copy of **Justicar Jhee and the Spectral Armada**, receive special offers, and hear about future books!

http://swiftnesse.com/spectral/

1

~

Living History

A seaweed-paper planner with several dates circled and a note reading "Pick one" awaited Jhee in her favorite chair. Jhee placed the planner on the end table and plopped into the cozy chair by the fireplace of their townhouse. The note had been written in Kanto's precise ornate hand. Both note and planner bore matching amethyst scalloped designs. The dates, Jhee presumed, were for counseling sessions. Kanto had been getting treatment for the lingering effects of his ordeal at the abbey. The process had prompted him to get on Shep and Jhee about their own neglected mental health and hygiene. Jhee admitted with a veteran's service center so nearby she had no excuse not to avail herself of her earned aid. But she had so much work to do between the academy, the law clinic, and consultant work.

Shep settled into the cushioned chair beside hers. He plopped a similar planner on the end table with hers.

"Where did he leave yours?" Jhee asked.

"On my exercise equipment. I have to give him points for persistence and knowing his targets."

"Could he be right? Perhaps we need to talk more about our experiences during the Flower Wars."

I

"Or how close we came to losing Mirrei."

"I'm not sure if I need the extra stress at the moment."

"Right or wrong, we agreed to be more open about our service, among other things."

Jhee rubbed the bridge of her nose. "I know. We should have just said 'no' if we didn't want to do it. Part of me wants to do it."

"And part of you wants to let the Trench swallow the anchors of the past."

"Yes."

Jhee and Shep brushed *escae*, the four-pointed, iridescent Makers' mark Water Folk bore in the center of their forehead. She briefly touched the scar that ran through Shep's right eye, which made it dimmer than the other. They nestled back into their chairs.

Between counseling and the reconciliation and living history projects, Jhee and Shep had over-committed on a topic they rarely spoke of in-depth: their service. Had keeping their experiences to themselves been proper or had doing so made it worse? Jhee extended her hand into the space between their chairs. Shep clasped it and stroked her knuckles with his thumb. Not long after, humming announced Kanto's return.

"*Denme*," Kanto said and squeezed Shep's shoulder. Then he planted a kiss on Jhee's lips. "*Denbe*. I see you both got my little reminders."

Kanto draped himself in his fireside seat opposite theirs. The embroidery on his amethyst and citrine robes echoed the decoration of the planner and note.

"Subtle," Shep said.

"Never," Kanto said. "So?"

"Give us a moment, we're still coming up with excuses to put it off."

Kanto grinned and shook his head, then hopped to his feet. "You two are incorrigible. Dearest wife, dearest brother-groom, when you come back from your night out, I expect the most amazing tale ever of why two are breaking your promise to me."

Shep grimaced. Jhee took a breath. Kanto knew how to hit them where it mattered. Shep and Jhee seized their respective calendars, circled their dates with finger quills Kanto provided, and handed them in to him.

Kanto peered at the calendars and nodded. "Excellent. Enjoy your evening out."

Once Kanto left, Shep and Jhee turned to each other.

"Drench, he's good," Shep said and raised an eyebrow.

They laughed.

For their night out, Jhee and Shep chose a gourmet restaurant a short transport ride away.

"Elaborate about what we ordered," Jhee said.

"Green beans almondine with a light caramelized butter glaze served alongside pan-seared whale-auroch with water chestnuts in oyster sauce with just a hint of truffle oil."

"Land meat? Are you sure about this?" Jhee asked.

"Trust me," Shep, her senior spouse, said. "The chef gives it a quick sear to seal in the flavor, then covers it just slightly with juices and simmers it in a covered pan."

The waiter arrived with their meals in short order. Shep took the eating utensils—knife and nail pike—sliced a piece of the red meat, and used his index finger to spear it with his nail pike. His teeth clinked on the pike as he slid the juicy morsel into his mouth. Jhee tensed and held her breath. As she watched for signs of an involuntary shift, her fingers hovered over the failsafe sigil on her arm. It remained cold and inert.

Shep swallowed. "Delicious."

He sliced another piece, then held it out to her. As she took a bite, they held each other's gaze. The tender whale-auroch had just the right amount of sear and seasoning.

Jhee had not had meat this rare in so long. She had indulged when she could during her stay in Galleon City, but Mirrei's ethical concerns put the damper on any enjoyment from the experience. Jhee found it hard to savor the meat while her youngest spouse watched with mild distaste.

"The trick to the perfect plate is not dissimilar to the trick to a perfect pour." Shep shimmered his amber, glowing eyes at Jhee. "Then there is the pairing of a wine to complement a brilliant meal. They have a lovely tasting selection for each course. They also have an exclusive house red I wanted to sample."

After the meal and several glasses of excellent wine were consumed without incident, Jhee's worries had dissipated. Despite the location, she and Shep indulged in hand-holding and a few kisses. Mere months ago, as a field Justicar in a rural district, she would have been scandalized to publicly carry on in such a way. In the capital as an academic, though, no one batted an eye at her behavior.

A few doors down, they visited a family-run zoba tea place crammed next to a darkened shop offering tailoring and shoe repair. Their introduction to the tart and tangy beverage was easily one of their best discoveries since moving here to the capital. The capital rarely seemed to sleep. Even now, pedestrians and transports moved by them often. This activity and closeness was a contrast to the ocean expanses of their former home in the Far Reaches. Though, when a Storm Wall fueled gale hit the Reaches, it made even full-sun's bustle appear tame.

Jhee swirled the zoba berries at the bottom of her lidded, clear tea bottle.

"How fortunate I am to be surrounded by such experts with respect to food and drink."

"Want to know another aspect of the perfect meal?"

She passed the bottle over to Shep, so he might have the last sip. "What?"

"The right companion." The smoldering tint to Shep's amber eyes suggested they should pay and make their way home. On the sidewalk, Shep swept Jhee into his arms and planted a kiss on her in full view of Makers and masses alike.

A man with a messenger bag and delivery logo on his jacket jostled them as he passed.

"Oi, sorry fel," the messenger said and patted Shep's robe a couple times.

As the man walked on, Shep immediately checked for his wallet, keys, and digital conch communicator. Jhee and Shep both recognized the old pickpocketing ploy. Shep removed his hand from his inner pocket and gazed at a glinting object in his palm. The command sigil on Jhee's arm switched from normal to burning hot.

Shep bounded after the messenger then grabbed him by the lapels and pinned him against the building, all with frightening speed. "What is this? Who sent you?"

"A *gul* just paid me to plant it on you as a gag."

"Who?"

"A gul. I don't know—an older lady with graying hair, maybe a little nervous."

"Shep, enough. Let him go."

Jhee got Shep to release the messenger. Shep held up his hands and backed away a few steps. While he paced like a caged animal, Jhee checked the messenger for injuries. The messenger had sustained some slight scratches and a bump on the head. Jhee apologized and also slipped the messenger a twenty-shell note.

The messenger rolled his head from side-to-side while rubbing his neck. He whispered to Jhee, "Your mister's got quite a temper there. Maybe he should see someone about that."

Shep fixed his good eye on the messenger to let him know Shep had heard that. The young man swallowed and scurried off. Jhee waited until the tempo of Shep's pacing slowed.

"Mind telling me what that was about?" Jhee asked.

Shep opened his palm to reveal a miniature representation of a kalacha war club, the preferred weapon of the berserker regiments. "Someone has a poor sense of humor."

"The berserker corps regiment pin. Who would send that to you?"

"I don't know." Shep's nostrils flared, and his eyes narrowed at something over Jhee's head, but he did not go on full alert. "Someone's there. The scent seems familiar."

Jhee turned. "Who's there? Show yourself."

The War Buddy

"Hey, *guls*, I see you got my message," a hesitant voice said. The figure of their old war buddy Ursula emerged from a shadowed doorway. She wore her hair in a slick ponytail. While her jacket was too baggy and loose-fitting, her other clothes appeared well-fitted, new, and clean, unlike the last time Jhee saw her some years ago. Overall, Ursula came across less frantic than their previous meeting. However, her gaze never settled in one place for long.

"Ursula!" Shep swept her up in a big hug and spun her around. "Urlibird! You old sneak."

"Sorry if my message upset you."

"You could have delivered it yourself."

Ursula shrugged and kept her gaze on a constant move. "Too many people. I'm not doing good with crowds these days."

"Understood."

"You two, though, are looking good."

"It's all surface waves, we assure you," Jhee said. She and Ursula hugged. "How are you doing?"

"You know. Hanging in there."

"Come on. Let's all go for a walk. We can catch up."

"Sure."

They grabbed another round of zoba teas then went for a stroll through the park along the lakebed. Few people would be there this time of night. They reminisced. Several times Ursula paused as if she wanted to say more.

"I owe you, Urli," Shep said. "What's going on? Why did you have a regiment pin planted on me?"

"I had to see your reaction. It was stupid. I didn't mean to upset you."

"Forgiven. I can't count the number of times you saved my skin over the years."

"Or you mine," Ursula answered. "So much has happened since we last spoke. I wouldn't even know where to start."

"Whatever you need, ask," Shep said.

Shep handed Ursula back the regiment pin, but she refused it.

"Keep it as a reminder," Ursula said.

Shep glanced back at Jhee. He frowned. That sounded like "goodbye" to him as well.

Ursula stopped to give them a long once over. "I still can't get over how good, how together, you two look," she said.

"You know how it is," Jhee replied, "the cozy life of an academic and civil servant. What are you doing for work these days?"

"A little this. A little that. I'm in a similar line as you were, Sniffer, private inspector work, and the like."

"My field work isn't so far in the past. Is there anything else we can do for you? Do you need a place to stay?"

Ursula smiled. "No, I got that covered. That's just it. For the first time in a long time, I can see a way through. I'm here to check in on you two. Thanks for the offer, though."

Shep pulled up his collar. "We're good."

"I guess that means you found your way through, too. The last of the unit, except Cap. It's been so long since more than two of us have been in the same place together."

Their walking slowed. Jhee allowed them to get a half a step ahead. Jhee had been their unit's liaison and wasn't a berserker, a war-trained full skin slipper, like Shep, Ursula, and the others. She accounted it an honor they viewed her as part of their unit if only partially.

Ursula glanced around her. "I have to get going."

"Make for Make," Shep said, invoking the tradition of hospitality in exchange for the berserker pin. "Take our private c-cards. Contact us if you need anything. Please."

Jhee handed over a numbered credential card to Shep, which he put together with his and a hand-carved shark's tooth. He touched them to his *esca*, Makers' mark, before presenting them to Ursula.

Ursula took the pin back long enough to touch it to her esca then stuffed Shep's offering in her coat. She turned to Jhee and pulled an object from the devotional pouch at her waist, likely Maker geld. Jhee dug out a geld coin she had stamped with the gear emblem of Jhee's path, Mechanism, which she brought to her forehead. Perhaps the Prime Maker's design would guide Ursula to the other side of her difficulties unscathed.

After Jhee and Ursula exchanged coins, Ursula seized her in an embrace.

"The Makers have blessed you. Don't forget that." Ursula refused to release Jhee immediately. "You enjoy the rest of your evening," Ursula said.

At last, Ursula released her. Jhee examined the small, smooth object she had been given. It turned out to be a circular, hardwood disc carved with the batfish or maye. While Jhee did not remember which specific Makers Ursula honored, she knew it wasn't the Maye King or Queen. The maye, though, was Ursula's preferred berserker form.

"Urli?" Jhee began.

Ursula had already slipped away. Jhee and Shep tried to locate her but lost her tracks by the lake along with her scent.

At home, Jhee and Shep concluded the evening in her bedchamber. Before turning in, Shep went downstairs to grab them some iced sweet-berries and cream. Jhee tidied up their discarded clothes along with others she had strewn about while getting ready for dinner. A shiny, jet black data shell clattered to the ground. It may have been one of hers or her students from the legal clinic. She threw it in her valise for later. Jhee took out Ursula's hardwood disc with the maye and wondered.

~

The Curious Academic

Days later, Jhee still puzzled over Ursula's visit and hardwood disc carved with the maye. The batfish or batwing maye was a sizable cartilaginous fish similar to a shark. Ursula used to leave this symbol to mark trails when scouting. Ursula had marked a trail for her, but to what? A few long-tides—weeks—passed, and Jhee all but forgot about it. She settled back into her regular routine of lecturing, advising the Academy's legal clinic, and giving arcane forensic seminars.

"We conclude from these records that the person was murdered," Jhee said. "Or more precisely, there is a high likelihood of their having been poisoned. And that concludes our virtual autopsy. Questions?"

Jhee signaled her teaching assistant to increase the lecture hall's lighting. Several hands in the arcane forensic seminar raised. Nevis, her colleague from the local Justicar's office who had been sent to evaluate the symposium, gave a grudging nod from the front row then scribbled on her evaluation sheet.

After the seminar, Jhee checked the time and gathered up her materials and slides. Plenty of time remained for her consult with the imperators and then refresh herself before tonight's evening out with Shep. In her haste, Jhee knocked over her valise and lecture materials. As she gathered up her fallen valise contents and slides, the jet black data shell she found the other day caught her eye. Following several failed attempts to decrypt it at home, Jhee thought to have someone at the office or clinic try. She stooped to pick it up. A floorboard creaked on the other side of the lecture bench.

Jhee grabbed the data shell and straightened up. A Water Folk individual standing by the lecture bench leaped back. She eyed Jhee and waited, hat clutched in her hands, looking sheepish. "Begging your pardon, Magistrate."

"Did you have questions about the seminar?" Jhee asked.

"Nay." Jhee gave the stranger a once over. Her clothes were threadbare. She continually twisted and worried the brim of the hat she held around in a circle. A sharp breath of the sea wafted from them. This was not a typical student or attendee. "This ain't about tome learning. You sees, a mutual friend gave me this card. She reckoned you might could help me."

The slight accent and pale body hair were peculiar to longshoremen and sailors from the Dales nicknamed sea dogs. The old sailor handed Jhee a credential card. After a quick inspection, Jhee realized the sequential number matched the one she had given Ursula.

"I have to head to my legal clinic. Walk with me." Jhee grabbed her valise, and she headed across the quad with the sailor. "What can I help you with?"

"I suspect this sea dog what I know be a med divisioner," she said using the sea dog dialect.

"I see," Jhee said cautiously. By "med divisioner," she meant a member of the Medical Protectorate. Between renewed interest in the Flower Wars and Medical Protectorate's recently uncovered unethical experiments, an obsession with war criminals had wormed its way into the popular consciousness. Folk had begun seeing them in every flower bed and suspecting every reclusive neighbor. "Have you brought your suspicions to the imperators?"

The sea dog handed her a copy of the complaint. "They laugh me off. I wants be sure before me goes back. I follow't along with your arcane detecting talks and be read your 'Dispatches from Arrow Point' adventures. Might I use some cypher or whatnot to prove me true?"

Jhee wrangled a few more details out of the sailor, but nothing that rose above the level of general war criminal hysteria. They arrived at the legal clinic where Jhee's grad students were sorting the files the Inquesters had brought with them. Consulting with Inquesters, the investigative ranks of law enforcement, comprised the other part of her new Justicar duties in the capital. At first sight of the Inquesters' insignia, her walking companion stopped short.

"Well, mum, many thanks for your time," the sea dog said and turned tail.

Had it been a generalized distrust of law enforcement officers that sent the sailor fleeing, or did she have more specific cause to avoid them? Hopefully, Jhee hadn't handled the card or incident report too much to get usable prints from them. Jhee tapped a finger aside her nose and proceeded to her consultation. A grad student handed her a stack of case files, and she went to work.

"There could be no denying it," Jhee said after examining a few reports. She peered through her magnifier at the images. Because of the lividity and bluish lip pallor shown in the images, Jhee suspected poison. Several victims' skin and body hair also bore pinkish blotches. This pattern seemed familiar. Jhee consulted the diagnostic tip sheet she had compiled over the years and compared it to the victims. Once she determined the cause of death to be poison, she had reached the end of her official mandate as consultant. All that remained was to turn her findings over to the local constabulary.

"Not all of these folk died of natural causes. You may be looking at a Maker of Death situation here. The calibrations and the alignments are key. Calibration: no common industrial link prior to their hospitalization. Alignment: all these victims show exposure to a rare pesticide present nowhere in their environment. This is a pattern I've seen before as a field Justicar in the Far Reaches."

"Folk can be so predictable. They always think they are so clever and have committed the perfect crime. They think they will be the ones to get away with it," the investigator said.

"Quite right," Jhee agreed. She tidied the bio-parchment printouts and handed the files back to the grateful investigators along with the clinic's and her grad students' findings.

"Thank you, Justicar. With your help, hopefully, we have enough to put this gutter guppy away," said the partner.

"My pleasure, Inquesters. Drop by anytime you need my help."

Later, Jhee might ask Shep what he thought. She had no doubt of her conclusion but missed talking through cases with him. Jhee pulled out her conch and recorded a summary of her notes. She double-checked her determination for good measure. Her notes concluded with the recommendation that a full murder inquiry be undertaken at once.

The Inquesters thanked her again before they left. Jhee basked in the sense of accomplishment.

Another conclusion expertly reached, but the job still felt half done. The urge to do more than make a determination had Jhee drumming her fingers on the case folder. She snatched up the folder again. Why give them the cause of death when Jhee could also give them the murderer? Jhee started running down the local suppliers of said pesticide. Only a few manufacturers produced it, but it had been prevalent amongst the older families. The pesticide mimicked the symptoms of a heart attack and was hard to detect. Until Jhee had helped discover additional markers that differentiated the pesticide-induced heart failure from a more typical one. With their favorite means to hide their crimes less effective, many in her home district switched to some form of direct violence. While the pesticide had a commercial use, it was an artifact being kept alive mostly via the Trench market by murderers. Had she single-handedly put a whole industry out of work? The Wolphin family from her home district might think so.

Unintended consequences. An interesting conundrum for another time. Jhee paused for humility's sake. This was not about her patting herself on the back; it was about getting justice for those who had no one to speak for them but her.

According to the wall-mounted clockworks, she had some time before she had to meet Shep for dinner. Jhee laid out the data shell, the card, and incident report. She plugged the data shell in and started another decryption protocol on it. While it worked, Jhee played with Ursula's disc.

Jhee continued to go through her files and review death records. A banded bruise on a body with the cause of death marked as accidental made her pause. Banded bruises like these often came from fingers. She projected the autopsy images and notes on the wall. She re-checked the cause of death and the findings on post-mortem lividity. With this heavy bruising and these injury patterns, how could someone have called this an accident? This person was badly beaten.

The coroner who called this an accident or natural causes had to be blind or corrupt. Some coroner late for a dinner or event took the word of a family member or authority figure. Jhee grabbed her conch to query the coroner. She noted the time. A few minutes and she might be able to tell which one this particular coroner was, and then she could hurry to meet Shep with time to spare.

Jhee now took her time and carefully went over the autopsy findings. She pored through reports from the time the body was found until autopsy. As she did so, she recalled Jeja's lessons on first principles and smiled. *Don't assume. Let the evidence lead.*

Sometimes the mortuary staff mishandled bodies, and without due diligence, post-mortem damage could be confused for pre-mortem. The logs showed no discrepancy. No mentions of anyone dropping the body. No gaps in the timeline. If the marks didn't come from post-mortem mishandling, that made it more unlikely this man died from an accident.

Jhee brought up full-dimensional images of the victim's body. Blunt force trauma to the head, contusions: she examined each injury's characteristics. Other bones showed evidence of old breaks and fractures, not all of which had set properly. From the depressed knuckles and metacarpal fractures, she determined this man might have been a pugilist of some sort.

A check of the fighter's lists, public records, and footage proved him not an extremely good or popular one. From his record, a minor one. He had a few low-level bouts, which he had all lost. He acted as a meat bag for up-and-coming fighters and a sparring partner. No fortune and glory for this one, his story ended in some dirty alley, and the injustice of his death may have gone unnoticed without her due diligence.

Jhee dictated her findings. *Should she investigate this one herself?* She checked his records for family. None. The matter had kept this long, and no one was breaking down the door to solve it.

This was not Jhee's mandate, and she was not a field Justicar anymore, she told herself. Her duty was in the lecture hall or lab like she had always wanted or to consult as the Empire required. She had gone from the assistant of the intrepid Jeja of Marpele to a bureaucrat and academic. This had always been the Path Maker's plan: the original course for her life, a position in academia. She slipped off her fingernail ink reservoir and laid a finger along her muzzle. Jhee missed the old days when she solved the crimes and judged them by her lonesome, but her life had changed. She longed to see a whole case through and not just review others' findings. This had to suffice. She had a household, a family to consider. Though, she might ask Shep, with his greater anatomical knowledge, his opinion on the autopsy injuries.

Family. Shep. Jhee viewed the time with horror. Her conch chimed, and she answered.

"Jhee, where are you?" Shep asked.

"At the legal clinic. I lost the time."

"Get moving. They won't hold our reservation much longer."

She grabbed her valise and dashed out the door.

2

The Caretakers

From the moment Jhee left her office, it was as if the Maker of swift travels conspired against her. Maintenance and construction delayed the routed transports. When she went on foot, she found herself caught up in the chanting crowds. Had she missed notice of a game, concert, rally, or other gathering happening at the university tonight?

A viewscreen Jhee glimpsed through a window displayed empire-wide protests over the latest revelations of the Medical Protectorate's atrocities. Morbid curiosity held her transfixed. The Medical Protectorate's Surgeon General had committed suicide after tests proved the grisly remains uncovered on Knifefish Island were related to the Haddondeep incident. Jhee closed her eyes. Deep inside a lock within released. A sense of ease and relief diffused through her. One architect of the Medical Protectorate's abuses, a caretaker of the House of Knives, was dead. Jhee walked the rest of the way in a daze.

When Jhee reached the grill, Shep frowned at her from the sidewalk. "They gave away our reservation."

"Dear one, I'm sorry."

"It took months to manage this. This is one of the best chefs in the Empire.

During her soft launch." Shep sighed. "We might be able to get a table at the eatery up the street."

Jhee hung her head. "Wait, let me fix it."

"It's fine. Just forget about it."

Jhee wanted nothing more than to make this better. She strode into the restaurant, past the line of diners waiting for a table, and approached the grillery hostess.

"May I help you?" the hostess asked.

Jhee affected her most official attitude. "We had a reservation."

"Of course, you did."

"Justicar, party of two, reservation for last-sun."

The hostess glanced at the time. "It's first-moon."

Jhee pointedly displayed her family and academy signets. Then, as she rarely did for personal reasons, she removed her billfold and brandished her Imperial Justicar credentials. "I know. Isn't there something you can do?"

The hostess flashed her umber-hued eyes and continued to appear unimpressed. If it weren't for the paperwork it would entail, Jhee would have used her siren module to command the woman. Instead, she displayed an instant note for fifty shell.

After the hostess consulted her seating chart and reservation listing, she said, "We had a cancelation. I can get you a table for two in the back. That's the best I can do."

"Thank you."

Jhee motioned for Shep to join her. A waiter led them to a table near the kitchens. Shep frowned. They sat down to their meal. They browsed the menu together, and Jhee, as usual, took his suggestions.

Every time Shep attempted to explain some nuance of the meal, a member of the wait staff burst out from the swinging kitchen doors with a plate of steaming hot food. Shep's mouth turned down at the corners, and eventually, he dropped into a sullen silence.

Jhee wracked her brain for a conversation topic other than the *dendes*—her junior spouses Kanto and Mirrei—or work.

"I located a rare collection of items from an estate sale. I believe it possesses some personal effects from one of Thaedra's students. Apparently, she was quite the cryptologist. The collection may contain the rudiments of what later became the first set of cyphering windings and gyrations. It'd be interesting to see how it all took shape. Many have a conception of arcana having sprang fully formed from Thaedra's head. Instead, from what I've learned, it was a collaborative effort refined by her with the help of her students. It's like what I want to do with the clinic and my teaching. If I could have just a tiny fraction of the impact on my students as she had on hers…. I don't know. I'd consider it one of my life's greatest achievements."

"Waiter, salt," Shep said. Jhee swallowed her wine as the scandalized waiter hurried to comply. Drench. Adjusting the seasoning of another chef's food. Shep was more keeled than she thought. "Is that what you were doing instead of meeting me for dinner?"

"No. I got preoccupied by some unusual cases… The Architect of Sorrows committed suicide."

Shep tensed. "So I saw. I had trench all to do while you kept me waiting."

Shep sank into an even deeper silence than earlier. They passed the rest of their meal without speaking. She picked up her glass of wine. A waiter bumped their table, and she nearly dropped the glass.

"I know this wasn't quite the night out you had in mind."

"Jhee, I told you about this *months* in advance. You knew how important this was to me. The head chef did a live cook demonstration."

Shep pushed food around his plate with his nail pike. Jhee folded her napkin in her lap and gave him her full attention, so he knew he was being heard.

"I had everything planned. We had seats front row center to the grill. Right over there." Shep jerked his thumb at the centralized grill in the middle of the room, now long cold and practically empty. "I had wanted to see the chef create a meal for months. We would be in the center of it all." Shep sighed. "Never mind, it's fine. Let's just finish our meal."

Once they finished eating, Jhee paid, and they left without saying much more.

"I understand how disappointed in me you must be, Shep. I'm sorry."

"The tardiness and absences are worse than when you worked in the field."

Weariness laced through his words. Jhee had no idea what else to say. When she went to take Shep's arm, he barely noticed. This passivity disturbed her more than if he had been loud and belligerent.

"Shep, please, yell, scream, something, just don't withdraw."

"Hey, guls," Ursula's voice called. Ursula's sallow gaze regarded them from a face haggard and bruised, unlike when they saw her last. Stains and small tears marred her clothes, while the tie on her ponytail barely held. "Did you see the lead item on the news? One down, a dozen more to go."

"Would that the rest of them were all dealt with so easily," Shep said.

"Makers make it so."

The two spat.

"You're looking more… wave-worn since last we met," Jhee said.

"Well, you know how it is. I haven't been sleeping much lately. I wanted to thank you guls for your Makers' blessings. It helped more than you know."

"A sailor came to see me at my lab about some med divisioners. They said you sent them."

Ursula's face became even more gaunt, and her gaze darted about.

Shep frowned at Jhee. "Come, have a bite, and a good night's stay at our place. There's a veteran's service center right up the road."

"You know I hate those places."

"Can we get you a ride somewhere, maybe?"

"No, thanks. I'll be fine."

Ursula seized both in a hug. "Until we are all remade," she said, then scampered off.

Shep stared after her long after she left.

"What do you suppose that was about?" Jhee asked.

"Don't know. I won't be good company for the rest of the evening," he said. "I'll call for a transport to bring you home."

Shep went to the edge of the transport lane and took out his conch. She turned to him when the transport arrived. He assisted her into it then shut the door before she could argue. The transport sped her home.

The automatic lights turned on when Jhee stepped into their townhouse's sitting room. She found Kanto asleep in her chair.

"Mamere, mamere," Kanto murmured in his sleep.

Jhee laid her hand gently on his shoulder. Kanto started awake. "Why are you sleeping out here in the dark?"

"I must have fallen asleep after talking to grandmamere."

"And how is the Lady Kaydence?"

"Ornery as ever."

Kanto's shiny, golden eyes dulled as he drifted into reverie.

Jhee said, "You were having a nightmare about your mother? Today is the anniversary of her death."

A disappointed expression came over Kanto's face. "I was hoping Mirrei would call. She must have forgotten with her hectic path as an activist healer."

"She will. I'm sure she had a good reason." Normally, Jhee might have said she would talk to Mirrei about being more considerate and not defended her third spouse. But after the muck Jhee made of this evening, paying lip service to scolding Mirrei was a feat of hypocrisy even Jhee couldn't accomplish.

Kanto glanced at the clockworks and yawned. "Where's denme?"

"Trenched if I know," Jhee said. She took a breath to calm herself.

"But you went out tonight together?"

"He needed to blow off some steam."

"Because you let matters slip again."

"Not exactly. Partially. Yes. We'll talk more about it later."

Kanto rose and offered her his arm. "Perhaps, what we all need is a good tuck away?"

"Perhaps what you need is someone to talk to about your mamere? I'll have tea brought up."

Bars and Hammers

Should I track Ursula down? Shep thought. Despite what she said, Ursula may have needed a friend as much as he did right now. She had been a big help to him when he first arrived. It was she that had referred him to the exposure therapy group, which had broken him of his extreme reaction to raw, land meat. Ursula said it had done wonders for her and might do the same for him, one of the many debts he owed her.

Shep caught up to Ursula. "Urlibird, how are you doing, really?"

"Better now that folk like that are no longer in the world." Ursula jutted her chin at the scrolling text relaying the details of the Architect of Sorrows's death. "Now, if only they could reach the rest of them."

Ursula's face became shadowed, her eyes smoldering orange. Shep touched her shoulder. "Why did you take off so fast last time?"

"It doesn't matter anymore." A manic light replaced the shadows. "Not when there's so much work to be done."

Work? That did not sound like the Urlibird Shep knew. "When was the last time you went for a run?" he asked.

"I've been trying something different. Come with me."

Ursula and Shep caught a routed transport to the seaport district. Shep gazed out the transport widows at the ever-wakeful city, and it's spindly, impossibly tall buildings that hid the sky and horizon.

After Jhee and the *denyes*—his co-spouses—left Tranquility Bridge's abbey, Shep had stayed a few more days. He availed himself of the peace and solitude of their garden. He slipped his Folk skin and ran the bluffs with Dari, his therapeutic shark hound companion. With Jhee not around, he even did some cliff diving. When the time came to leave, instead of taking the barge to the capital, he hopped a steamer where he worked as a member of the crew. It had reminded him of the months he spent out to sea as pre-jubilant, learning the diving trade. He had left the Far Reaches a scrawny kid with corrective lenses and came back a stout diver and one of the best swimmers in the whole district.

Fight. Protect. Survive. The old berserker mantra kept going through Shep's head. It had a clear, simplicity to it—clarity he sorely missed. Shep turned over this evening's events from Ursula to his anger at Jhee again and again. One thing he did know was the absolute last thing he wanted to do now was talk. A good run might clear his head. He had not had one in a while, and neither had Dari. Even that did not feel like it would quell the storm raging within him. This place did not afford him the space and privacy to go all out as he might have in the Reaches.

This city did not move right. Shep barely felt connected to the waves and the sea here. Perhaps it was that they were so far inland. How could Jhee and the others not notice? Whatever the cause, Shep just felt so boxed in. Is that what was affecting Ursula? Many accepted into the Skin Slipper program had come from the Empire's outer rim islands like the Reaches. Ursula was one of the few inland berserkers he knew. Maybe it was just some aspect of their berserker nature, which would never be at ease amongst the ordinary folk?

When was the last time Shep felt at ease on this strange isle? He did not have to think long to come up with an answer: the retreat. While Jhee and the *denyes* had stayed in Galleon City, Shep went ahead to get their home ready. At least, that was the excuse he gave. What he had done besides that was seek treatment because of his losing control at the abbey. He stayed on a few extra days at the abbey, then sought counseling meant to get his berserker instincts under control. No matter how it happened, Shep could not allow another incident like that.

Ursula led them to the docks. His fur raised at all the random toughs milling about. Some paced. Some toked smoke root. Others sat still and tensed watching the others with shifty, watchful gazes. His hackles rose. Berserkers. A foghorn sounded in the distance. The gathered berserkers snapped to attention.

The shadow of a ship loomed large over the dock crowd. A gangplank lowered for man and a woman to disembark. They assessed and sorted the group.

The couple led the selected folk, Shep and Ursula among them, up the gangway to the deck. The transport ship carried them beyond the harbor to one of the most extensive mobile gyms and obstacle courses Shep had ever seen. Shep fingered his facial scar as he inventoried the set-up: grab bars, rope swings, wheel runs, climbing walls. He whistled.

Ursula smiled. "Better, right?"

"Amazing. What's the hitch?"

"I did some work for the owners, and they let me use the place whenever I want. I can even bring a friend. Tonight, that friend is you."

A little while later, Shep and Ursula sparred. The freighter pair pointed at and consulted about various folk using the equipment. They came to a stop in front of Shep and Ursula. "Skin?"

"Maye," Ursula answered.

They gave Shep a once over, pausing on his scarred face. "What about you, gorgeous?"

Shep fixed them with his good eye. They were asking the easiest skin they slipped into, their base skin. "Orcinus," Shep answered.

The orcinus or the whale crusher was a hulking black sea mammal covered with white splotches. The man did a double-take. A smile widened across the woman's face.

"Excellent," she said. "Don't get many heavy-class. We'll find something for you."

"Best reinforce the equipment first," the man said.

While Shep grabbed a swig of water, he saw them slip a few notes to a solidly-built Water Folk with straw-colored hair and missing a chunk from one ear.

Some time later, the transport ship returned to bring everyone to the docks. Berserkers slunk off into the night. After the blare of the foghorn signaled their hosts' departure, Shep, Ursula, and a few stragglers lingered, wondering what to do next.

"What'd I tell ya?" Ursula said.

Shep stroked his scar, ashamed he had enjoyed hitting the heavy bag so much. "I needed that."

Someone bumped into Shep nearly, knocking him off his feet.

"Out of the way, pup shark," the half-eared Water Folk growled.

"You bumped into me," Shep said. He felt a twinge of anger at the use of "pup shark." A name that hit too close to home.

The man gripped his gym bag strap and puffed out his chest. "Oh, really. Are you looking for an apology?"

Shep shook his head. "Just forget it."

Shep turned back to Ursula. A hand grabbed his shoulder and roughly spun him around.

"Nobody turns their back on Hammad the Hammerhead."

"Hey, gul, sorry. It's all good," Shep said though he felt the faint stirrings of annoyance. He had just reached equilibrium again after his recent upsets. He held up his hands.

"What if I say it's not?"

Hammad the Hammerhead poked his finger in Shep's chest.

"Tell you what, gul. Why don't you let me and my friend buy you a drink?" Ursula said.

Hammad hesitated then fixed a mean expression on his face. "Hammad the Hammerhead buys his own drinks."

The remaining berserkers had gathered around them. Clearly, Hammad was spoiling for a fight. Shep wasn't about to give it to him. He must keep his violent impulses in check. Besides, he already imagined having to explain himself to Jhee and Kanto after having brawled like some stripling.

"Come on, Ursula. Let's leave."

Shep patted Ursula's shoulder, and they began to walk away.

"Nobody walks away from Hammad the Hammerhead."

Shep's senses narrowed to the sound of Hammad's gym bag dropping and a shoe squeak. Shep and Ursula dodged in opposite directions. The slow, clumsy haymaker punch missed them by leagues. When his fist failed to connect, Hammad caught himself before faceplanting. The brute glared from Shep to Ursula, picking his target. A menacing mask settling in on Hammad the Hammerhead's face informed Shep he had made his choice. From the narrowed eyes when his gaze settled on Shep, Shep had a fraction of a second's warning before The Hammerhead lunged at him with a yell. Shep brushed aside the charging brute.

The Hammerhead's face reddened at being denied again. "What sort of berserker are you? You run like a coward. Fight. Protect. Survive."

Shep sighed and squared up his fighting stance. "I'm not running now."

The Hammerhead grinned. He matched Shep's stance, and they circled each other. Hammad the Hammerhead went right into a series of hooks and jabs, likely the set up for a decisive body blow or uppercut.

Shep had a moment to react when he caught the telltale signs of the wind-up. He hopped back. The miss overextended Hammad again. Shep caught the vulnerable arm in a lock, which brought the Hammerhead to his knees. As the Hammerhead struggled to free himself, Shep made fast his hold.

"Stop struggling, or you'll break it," Shep said.

Hammad made a groan of impotent fury. His eyes smoldered orange rage at Shep.

"Raise your chin," Shep said. Hammad complied. "Higher."

Hammad raised his chin higher. Shep drew back and knocked the man out cold. The berserker crowd cheered and jeered. Folk bore him and Ursula off to a bar. After several rounds, silence fell over the bar. Hammad the Hammerhead filled the bar doorway. The patron's parted as he lumbered toward Shep. Shep rose. They stood just an arm's reach apart.

The Hammerhead grinned. "That was magnificent! Get this man another drink. On me. Hammad the Hammerhead buys the drinks."

Shep reacted with dumbfounded paralysis as the man crushed him in a hug then ruffled Shep's hair. They spent the next hours drinking themselves stupid. By the time he and Ursula stumbled out of the bar with Hammad in tow, the three had taken to singing sea shanties at the top of their lungs.

Their singing and camaraderie caught the attention of two uniformed imperators on patrol. Hammad the Hammerhead took loud exception to this and did what he did best, started a fight.

The Man or The Beast

Some friend of Hammad's showed up and spoke to the imperators' wallets. Both parties to the transaction had taken it in stride. "See you in a few days," Hammad said once they were released.

The sleepy friend, a woman, approached their gang of three. "Is it too much to ask at least one long-tide go by where I don't have to come out here?"

Hammad grinned.

The woman rubbed her eyes and looked at Shep. "Who might you be?"

Hammad answered, "This is Hammad the Hammerhead's new chum."

The woman fluttered her eye color in frustration and offered Shep a credential card. "Counselor Medea, caseworker from veteran's outreach. Here's my c-card. If you keep hanging out with him, you will need it. Now, I'm going back to the center to get some sleep."

Shep tucked away her card. "May I ride back with you?"

Counselor Medea sighed. "Fine."

In the meantime, Ursula had slipped away again. Shep paced in the transport car, surprised he, Ursula, and Hammad had not ended up in jail. At last, he sat down.

"How'd someone as even-keeled as you hook up with the Hammerhead?" the counselor asked.

"A fight," Shep answered.

"Of course."

"You work at the veteran's center? I live near there. I kept meaning to go."

"Why haven't you?"

"Those places never helped me."

"What did?"

"I used to love diving.," Shep said. "I was a great diver."

"What happened?" Counselor Medea asked.

"I had to stop. My wife became deathly afraid of the water. We couldn't dive together anymore. When I went out on my own, I'd return to find her pale as a morning mist, waiting up for me. She didn't used to be that way. I remember when we were younger, how much she loved the water, even until secondary school. The whirlpool of fate stole her joy of the sea from her. 'What a thing to see, a Water Folk who hates the sea.' I poured my efforts into being a great husband."

Then it was as if a dam within Shep had burst and expressed his frustration about the night and the move to the capital. The counselor nodded along and interjected supportive or clarifying comments. Eventually, she yawned.

"Excuse me. We'd be more comfortable at the center." Counselor Medea dropped into a mumble, "Padded chairs, fresh-brewed kolal. A chance for me to review your case files during decent hours."

The counselor scribbled something down on a bio-film sheet, then handed it to him.

"What's this?" Shep asked.

"A veteran's retreat. Gardens. Sea views. Great diving. Other berserkers to talk to. You just get some quiet time with other folk who might know what you're going through."

"I just came from a monastery like that."

"Where I can sense you felt calm and at peace."

"I did. It didn't stop me from going into a frenzy, anyway."

"It happens from time to time. What you have to decide is if you will let that possibility rule your life forever? Decide which you want to be more: the man or the beast. Then find a way to reconcile that choice. This is my stop. Please, I encourage you, stop by the center."

Shep refused to meet her gaze because he knew how unlikely that was to happen.

"Right, not helpful," continued Counselor Medea. "How about this? Exercise with your dog or therapeutic companion at the section nearer the center. Join the center's pet walkers' group. Maybe you'll even be tempted to go in."

Shep nodded, though confused how she knew he had a canine companion.

"Dog hairs," she said.

Shep almost laughed out loud. One would think after all these years with Jhee, he would recognize that trick by now.

"Who knows? Maybe we'll run into each other some time?" Counselor Medea said and exited the transport.

The light from the first dawning of the lesser sun had just illuminated the world when Shep carefully slipped into the house via the kennels. He crept up the backstair making as little noise as possible.

Jhee would know he hadn't joined her in her chambers. Hopefully, no one would know he hadn't slept in his rooms either. Shep checked the hour and winced, as much from his bruises as the time. He had a barber's appointment with Kanto soon. Shep had to find a way out of it. If Kanto saw him like this, the young spouse would run straight to Jhee.

Last night's events still fresh in his mind, Shep removed his shoes. Generalized anger at nothing and everything still had him in its grip, and he was not sure if he was ready to talk with Jhee yet. It had been so much easier to express himself to a virtual stranger. The time at the gym with other berserkers had done him good, too. He had needed to hit something to let off steam.

Shep had just reached his door when her chamber door opened. He pressed against the wall out of sight. Kanto emerged, followed by Jhee.

"Everything will be fine," Jhee said.

"Thank you for letting me stay," Kanto said. They embraced a long time then touched escae.

Shep's dander rose until he realized he had his excuse, his pretext. He revealed himself.

"Denme, morning," Kanto said with a warm smile. Shep puffed up his chest. Kanto and Jhee's smiles faded.

"Shep, I know what this looks like," Jhee said.

Shep growled then slipped into his room. He slammed the door, pressed his ear against it, and listened.

"He doesn't think we…" Kanto began.

"I'm unsure," Jhee answered. "I'll talk to him later and explain the situation. Let's give him some re-centering time for the moment."

Aim achieved. A twinge in Shep's side reminded him of what state he was in. Shep showered and performed field healing on his bruises until they had mostly faded and were no longer tender. As long as Kanto, or especially Jhee, did not get too close for the next day or so, they'd be unnoticeable.

3

～

The Invitation

Lunch the next day dragged by in awkward silence. Jhee monitored Shep for signs of violence. Her arm sigil tingled with the residuals of his anger, but it remained at the same intensity as it had since the previous night. Even when he had seemingly caught Jhee and Kanto being unfaithful, the sensation had not increased, although the sigil had been less of a barometer of his mental state lately.

The day schedule was the chosen mechanism by which their household operated. Other cohorts had their arrangements, this one was theirs. From breakfast to breakfast, each day of the long-tide belonged to one of Jhee's spouses except the last, which was an open day. On the designated spouse's day, Jhee spent time exclusively with that spouse unless otherwise agreed or an emergency occurred. Jhee and the day's spouse decided upon their activities together, though she usually deferred to their favorites. They became her primary consort, and the others, especially in romantic terms, became friends. The last was where the misunderstanding had come in. There was leeway, but it had to be mutually agreed upon, or else it was considered a violation of trust. Their family decided Jhee would not be a snipping thistle crab hopping bed to bed throughout the night.

Shep had yet to let her explain. Jhee stuck close to Kanto's side just in case. It served multiple purposes. One, to be there in case the young man still needed someone to talk to; two, to selfishly use him as an emotional buffer between her and Shep; three, a precaution if Shep instigated a delayed quarrel with him.

The door chimes rang. A moment later, their housekeeper, Irina, informed them an imperial messenger had arrived. Kanto bounded to a standing position and adjusted his dressing gown. He shook his head at both Jhee and Shep's appearance. With barely contained excitement, Kanto shooed them out to the entryway.

The messenger's livery was of the finest make. He dipped his head and held out a silver tray bearing a bio-film invitation which had been expertly folded into a flower shape.

Once Jhee had taken the invitation into her palm, and her credential ring lit in response verifying its authenticity, the messenger spoke, "Sirs, my Lady. On behalf of the dual thrones of Emperor and Empress of the Blessed and Glorious isles of the Empire of Narhiya, you are invited to attend the Imperial Electors at their Summer Sojourn held at the imperial resort on Sovereign's Isle in two long-tides."

"An invitation to the imperial resort," Kanto said.

The messenger raised his head and waited. Drench. Jhee glanced at Kanto's excited expression and Shep's annoyed one. She had little choice. The invitation was now or never. Marital difficulties would not be accepted as a reason to refuse an invitation to the Imperial Sojourn.

After Jhee touched her credential ring to the message's response plate, Jhee unfolded the invitation and went through the formality of reading it in full. The messenger bowed, then took his leave.

"It's so exciting, isn't it?" asked Kanto.

"Thrilling," Shep replied.

"I've got to get to work on new outfits for us. We'll need a whole new long-tides worth of clothes. I'll need to hire assistants; there's no way I'll be able to design and finish a new holiday ensemble for us in time. These are such problems to have."

"We'll leave it to your expert judgment."

Kanto clapped his hands together in happiness, then summoned retainers. Jhee watched Shep to gauge how he viewed the matter. He shrugged. She supposed that was an improvement from his breakfast demeanor.

"Of course you will," Kanto said. "Color schemes, patterns. Oh my. I just happened to have received bolts of custom fabric back from the textile shop. You both need to give me your opinion on it. I designed a new house insignia and colors based on the combined motif of our houses. I think it's quite clever if I do say so myself. Also, we'll need to do some briefings so you can have a rundown of the players before we get there. No need to start an Imperial incident."

"I need to work on my lesson plans," Jhee announced. At least, Kanto was looking forward to this. She would have to have another instructor fill in for her. Usually, it would not be a problem this late in the academy year, but she had signed up to teach some courses in the extended season.

"Dari and I will go for a walk," Shep said.

"Let me take your measurements before either of you go anywhere," Kanto said. "Then, we'll have to do fittings."

"Perhaps later," Shep said over his shoulder. He grabbed the leash and headed for the kennels. Kanto waved him off.

While Kanto measured Jhee, she worked through her lesson plans on her conch. The house buzzed with excitement.

A delayed message from Mirrei arrived. It glitched and warbled.

"Sorry... Tried several times to get through." The skies behind her were dark, gray, and overcast. Half the message lost itself to the storm. "I really think I'm doing some good here. Miss you muchly."

The message cut off. Kanto hummed a bright tune now as he measured Jhee. Jhee glanced out the windows of their home to the clear skies and near-constant lack of storm clouds. The capital really was like its own little bubble. She smiled.

Kanto and Mirrei had found their paths. Jhee gazed down the hallway to the kennel. Shep, however, seemed more adrift than ever, and she did not know what she could do to reach him.

Shep had been keeping his own counsel more and more as of late. They used to be able to talk. Maybe not about everything but more than this. Was it being cooped up at the capital that was doing it? Or the visits from Ursula? His time in the service, in the berserkers, was catching up to him in a way it never had before. She had thought he had adjusted well, but maybe that was because they were just so far away from society in the Far Reaches. Here they were in a large city, one of the busiest in the empire. This many people living on top of each other may have been too much for him.

"I think I have what I need for now," Kanto said, in buoyant waters, after the message from Mirrei. "If you hurry, you can catch up to him."

"Thank you," Jhee said.

Kanto shook his head, already furiously at work in his sketchpad. "So much to do. So much to do."

Jhee walked up the mahogany steps to her room. The house was brilliantly appointed because of Kanto's excellent eye. She paused briefly at what they had intended to be Mirrei's room. All of her belongings sat still neatly wrapped. Jhee was not sure if she should have them unpacked and put out. It seemed like wasted effort if she would have to send them along elsewhere. Mirrei had still yet to mention if she had wanted a divorce. Somehow their calls always ended before it reached that point. Jhee, though, preferred to prepare herself for the inevitable.

She dressed and caught up to Shep and Dari at the park. Jhee spread her hands in askance. Shep offered his hand. Jhee took it, and they touched escae while Dari looked on, tongue lolling in seeming approval.

"You are wind and waves, my lady of the Isles," Shep said.

Departure

The intervening long-tides between the invitation and the departure date for the sojourn rushed by on rip currents. So fast, Jhee still found herself working on lesson plans and presentation materials the day they were set to leave.

"Jhee, what are you doing? We're going to be late," Shep said.

"A few more minutes," Jhee said. "I have to finish this lesson plan."

Along with her lesson plan, Jhee had spent a lot of time studying Saheli's last sermon. True, it had influence from the fell text, but it did not account for the whole of the formulations. They were innovative. She verged on calling them revolutionary. Jhee's experiments with her siren module and templarite dust were at a critical stage. After her experience in the mines of Galleon City, she deduced her module used templarite in some fashion. It reacted similarly to the synchronator regarding the mist. If she could have had just a few minutes to try out some fabrications…

Then there was the stack of case consults she had to sort through. She still saw those Albatross files. She opened up the file packet for another quick peek. Perhaps, something new would jump out at her that didn't the last time.

Shep blocked her conch screen with his hand. "You know how Kanto gets. We were supposed to be ready for his final inspection by now."

"He's worse than our training inspector. I have to get this done."

"You should have managed your time better." Shep shook his head and put on his sashes. He tugged at them while frowning. "I'm not sure I like these color choices. Don't you think they are a bit brash?"

Kanto gave a rhythmic knock before breezing in from the adjoining room without leave to enter. "It is a perfectly good complementary color palette. I already toned them down. If you think they are too much, wait until you see some of the flamboyant colors of the other houses."

Kanto stopped dead when he saw Jhee was still in her dressing gown. Jhee swore under her breath and braced for the admonishment she knew was coming and deservedly so.

"You're not even dressed?" Kanto turned on Shep. "Why isn't she ready? You said you would see to it."

"You know how she can be. One more lesson plan," Shep answered.

"That's what she does. Always one more experiment, one more derivation, one more puzzle. We keep her grounded, so the other things don't slide."

"I'm right here," Jhee said.

"Good, so you are hearing the tongue-lashing my denme is getting, which rightly should be yours. Now finish up quickly."

Kanto flounced down in the chair next to her, looking profoundly piqued and bored.

"I can't with you hovering over me. This will go much faster if you just go get Shep ready."

"Shep is ready. We're both ready. Everyone is ready except you. After you get dressed, I still need to touch up your hair and trim your nails."

"I have to get this done. Go on ahead without me."

"We will do nothing of the sort. The resort is close to Emperor's Isle. Two males can't wander about there, let alone arrive at a court function without their denbe. Without notice of intent papers, we'll be stopped every fifty feet or worse detained if you aren't with us. It would serve you right if the two of us were added to the imperial companion collection."

"Oh, all right."

Shep gave her a smug smile. Jhee typed with one hand or narrated into her conch as Kanto and Shep helped her dress. Eventually, she handed her free hand to Kanto so he could begin manicuring her fingernail claws.

Now and then, Jhee forgot and attempted to adjust or scroll something with her "free" hand. He refused to let go. Once he had finished trimming and painting the first hand, Kanto switched to the other. He slapped the back of her finished hand every time she attempted to lift it off the table. Now, she had no hands to use to finish. Shep chuckled before he left to oversee the servants and their luggage. Eventually, she sat there with both hands flat on the table. A firm flick from Kanto greeted any attempt to move.

Jhee waited quietly, watching her lesson plan's sample cypher derive. The conch had been left at an odd angle, so she had to strain her neck to monitor its progress. She leaned over and painstakingly used her nose to move her conch into a better viewing position while her nails dried.

Kanto wrinkled up his snout. "Really, denbe?"

Jhee grinned. "I couldn't see it."

They burst out laughing. Shep returned to the room. He saw them sitting there with Jhee's freshly trimmed and lacquered hands clasped in Kanto's. Shep shook his head then exited. Jhee and Kanto burst out laughing again.

"I heard from Mirrei again," Kanto said.

Jhee sat back and smiled. "Me too."

"She wants to set up a remote meeting for after we return." Kanto looked smug. "She tries to hide it, but I think she misses us."

"I think she does, too."

"I never doubted it for a moment."

Jhee raised an eyebrow.

"Maybe for a moment. I haven't told her about the work I've been doing at the center. I wanted it to be a surprise. When she calls again, I'll tell her all about it."

"She'll be thrilled."

"I know. I told her I was proud of her. We're in a good place right now, I think."

"Let her know what an inspiration she's been to you and your philanthropy work."

"Good influence on me? Hey, I started it all back at the abbey. If it weren't for me, she would still be lying abed like some wasting whelk."

"You know, *dende*, one of the many things I admire about you is how humble you are."

"I know." Kanto stood. "Now, hurry, so we won't be late."

Jhee's conch beeped to indicate her derivation had finished. The fabrication station beckoned Jhee. She almost grabbed her tools and started working immediately but remembered at the last moment about her freshly manicured hands. She held them delicately as if covered in goo or slime and stepped away from the fabrication station. Far be it from her to ruin Kanto's gorgeous work!

Shep entered the room again. "Yav-yav, everyone. The transport will be here any minute," he bellowed in his military voice.

He grabbed her conch and walked out with it. What could she do but follow? Her hands held up, Kanto somehow put a coat on her without so much as brushing her nails.

The amphibious transport arrived at their manse promptly at mid-dusk, the time after the elder sun had set. Realizing she had forgotten her tabard, Jhee turned to retrieve it. Shep intercepted her and escorted her into the transport.

They spent the transport ride to the pier politely nodding as Kanto tried to brief them on the power players while interspersing a lot of court gossip. She should have learned her lesson about paying attention to these, but it was so dull.

Jhee and Shep made eye contact. He gave a slight smile, knowing exactly where her thoughts must have been. He knew her so well.

"Are you two even listening to me?" Kanto asked.

"The vizier from Graydale hates crustaceans," Shep said.

"No. He is in a feud with the Cetaceans over a broken shipping lane contract."

"Right. Right."

"I won't be able to do all the talking there." Kanto frowned and clutched at his robes. "If either Shep or I so much as make eye contact with the wrong woman…."

Jhee touched Kanto and Shep's hands. She recalled now why she detested these imperial functions so much. The Imperial grounds were like stepping back centuries in time. Yet, Kanto enjoyed the opportunity to mix with the Imperial family. "You know I won't let anything happen to either of you."

Jhee's arm sigil warmed. Shep had, also, straightened up while watching the assembled nobility.

"What is it, Dawn Wolf?" Jhee asked using Shep's outside name, a social name for use outside the home in mixed company; now become quite old-fashioned.

With a shrug, Shep sank back into the cushions. "I don't know. Just thought I saw someone I know from the gym."

"It's not impossible," Kanto said. "Imperial consorts have some odd pastimes."

Shep worked his jaw. "I didn't say it was them."

A tingle from the sigil grafted to Jhee's arm and bound to the brand on Shep's neck indicated his distress. Jhee rubbed each husband's nearest arm in turn to ease the growing tensions. "It could be just someone who looks like them."

"Perhaps you're right," Shep said.

Kanto took a breath. "Please, esteemed spouses, I know the gossip seems a bother, but take heed to these trifles anyway. Wars spring from less."

"All right, denye," Shep said.

"Now, the scuttlebutt in Graydale…"

Graydale, also known as Greater Dale, was the largest of the Dale island group, another group of rim islands like the Reaches where Jhee and her house-hold had grown up. And like the Reaches, it supplied numerous Folk to the war effort. Her thoughts returned to the sea dog who suspected her neighbor was a war criminal. First Ursula, then the sea dog, it must be catching.

The transport pulled up to the pier. Jhee and her husbands joined the other dignitaries lined up to board the Imperial yacht to the Imperial Isles.

~

A World Apart

A dedicated group of Imperial porters greeted each retinue upon their arrival on Sovereign's Isle. A taupe-colored woman porter whose arm bore a band with Jhee's house colors and crest gave Jhee a slight bow.

"Welcome to Sovereign's Isle, my Lady Justicar. I am Pela. It will be my team's pleasure to serve you during your stay."

The woman made a discreet gesture, and her team of porters spirited away their luggage. Meanwhile, Pela escorted Jhee and her husbands to a covered beach skimmer equipped with iced mango punch. They sipped punch as Pela narrated the island's history and pointed out various landmarks. The tart punch with a hint of citrus tasted almost the same as Jhee remembered. One sip transported Jhee back to summers at Hillside with grandmamere and gram-gram. By the time Jhee's house-hold arrived at their quarters, porters had almost completed furnishing their rooms and unpacking according to the detailed instructions Kanto had sent ahead of them.

"Allow me to show you to the hall of alcoves so you can make your devo-tions," Pela said before Jhee could ask to be shown to their shrines.

The hall of alcoves contained many and sundry variegations and representa-tions of nearly every Maker, great and small, Jhee might name.

"How many Makers do you worship here?"

"It's hard to say, my Lady Justicar. Hundreds, perhaps. It depends on who currently occupies the isle. I believe you'll want to visit the First Makers archi-traves, then I'll allow you to pick which variant of Futou, Lashae, and Pascoe to commemorate."

"You have more than one shrine to them?"

"Dozens for each."

Jhee performed her First Makers' devotions at the pillars and basins under the enormous architraves. She gave offerings of the four elements to the trio of sky, earth, and sea, plus the Unknown Maker. The eyes of more than her ancestors watched her. The more of this sojourn she saw, the more of a backwater rustic she felt. Mechanist devotions were much more personal, and she would perform those in private later.

The rest of their first day at the sojourn saw them attending a series of lavish receptions. Lengthy feast tables bore fare of every description from any isle one might name: Laruscan pork, Dalesian watercress, aged Valerian cheeses, rare Chalumet wines.

Similarly, the guests hailed from every corner of the empire. They brushed metaphorical fins with Findari, commonly known as Water Nomads, nobles, and teal-eyed, blue-black complexioned imperials. The dark skin-tone implied highborn ruling elites while teal eyes meant they had Fire Folk ancestry or had resided in the Scorched Lands long enough for their eyes to change.

The clothing ranged from simple wraps and pullovers to glittering dresses with elaborate embroidery. And then, headwear. The headdresses ran the gamut from scarves and jeweled turbans to hats with outrageous fascinators or brims so wide even Jhee's mentor, Jeja of Marpele, known for her impressive hats, might weep at the sight of them.

Jhee and Shep went about trying to mask their astonishment, while Kanto introduced them to all the right people. As the junior spouse, he could not have pride of place on her arm, but somehow still managed to call the tune.

"We should suspend the schedule while here and let Futou guide our play," Kanto said, and they agreed.

While Jhee and Shep may have been the veterans, this was Kanto's battlefield. Shep held back half a step and let Kanto walk by Jhee's side. It was his night, but he knew it would make a better impression if she walked in with the gorgeous, decked out Kanto. Shep would present as a protector spouse, but Kanto was the showpiece with his impeccable grooming and flawless body lines. His steps were graceful and lithe. He never overtook Jhee at any point. He never spoke to anyone except without her presenting him to them and speaking first. Kanto gave her subtle nudges as to who and when to introduce him to someone, a slight tug in the direction he wanted to go or a gentle touch to her elbow. He led her through the political maze, with no one being the wiser. She made occasional eye contact with Shep to check in on him.

By the next day of the sojourn, fun and games, Kanto had secured them a weirs match with the Vizier of Finance and the official in charge of trade.

After a rousing game, the vizier asked, "Now, Justicar, what is this I hear about you having one of the lowest overturn rates in the circuit?"

Jhee inclined her head, and they clasped forearms. "Not much to say about it other than that. That was in my field work days. Now, I'm strictly an instructor and consultant for the Justicar Annex."

Kanto took Jhee's arm. "Denbe is being modest. She also had one of the lowest requests for appeal."

"Indeed?" the Vizier asked.

"Yes, Vizier."

"Is that terribly hard?"

Jhee answered, "It can be. A lot of reviews are triggered by unsatisfied litigants. I usually did my best to explain to my litigants the full extent of my ruling and also mete out a fair punishment."

"I'm inclined to think a criminal never views their punishment as fair."

"Not in the main. However, it is rare for a criminal to commit their crimes out of a wholly criminal mindset. Many crimes are done by people at their limit or desperate, justified or not. The crime is their way of trying to fix an imbalance in their lives."

"Denbe is being too modest," Kanto said.

"Tell her about the opening," the trade official urged.

"Oh, yes. I have it on good authority one of the chief reviewers of the judicial archives will be stepping down soon. She will need to be replaced. The Chief Justicar will be putting in an appearance at the sojourn, I'm sure. You might want to talk to her when she arrives."

"We've never been introduced."

"I'll introduce you. She's currently in the process of screening nominees and considering replacements. With your record and reputation, I'm sure you would be a logical successor."

"Thank you, Vizier. I look forward to the meeting."

"Care for another match, Justicar?"

"I suppose I could let you embarrass me again. You are one fierce player."

Kanto beamed at Jhee as they walked back from the weirs field. He took her arm. "See, this has already been a productive trip. Aren't you glad we came?"

"Perhaps."

"We are at the Imperial Sojourn, teeming with a surprising number of eligible companions. Not a bad place to catch the imperial eye."

"I thought we settled this before, Jhee."

"I meant for me."

Kanto slapped Jhee's arm. "Being one of what—ten, twenty spouses—would be an improvement in either of our situations, how? I can barely deal with being a second, let alone a tenth. This is not to be squandered so."

"I stand corrected."

"Duly so."

"What if I'm not speaking of improving your situation, but one of companionship, solely for your benefit?"

"Companionship isn't a complaint I have at the moment. Only a desire to feel more fulfilled and serve the community, which my work at the youth center helps."

Jhee spared a thought for Shep, who had mostly chosen to closet himself in their rooms. Kanto pecked Jhee on the cheek. They went on a walk, which took them back to the pier where the Imperial yacht had appeared again, dropping off another round of attendees.

4

~

Breath of the Past

That evening their household dined together in the great hall on a feast of halibut and sea urchin, all poached in a lovely butter sauce with a hint of tarragon. Jhee and Shep ate it with great relish.

"Such compliments to the chef," he said.

"Yes, yes," Kanto and Jhee agreed—Jhee, if only because Shep had found something to enjoy during this trip. Whatever haze he had been in appeared to have lifted.

The doors of the great hall opened with great fanfare, and a bustle of people arrived.

"As I live and breathe," said a statuesque Water Folk woman who shared Shep's chestnut coloring. The recent arrival, attired in a billowing sun cape and summer lenses, breezed into the dining hall and made straight for their table.

Shep stopped mid-chew. "No," he said, "no."

Jhee choked on her sea urchin. "It can't be."

"Ah, brother dear." The woman passed off her lenses to a companion and held out her hands to Jhee and Shep. "Don't be like that, kin. Give us a kiss."

Shep stood and clasped forearms with her. She kissed him on each cheek. Jhee expelled a slow breath and rose.

"Sharlet," Jhee said.

"Sister-in-law, lovely to see you, too. I see you've been taking excellent care of my dear brother. How are you, though?"

Jhee gave Sharlet a half-hearted clasp because she was sure the Imperial family would disapprove of her stabbing another guest.

"I'm well. What of yourself?"

"Well, see for yourself. I'm simply marvelous, and it's great to see how far the three of us have come. Who would have thought two divers' kids from Briny Town and a smuggling, monogamist's spawn would wind up at an Imperial Sojourn? Who would have thought events would turn out this way when we were younger?"

"Indeed."

"All right you suckerfish, where's my drink?" A retinue of sycophantic assistants hustled off to do Sharlet's bidding. Her eyes zeroed in on Kanto. "And who might I ask is this fine drink of water here?"

"I'm Bright Harmony," Kanto said.

"My second," Jhee said.

"Really?" Sharlet laughed uproariously and continued on for some moments.

"You are truly Shep's sister?" Kanto asked.

"Guilty as charged. Oh, look at you. I see sister-in-law's taste in men has improved. Oh, Makers my, whatever possessed you to throw in with these two?"

"It's purely physical I assure you," Kanto said.

"Is it now? Gorgeous and with such a glorious sense of humor, too. Well, I'll be having a salon later. You are, of course, invited. You can even drag these two along if you wish. Though, I don't recommend it." She leaned in and whispered, "Bad blood. Maybe one of us will tell you about it one day."

Jhee clenched her jaw and contemplated how quickly she could be at the woman with her nail pike.

Sharlet addressed Shep, "Brother, you going to let your wife do all the talking for you?"

Shep sat.

"Bright Harmony, pleasure to meet you, and remember, my invitation still stands if you wish."

Kanto gave a polite bow as Sharlet and her entourage left to make the rounds; Jhee and Shep didn't bother. Kanto took his seat. "May I ask?"

"No, you may not," Jhee snapped, then mitigated her tone. "Apologies, not just now. Perhaps when we are back at our rooms, and I'll be at my leisure to rage and yell with full abandon."

Kanto cocked his head at her and brightened his golden eyes. "That bad?

Look alive, Jhee, isn't that the Chief Justicar over there?"

At Kanto's urging, they met the Chief Justicar as she shook hands and received people, but Jhee was in no mood for politicking at the moment. However, Jhee straightened her posture and tucked her hands into her robes.

"Ah, Justicar, you're the one in charge of the Far Reaches?"

"Just so, Chief Justicar."

"Please, call me Elver. Exemplary work out there. You truly brought law and order to District Sixteen. The number of complaints I had on your predecessor. It was a nightmare over at review. You, however, were a breath of fresh air."

"Thank you, Elver. If you will excuse us."

"Yes, yes, of course. Have your social secretary contact mine, and maybe we can play some weirs while we're here. I've been eager to ask you about some of your cases."

Jhee made a curt response. As Kanto bowed and smoothed things over, she took her leave.

"You must excuse, denbe," Kanto said. "Dinner didn't agree with her."

"Of course. You better run and take care of her. Have her contact me."

"I will do that, Chief Justicar."

Jhee and Shep quickened their pace. Kanto scrambled to rejoin their side. Shep outpaced both, leaving Jhee to decide if she should speed up to catch him or slow down to insure they didn't lose Kanto. Jhee commandeered a spot between the orchestra and the azaleas. If either husband wanted to join her, they were perfectly welcome. Kanto did so immediately. Not long after, Shep reappeared with a drink for each of them. Kanto excused himself, and Shep replaced him at her side.

Jhee took the fluted glass from him. "That wasn't so bad, was it?"

"He makes it look so easy," Shep said and gestured his glass at Kanto, who had begun to enchant the gathering.

"But this is for us. He knows what needs to be done and who needs to be flattered. A lesson you think we would have learned after all these years."

They both dropped into silence. "Our solution was to hide once we came home."

"I know, but that's no longer an option. This is our new home. That crumbling pile of stones is just barely above water."

"Me too," he whispered. "We had pleasant times there, though."

"And just about as many bad," Jhee said wryly. "I have to admit, while I don't like everything here, it is growing on me."

Shep took a drink. "Not me."

As Kanto kept his charm offensive circulating among the guests, Sharlet never seemed far behind. Jhee set down her drink when Sharlet snuck up behind Kanto and wheedled her way into conversation with him. Once Sharlet pulled out her conch, Jhee's curiosity propelled her across the room with Shep in tow.

"That's clearly you. That's Star Mirror's mamere," Kanto was saying. By "Star Mirror," Kanto meant Mirrei. That was her name for mixed company. "Denbe, denme, Miss Sharlet was showing me images from your old swim team days."

Jhee flushed while Shep tugged at his collar.

"This smart-looking young lady with the clipboard and cap, trying to fade into the background, has to be my esteemed wife. Is this slick slim swim boy the infamous Rennie Crag Hall?"

"Guess again," Sharlet said. "If you like those, I have some even better ones to show you. Guess who this scrawny male with the gigantic head and lenses nearly the size of his face is?"

"Shep, I mean, denme?" Kanto took the hand viewer from Sharlet. He scrolled a few more images along. By the end, Kanto was practically in hysterics. "Well, I'll be Futou's fiddledrum."

Shep's skin had reddened, and his eyes widened from all the attention. Jhee brought up images of Shep from her academy days. Jhee handed Kanto her conch.

"Ah, that's more like it. Hm, no scar. This is how I imagined he looked when younger. You had one drench of a bloom, denme," Kanto said. "You bulked up quickly."

The corners of Shep's mouth drooped. "Courtesy of the M-Prot exercise regimen."

Kanto handed Jhee back the hand viewer. "I'm sorry."

With a desire to steer the conversation away from the Medical Protectorate, Jhee brought the topic back to their swim team days, "Shep showed up the rich jerk, beat the bullies, became captain of the swim team, and won the girl of his dreams."

Jhee finished the recitation with a smile.

"You," Kanto stated.

Sharlet answered first, "Mai."

Jhee tucked away her conch and sought to put a positive frame on it. "Her family did not approve. I used to cover for them so they could date."

In a way, Shep besting Rennie Crag Hall and getting together with Miramar had felt like her victory as well. A mirthless chuckle escaped Shep. Any hope of a pleasant close to conversation left with the tide.

"That's the way it went," Shep said. "Families like theirs undulated over who got to be at the crest or the trough. What remained steady, though, was that families like mine were always beneath theirs. We didn't get to go to Imperial Sojourns unless we were delivering the catch."

An Odd Couple

Was this truly the path Jhee wanted to travel? Jhee sat stoic as Sharlet received guests and circumambulated the room. How had Kanto convinced them to attend?

"If you want to know what she's up to, you need to monitor her. What she does. Who she talks to. The salon makes a perfect cover for her to conduct business," Kanto had said.

Sharlet kissed cheeks with a blue-black furred high Imperial. "Welcome, gentlefolk, distinguished guests."

"I'm sure you will love the treat I have in store for you," the High Imperial said.

"I'm sure," Sharlet said. Her voice oozed that false note Jhee despised.

Jhee's attention went to the two large Fire Folk companions at the Imperial's elbows. Their eyes scanned the room but showed nary an expression. They held themselves stiff but ready.

Shep's instant focus on them told Jhee most of all and confirmed her suspicions they had served. He examined them extra hard. His nostrils flared.

"Berserkers," Jhee said.

Shep gave a curt nod.

Berserker Fire Folk. Jhee's back went straight and rigid. Only one regiment of berserkers had ever been Fire Folk. What was Sharlet up to?

Later, Jhee and her husbands walked into one room of the gallery. The High Imperial's pets waited in the center naked.

The High Imperial leaned in and whispered something to them before she handed them a small vial of reddish liquid: bioplasm. But from what creature?

"Whenever you feel ready or comfortable," the royal said.

The male of the couple knocked back the infusion then started huffing and puffing. The woman took hers. She joined him in the huffing and puffing.

The pair pumped their arms. They went into a series of strong exhales and stomps until they started to sweat. The crowd had gone uncomfortably silent. The pair worked their arms and jumped up and down.

Both Jhee and Shep had gone still. Jhee stroked the sigil on her arm.

At last, the manfolk's eyes went red. Other features changed. Shep tensed when the womanfolk's eye turned red also. They were forcing themselves to skin slip.

For most in the Outer Reaches, it was a gradual process, one adapted a little as they went about their business. On occasion, someone did not look quite the same: sleeker fur, finger webbing, bigger or larger ears, mostly slight changes. Then the next time one saw them, they were back to normal. Jhee had heard inlanders could do it too, but it was much rarer.

However, the only way most went into a full skin slip was traumatic, sudden immersion into an extreme environment. Unless one underwent the berserker procedure. For a creature other than their base skin, animal shifters usually required a fresh infusion of bioplasm from the target animal.

Jhee waited for the berserker pairs' limbs to twist and shift into some sea crea-ture's shape. Folk in the Far Reaches sometimes did this as a parlor feat at parties back home. Not everyone could go the full way, especially if sharing one bioplasm infusion. Shep had been one of the talented few that could. Given how matters turned out, would that he couldn't.

Instead of the pair's limbs changing shape, their esca did. The Fire Folk's distinctive teardrop-shaped mark transformed into the star shape associated with Water Folk's esca. Their furred skin likewise changed from the Fire Folk's signa-ture stripes to solid brownish in color. Their hands had become less claw-like, and their size had decreased by about a factor of two.

Jhee and her husbands gasped. The attendees, as well, once they realized what they saw before them were two Water Folk where once were two Fire Folk, down to the eyes going from teal to gold.

Applause broke out. Shep sat there with a snarl and Jhee with her mouth agape. Even Kanto frowned. Jhee stroked the arm sigil as much to calm herself as Shep.

This technique or condition those from the Far Reaches had was not a party gimmick. Transformations such as this had serious consequences. This was a mockery. They took it seriously, and what they certainly did not do was mimic the Other Folk. Other Folk's composition was too similar to Water Folk, which is the reason one did not shift into them. It might wind up being permanent. Despite what Water Folk thought of the Fire and Other Folk, this proved they weren't such a unique sort as the propaganda would have many believe.

Attendees had approached the berserker pair to fawn and fondle them. Kanto sensing his household members' distress, began subtly maneuvering their group towards the door. Sharlet headed their way only to be intercepted. The High Imperial caught up to them all at the same time.

The High Imperial addressed their hostess. "What did you think of my little entertainment?"

Sharlet, whose smile remained plastered on her face though the corners of her mouth twitched, replied, "Quite illuminating, high born."

"Excuse me," Shep grumbled.

Shep cut through the crowd unceremoniously and left. Kanto replaced Shep at Jhee's side and prevented her from following by grabbing her arm. For Jhee to leave the conversation in such a manner too, without basic pleasantries, was a social misstep bordering on an insult.

"Sorry, did you think that was dreadfully gauche of me?" the High Imperial asked.

It was an abomination, Jhee wanted to say.

"I'm given to understand that many of the folk from your region have similar abilities."

"Yes," Sharlet answered, "many say it is a side effect of being so close to the vagaries of the open seas."

"Sounds probable. It is remarkable, though, that some good could come out of those atrocities. The Medical Protectorate research appeared to have perfected the process in the berserkers."

"Apparently so." Jhee drained her glass and tried to keep her expression blank.

"The trick I found is not to trigger them like the berserkers via combat and violence, but with basic excitement and adrenaline. Hence, all the arm-waving and huffery and puffery."

A man bearing an island senate badge approached and asked leave to join the conversation with a slight bow. After they acknowledged him with a nod, he spoke, "Indeed, it seems to be quite effective. Your companions had me completely fooled. I thought we were being invaded. It appears those freaks over at the Medical Protectorate did something right for all their dreadful experiments. I hear the Medical Protectorate were on the verge of taking it even farther."

"How much farther can there be?"

"Total mimicry. Not simply general characteristics of the Other Folk, but the specific features of a specific individual. There's also mimicking plants and objects. I heard their first experiments were quite… messy. Folk losing coherence and degenerating permanently into puddles."

"Sounds dreadful."

"But you have to admit the intelligence applications would be enormous. You were in the intelligence pool, my lady Justicar. Wouldn't you agree?"

Jhee swirled her drink. "I can see the benefits. The berserker program was not without its drawbacks. I'd say it'd be much simpler to meet such aims with more mundane means such as disguise."

"Or arcana perhaps. Eh there, Professor of Arcane Forensics?"

Jhee chose her words with care and tried to sound casual, "There are some glamors which allow the manipulation of appearance. You also have to take voice and mannerisms into account. However, without close study of the subject, the effect is uncanny like bad prosthetics. The illusion can often be shattered under fast movement or the constant challenge of, say, heavy rains."

"Ah, but therein lies a situation in which physical mimicry of the sort we are discussing proves its worth."

"You have me there, Senator."

Another person, a duchess of some sort, said, "I'd prefer plants and objects. I, for one, find the prospect of someone else running around out there with my face downright disturbing."

"Unless, of course, they could take your place in commerce meetings," the senator responded. "Am I right, Duchess?"

"How right you are, you scoundrel. Though a potted plant could replace most of the folk in those and it wouldn't make much of a difference."

The High Imperial gestured with her glass toward where Shep had left, "I fear my little demonstration did not go over as well with everyone."

"Not at all, your highness," Sharlet said. "There are still some residuals which he has trouble dealing with from the service. He merely needed some air."

"Oh, my word, forgive me. Your brother was part of one of their programs, was he?"

"Yes, he was."

"I did not mean to offend. I simply wanted to show off the talents of my consorts. Forgive me."

"It's not for me to tell your highness what she can or cannot do."

"Marvelous, perhaps you can have him demonstrate his transformation technique for us sometime."

Jhee's jaw clenched. A few choice responses for Sharlet and the High Imperial took shape in her head. Her posture tensed, and she opened her mouth.

Hedge Maze Timeout

"Perhaps," Kanto said before Jhee or Sharlet answered. Right after agreeing to that, perhaps Jhee would sail a raft out to the breakers by the Rock of Woe and go for a swim. Even joking about being alone in those waters made her break out in a cold sweat and quickened her breathing.

Kanto tightened his grip on Jhee's arm. It was enough to make Jhee reconsider her actions.

"High born," Sharlet said, "isn't that the Earl of Marsh, conversing with your companions?"

The High Imperial set her drink down on a passing server's tray. "My word, I need to rescue them before that lecher gets too handsy."

As soon as possible, Jhee and Kanto excused themselves. They found Shep on a balcony. Before they could say anything, Sharlet joined them.

"I'm sorry, kin," Sharlet said. "Not only was that display offensive, but it was also tacky in the extreme, and I would not have allowed it if I had known."

Shep regarded his sister with his brighter, unscarred eye.

"Kin, you still can't be upset about that? I did what I had to do to protect the family. Your drenched hormones brought us to the verge of ruin. Someone had to be pragmatic."

Jhee itched to go for the utensils, fireball her, or maybe just cut off her air. "I suppose your special appointment helped. Where was your protective instinct when the lottery came up? Perhaps you should have protected Shep instead. Then maybe we wouldn't be so upset. You could have protected your family without abandoning him."

Sharlet raised an eyebrow. "By throwing in with you?"

"I won, didn't I?" Jhee said.

"Of course, you did." Sharlet smiled and addressed Shep, "You know it wasn't just my call. I was only a pre-jubilant, not much older than yourselves. Mamere and papere had the final say. Please, don't be this way, brother. For all we know, it's just you and I left. We should make amends."

Shep continued to fix Sharlet with his eye and remained silent. She wrinkled her nose.

"Well, if you are going to continue to be so unreasonable, I'm going to find better company until you decide to act civilized."

"Hence why we haven't seen you in ten years," Jhee said.

"I've been around. I didn't hear my conch chime either."

"Ah, Lady Sharlet, there you are," the island senator called. He had tracked them down and now stood at the threshold of the balcony. "Sorry to disturb, but we need to finish our conversation, sooner rather than later."

"Of course." Sharlet raised the corners of her mouth in a not-quite smile. "Ta for now, and do look after yourselves."

Once they were alone again, Jhee placed her arms around Shep and rubbed his ears with her thumbs. She traced her gaze along the scar running down his face through one eye. Then Jhee frowned and faced out over the balcony. The eye's light was dimmer because of a dagger's damage, her dagger's damage. She wanted to wrap her arms around him longer to comfort him. Yet, the venue and the party made it impossible.

"Let's go find Kanto," Jhee said.

They found Kanto inside commanding the attention of some younger party-goers. They pried him away to sit down for another quick course of drinks and food. Jhee chose a neutral conversation topic, Kanto's work at the youth center.

"Is volunteer work not paying off like you hoped?" Jhee asked when the topic made Kanto wistful.

"To see children develop a passion for music every bit as deep and abiding as House Kenyatta used to be known for. To see the passion for music developing in those youthful faces matches the ecstasy of performance. On the other hand, having to work around the education council's rules and regulations is quite a pain. It would be nice to take a hand in getting the regulations cleaned up."

"Fancy being a Vizier, do you?" Shep asked with a hint of sarcasm.

Jhee brushed it aside, "Aren't you happy at the youth center, dende?"

"The children are brilliant," Kanto said, "the bureaucracy though... So much of my frustration is chronic and systemic to the institutions themselves."

Shep sighed. "Vizier Kanto to the rescue."

"If only. In most cases, you need to be a veteran. Or an imperial lickspittle to even be considered."

Jhee nodded. "True. A history of military service increases one's odds of becoming a vizier by almost forty percent."

"You, in the service?" Shep scoffed.

This time Kanto could not help but notice Shep's mockery. Jhee glowered at Shep's uncharacteristic rudeness to Kanto.

"It appears it might also improve my chances of being taken seriously one hundred percent. I require refreshments," Kanto said, bowed, and returned to the salon.

"You know what Shep, let's get you a timeout. Look out there. You see that? They have a lovely hedge maze. I think I would very much like to see it in person."

Shep nodded in recognition of the escape she offered him. A chance to get away from the crowds and people suited him fine. "It would be my honor."

Shep presented Jhee his arm, and she looped hers through his. A servant directed them to the hedge maze entrance. If it would not have been a social insult, Jhee would have allowed him to stay home. Though, was more time alone truly what was best for him? He did not do well at these events. This was among the reasons he had sought a second. As second, Kanto handled all the balls and social events required at court and the capital. The invitation to this retreat, though, had specifically named Shep and Jhee, as some form of recognition for their military service.

"Sheepdog and Sniffer, you dog-eared bastards."

Shep and Jhee paused at the threshold. A giant walrus of a male lumbered towards them, supporting his weight with a cane.

"Captain Odo?" Shep asked.

"Yep, I see you got my invitation."

"It was you who invited us."

"Least I could do once I heard you had taken up residence in that Maker-forlorn city. Sniffer, how are you doing?"

"Captain Odo, you old bag of blubber," Jhee exclaimed.

Odo shambled closer and pulled them into a crushing embrace.

"So, we have you to thank for trapping us here?"

"You don't think I want to suffer through this torture alone. I figured I'd share my misery with others. Is that young bull gadflying about yours?"

"Yes, Bright Harmony," Jhee said.

"My second," Shep said.

"Har!" Odo said. "That pretty boy is living with you two curmudgeons. Now, I've seen it all. Going to the maze, eh? Allow me to give you the tour."

"Unnecessary, old friend."

"Nonsense. This way. None of this queuing business. Sure way to get lost." Odo took off in a manner that made it clear he expected them to follow. And surprisingly fast. Jhee and Shep had to hustle to catch up to him. "I presume you've heard about this tribunal nonsense."

"Which tribunal?"

"Which? Have you been under the rocks? Ah, yes, I forgot who it was I was speaking to. The jelly-hearted politicos have decided to open up a tribunal into the Medical Protectorate's atrocities."

"We're aware," Jhee answered, "but there are multiple. Which do you mean?"

"The House of Knives."

Jhee and Shep stopped dead calm.

"Exactly my reaction, too. No one needs to go poking about those old wounds. Come on now. This maze isn't getting any easier."

They followed Odo through a secondary entrance to the maze. They eventually found their way to a dead end.

"I thought you said you knew how to get through without getting us lost," Shep said.

"He's not lost," Jhee said. "We're exactly where he means us to be."

"Sniffing out the truth as always," Odo said, his voice serious and low, "ever the precocious Justicar."

Shep bristled up his fur and stood at Jhee's side. "Explain yourself, cap."

"Calm your seas, Sheepdog. I wanted to make sure we lost our tails, so we had privacy for our chat."

"I can provide an additional guard against eavesdropping," Jhee said.

"No, that would only draw attention to us. They are at least as good at detecting as you."

"You mentioned the tribunal and old wounds."

The captain wrinkled his mouth. "Ursula's gone missing."

"Not surprised," Shep said. "She's had more trouble adjusting than the rest of us."

"True, but recently," Captain Odo began then shook his head, "she had been doing better. Then I saw her a long-moon ago."

"So did we."

"She was paranoid, raving about the tribunal. She said she saw death, and it had her face. I'm worried about her."

"You're the one with imperial clout. Why ask us?" Shep asked.

"The situation is delicate."

"You never told your wife about Ursula," Jhee stated.

"I was a dutiful boy. I told the Princess Regent all about it. She took no action but set a condition I was never to see Ursula again. If my Imperial wife learns I've met with her twice, let alone once, I fear it will be worse for Ursula than me. I'm worried, though. This last time I saw Ursula, it was different. I'm afraid she may have done something to herself. Track her down and get her help if you can."

"We'll do this for you, cap. And for Ursula and the others," Shep said.

"We will see what we can do, Captain. Where was the last place you saw her?"

"Packer's Pier One. Thank you. Best get back before we're missed."

Jhee's mind had already begun to turn over the puzzles. Death had her face. She had been witness to some of Ursula's episodes, and she had said nothing like that before. The three of them returned to the party in silence, and the captain went his separate way. Jhee's arm sigil remained inert. She watched Shep but could not get a good gauge on his mood in the dark. He had put on his stone face. Jhee suspected she had as well.

<h1 style="text-align:center">5</h1>

Old Wounds

By the time they saw Kanto again, he stood amongst a group of youthful men indeed decked out in color schemes fathoms more daring than his. Kanto raised his glass to his spouses when he saw them. Jhee hailed Kanto back before taking a walk about with Shep.

"If something's happened to Ursula," Shep said, "That means I'm the last of my berserker gang. We should've done more to help her when she came to us."

Jhee glanced about to see if they were being watched. She stroked his ear with her thumb. He rubbed his head against her hand a moment before they continued to stroll the gardens. The skies here were clear, with barely a hint of lightning or the Storm Wall's ever-present glow. Imperial artificers likely had much to do with that. The arcana that infused it still reached her. One would have to leave the isles and probably travel all the way to the Scorched Lands before that would ever not be the case. Or ascend the Grand Tether to the Stars.

Jhee and Shep stopped on a footbridge, which offered an unobstructed view down the river channel to where the Tether touched the ground on Tether Island. The thin granite line bisected the horizon view. A lightning flash every few minutes illuminated it towards the top where it disappeared into the clouds. The Tether led directly to Equilibrium Point Station at the heart of the Three Worlds' orbit around each other, remnants of the Prototypes' tech. As a feat of mortal design, only the Storm Wall had even come close to matching it.

The wall had been Jhee's hope that horrors like the Medical Protectorate and what happened to Shep and the berserkers would never happen again. She stepped closer to Shep and laid her hand on his shoulder. The Fire Folk may have been stymied, but their off-world counterparts, the Other Folk, were as belligerent as ever.

Later that night, after Jhee and her husbands had retired for the evening, Shep knocked upon her door. Shep regarded her with more intensity and passion than he had in a long-month. They fell into each other's arms. Too soon, Shep sank back into an unreachable silence. He flinched when Jhee reached out to him. Then he rose and paced the floor. She sighed.

"It's fine, Shep," Jhee said.

Shep grabbed a dressing robe and shoved his arms into the sleeves. "No, it's not."

He sat on the edge of the sleeping pallet and rested his head in his hands. At last, he laid back down. Jhee traced one of the scars that left a line through his graying fur and brushed one of the smooth patches where scar tissue had prevented hair from regrowing. Overall, Shep's body hair was coarser and more unruly than Kanto's. Whereas the latter was all slim and sleek, everything about Shep took up space: from his bushier, curlier hair to his wider frame and features.

"I've yet to see those pictures of you in the lenses or any of the ones before secondary school," Jhee teased.

"That's because I thought I'd destroyed them all. I hated the way I looked then," Shep said. His rhythmic breathing hitched, then continued. "Kanto is smooth. No scars. I've seen him bathe. Not a blemish anywhere on him except for his gentleman's scar. I was never that beautiful, even at his age. Noblewomen are judged by the quality of the things they keep around them. He's a much more suitable choice to be on your arm than me. For your introduction to court society. I don't think he's ever known a hardship."

"His hardships don't leave scars on the outside."

"Like some of ours. You should afford yourself of his company more often. You spend half your supposed days off with me. Give him both Mirrei's days. You have my permission. Virility was one of the criteria I selected him on."

"You think I care about any of that," Jhee said. "All I ever wanted was you, and you, me, and Mai, the whole of the Far Reaches, suffered years for it."

Much as the tides, Reach feuds ebbed and flowed. It seemed terribly fitting that the fight, which had once been Jhee's and Miramar's and had spilled over to their families, became theirs again in due course. Jhee did not know who she intended to hurt more with the marriage: Miramar, her family, or the Reaches.

The rules would have to change. As Jhee had reached accommodation with Kanto and Mirrei, the relationship between her and Shep had become unmoored. As she had found roles in her life for the younger spouses, Shep had lost some of his. While it had been as he intended, he was not ready for how it would feel.

Jhee had suspected this might happen. She had resisted becoming attached to her younger spouses. Shep, though, had been driven to find a second husband for her: one more suited for high society, one with all the graces he lacked and who would provide her what she needed to survive the political battlefield of the capital.

Now, Jhee must do the same for him. To survive here, Shep had to know he was still essential to her and had not trained his replacements. She had taken it for granted no topic was off-limits between them, even Miramar. She owed him some small peace of his own in exchange. He sacrificed the actuality of his singular and central role in her life. In exchange, she offered the illusion nothing had changed.

"New rule," Jhee said. "When we are together, we don't talk about them. This is our time. Do you remember how we met?"

Shep sat up. "I think I was bringing in the family nets."

Jhee snuggled up behind him and draped herself on him. "You'd been diving. You emerged from the sea like a sea king of old must have. It must have been cold that day as you had turned more seal than otter. Miramar and I were both instantly smitten."

"I'm not sure if I've ever deserved your devotion." Shep closed his eyes then turned away. "I took a fathership test, Jhee. I needed to know about Mirrei, even if you didn't. She's not. I would have put a stop to this marriage otherwise. You were right to have suspected, though."

As if Jhee had been burnt, she snatched herself away from Shep. The relief was bittersweet as it confirmed what Jhee had never wanted to know: he had had an affair with Miramar. The three of them—Jhee, Miramar, and Shep—were once the best of friends and inseparable until Shep and Jhee eloped in her academy days. Miramar was Mirrei's mother and the woman whose ghost hung over Jhee and Shep's marriage for almost a full jubilee. She had needed the sliver of deniability. Now, it was gone. Jhee left the bed and slipped on a casual robe.

Shep grabbed her hand. "Jhee?"

Jhee tugged her hand loose. Before she left, Jhee asked without turning around, "Congratulations, you've succeeded in pushing me away. One more question: Mirrei's crush was only one way?"

"Yes."

She recited cyphers and statutes in her head to maintain her composure. The First Makers' Design guided her steps to a quiet place in the gardens where her Imperial shadow's presence wouldn't be too noticeable. She pulled out her conch and pored over charts and derivations while small sobs shook her body.

A Search for Equilibrium

Once Jhee had poured out enough tears, she petitioned her Maker within for equilibrium. She returned to the main building and endeavored to find a nice quiet study. A lengthy reading session would recalibrate her. As Jhee reached an enormous set of ebony doors, they pushed open. An imperial lady with saffron eyes and a lithe, sinuousness which reminded Jhee of a water snake swept out nearly leveling Jhee in the process. The imperial paused to raise an eyebrow at Jhee then turned her back on Jhee with a grand sweep of her skirts and haughty, dismissive wave.

Through the open doors, Jhee's search bore fruit when she spied an enormous library. Shelves bulged from floor to ceiling with bio-films and bound seaweed paper tomes. She touched the palms of her hands together at angles before she entered and ran her fingertips over one gorgeous volume bound in burgundy sharkskin, *Imperial Births and Lineages, Volume Twelve*. She let her fingers linger on the pitted, rough pores of the material.

A cup rattled with small items behind her. "Care for a game?" a feminine voice asked.

Jhee gasped and whirled toward the corner from where the offer had come. A dark-skinned, feminine hand holding a dicing cup poked out from an over-stuffed chair in the corner.

The woman shook the cup again. Jhee approached cautiously and respect-fully. The woman's robes were fine, yet studiously devoid of any insignia or identifiable pattern or crests Jhee could attribute to any house. "All pardons, I thought I was alone."

"No pardons necessary. Please, sit."

Jhee took the chair opposite the woman at a *gammancala* game set. Even with the lack of identifiers, the woman's demeanor carried the force of rank, though, from military service or Imperial blood, Jhee could not fathom. Her dark, blue-black skin suggested the latter.

The woman poured them tea from a nearby tea service. Jhee slipped the insulated sleeve over her cup, then turned it three times before picking it up in both hands. "All honors...."

"Lady Amani." The lady turned her cup twice. The number of turns indicated rank based on the degree of removal from the Imperial line. Jhee did not believe for a moment that this woman was only one step closer to the succession than her. Nevertheless, she had to abide by it. Jhee certainly was in no position to challenge the assertion. She was sure to learn the truth fast enough if Jhee crossed the woman's line. The ones who wanted to blur the class lines were often the most dangerous when crossed. Lady Amani picked up her cup, "Honors to you as well, Justicar."

In accordance with high etiquette, Jhee drank a moment after Lady Amani.

The game board had already been set for two. "I hope I didn't interrupt, my lady."

"A habit. My playing companions are limited. I've had to play both sides of the board lately. It's an excellent way to keep oneself sharp. Though I always welcome a new player. Keeps things fresh."

Jhee chose not to mention the woman she had seen stalk out of here. "Just so."

They diced for a while in high spirits. Once they switched to playing a two-person trick-taking card game, Jhee's Maker within answered her petition. The gears began to grind in Jhee's head about how to find Ursula. Perhaps the pier was not the best place to start the search for Ursula. She might want to start with the sailor who had come to see her. Also, there was that hardwood disc Ursula dropped. Jhee had no time to dwell on old betrayals. Her old friends required her assistance in the here and now.

Lady Amani won the first play due to Jhee's distraction. Jhee recovered and won the next two tricks. The game eventually ended with a draw, the preferable outcome to Jhee winning until she knew what kind of noble Lady Amani was. With her mind focused on the Ursula matter, Jhee might miss any warning signs for poor sportsmanship.

Communications on Sovereign's Isle were limited and heavily monitored. Jhee understood that before she accepted as it only made sense. The Regent might intercept a direct search for Ursula while here. It was the sort of pragmatic action Captain Odo's wife, the Regent, would take to keep him honest. With her composure regained and renewed purpose, Jhee excused herself.

To Play With the Courtiers

Kanto touched his credential ring to the verification stone. "I accept. I would also be honored to play with the courtiers' orchestra."

"A servant will contact you about accommodating whatever instrumentation you may require."

Once the messenger left, Jhee gave Kanto a playful clap. "Seems as though you made quite an impression. An invitation to the imperial spouses' luncheon and to play with the courtiers' orchestra in the petite hall!"

He bowed slightly. Then a look of panic spread over his face. "By the First Makers, I need to practice. I also need to brush up on my notation reading. And do I bring my own lute? It would surely be too plain beside what the Imperial courtiers would have. Should I use one of theirs? Then I would have to acquaint myself with the idiosyncrasies and peculiarities of a new instrument on such short notice. What if they give me one from the Imperial collection? What if I drop it or snap a string? Some of those instruments are hundreds, thousands of years old."

Kanto bolted to the next suite and spent the rest of the evening going through outfits and examining his instruments. Once he had finished with that, he practiced on his lute for most of the evening. He swore as he messed up notes over and over.

"Calm yourself, dear one. It's the anxiety. You are putting too much pressure on yourself."

"I know. Gah. I'm just so nervous. I want to make a wonderful impression. This is it, Jhee. The Imperial family. It doesn't get more upper class than this. Aside from an audience with the Grand Sovereigns themselves. If that were to happen, I am liable to pass out and die."

"Stand up," Jhee said.

"I have to practice."

"I said, 'stand up.' Obey your denbe."

Kanto sighed and reluctantly got to his feet. Jhee dropped into a wide motion meditation stance. "I don't have time for this."

"Yes, you do. What you need to do is meditate. Clear and center first. Then you can go back to practicing."

Jhee guided Kanto through motion meditation sequences for several minutes. "Now, try again."

Kanto sat down and picked up his lute. Beautiful, dulcet tones flowed from it as he played along with a piece he had never tried before. He finished the piece to great applause from Jhee.

"Thank you. It was the first time I tried that piece."

"See. Clear and center. Now what you also need to do is rest, so you are fully refreshed for your performance."

"By the Maker's plan, you are right. If I don't get enough sleep, I'll show up with puffy eyes. What sort of impression would that make?"

"One, I'm more than sure your make up skills could turn around."

"Thank you, Jhee."

"No 'thank you' required. It's an honest assessment of your skills."

"No, I mean for everything." Kanto came over and put his arms around her waist. "I dreamed of being at the imperial palace, meeting the Regent Sovereigns when I was young. Now, because of you, I just about realized that dream."

Jhee's face felt warm. "You would have found a way."

"No, nobody but you could have done that for me. We did it together. This is why I never regretted marrying you. Even when you were acting like a complete saphead."

"Thank you for putting up with me while I came to understand your worth."

Kanto grinned. "I'm flipping priceless and don't you forget it."

"Wouldn't even dream of it. Never crossed my mind. Not in a millennium."

"You know what, Jhee? You are too."

"I'm glad you can see that despite how I acted."

Jhee worked with Kanto up until a messenger collected him for practice and staging. At the petite hall, Jhee was seated in the section reserved for performers' guests and imperial benefactors. Shep was nowhere to be found. Eventually, the seat to one side of her was taken by a flamboyant yet dignified older male. A slender male with statelier, single-colored robes and sandy hair took the other seat beside her.

When Kanto played, Jhee perched on the edge of her seat, almost as anxious about his performance as he was. She restrained herself from clapping like a ninny once his group finished. Jhee caught his eye, and they shared a smile.

"Talented companion. Yours?" the sandy-haired male asked.

Jhee nodded, though she bristled at the notion of Kanto as property. Then a feeling of hypocrisy set in. Before Jhee could dwell on it, she spotted Shep's sister Sharlet talking to the same island senator who had collected her after the appalling slipping demonstration at her salon. The sandy-haired male continued to make small talk while Jhee watched Sharlet and the senator speak.

The Return to "Normal"

The rest of the sojourn proceeded without event, though Jhee and Shep kept their distance from each other. Kanto was the star of the show. At least, he had enjoyed himself. He remained ecstatic after they left the sojourn. Jhee tried to match his enthusiasm. She and Shep grudgingly acknowledged each other when they had to.

Kanto checked their messages. There was a message from Mirrei. "Hi, kin. I know you are at the Imperial Sojourn, but I just wanted to say 'hi' and 'I miss you.'"

Normally, Jhee would have been ecstatic, but Mirrei's face, the spitting image of Miramar, at the moment was only salt in the wound. "I'll be in my study," Jhee said. She went to her study and closed the door. She took a finger quill and began to list every data point she had for Ursula.

At Captain Odo's suggestion and her own common sense, she delayed her search for Ursula until they left. Upon their return to the normal world, Jhee threw herself into the search. She spent her first night home locked in her study, contacting folk via conch.

Jhee tapped the data shell Ursula had dropped against her esca. She weighed the invasion of privacy against its evidentiary value. Before it came to that, Jhee had other less invasive means to find Ursula. She used her credentials to access the Justicar code base and check the death records. None of the local morgues or body disposal facilities had a record of anyone matching Ursula's description, nor did the veterans' last repose societies and services. A dread notion within her released. Though, they just could not have found the body yet.

Next, she checked with local hospitals, mental institutions, and veteran care facilities to see if they admitted anyone with Ursula's features. Last, she checked the major imperators' branches for anyone arrested who might fit her description. All came up empty.

Ursula might still be alive. She was resourceful and had a small military pension-provided residence, which came as part of their separation benefits. Checking that out would be the first item on tomorrow's agenda.

Jhee had fallen asleep in her study and encountered Shep on her way to her rooms.

"Come with me to exercise Dari?" Shep asked.

The morning run was usually his alone time, except for Bax and Dari. Despite their estrangement, Jhee felt honored. The run was Shep and Bax's exclusive routine with Dari because the pair and Dari had bonded in a way Jhee would never know, a way she and Shep used to be. They had started the routine when the pair went ahead to set up their house while Jhee and the younger spouses stayed at the villa of an old schoolmate on the outskirts of Galleon City.

Shep and Jhee walked arm-in-arm to the area of the park where many did their morning exercises. She participated in one of the devotions-in-motion gatherings. He removed Dari's leash and let the shark dog run about and play with the other hounds.

Jhee picked up a stick and played fetch and retrieve with Dari. The shark hound served as a cautionary tale of where Shep could end up if he neglected his health. Dari ran into the distance and dutifully brought back the stick. Her tongue lolled out in expectation of praise. Jhee knelt and ruffled Dari's fur. "Good girl. Good girl."

As Jhee fought off the shark hound's rough tongue, she noticed Shep scanning the park.

"What is it?" Jhee asked.

Shep shrugged. "One of the other hound owners who normally exercises their dog around this time isn't here."

"Schedules change from time to time."

"True, we've only been here a few moons. Yet, every day like clockwork, she was there. It's unusual is all."

"Is there some other reason you're worried?"

"I think she ganged."

"Another berserker? Are you sure?"

"No. I'm not sure," Shep snapped. He contemplated the ground. "They, we, have a look, one you can recognize on others. You've seen it. A way they carry themselves. Also, some things she said. I couldn't put a finger on it. Sometimes you just know. What with Ursula missing...."

Jhee took a breath. "Do you want me to ask around while I look for Ursula?"

"No. No. I don't suppose we should. She was practically a stranger, after all."

Jhee hurled the fetch stick so hard she nearly wrenched her shoulder, and Dari ran after it again. Shep continued to search the faces of everyone who passed them by in the park. Jhee didn't want to name what she was feeling.

Eventually, Jhee and Shep put Dari back on the leash and stopped at one of the beverage carts for kolal and pastries. She thought through her plan to locate Ursula because it kept her mind off other matters. Jhee had a cinnamon-raisin twist while Shep ate a peach tart. Dari panted at them expectantly.

"None for you, old girl. You're on a strict diet."

Jhee and Shep found a bench nearby on which to sit and watch the suns rise higher. Off in the distance, the shadowy outline of the Grand Tether split the skyline. The sinking feeling Jhee got when Shep mentioned the hound-walking woman had taken her by surprise. It reminded her of the dread she carried after finding out Miramar and Shep had corresponded after their marriage.

"Mai told me, you know?" Jhee said, unable to state her feelings more directly than that. "When the situation was at its worst, she threw it in my face. To be honest, though, I shouldn't have been surprised. You cheated on her with me."

"The woman with the hound is just a friend, a counselor from the veteran services center on the other side of the park," Shep said, having discerned the source of Jhee's anxiety. "She works with gangers. I thought maybe, Ursula, us, too."

Jhee gave a nod. She and Shep brainstormed all the places they would expect to find Ursula.

"Where would Ursula go if she were feeling agitated?"

"Many of us like calm places full of greenery; parks; gardens. It's the flip side of our conditioning. How they calmed us down."

"I remember." They held hands, and he ran a thumb over her knuckles. "We'll start with other parks. You should stay here."

"But, I can help."

Only the top floors of the veteran's service center could be seen when Jhee gazed in that direction. She had attended a counseling session as she promised she would, one single session. Shep, though appeared to have kept his word better than she had on that score. Jhee talked to Shep about everything. Where did she go to talk about him or the self-doubts she did not want to burden him with?

Jhee brushed Shep's facial scar with her thumb. "I have no defenses when it comes to you. You'll be more of a distraction than anything if you come along. You blind me in a way nothing else does."

"Please, Jhee," Shep said.

"I will take Bax. I'll let you know when I return."

6

____

~

The Search Begins

Jhee summoned Bax, and they called a transport around. "Bax, are you familiar with those Shep talks to while he is out with Dari?"

"Aye, Justicar."

"Are you familiar with the hound owner? The one who he is concerned about?"

"Aye, Justicar. I may have seen them speaking in passing."

"Did you see her speak with anyone else?"

"A few other hound owners. As I said, Justicar, I only saw her in passing."

"Was she there on the regular like Shep says?"

Bax fidgeted. "Aye, Justicar."

Ursula missing and also Shep's acquaintance: one definitely a berserker and the other allegedly, or at the very least, berserker adjacent. Jhee worked over in her mind what it might mean. Coincidence perhaps? She needed to keep her Maker's eye open and not let a preconceived notion blind her.

Jhee decided against visiting Ursula's last knowns and old hangouts, flashing a picture of her. If Ursula were just lying low, that would be the quickest way to ensure she'd go to ground. Then they might never find her.

Jhee and Bax spent the better part of the day checking parks and gardens, including several zoological ones near areas Ursula had been known to frequent. After a while, Jhee's knees and feet ached fiercely. Some park, preserve, or another occupied every patch of this Maker-forlorn city. That did not even count the numerous private courtyards. Jhee pinched the bridge of her nose.

Perhaps they should have started closer to home with their own park. But Jhee had needed distance from Shep.

Jhee and Bax made more inquiries, which also came up empty. Perhaps she should not have been so quick to prevent Shep from joining them. She had meant what she said about him being a distraction. Her feelings were in flux between the confirmation of the affair with Miramar and the knowledge of this dog walking friend of his.

"Did you follow him that night?" Jhee asked Bax. "Do you know where Shep went that night he took off after Ursula?"

"Aye, Justicar. You came home from date night alone, and you seemed sore worried."

"And?"

Bax fidgeted some more. "Begging your pardon, Justicar, but I'm asking your leave to keep that between me and Mr. Shep."

While Bax was Jhee's head servant and trusted adviser, he also claimed to be a distant relative of Shep's. Bax came into her employ after she saved him from being mutilated by the previous Justicar of her home district. He pledged his life-long service to her because he owed her a life debt, as he put it. Even if Bax's claim of kinship to Shep was dubious, he became almost as loyal to Shep as to her. Because of Shep's bond and caring for Dari, Bax behaved almost as an uncle to Shep, too. Did where Shep go that night involve Dari? That might be the only topic that could split Bax's loyalty this way. Jhee respected the old man enough not to force him to betray Shep's confidence, yet.

Bax and Jhee went to Ursula's apartment. He rubbed his chin and grunted approval at the lock. Though she had no doubt Bax could have gained them entry without it, Jhee produced the key Odo had given her. This was not her jurisdiction, and she had less latitude, though Captain Odo had given her an open, notarized writ for emergency use only. Jhee chose not to question Odo about why he had the key, but she would revisit the matter with him later. She suspected a stronger connection between the captain and Ursula than he let on. Until it became immediately relevant to her preliminary inquiries, she would let him keep his own counsel. Jhee had been doing that a lot lately. Perhaps she should start demanding more candor from the men in her life.

"Perhaps we can enlist some other members of you and Mr. Shep's old unit to help track her down?"

"Shep, the captain, and Ursula are the only ones left. The other problem is, Bax, Ursula was the unit's scout and tracker. If it was someone else who had gone missing, she's who I might send to find them. Which means if she doesn't want to be found, we'll need Lethys Luck to find her."

"Then, we best give libation to Lethys and the Rum Toad at every shrine we come across. Couldn't hurt."

She chuckled. It was as fine an idea as any she had.

Jhee had not been sure of what she expected to see on the other side of the door. The neat and cleanly kept apartment was not it. Between what the captain said and their knowledge of Ursula's condition, she had expected a mess; empty or half-empty liquor bottles; trash. This is not the apartment of someone unable to take care of themselves. This almost made no sense.

"You're probably right." Jhee touched her palms together at angles in a minor act of blessing.

Jhee walked through the apartment. A cleaning or home care service might have done it. But a closer inspection showed the neat, well-maintained folds and alignments of military discipline. Ursula still kept the apartment to the nines, regimented like during their service. The order, the discipline must have been what Ursula needed most once she returned home. Shep had been the same. The lack of structure sometimes drove him inward.

At last, Jhee discovered a bound picture of Ursula and Odo, a recent one. She picked it up and felt a bulge in the back of it. Removing the frame's back exposed an envelope. Jhee read the contents. These were intelligence credentials, signed by Captain Odo, which designated Ursula as a confidential informant or asset.

Saw her only occasionally, my snout, Jhee thought.

An Empty Plate

Jhee and Bax returned home from their day's adventures empty-handed, disappointed, and with more ambivalence toward Shep than ever. She had done what she could and found neither hide nor hair of Ursula, let alone some random hound-walking woman counselor. Shep and Kanto laid out pots and utensils in the kitchen together. She paused to observe how they got on without her influence. She was also loathed to break the mood with her lack of progress.

"You can't cook in that," Shep declared.

"What's wrong with what I'm wearing?" Kanto asked.

"Your sleeves. No sleeves or narrow sleeves are best for cooking unless you plan on catching them on fire or trailing them through grease and sauce. Once you change, the first thing I'm going to teach you is called a reduction."

"Why did we set up Mirrei's chemistry lab in the kitchen?" Kanto asked.

Shep sighed. "It's not a chemistry lab. It's molecular gastronomy equipment. Some sort of fancy way of cooking she was just getting into. I meant it as a surprise, but now I think I might want to learn it myself."

"Oh, I've seen and heard some of what they can do with their dishes. A chemistry lab, as I said. It is kind of ingenious. You'll be able to make creations like those with these kitchen stations?"

"Maybe. Though, seems like an awful lot of trouble. A good sous vide. A nice sauce and done is my usual go-to."

"But molecular gastronomy makes it the pinnacle of high art. It takes the dining experience to another level."

Shep slapped down a skillet on one of the burners. "The pinnacle of the dining experience is having a good, tasty meal. Everything that doesn't contribute to that is a waste and a distraction from that. Food preparation, the serving of a good plate, meals are about the people. Giving them great tastes to nourish their bodies as well as their senses."

"I'd argue that last part is what molecular gastronomy is trying to do. Feast the senses as well as the appetite. But this is your area of expertise, and you know better."

"Nice to see you agree," Jhee said and pulled up a stool at the kitchen island. Two empty place settings waited there: one for her and one for the Lost Makers. An empty place for the Lost and Unknown Makers was an old outland tradition. They could have fed an army in their kitchen. They had each put their imprimatur on the house. All she had wanted was a study and an arcane workshop, preferably connected. For safety reasons, they had convinced her to put her workshop, which housed her more volatile experiments at a remove from the house.

Jhee admired the impressive, state-of-the-art kitchen Shep had designed. Each member of the household got to put their stamp on the house. Shep and Mirrei planned out the kitchen. The kitchen was Shep and Mirrei's passion project. Shep and Kanto largely designed the landscaping and hardscaping except for the plants and gardens. She and Mirrei had masterminded those: herb gardens, hot houses, and even an algae pond. Kanto and Mirrei had planned many of the connective and social aspects of the house's functions. Music systems, redundant power arrays, extra tethered and ether connectivity. Jhee and Shep worked on the physical security. Ever the cautious ones, they put in a panic room and a few secret hiding spots. She, Mirrei, and to a lesser extent, Kanto had overseen the learning areas like the studies and entertainment rooms. A winding practice space and a small place, which could be a mini-lecture hall. A workshop or craft room or studio for each of their interests. Kanto, herself, and Shep had overseen the layout of the exercise room.

Shep turned to Jhee, expectant. She shook her head. While Kanto left to change his robes, Shep plated some pasta and set it on the table in front of her.

"Bax and I checked every park, garden, and bush from one end of the city to the other. I checked her apartment, with the morgues, etc. Nothing. Not a trace of her."

Shep's expression fell. Jhee chose to hide her disappointment. Ursula was Jhee's friend, too, maybe not like she was to Shep. Jhee still had the folk from her old intelligence unit that she would drop everything for in a minute. Jhee had been the liaison officer to Shep's berserker gang; the closest she had been allowed to get to their unit due to the conflict of interest it presented. Jhee had, however, used what influence she could, where she could on their behalf. The shaky ethics of it had been justified, she told herself. At the time, they were still fighting the machinations of Houses Mitsu and Crag Hall. They tried to make conditions worse for him, and she countered to ease his burdens.

"Well, you did your best," Kanto said upon his return. "You did do your best, didn't you?"

Jhee nodded, even though she was not sure.

"Now, what is it you think you can teach me about good food, denme, that I don't already know?"

"You know about good food and good wine because you've read about them or seen them in a publication," Shep replied, "or you've seen them on a list somewhere. I want to teach you both why they are good, and that inexpensive ingredients can sometimes be just as good."

"They taught me to enjoy good food at finishing school."

"Correction: they taught you to pretend to like good food. I'm going to teach you how to truly appreciate it."

Kanto touched Jhee and Shep's hands. "Who knows? Maybe your friend will turn up safe and sound, and this worry will have all been for nothing?"

Jhee smiled. She might have been won over by Kanto's optimism if she and Shep had not exchanged looks. Neither of them said it, but they were sure Ursula was dead or worse.

~

The Commission Files

The search for Ursula fell by the wayside as Jhee resumed her duties. While she was working at the legal clinic, she received a visit from the academy dean.

"I'm sure some of you are aware of the ongoing tribunal about the Flower Wars and the abuses of the Medical Protectorate," the dean said. Xe straightened the burgundy sleeves of hir dean's robe. "The clinic has been asked to catalog some findings, help identify victims, and perhaps triage many of the cases to determine if they should be included in the tribunal. This will be the prelude to the establishment of a reconciliation commission to address some wrongs the Empire did to its citizens and others."

"Wrongs done? The empire has done nothing but protect and defend its citizens. These people should be grateful."

The comments were greeted with furious knocks on the tables. Several of the students shook their heads. Jhee folded her arms.

"My Lady Justicar, I wanted to ask you and your clinic if you would be interested in spearheading our efforts, as a veteran yourself."

The Knock Brigade now regarded her with a touch of admiration. "I'll do what I can, Dean."

"Thank you. Who knows, Justicar? Do a good enough job, and they might appoint you to the tribunal or reconciliation commission."

After the dean left, Jhee pulled out the case files xe had left behind.

"You served, Justicar?" one student asked.

"Yes," Jhee replied.

"Where?"

"Wherever the empire needed me."

Another student spoke, "But you were an influential noble, so you got kept off the front lines?"

"Did you kill any barbarians?" another student asked.

Jhee shut her eyes to block out the images, but that only made it worse. She sneered, then marshaled herself to stillness. "Never ask a veteran that. I was in the intelligence pool, which, as has been aptly noted by some, kept me off the front lines. We pushed paper and deciphered messages."

"I heard the intelligence pool was full of spies," a fourth student remarked.

Jhee sighed. "It was full of those wealthy and powerful enough to get themselves out of combat—in case they could not find some other way to manipulate the lottery. We should get back to the task at hand. We're going to go through each of these case files."

The e-tech gul arrived, and they spent the day setting up students with limited access to the judicial archives. Jhee watched them eagerly work while she found it hard to open the case files. On the occasion she did, she saw all the acts she had done in service of the Empire.

The tribunal had been mainly convened due to public outcry from the families of the victims after they found out the truth of how they died. During the decommissioning of one of the old Medical Protectorate buildings, a mass grave was found. The island facility had been due to be sunk. Instead, some enterprising person had bought the property, which was little more than a bit of island and dirt poking out of the ground and planned on turning it into cheap, refugee housing.

Until they discovered the macabre remains on the site.

Soldiers and knights who had been reported killed in battle or, as was the standard explanation, lost at sea, LAS.

Jhee shuddered. She thought about her two older sisters. She thought about the hardships she and those like Shep had to endure. The popular consciousness dubbed the main Medical Protectorate facility, the House of Sorrows. Those experimented on there had another name for it: The House of Knives.

Her disappointment in the Storm Wall resurfaced. Would it never end? Would the Empire always betray them? In the end, what did it matter? Those skin-scrapers would find some new ways to steal their blood, sweat, and tears. And then come up with some new way to do it all again.

Jhee rested her head in her hands and thought about Ursula out there. The Empire had used her as a chew toy and spit her out. When had Jhee last checked in with veteran services? The Empire had managed to get proper care for their physical wounds right at least. The veteran services division, though, had fallen woefully short on services for the wounds that mainly showed on the inside. The closest they came was the therapeutic companion program Shep and Dari participated in—even that, though, had its own peculiar drawbacks.

Ursula and the tribunal still weighed on Jhee's mind as she returned home. Shep and Dari relaxed in the study while Kanto played his lute for them. She sat down on the arm of Shep's overstuffed chair. She rubbed his shoulders as they appreciated Kanto's lovely playing. This is what it was all about: their family.

Jhee pulled out her conch and made herself comfortable in her armchair beside Shep's. The four, Shep, Jhee, Kanto, and Dari, sat wordlessly together. No strife. No worries. It occurred to Jhee this was what she and Shep had fought so hard for. The person beside you is who you fought for. Did this make it all worth it?

Jhee closed her eyes and allowed Kanto's playing to transport her to another place and time of youthful optimism and vast, empty homes where sadness appeared to be a part of the walls themselves, a House of Sorrows all its own.

Shep and Miramar: it was like a wisp fancy. Jhee was enamored of both of them and the idea of them. She could go home to a cold, humorless, empty, dark house where her parents did nothing but cry all day, or she could hang out with them: two young, carefree lovers living their fullest lives. The oppressive atmosphere of Hillside only worsened once she went away to the academy. She hated coming back there.

Jhee opened her eyes when Dari began to whine. The shark dog had gone on point.

The door chimes tinkled. They had dismissed the servants for the evening, so Jhee took it upon herself to answer the door.

Ursula waited on their doorstep, wide-eyed and in deplorable condition.

"Shep!" Jhee called.

Shep and Dari bounded into the entryway. He stopped short.

Ursula clutched them. "Thank the Makers! I didn't know where else to go. Sniffer, Sheepdog, you have to help me. Death is after me."

With that, Ursula collapsed. Jhee and Shep caught Ursula, punctuated by more whining from Dari.

The Gray Lady of the Deeps

Jhee and Shep had Kanto make ready the secret room for Ursula. Meanwhile, Shep tended their fallen friend and kept her comfortable as she lay unconscious. While Shep strove to diagnose her condition, Jhee took charge of Ursula's clothing.

"Sheepdog," Ursula said in a hoarse whisper.

Shep used a wet cloth to wipe the woman's brow and gave her a sip of water. She gulped at the glass. "Easy, Urlibird. You're dehydrated and malnourished."

Ursula fell back on the bed. "Thank you."

"Now, Urli, tell us what's going on, if you're up to it," Jhee said.

Ursula nodded. "I saw the Unmaker. In the guise of the White and Gray Lady of the Deeps, except she had my face."

"What does that mean, Urli?"

"The Unmaker is coming for me, coming for us all."

"Yes, we all die."

Ursula shook her head, then fell back on the pillows in frustration.

Jhee tried again, "What are you trying to tell us?"

"Jhee, enough," Shep said. "Let her be."

Ursula lapsed back into a fitful unconsciousness. Jhee pulled Shep aside. "Do you have any idea what she means?"

"Outside my depths."

"When she's stronger, perhaps I'll use inspiration on her."

"No, you won't." Shep looked apologetic when Jhee pursed her lips. "*Our friend* needs time to heal. Her system may not be able to handle anything so invasive."

Jhee tucked her hands into her sleeves. "Do you think it was the news about the HOK?"

"Could be. Why did they have to go poking into that? Why couldn't they just let it lie? We'd made our peace with it."

Jhee pressed her hands together inside her robes. "Ursula hadn't. I didn't tell you this, but Ursula came to me a few years ago. She wanted to know how to convene a tribunal. I gave her the names of a few contacts. I didn't think much of it at the time."

"And you never told me?"

"I figured it was just Urlibird being flighty. She seemed desperate for someone to listen."

Shep tugged on his arm hairs. "Of course, of course. Do you think Ursula is one of the anonymous plaintiffs?'

"Would that track with what you know of her?"

"Yeah. Do you think someone would be willing to kill her over it?"

"You tell me, Shep."

"Maybe. None of us wanted to revisit it. Many of us told her to let it lie. It's one of the reasons we drifted apart. Maybe I should have listened."

"Could any of those who wanted it that way have wanted it badly enough to silence her permanently? That could explain why she thought the Unmaker was coming for her."

"It could."

Jhee tapped a finger against her nose. "But why would she say it had her face?"

"Either way, we should tell Odo we found her. He would want to know."

"I think we should hold off for the moment."

"Why, Jhee? Surely, you don't think Cap's in on this?"

Jhee showed Shep the image she found of Ursula and Odo she found. "The captain is not telling us the whole truth at the very least. It might be best if no one but us knows she's alive and where she is for now."

"I'll defer to your wisdom."

"I think we should examine her clothes. Perhaps we can figure out where she's been all this time."

Kanto held out his hands for the bundle. He wrinkled his nose once he got a good whiff. After he recovered, he turned out the pockets, patted the garb down, and checked the hems.

The lining of Ursula's overcoat bore fruit. Kanto held up a slim, leather-bound journal. "Jhee, this leather is expensive and well-maintained. I thought you said she was broke and practically homeless."

"She was." Jhee took the journal from him and undid the clasp. It was a volume full of illegible cacography. It did not resemble the basis of any arcane cypher, though it did have the characteristics of a traditional cipher. "Maybe this was why Death was after her?"

With a little more thought, it reminded Jhee of finger sequencing mazes. Though not one Jhee had ever seen, and there was no starting sequence, a must if you were to figure out the movements required to solve a watchwork puzzle. The journal also contained identification belonging to Ursula, but an address that matched none from her public records. What sort of dual life was Ursula leading?

"I'll cook her some healing broth," Shep said, "and see if I can follow along with one of Mirrei's healing draught recipes."

"Good. Good."

"Death had her face."

Jhee tapped her snout some more. She might check out the new address at first-sun tomorrow. A return to her legal clinic might also be in order. The tribunal files were sensitive enough no one was allowed off-site access, not even the low-level data being worked on by the legal clinic students. She would examine the tribunal records and see if there was a clue contained there. If Ursula was one of the anonymous plaintiffs bringing the suit, she needed to know who would have the most interest in keeping Ursula quiet.

Jhee waited with Ursula while Shep concocted a healing draught. The data shell Jhee found some time ago rested in Jhee's pocket. She brought it out and considered again if she should read it. After a moment, Jhee realized Ursula had regained consciousness again. Her eyes fixed on the data shell.

"Urli, you planted this on me, didn't you? May I have your permission to look at it?"

Upon seeing the data shell, Ursula set her jaw, and the sharp shades of anger infused her eye color. "I don't care. It's no use to me anymore. I never want to see that again."

"May I look at it?"

"Do what you want."

"I'll need the access code."

"I don't have it."

7

———

∼

The Face in the Mirror

The tribunal files remained as inscrutable and disturbing as before. Dozens and dozens of folk like Shep and his unit gave their accounts. Jhee tried to focus on the puzzle, the mechanics of the matter. This was about getting to the truth and not about her family or their grief. No. She shook her head. Her sisters were heroes killed in combat. They had not met this fate. She could not afford to think anything else and be distracted.

Eventually, Jhee closed her eyes and rested her head in her hands. She needed a break. The cafeteria would be closed. Instead, she prowled the halls for a food dispensary. When she eventually found one, she stared through the banks of heavily processed treats and snacks. Jhee sighed. The noodle nook on the corner might be the better option. A nice sit and some kolal or spiced zoba tea might allow her to focus better.

The fine hairs on the back of Jhee's neck stood up.

She stilled herself and glanced in the reflective surface of the dispensary's front. Nothing behind her. She turned her head one direction. Nothing but shadows. She turned her head the other. Only shadows there, too. She relaxed. Then one shadow moved.

Jhee stepped back in alarm. So did the shadow. Jhee dropped into a stance.

The shadow mimicked her. She prepared a cypher. The shadow matched her movements. Exactly. Then Jhee noticed the background behind the shadow matched what she had seen as she came down the hall.

Jhee realized with a chuckle she was looking at a mirror. She approached it and had another laugh at herself. Hands reached out of the mirror and grabbed her shoulders.

Jhee jerked awake, still at her desk in the clinic with the tribunal files arrayed on the desktop before her. The siren module in her neck ached something fierce from the odd way she had slept.

With deliberate slowness, Jhee pored over the tribunal files. Case after case after case, a pattern emerged. Not about misreported deaths, but about the address where many of the pension drafts were being sent. Seven of the sixteen families received their death benefits drafts at the same address. They may have signed the pensions over to a settlement service in exchange for a lump sum; except when Jhee performed an address lookup, the address resolved to the middle of the East Harbor.

Next, Jhee researched the families and crosschecked who they claimed as their qualifying veteran. The trail led away from the parties to the main suit, to an unrelated group of service folk. According to services records, half of the veterans had no family on file. Half those whose deaths the tribunal sought to answer had no family on file. Then who were the folk pushing for the reconciliation council?

It may have been extreme expunging. Some deep cover operatives had their records erased during their assignments. Or the complementary process where they had created a series of deep assembled identities that could be used in a pinch. What if those identities had been put to a different use by the Medical Protectorate? False identities created for experimentation victims. Perhaps not volunteers or criminals but everyday folk kidnapped and sold to Medical Protectorate like the refugees trafficked at Tranquility Bridge.

Jhee laid a finger aside her nose. Her mind went back to the Imperial Sojourn and the two companions who could skin slip into Other Folk. The questionable veterans may have been killed or died in the Scorched Lands in one of the Empire's numerous deep infiltration operations. The chosen operatives would live out their lives reporting back to the Empire from deep within the heart of the Other Folk's territories. For that matter, were these folk even dead?

The bodies were real enough, but those could have been swapped for others no one would miss.

What was Jhee going to do with this information? This was a matter of Imperial Security, and that meant the Abyssal Constabulary might be involved. If she told anyone else about this, even an official such as she could be made to disappear. Jhee scrolled through the records. *Stop now.* She did not have to keep looking into this. *Let it go. Protect your family.* They mattered most. Right?

Right. Jhee gathered her papers and packed to leave. She would let this rest. A montage of all the damage her selfishness had caused in the past replayed in her mind. Recently, she had almost made that mistake again twice. There would not be a third—not if she could help it. She would not go down the path of the puzzle, the game, at all costs again. Family is what was important. Family is what mattered. It had taken her so many years to rebuild her family, Jhee would not risk it now.

Jhee tucked her valise under her arm and walked out of the clinic and back to the loving embrace of her family. The family plus one ate their dinner of halibut.

"What was it like being in the service?" Kanto asked. "Growing up in the Reaches, I remember the posters of those proud, resolute folk in their bespoke uniforms. Noble-looking folk with bright eyes, bold stances posed above messages to join the military for a chance to prove your quality. Not only that, but it was also your duty and obligation as a citizen of the Empire."

"And I knew folk who joined because it meant they got to kill 'barbarians,'" Shep said.

Ursula pushed some food around her plate. "For every two military recruiters who candidly wanted to ensure I knew what I was getting into, there was one who only cared about the recruitment bonus. They promised easy assignments in exotic locales."

Shep smiled and nodded. "Instead you got stationed on some polluted, hardscrabble atoll or in a Scorch hole with spider-mice the size of dogs. Do you remember that one Lockjaw shot with the forty-cal? I think he just pissed it off. You should have seen it, an entire squad fleeing from one spider-mouse."

"Um, yes."

Jhee laughed while holding what she had uncovered close to her heart. Ursula kept poking at her halibut with her nail pike. This was a much more stable if taciturn Ursula than Jhee was used to seeing. Despite how she turned up on their doorstep, the wasted away aspect of her appearance had gone as well as the pall that had hung heavy on her.

After dinner, Jhee pored over the Albatross dossiers again with an eye toward different irregularities, safer irregularities. Having once seen the pattern, she could not help but notice it anyway. How could she not be horrified by what she had found?

"Denme," Kanto said.

Jhee reacted with a startled, "Hm?"

"Everyone's retiring."

"Yes. Yes. Help Ursula up to her room if you would."

"What about you?"

"I have work to finish up for the evening. Keep her company. I'll be up soon to say good night."

In her study, Jhee stared at the Albatross dossiers. Something must be done. *But not by you.*

Jhee left the study. Kanto and Ursula were still enjoying drinks in the sitting room.

"Miss Ursula, why don't you have brands like Shep?"

Ursula lifted her pant leg. "A brand? I do. Right here. Ain't she a beaut? Says I'm property of the empire."

"Shep has that, but he has an extra one on his neck."

"Couldn't tell you anything about it, son."

~

The Youth Center

Jhee wandered the capital streets, allowing the Path Maker and the First Makers' Design to guide her steps. The impulse to visit Kanto seized her. She hailed a transport, then did not hop out until in front of Kanto's youth center.

The youth center's neighborhood was not all that different from the area near the free clinic she supported in Galleon City. It was the same in most cities and towns. The poor gathered where they were allowed, where the affluent seldom frequented. Noisy transport hubs, dumps, and industrial areas housed those who had no options or resources to find alternatives. Anywhere else until the more well off in a search for bargains arrived to push them out by driving up costs. Then the cycle began anew elsewhere. In these areas, the poor always remained because the risks still outweighed the bargain.

Inside the youth center, a volunteer pointed Jhee to Kanto's location. Kanto's bright citrine and amethyst trimmed robes contrasted with the dingy classroom and similar but dirtied colors of the children's toys. Muddled light beamed in from frosted windows covered with rusty security grating and in need of a good cleaning. Jhee took a moment to watch him with the children.

Despite being in an environment Jhee was sure he would not be caught dead in as little as a year before, Kanto appeared the happiest she'd ever seen him. He and the children bounced along to the beat of the radio as it played one of those songs she had been hearing everywhere. A presentation board behind him bore musical notations and the lyrics. She puzzled out that it was one of the other songs she had heard many of her students enjoying. That was an excellent teaching technique she sometimes used herself: relate one's lessons to a cultural touchstone that would be of interest to the children.

Many of the children and Kanto sang along. Jhee never recalled hearing him do more than hum. At the chorus, all the children joined in, and he performed some trendy dance move. Had she ever seen him dancing in such a common fashion? Jhee knew him to be a gifted dancer, but all she had ever seen him perform were the formal tunes of courts and the partner dances.

Kanto smiled when he saw her. Jhee gyrated along with her head at least, but she knew it looked awkward and offbeat. The song ended, and Kanto turned off the broadcast receiver.

"See what I mean about the timing and rhythm patterns?" Kanto asked his students. "It's very similar to those played by our ancestors of thousands of years ago, or even the First Ones. Folk are wired for music. Some beats may be universal and have a similar energizing effect on folk today as they did back then. Now, get out your toy flutes, and we'll try to play it ourselves. I'll be back in one moment."

Kanto touched Jhee's waist and gave her a quick muzz on the cheek. "You're a natural," Jhee said.

"I learned by watching the best. My, this is a pleasant surprise."

"I haven't been here since you first started and wanted to see you work."

"I'm glad. Though, your anonymous donations have been much appreciated."

"Anonymous donations?"

"Don't be coy. I'm privy to the household finances now. Both you *and Shep* have been giving the center money. I also suspect he's the one who's responsible for the long guard who make sure I get to and from here safely."

"That's me."

"Then he must be behind the toughs across the street who keep the area around the building clear."

"Sorry," Jhee said. "We know you wanted to do this all by yourself."

"I'm not complaining exactly. My ego is less important than helping these kids. I'll be finished in an hour or so. Stay, and we can go home together?"

"Agreed."

The children acted moths to Kanto's charisma. They crowded him and leaned in as he demonstrated techniques on the harp. He sat one child on his knee and had them blow into a horn. The noise was loud and Maker shaming. The children covered their ears and giggled.

Few by few, parents or siblings arrived to collect the children. A few of the older children went home on their own. Kanto and the other volunteer waited with the last child. They kept a positive face for her but gave each other frowns. Jhee waited with the little girl while Kanto and the volunteer locked up. The four waited together on the front steps some more. It was practically last-sun when a little girl, dirty and barely older than the one they waited with, arrived.

"Baba's sick… I'm sorry. I'm sorry." The older girl repeated it over and over while she smoothed out the younger child's coat and escorted her down the steps. The task barely kept her embarrassed tears at bay.

Jhee watched and pursed her lips as the two children hurried down the street. "Shouldn't we walk them home?"

"It will only make it worse for them. Their baba's sick from drink and doesn't like them being here," Kanto said and held up his conch. A blinking, red dot on a city grid moved away from the center's marker. "Here's us. Here's where they live. We'll wait until they reach it. There is not much else we can do about what comes after. The classes are their time to be happy, to be kids."

Jhee watched the dot without breathing. Once the dot reached its destination, she breathed again. She sighed but could not help but think of what would happen after. Kanto presented Jhee with his arm, and they headed for home.

Kanto remained quiet during the ride, not full of his usual gossip and details on scandals. Jhee missed the chatter a bit. More than once, it had turned out to be useful, and she had to admit having lived with too much silence over the years. Information she had been too obstinate to realize until he had patiently proved it to her. Had he matured, or had she mellowed? She instructed the transport to leave them at the foot of their driveway. She savored a few more minutes like this with him, such a marked difference from where they were before. Even more, his excitement for life had grown on her.

They reached the main door. When Jhee placed her hand on the ornate handle, Kanto touched her wrist. She waited for him to speak.

"I want to join the services," he said.

Jhee closed her eyes and gripped the handle tighter.

"Nothing?" Kanto asked. "You're not going to try to talk me out of it?"

"Do you want me to?"

"Yes. No. I don't know."

"If this is because what Shep said at the resort… You don't have to serve."

Kanto sighed. "I know. You and Shep, both did. I feel as though I should be giving back more. What you two went through, so Mirrei and I can have options."

"Exactly. We did so others like you and she didn't have to." Jhee cut herself off. "I know you don't think I fought hard enough for Mirrei."

"I was wrong. That's not why I'm doing this."

Jhee laid her hand on Kanto's cheek. "I want to respect your choices and treat you as though you know your own minds. If I don't fight you on this, please know it's not like it was before. I value you and your place in our family. More than that, I respect you. I can't speak for how Shep will react, though. If your mind is not already made up, and even if it is, if you have questions, I'll do my best to answer them without trying to push you one way or another."

"Thank you, Jhee."

Jhee and Kanto touched escae.

~

The Turquoise Typhoon I

A curious quiet greeted Jhee upon her arrival home a few days later. She set down her valise in the entryway. No music played as was Kanto's wont about now or other acknowledgment came from her husbands.

Shep entered the foyer from the sitting room, wild-eyed. He hustled to her. "Turn around. Leave. Quickly," he whispered.

"Is that her?" an older woman's voice called from whence Shep had come. "Tell her to get her tail in here."

Jhee matched Shep's grimace at the sound of the voice: the Lady Kaydence, Kanto's grandmamere. Would Jhee be able to run for it?

"Well, get in here. I know you're out there."

Jhee inched around the foyer door. Kanto sat in his favorite spot, head down, hands folded in his lap. He glanced at Jhee, seeking some form of mercy or relief.

"Get us a drink, yes?" Lady Kaydence directed him.

"Straightaway, grandmere."

Kanto ran off. Lady Kaydence smiled after him. A moment later, her smile dropped. She whipped her turquoise hover chair—which matched the color of her robes—around to face Jhee without so much as bumping the end table. Jhee took a step back.

"Lady Kaydence," Jhee said, "to what do we owe this lovely, but unexpected visit?"

"Clam it. Did you think I wouldn't find out?"

"Find out?"

"About that one trying to join the military."

"Lady Kaydence," Jhee said, "both Shep and I have spoken with Kanto at length. This is something he wants to do."

"Fix. This," Lady Kaydence finished sweetly.

When Kanto returned with an iced melon drink, they gossiped and made small talk. Shep used playing host as a reason to leave every so often. Over Lady Kaydence's drink, Jhee received stares so cold they should have frosted the rim of her glass. When the lady said, "fix this," she meant it.

"Your idiot cousins are still idiots," Lady Kaydence said. "I swear you are the only one of this generation of Kenyattas worth your salt."

"What of my sisters?" Kanto asked.

"Your sire's children are fine. Last I heard, they are making plans to relocate to the inner isles, too. Like everyone else."

"I shall have to look them up."

Lady Kaydence frowned, then sighed. "Enough of that. I'm sure it hasn't been nonstop parties and fashion. What else have you been doing to keep yourself busy?"

"I've been volunteering my time at a youth center. I give underprivileged children music lessons. You should see how eager and precocious they are. They are quite adorable children."

"I bet they are. What of children of your own? I'm not getting any younger. I want some grand-grands to dandle on my knee or more accurately give hover rides to. These taffies won't eat themselves."

Kanto sipped his highball and glanced at Jhee demurely. A sudden rush of guilt made Jhee face away. She wanted nothing more than to make a hasty exit again.

"I'm on a breeding cycle with Shep," Jhee blurted out. "It's just taking longer than expected. Once it resolves in children or not, Kanto and I will discuss the matter further."

"Also, still a second, I see," Lady Kaydence said. "You told me you'd be denme by the time you reached the capital."

Kanto wiggled his shoulders defensively. "It's proved to be more difficult than I imagined. Jhee and Shep are very close. He deserves his position. Besides, at the Imperial functions, I am given pride of place on her arm. You should have been at the imperial resort with us, grandmere."

"At my age, I've got no cause to be running around an island resort with a bunch of backstabbing phonies. Could you see me and this thing on the weirs courts?"

"Nonsense, grandmere. You were kicking my tail for years after you got that thing."

"That's because you let me win."

"No one lets you do anything."

"You better remember that."

"The Imperial Sojourn was everything I hoped. I think I glimpsed both the Regents. We attended the private opera. A select group and I were asked to perform at a private event where they attended. They must have been practically within arms' reach."

"You were quite the highlight," Jhee said. "How many lords and ladies asked you to tutor them or their relations?"

"Too many to count. I'm still considering it. I have some time left in between the center and my charity work. I could fancy being an Imperial tutor."

Kanto's expression clouded over for a moment from the specter of the abbey and the vizier in residence. The vizier had been an imperial tutor once and had abused her position.

"I always knew our isle was too small for you," Lady Kaydence said.

After Kanto set down his drinking glass, he stiffened his spine, "Grandmere, I know why you're really here."

Lady Kaydence glared at Jhee, then whipped back around to Kanto. "You mean this nonsense about you joining the services? Of all the dunderheaded, misguided notions. These two were supposed to be pampering and taking care of you, not letting you sit vigil over dying women or go haring off to die."

"Grandmamere," Kanto said, "it's peacetime."

"Save it. That only shows how naïve you are. There are plenty of places for you to wind up stationed even in peacetime: a barbarian breach here, an uprising there. The Shield can't save you from those."

"Please, Lady Kaydence," Jhee began.

Jhee lost her thought process when the grand dame rounded on her again. "As for you. I agreed to this match for you to lavish affection on him and keep him in the style to which he was accustomed. Not for you to fill his head with jingoistic nonsense."

"Grandmere, they didn't. They have been nothing but frank and candid with me." Jhee placed a supportive hand on Kanto's shoulder. Shep moved in behind them. Kanto took courage from a glance at them before he faced down his grand-mamere. "It's my decision."

Lady Kaydence sneered at them in turn. She zoomed her chair right up to them. As Lady Kaydence fixed each of them with a glance, Jhee swallowed. Kanto clutched her hand.

Lady Kaydence scoffed and held out her arms. "You impudent, young pup."

Jhee, Kanto, and Shep relaxed. Kanto went to his grandmamere's arms in relief. "Thank you, grandmere."

"I couldn't be prouder of you."

Kanto blushed. Lady Kaydence pulled a paper-wrapped lace root melon taffy from a compartment in her hover chair.

"Grandmere, I'm too old—"

"Ah." Lady Kaydence held the taffy closer, and Kanto took it. She patted his cheek. Lady Kaydence dabbed her eyes. "Now, Jhee, you best show me around this manse of yours, so I can acquaint myself while I'm here."

"I can do it, grandmere."

Lady Kaydence held up a hand. "You've played host enough for the moment. It's your denbe's turn. However, if you want to have a quick tea in my quarters before I retire, that would be acceptable. Only the two of us like old."

With a smile and taffy proudly consumed, Kanto set about having the servants clear their drink service. "Yes, grandmere."

The Turquoise Typhoon II

With envy, Jhee regarded Shep when he excused himself and made his escape. Jhee led Lady Kaydence down the hall. Their townhouse had been outfitted with access ramps in anticipation of accommodating Mirrei's mobility chair. They served just as well for the grand dame's use. A twinge of regret over Mirrei made her pause.

Lady Kaydence did not allow it to last long. "Do you think you can dissuade him with Imperial music lessons? I raised him more determined than that. It's times like these I regret it. And, another thing, if I wanted him saddled with another dying woman, I would have kept him at home with me. He needs someone to caretake him for a change."

"Kanto is grown and fully capable of making his own decisions."

"Which is why you have to be extra devious about making him think the decision is his. He can see through most common ruses."

"To what end?"

"To keep him safe. I presume you have contacts, misfile his documentation. Do anything and everything to delay him until he comes to his senses. Barring that, exercise every influence to not have his service interfered with like your first husband's. I figured after your go around with the Mitsus and the Crag Halls, you'd have built up a healthy contingency of favors and leverage points. You don't want history to repeat itself."

Jhee clasped her wrists behind her back. "Trust me, I have no intentions of letting anything like that happen again."

"I should think not. With my dowry and those you gained from other families over the years, you'll have one and a half, maybe even two full shares of M-corp preferred company stock—if the nightmare with the Mitsu estate is ever sorted out. Enough to make you an elector at the very least. If you don't now, you definitely will once I pass and all mine pass to him and by extension you. He can't inherit my seat, and I don't trust any of the other heirs with it."

"That's none of your business."

"Don't be so naïve, girl. If I could find out, you are drenched sure these Imperials will, eventually. They'll be courting you soon if they already haven't. With the way the succession fights are going, one vote more or less could make all the difference."

By "M-corp," Lady Kaydence meant MANTEL. The MANTEL corporation held nearly all the mineral, land, and natural resource rights in the Empire. Its charter expressly forced the passing of shares and, by extension, voting rights through the female line. As a male, even if Kanto possessed shares, he couldn't be seated on the MANTEL board or participate in the mineral rights exchange council.

"I will protect my grandson and won't have him treated as a tile like they did to Shep. You think all is forgiven now that you've moved to the capital. If anything, your parting act as the district's Justicar cemented the old grudges for those who wound up on the wrong side of the Spectral Armada fiasco. Even my own Kaisonia was never so petty, and believe me she could be petty, to Kanto's detriment."

"Which is why it's so important I don't undermine him or his decision."

Lady Kaydence sighed. "I was never so disappointed in her as I was when he was born."

Jhee gripped her wrists harder.

"Don't mistake me. Her behavior…. I hadn't truly seen her for who she was until then. I was so grateful to still have her I'd spoiled her. We Kenyattas are a proud lot. I hadn't realized how much I had taught her to be cruel and undervalue family. It's a hard lesson when you thought you raised one kind of child, and she shows you she's another. You do what you can to raise them the best you know how. You may even think you've done a good job."

The Kenyattas were one of the families who lost the most the day the ferry sank. Jhee reached out hesitantly to Lady Kaydence's shoulder. "I'm sure you did your best. That was a tough time for everyone."

"You don't have to flutter foot around it, Jhee. My heirs were a bunch of morons and trenchers, and now most of them are dead. I've made my peace with it and tried to do better with Kanto. Your sister, may the Makers and Waves keep her, is the only reason I didn't lose Kaisonia."

"Is that why you threw your support behind me?"

"I was neutral."

Dubbed the Turquoise Typhoon, by those who had the misfortune to stand in her way, even if she had not thrown her full support behind Jhee, it was enough that she had stayed out of it.

"How long do you have?"

"By all rights, I should be under the waves already. Does he know?"

"I have not told him, but I think he understood what you were up too."

"Of course, he did. He's my grandson. He's quite clever, you know. Don't let the appearances fool you. I wish I had told him that more."

"I think he knows."

"What of you, dear? I had hoped to have some little squirts to spoil with taffy by now."

"It's complicated."

"Uncomplicate it. You're not a hermit, Jhee. Don't wait until you're like me to realize it. Now, you best show me to my room."

Jhee brought the grand dame to her suite, where Kanto awaited them with a freshly set tea service.

"Everything arranged to your liking, grandmere. The tea will be prepared momentarily."

"Such a good grand prawn. Now, let's catch up. You are excused, Jhee."

Lady Kaydence piloted her chair into her suite. Jhee kissed Kanto on the cheek. Jhee had already reached the hallway when she realized she had just been dismissed in her own house. Kanto caught up to her.

Kanto gave a quick glance at the door to the grandmamere's suite. "Whatever she asked you to do, don't do it."

Jhee glanced around. Now she was keeping secrets in her own house. "I hadn't planned on it."

"Did you get lost?" Lady Kaydence called. "This tea sits too long, the flavor will be even bitterer than I."

They touched escae, Makers' marks, briefly. "Coming, grandmamere."

Some time later, Kanto entered into the kitchen where Jhee was constructing a sandwich. Kanto entered and plopped down at the kitchen island opposite Jhee's sandwich fabrication station.

"Grandmamere has finally gone to bed," he declared.

"Blessed be the Makers." Jhee bisected her sandwich and pushed half toward him. "How did it go?"

"I held my ground." Kanto munched into the sandwich. "Wow, this is good."

Jhee may not have been able to plate a meal like Shep, but no one made better sandwiches. She savored a bite of the sea salt mixing with the dressing. "I meant what I said. It's your decision, and I'll respect it. But I'll answer any questions you have."

"What was it like for you?"

"My two eldest sisters had secretly joined the navy. I later joined too. I wanted to do my duty…. They went to give me my seaworthiness test, and I froze. The incident was quietly scuttled because of my status. I was excused from normal naval service and sent to the intelligence pool because I could artifice. Most importantly, it still was considered the navy. For the daughter of a prominent family to join the army, just wouldn't do. No one was the wiser. My family got to save face. I never told anyone that. I'm not even sure if Shep knows the details."

"There were rumors in the Reaches."

"I know. Spread by the Crag Halls with help from the Mitsus."

"The two sides of Mirrei's family. I'm understanding more and more why you and she chose to marry to end the feud."

"The Crag Halls had to save face once I broke the marriage contract and eloped with Shep. In primary school, our youth cohort declared, we would be different. We would put all the old family squabbles out to sea. Generational feuds? Anchors of the past. Instead, we elevated feuding to a level where you would have to look up from Equilibrium Point Station to see it. Don't feel as though you have to compete with us."

8

———————

~

Dinner Guests

"So, Sheepdog here goes charging in, screaming and waving his arms like a madman," Odo said. "It turned out to be a bunch of pre-jubilants on a fishing expedition. They take one look at him, drop their things, then turn tail and run. He picks up their equipment and proceeds to spend the rest of the day diving. He caught enough sea meat to keep us fed until our supplies arrived."

Jhee sipped her wine, and Shep even smiled. *Those teenagers never knew how close they came to death,* Jhee thought.

Kanto laughed, "Sheepdog? Sniffer?"

"Ah, those were the days," Odo said. "Sheepdog, here, is the one who always did his best to keep us together and looked after."

"That explains 'Sheepdog.' That's precisely what he does with us, too. Why do you call denbe 'Sniffer?'"

"Because she was allergic to everything but the truth which she was relentless in sniffing out."

Shep grunted.

"Sheepdog's better than his original name, Cooky," Captain Odo said.

Kanto barely contained his laughter. "Cooky?"

Shep's nail pike clattered onto his plate. "Lot of units called the gul who

85

prepared the food Cooky. But it got confusing if more than one unit was stationed together."

The captain fished out an image from his inner pocket. "This is our unit, the Dawn Wolves."

Kanto practically snatched the framed and bound image from Captain Odo's hands. "Dawn Wolves? You chose your married name from your war unit, denme?"

"I'd resolved not to choose a married name at all in those days," Shep said. "I was a modern man, and veiled names were a relic."

"So, you and denbe were married when you served? I thought married men were excluded from the lottery?"

"I didn't serve because of the lottery."

"You volunteered?"

Shep's mouth twitched. "No."

Kanto took the hint and asked, "When was this taken?"

"Right around our discharge," Captain Odo answered.

"Shep still doesn't have his scar."

Shep had begun to tug on his arm hairs. "The scar happened after I left the service."

"I always assumed you got your scar in the military. Did you get into a street fight?"

"We can talk about that later," Jhee said. She stroked the command sigil, as much out of reflex as to calm Shep. "What say we have a game of tiles?"

"Excellent suggestion, Sniffer."

Servants cleared away the dinner plates and glasses. The four of them retired to the parlor.

"Overrun... Sniffer," Kanto teased.

"That's Puzzler to you," Jhee said.

After the quick game, Jhee broke out her best brandy. Odo pulled out a cigar case. "May I?"

Jhee looked to Kanto, who answered, "This once. Only because you are our honored guest."

"Bah, naw, you've been such a gracious host. I'll go outside. Sniffer, Sheep-dog, care to join me?"

"Go," Kanto said. "Reminiscence with your friend. I'll square everything away."

They retired to the rear veranda attached to Jhee's study. Odo produced the cigar case again. He took out a tightly rolled smoke root cigar and drew it under his nose. He offered one to Jhee and Shep, but they declined.

Odo clipped the cigar end, then used a finger flint to spark the end with fire drawing. "One of the few the missus lets me do. How are we doing with the investigation?"

Shep opened his mouth, but Jhee interrupted him.

"I'm sorry, Captain," Jhee said. "We looked everywhere. If she is still alive, she doesn't want to be found."

Odo took a long draw on his cigar. The tip glowed an intense orange, matching his eyes then ashed over. A white wisp of smoke floated away on the breeze. "Drenched shame. She was the best of us Wolves. She deserves better than to be chewed up and spit out like leaf mash."

"We all did," Shep said.

Odo nodded. "True. True. I only wish there was something we could have done for her. In your search for Ursula, you didn't happen to come across an old attaché case, did you?"

"No, why?"

"It contained some sentimental items of mine. Old photos, mementos, and keepsakes from our time in the service. I gave them to Ursula to see if it would snap her out of it."

"Keepsakes and mementos? I didn't find anything like that, but then again, I wasn't looking for them. What's really in the case, captain?"

Odo grimaced. "No fooling you, is there, Sniffer? They're of a rather explicit nature. I wrote Ursula off and on over the years. The life of a secondary spouse is a lonely one. I wrote to her. She wrote to me. We saw each other in person only occasionally, I swear. If the contents of our correspondence should become public and the missus were to see them or learn about them…. Well, I don't think you want me moving in with you."

Jhee stared at the captain. "I'll take another look, but still no promises. This is it, though. From here out, no more lies."

"I swear. Thank you, Sheepdog, Sniffer."

Jhee wanted to believe him, but her Maker within urged caution. "What else do I need to know?"

"Ursula may have been pregnant."

"Yours?"

"Presumably."

They returned to the parlor. Kanto sat on the couch, streaming the day's testimony from the tribunal. The three, Shep, Jhee, and Odo, perched on the edge of their chairs. A bold and brash vizier in the finest of suits and groomed to the quads occupied a driftwood bench before the balustrade and assembled judges.

Shep sneered. "So, that's her, is it? The one who signaled it all; the one who signed off on all the experiments?"

"Yes," Odo hissed. "The butcher of Haddondeep. The Architect of Sorrows."

The sigil on Jhee's arm burned with Shep's hatred. Jhee kept her own counsel. The vizier presented about how Jhee expected her to look, every bit the arrogant bureaucrat who thought nothing of ruining lives. They were all just numbers on a screen. But for a few quirks of the Divine mechanism, could that have been Jhee on another Path? One who did not see people as folk but as resources to be used and discarded like Shep and the Dawn Wolves.

Jhee would never know the full extent of what the Dawn Wolves went through. She had only been a liaison. The Dawn Wolves were specialized in abyssal missions and infiltration. She had used her family's clout to track down the Dawn Wolves and get herself embedded with them in violation of service rules. Though Jhee had been one of the few field trained artificers at the time, so they had had little choice. Jhee and Shep were discreet and kept their relationship under wraps, a habit hard to break once they returned to civilian life. They were always mindful of public displays of affections, even beyond what propriety had demanded of an official such as herself.

Even now, there was a distance between Jhee and Shep, one she could not always attribute to their service. The open affection Jhee could express for Kanto had become a relief. The distance went beyond their war service and kept coming back to one woman, Miramar. The distance was born of the knowledge Jhee always tried to hide and hated to admit: Shep may have loved Miramar more than her. When Shep lost the lottery, Jhee, not Miramar, had done everything she could to stop him from being sent to the front lines and track him down once he had disappeared into the bottomless trench of bureaucracy. Shep had been grateful, but gratefulness is not love. Shep's affair with Miramar had simply driven it home.

"Odo?" Ursula said.

Captain Odo's face brightened. "Suli."

"I thought I'd never see you again."

"Me too. I thought the regent..." Captain Odo swept her up in his arms. "Suli."

"I had to show myself when I heard your voice."

Odo cast a dark glance Jhee and Shep's way. "You were here this whole time?"

"Don't be angry. Our friends only did as I bade. Come, my love, whisk me away from here."

Jhee approached Ursula in the hidden room as the now chipper woman packed her what few belongings she had.

"You're leaving?" Jhee asked.

"Why yes, you've been such true friends. But now I think it's time I get out and face the world again."

Jhee held out the data shell. "Don't forget this."

"Oh, that. It's nothing, a bit of file work from a troublesome client. Do me a favor and throw it away."

After Ursula and the Captain left, Jhee and Shep had a quick discussion.

"Pregnant?" Shep mused.

"Did you see any signs of breaching or pouching when you examined her?"

He shook his head. "No obvious ones."

Shep paused. His eyes worked back and forth, weighing if he should add more. He shook his head again.

"The captain said 'might.' Perhaps she wasn't. Perhaps she only thought she was. Perhaps she…"

"…lied," Shep finished. "To get Cap to leave the Regent."

"Perhaps." Jhee rolled the data shell Ursula had left behind between her fingers. "That doesn't seem like her, though."

"Nothing seems like her these past long-tides."

Jhee tried to reconcile all the different facets she had seen of Ursula since Jhee served as their unit's liaison: from the manic one determined to mete out justice via tribunal, to the self-possessed one checking in on them. Next came the beaten down, broken one and then back to a more stable if mercurial one who just left.

Shep stretched in his chair. "Time—desperation—changes folk."

"Perhaps." Captain Odo had acted strange, as well, and lied to them several times. Was Ursula trying to keep the data shell away from him?

"Jhee, I can see the gears grinding in your head. What are you thinking?"

"Nothing concrete. Only nascent doubts."

The Passing of the Storm

"Explain this, Justicar," the man with an island senate badge said.

Jhee took a moment to focus on the parchment the senator had thrown on her desk at the legal clinic. He had been at the Imperial Sojourn and spent time talking to Sharlet, Shep's sister. She knew she should have recused herself. Nothing connected to Sharlet ever turned out to her good.

Jhee sighed. "It's a criminal referral. What's to explain?"

"What's to explain? It's against me, you backwater twit. You're calling me a murderer."

"Our legal clinic only made a referral. I suggest you engage a legal team and consult them and the Inquesters' division."

"Withdraw this accusation you piece of swamp trash, or so help me, I'll see you sent back to whatever marsh spawned you. You don't know who you're dealing with." He leaned in. "I have imperial favor."

The island senator left with a smug smile. It turned out the senator had been the benefits director administrator for the scam she uncovered. He had been on the verge of being discovered by a lower-level official who either blackmailed him or threatened to expose the whole scheme. They found the lower-level official murdered, and the senator was suspected of killing him to keep him quiet.

The data shell Ursula left behind had some information about the Albatross dossiers, as well. Ursula may have stumbled onto it in a similar manner as Jhee, just from the opposite angle. Ursula wound up at the veteran services center hunting for answers but dead-ended in their fake identities. She had also uncovered another three missing minor officials Jhee had not.

Another three missing low-level officials... Jhee checked the public records and judicial archives on them; no liens against their homes; no public judgments against them. All of them, however, disappeared under mysterious circumstances. She dug around a bit to finesse her way into uncovering their Imperial identification codes. She would not be able to read the code itself, but she could transmit it and have records requests run on it. She accessed the birthing records, nothing too unusual, born and raised at the central facility on Princess Isle. Many nobles and rich had been. They had the best Academy prep program. They guaranteed their graduates would pass the civil services exam, which would make them eligible for public office. Once Jhee had come to accept the truth of the Divine Mechanism, she had developed a skepticism of coincidence. Sometimes it did hold, but on a case such as this, in a time such as this, it strained credulity.

Nevis might have better results. Jhee left a copy of her findings at the adjunct office for her colleague and headed home. Jhee stared at the cold, dark multistory townhouse. It was beginning to have the feel of Hillside back home, a house of deep loneliness and mourning.

Jhee steeled herself and trudged up the steps. She juggled her conch, valise, and keys, as she left a message for Nevis, "I left some files for you at the adjunct office. Would you run background checks or check the deep records on those folk, please?"

The automatic lights turned on when Jhee stepped into the sitting room. A sob followed right after. Kanto sat in his favorite spot, holding a dispatch.

"Kanto, what is it? Why are you sitting in the dark?"

He gazed at her, his golden eyes swollen and dull. "Grandmere... she's— she's.... Grandmamere has passed. She knew it might come to this. So, she sent me away. In her opinion, I had spent enough time caring for an ailing woman. She wanted me to be happy."

Jhee knelt and took the dispatch from him. She read it briefly. They touched escae. They held each other a long moment. Their gaze met. Kanto pressed his mouth against her firmly and urgently. She thought about pushing him away. Instead, she pushed the thought of houses of mourning and denying him out of her mind.

～

Of Rules and Regrets

Shep crept up the backstair, mindful of the creaky boards. He had to think up an excuse to miss his barber's appointment with Kanto. When he heard movement from Jhee's chambers, he found the shadows and concealed himself. Kanto emerged from the door, putting on his robes. He turned back and kissed Jhee. They embraced for a long while.

Kanto grasped her and nuzzled her neck, seemingly intent on pushing her back into her chambers. She pushed him away and put a finger to his lips. "No. Tomorrow."

"Tomorrow," he repeated. "I'm not sure if I can wait that long."

Kanto scooped up his dropped robes. He turned to regard her with longing before quietly slipping into his room. Jhee smiled. Once his door closed, her smile faded.

Jhee leaned against the jamb of her rooms. "I shouldn't have done that," she whispered.

Shep shifted his position and stepped from the shadows. Doubt left her face at the sight of him. They caught each other's eye. She jutted her chin defiantly in the air. As if she had already not been inconsiderate enough, she had taken Kanto to bed on his night. He clenched his jaw. Pain lanced through it. He flinched.

Shep's dander rose. This time there was no misunderstanding what had happened. He had signaled shark—raised a false alarm—and the Makers had implemented his design. Jhee showed him her back with a crisp turn before closing her door to him. Shep expelled a breath. She had not seen how he looked.

A knock upon his door came a few minutes later. "Shep," Jhee called.

She knocked again and louder when he did not answer. She kept knocking. Shep cracked the door and peered at her.

"We must talk," she said. "I debated letting this lie, but I feel I owe you an explanation if not an apology."

"We'll discuss your infidelity later," Shep said and closed the door before she could say more.

Shep tried not to work himself up too much as he showered and enacted healing on himself. Now, he no longer wanted to skip his barber appointment. He marched down to Kanto's workshop and waited in the barber's chair, eager for the young man to arrive. This was a clear challenge to his household status. He and Kanto would discuss this violation of the rules.

After a few moments sitting, Shep's eyes felt heavy. He awoke when Kanto entered and went over to the mortar and pestle with barely a glance at him. He poured in his soaps and tonics. Clink-clink-clink went the pestle against the bowl. Shep's head pounded. The sound of the pestle striking the bowl got louder and faster. Shep's annoyance grew with it. Despite how he had spent the evening, he was still spoiling for a fight. Shep left the chair and loomed over the upstart. Kanto slammed the pestle against the bowl. Shep tensed. Kanto picked both mortar and pestle up and dashed them against the wall. He hunched over the countertop. Sobs shook his slim frame.

"Kanto?" All thoughts of putting the young pup in his place fled. Shep gently put an arm around his shoulders.

"Grandmamere wanted grand-grands, you know? I wanted to give them to her. I wanted them for myself. I always imagined what it would be like to be in a house full of happy children with their screams and their laughter. I want a house full of children. Yours. Mine. It doesn't matter. This big empty house needs children. As many as we can stand. When you and Jhee are off your breeding cycle, no matter what the outcome, I want Jhee and me to have children of our own. I want to be a father, Shep, not a sire. I wanted to ask you before I bring it up to Jhee."

Shep pulled the young man in against him. Birthing cycle? Jhee and Shep were never on a birthing cycle. They had decided against it long ago. It seems she had lied to him too. "Whatever you wish, denye, my brother groom. We'll discuss it with her together."

Shep cradled the young man and just let him cry. So last night had not been some random tryst to spite him. The young man's grandmamere had died. The Lady Kaydence had died, the last full-blooded matriarch of House Kenyatta. Kanto was the last of the primary birthline of his family, a harsh reality for the proud line of song and music makers. Of course, the younger man wanted children, preferably ones not sired. Kanto could not inherit the bulk of the Kenyatta estate as a male. All anchor holds and proprietary cyphers had to pass on to a female. The deal Shep and Jhee had made with Lady Kaydence was that it would be Jhee until such time as they produced a female heir from her and Kanto. Even so, until that heir came of age, Jhee would have control over the inheritance.

Eventually, Kanto pulled away. "Sorry. I must look a fright. You certainly do. Come. Sit. Let me have a moment to whip up some new lather and pull out the clippers. I can't have my denme looking like a leviathan chewed him up and spit him out now, can I? I'll have you looking like the most distinguished gentleman of gentlemen in no time."

Kanto patted the barber chair. Shep waited patiently. He soon came over with soap and a cape. He secured the cape around Shep. He hummed as he applied the lather. Every so often, Kanto choked back a sob or the melody caught in his throat. He shaved Shep quickly and expertly.

"I'm sorry about last night," Kanto whispered. "I crossed a line. Thank you for understanding. It won't happen again."

All that remained was to straighten matters out with Jhee. Her lies had to stop.

Sealed and Dated

"Are we going to talk about last night?" Shep asked.

Jhee sipped her tea, then folded her hands in her robes. "Not if I can help it."

"So, you are just going to run away from it?"

"What do you want from me, Shep? You're the one who shut the door in *my* face. Why are you shutting me out?"

"The irony of that coming from you."

"What is that supposed to mean?"

"Nothing, Jhee. Nothing."

"Don't do that. This is precisely what I'm talking about. You are shutting down on me, and I don't know how to reach you anymore."

"Too busy with other things."

"Is this about Kanto? Are you feeling threatened? It was your idea to marry him."

"I know, I know." Shep threw up his hands.

"I'm trying, Shep. All I want is a peaceful house, calm and order."

Jhee trailed off to watch Shep pace, unsure of how else to continue.

Shep halted and spun on his heel to face her. "Is that why you don't want children? I spoke with Kanto. He's of the notion we're on a breeding cycle. There's only one place he could have gotten that idea. Although, by my reckon, you and I had decided on exactly the opposite."

"I panicked. Since we've settled in the capital, he speaks about children more and more. It's been so long since that was an option. Even after we fully accepted him into the household, it's remained an unspoken matter between you and me."

"You claim you're denying him on my account?"

Jhee pursed her lips. The new spouses had shaken up their household for both good and ill. The increase in household numbers multiplied the emotional complexities of every household decision and interpersonal conversation. "Not wholly. I don't have an honest answer to give him."

"Jhee, don't deny him on my account. Kanto's young. He's fit with an excellent pedigree. The anchors he carries inside are different. And he wants to give you children so your line can continue."

Jhee rubbed the bridge of her nose. She thought back to the Far Reaches when they used to cliff dive as youngsters. In those days, even though she was a weak swimmer, she took the leap as fearless as anyone. Shep's eyes turned a more muted shade before he dropped into his easy chair beside hers.

Shep said, "The M-Prot experiments' effect may not be solely on my potency. We don't know the extent of what Medical Protectorate did to me. We don't know if what they did could affect our children."

"We don't know the extent of what they did to either of us. More than that, though, I like what we have. It's safe, comfortable."

Shep held his hand out to the side in the distance between their chairs. She reached over and took it. "You're scared. Don't you think I am too?"

"Are we parent material? What kind of mamere would I be? I'm careless and preoccupied. I let important issues slide because I don't realize how much they matter to others. Think about my recent behavior. Will I disappoint our children the way I disappointed you?"

"Will I lose my temper or shut down like I did with you?" Shep and Jhee interlocked fingers. "It wasn't all you. I don't know where I fit anymore, Jhee. New house with plenty of servants to do whatever we need done. You don't need me to help you out with cases or security. Then there are the more personal matters."

"I'll always have a place for you in my heart."

"I'm not sure if that's enough anymore. Do you know where I was last night?"

Jhee swept her gaze over him quickly. He had showered and shaved. There was the faint yellowing of old bruises. "A street fight?"

"Close. I found an unsavory all-night gym filled with unsavory gym rats where I sparred and beat the Trench out of the heavy bag. It felt so good, so simple to just hit something again. For all that happened to me during my service, it had a visceral simplicity to it. Fight. Protect. Survive. You're not the only one who longs for order, discipline, something to make sense of it all."

Jhee grunted. "Maybe you should take up arcana and teaching, and I'll do the hitting things."

"To calm the chaos with violence. To find the obvious with the arcane."

"Pastimes, causes," Jhee declared. "We should find you more productive interests outside the home. It may do you some good. Kanto has his volunteer work. What about you? Are there subjects or causes you are passionate about now? The city is the hub of so many paths. Maybe you can find a charity or center which needs help. Maybe something with veterans. The local service center always needs help. Maybe you can see what you can do there."

"Maybe." Shep touched his hand to his chin and nodded. "I have some morning exercise buddies from there."

"It's been just us for so long, and now we're in such a lively place where you can meet all manner of new people."

"Jhee," Shep said, his tone more somber. "Consider what to do about Mirrei's days. We don't know when or if she's coming back. Give them to him. At least for the while. He needs your support more than I do right now."

"Are you sure?"

"I need time to figure out how to just 'be' with our new status quo."

Jhee rose and placed her hands on Shep's shoulders. "About last night. I'll try to do better. Nay. Scratch that. I will do better, by you and by Kanto. I've been a poor denbe of this household. Keeping our house together can't solely be you two's responsibility. I must stop shirking my part of the burden."

"A household sit-down is in order, Jhee. We need to either redefine or recommit to the household rules."

"Mirrei wants a remote meeting. We'll do it then."

"Those of us here need to consult sooner. Especially given his desire for children and to join the service. You can't keep lying to him. There was no excuse for it. You should have told him how you felt all along. Together, the three of us will discuss our options. The death of his grandmamere has hit him hard. We'll need to hammer this out, especially if he is also still intent on serving. A front-line assignment may be out of the question. It will affect his service options if he wants to go the parent route."

"You are as always right, dear one. We need to clear the air. How about tomorrow night? I'll leave work early. Pick us up some crescent pies."

"From Bartir's. Extra garlic. Extra anchovies."

"Deal: sealed and dated." Jhee and Shep stood up. "About Mai."

"Jhee, don't."

When Jhee risked those cliff dives, she only did so because those she loved and trusted, Miramar and Shep, awaited her below. "I understand. On some level, I do. You weren't the only one Miramar tried to seduce. I assumed she had come to me after you had ended matters."

"That fits with her operating mode." Shep refused to face her. "You've spoken about a Maker within that guides you. What's inside me doesn't feel like that. It's an Unmaker. I have an animal within. It's a struggle to ignore its guidance."

Jhee touched her esca to Shep's. She left him alone in the sitting room.

9

A Reminder of Briny Town

Jhee locked her office for the day. "Bax, what are you doing here?"

"Begging your pardon, Justicar. I found out more about your friend, Miss Ursula."

"Couldn't this have waited until I got home?"

Bax looked this way and that. He continued to squeeze and mangle his hat. "Nay, Justicar. I think you should follow me. These folk don't stay put long."

Jhee took her valise under her arm and headed out with Bax. He brought them to a seedy area down by the docks. Jhee immediately felt out of place in her professor's robe, carrying a valise. Bax led her to a darkened booth in a corner where an old, grizzled woman in a sea captain's hat sat. She looked up at them with one squinty eye when they approached. Jhee and Bax slipped surreptitiously into the booth with her.

"This is the one I told you about," Bax said. "She can help."

The captain sniffed and flared her nostrils as if trying to get a definite scent of Jhee. Between that and the way she moved her head, Jhee knew instantly she was a berserker. "The one you were looking for has been in here a few times. Asking questions just like you. One day she shows up with another fancy woman in tow, pretty much like yourself. They get into a huge argument, and your friend pulls out a weapon. The other woman just laughs at her. Probably cause your friend's hand was shaking so bad. Looks as though she had the shifty shakes. I've seen it plenty of times. We berserkers sometimes need a little something to take the edge off. What's more, a skin brother of mine's gone missing, too."

Gears of thought engaged within Jhee. A third missing berserker, if indeed Shep's lost hound lady was one too. They left the bar and headed for the transport lane. The more the gears turned, the less this felt like a coincidence.

"I've left it be for long enough, Bax. Where did Shep and Ursula go? And what can you tell me about Shep's walking Dari along with this *friend* of his?"

Bax opened his mouth to speak, but no words passed his lips. He carried a look of thoughtfulness.

"Spit it out, Bax. This is not just a jealous wife's probing. A friend of ours is troubled and might pose a danger to herself and others. If Shep put the two women in contact… If you know something, say it."

Bax's gaze darted this way and that as if he wanted a means to escape the transport. "Shep did not always go to the park. There's a place nearby, a bar, where the hound owners, the ones who gang at least, go. They also went there that night."

"Direct me there."

"Justicar."

"At once, Bax."

"Aye, Justicar, but you might not want to go dressed like that."

Jhee regarded her blue and topaz robes of rank, house, and occupation. "I see what you mean."

She removed her over robes and sashes down to an outfit more resembling her teaching garb. She switched to a basic suit and left her sashes and top robes home. Old Jhee might have thought of that sooner. It was so easy to let the details slide here. Her comfortable teaching job had dulled her instincts. She patted down the robes until she found one of Kanto's surprise pockets of essentials. This robe contained some makeup for disguise and a little emergency kit for field injuries, complete with the inclusion of a few gauzes and poison neutralizer draughts. The last, no doubt a suggestion from Mirrei.

"Will this suffice?"

"Aye, Justicar, it will do."

Jhee stepped inside the seedy bar. The establishment was indeed the tough and tumble place Bax implied. She took in the patched holes in the walls along with chairs and tables held together mostly by prayers. It was still early in the day, and she surveyed the patrons who would be here so early. Many had the ruddy complexions of hard drinkers. One gul had already passed out in the corner. Bax seated himself a few stools down and disguised clearing any obstructions to his sleeve knife by taking out his pipe and tapping out the old pack.

"Hey, sister, what can I get for ya?" the barwoman asked when Jhee approached.

"Ale. Whatever you have on tap."

"Right up."

The barkeep placed the ale in front of Jhee. She gave Jhee a once over as if wondering what threat Jhee might pose. "First time? Definitely not a regular."

"I'm just here to have a drink and check the place out."

"I get it. You're a few hours early. Action doesn't really get going until long after last-sun and not here. You won't find any participants here yet either. All that happens elsewhere. You'll be informed."

"I like to assess things myself."

"Eager. I like it. I think I'll put my shell on you. You have a dangerous, shrewd look to ya."

Shep had found some kind of peace here. What would Shep be doing in a place like this? What did it offer that she had missed? It reminded her of some areas in Briny Town back home. She pursed her lips. It had been so many years, she had almost forgotten. Shep came from Briny Town. A place such as this might feel like home.

Jhee tipped the barwoman and left. Bax slipped out soon after. "What now, Justicar?"

"Keep up what you've been doing and keep an eye on this place."

"Aye, Justicar."

While waiting for a transport, she called her colleague Nevis. They met at the cramped Justicar Annex in at the imperator's station. Nevis was the official Justicar for the capital district, largely a legacy appointment. Both their positions were. Their jobs focused on teaching and consulting with the local imperators' division.

"Did you look into those names?" Jhee asked.

Nevis took her by the arm. "I did. They're dead."

"Dead? All of them?"

"Yes. Also, several had complained to friends about having their homes and transports broken into and a dead toad or frog left behind. Justicar, what's this about? You may have stumbled onto something here. Running the check triggered the algorithm. They have been auto-flagged for follow-up by the system. It's an active case now. I can't share anything with you about it anymore. Since my search triggered it, I'm going to be questioned."

"Is there anything else you can tell me?"

"They were all beaten to death. That's it. Now, don't contact me about this until it is all over. I'll keep your name out of it if I can."

"Thank you. I'd appreciate it."

Jhee thought about what she had learned. All beaten to death like her homeless vets. Again, the Divine Plan made her skeptical of coincidence. She must play this smart. She convinced Nevis to give her a copy of her records on the data shell Jhee provided.

Jhee contacted Inquester Paij from Galleon City. She was not sure if her local imperator department and Justicar contacts needed this kind of heat.

"Well, if it isn't my favorite, way too reasonable and noble Justicar."

Jhee cleared her throat. Abusing her contacts and friendships this way for any but the direst of circumstances still did not sit well with her. For all she knew, this could be nothing. "May I ask you to do something for me?"

"Ask, and I'll decide if I'll actually do it."

"Would you run background checks or check the records on the following people, please?"

"That it? Couldn't you have done that yourself?"

"They may be flagged. Perhaps do it over lunch at the Stingray Club."

"Oh," the inquester's tone took on a serious note. "Understood."

～

Another Slip

Another day passed, enough time for Jhee's household to coordinate schedules for the family meeting about children. Rather, Kanto had coordinated by trailing Shep and Jhee and keeping after each one until they agreed. She pulled out her conch to send ahead her order for crescent pie from Bartir's and found an urgent message from Inquester Paij. Jhee closed and locked her office for the day, as usual.

"Learned a lot over lunch at the gentlewoman's club. Let's chat. I'll come to you."

Whatever Paij had learned at the Stingray Club must have too sensitive to send via ether. Inquester Paij met her at the capital's natural history aquarium. The woman with her short hair and short robes worn over ankle-length pants looked more at home here than Jhee did. Paij regarded her with a bemused half-smile. Despite the need for discretion, they indulged a friendly forearm clasp between the preserved lesser drake skeleton and a prehistoric leviathan skull.

Paij had been instrumental in the fight to save Mirrei's life and talked Jhee down from a few actions she might have regretted in Galleon City.

They purchased some roasted nuts and strolled along the pier with its selection of ocean-side exhibits. Jhee kept her gaze focused in the distance. The pier passed over breakers, which reminded her too much of Wailing Point back home. *Storm Child, Storm Child, not today*, Jhee recited in her head. A mantra her grandmamere had taught her for when the seas got too rough. The Storm Child and the shell drake were said to be the cause of all roughs seas and ill weather.

Paij passed Jhee the bag of roast nuts. Jhee slipped a data shell in it.

"I can't leave you alone for a moment, can I? The second I turn my back, you couldn't help but poke the Ink again," Paij said.

The Ink: Inkerton Enforcement Solutions or Event Solutions or whatever MANTEL needed them to be. Also known as IES or the Squids, they were the enforcement and long arm of MANTEL. Both had many ties to the imperial family. Jhee was shocked, but not surprised. She hadn't meant to tangle with them again so soon.

"I see." Paij noted her reaction. She attached the data shell to a port on the Sensor Suit she wore under her robe. While Jhee had her siren module, Inquester Paij, Galleon City's finest, sported experimental Sensor Suit technology, a thin mesh garment with recording, remote device access, and defensive capabilities. They continued their walk. "They certainly do turn up like scum on water, don't they?"

At the end of the pier, Paij handed over the bag of nuts and the data shell.

"It was good to see you anyway, Inquester," Jhee said.

"Likewise, Justicar. You still owe me a visit to your noble estates. Maybe we'll get together with the misters sometime for dinner."

"Misters? Dinner? Oh Trench, not again."

The crescent pie and the family meeting. She had forgotten all about them. Jhee winced and palmed her esca. She gave the inquester's forearm a farewell clasp, grabbed the bag, and hurried home. She stepped into the sitting room from the foyer with only her valise and the bag of nuts. Kanto and Shep met her with keeled expressions on their faces.

Kanto strode up to her with an accusing frown. "Why would you lie about being on a breeding cycle? I had to learn you weren't from Shep. Were you ever going to tell me?"

"I expected us to find a new situation for you before it became an issue."

"And after? Once you knew I intended to stay? Or when grandmere asked you? Or how about the night I learned grandmamere passed?"

Jhee laid her hand on his upper arm. "Kanto, I'm sorry."

The young man shook it off. "I thought we were past this, Jhee."

Kanto turned and went upstairs. A moment later, a door slammed. Jhee glared at Shep.

"He had a right to know. He is my denye, and I won't keep those sorts of secrets from him," he said and folded his arms.

"If I actually thought that was why you told him, then I'd consider this punishment fairly meted. But it wasn't a noble or principled act."

"If you were here, maybe you could have told him yourself, pleaded your case, mitigated the damage. But you weren't. Like always. What was it this time?"

"I think I stumbled onto something. It may have to do with Ursula."

The self-righteousness slipped from Shep's affect. He unfolded his arms. "What did you find out?"

They brought the data shell she received from Paij to her study. As they reviewed the data, Jhee realized she had been given dozens, perhaps even hundreds of death records and redacted Medical Protectorate files. It would take forever to sort through without explicitly knowing how to narrow her search. If only Mirrei were here with her algorithmic expertise!

"So empty holds, yet again," Shep said. "This is what you stood us up for?"

"My contact wouldn't have given me useless data. There must be something here. I'm just not seeing it yet."

Shep scoffed. "This was a waste of time. Figure it out on your own, Jhee, like you do everything else."

"Wait, Shep, don't go." Jhee followed Shep as he retrieved his overcoat from the coat closet. "Where are you going?"

"To the gym. To look for Urli on my own. I don't know yet. Don't wait up for me."

Shep slammed the door after himself. Jhee stared at the front door glass for a long while. A loud bang outside made her jump. Had Shep returned already? By the time she flung open the door, no one was there. A folded note lay on the mat. A plain, hand-written message read, "We didn't do this. The chamber targets all war criminals regardless of side or division. Your victims had ties to Medical Protectorate only. The chamber wouldn't be that specific." It was signed by "The Star Chamber." Jhee scrambled to seal the note in an airtight container. Before Jhee found one, the letter flashed and consumed itself without a trace of smoke or ash.

Jhee went to the coat closet to hang up her cloak. Her foot hit Shep's gym bag, which remained at the bottom of the cloakroom.

The Proctor

Jhee spent the night sitting in her comfy chair in the sitting room, waiting for Shep to come home. In between bouts of worry, she examined the records her contact had provided her via Inquester Paij. With the watchdog systems active, she would have to be extra careful and oblique about accessing the files of the victims she had identified. Perhaps Bax knew someone who could help. She wished Mirrei were here for more reasons than one—the least of which was her know-how of systems' code. Another of the many fascinating facts she had found out about the woman now that her pretense had ended.

After promising to be better, Jhee had screwed up again. Jhee sighed. She was disappointed in herself. She was failing her family, and she did not know how to stop herself. Her household was imploding, and she did not know how to stop it. In fact, it was her failings causing it. Why had she truly lied to Kanto? Why had she kept lying? All she wanted was an orderly house. Was that too much to ask? She liked it calm and peaceful.

She thought about the first of her siblings her family lost, Gascal and Gabi, for the first time in years. When they died, she was so young. She barely had any memory of them. Then there were her older sisters, Gwyn and Gloriana. Both were war heroes, lost at sea, in separate incidents. And last she thought of Ghele, the first hero of her family. Jhee had another sister, but no one had seen her since shortly after her parents' memorial. She just took off one day and left Jhee to be raised by their aging grandmamere.

Jhee was never meant to inherit one house, let alone three. She was meant to be an academic. Now Jhee was the sole bearer of the fabrications and schematics of three lines. She had a responsibility to make sure all those works did not die out. Familial duty had not always driven her. Though by the time it came to negotiate Kanto's marriage contract with Lady Kaydence, Jhee had learned if she did not take on the burden, then many of the Outer Reaches' family legacies might die out—a sentiment the Lady shared.

"Even in death, Kaisonia declared contempt for him via her will. She didn't just leave the special holdings to her nearest female relative, she left everything to her nearest female relative, which luckily for him turned out to be me. I think she still held out for a daughter. I, however, intend to leave everything I can to him and his wife—should he choose to marry. The rules of inheritance prevent him from inheriting either of our anchor holds. Those will have to go to one or more of the idiots. Which are unfortunately the bulk of our

estates. Unless he's married, he's screwed. Convince me the woman he should marry is you."

Jhee had understood more than Kanto realized about how it was to grow up practically parentless—with a demanding grandmamere, who wanted nothing more than to fill the void they left behind, but who had her own burdens. Jhee had used that understanding to ingratiate herself to the Turquoise Typhoon long enough to put her marriage offer over the top.

The litany of Jhee's departed family members ran through her head again.

Mamere, drowned; Babere, drowned. Gloriana and Gwyn killed in action or lost at sea, presumed dead. Gascal lost to fever; Gabi kidnapped by barbarians. Gamaje just disappeared one day; Ghele killed rescuing Jhee and other children from a capsized vessel. Had that been what compelled Gloriana and Gwyn to be so ethered up about joining the service, living up to that heroic legacy? Her family gained a measure of love and respect throughout the Reaches despite their crazy grandmamere and criminal past because her sister had died saving so many. If Jhee could swim, could she have saved her? If she could swim, would Ghele have taken one less dive and had the energy to save herself?

Jhee shook her head. No, her first duty was to the husbands who cared for her. She needed to fix this, whatever it was. She did not know if there were any way for her to make amends. Shep had been right. Life had been so much simpler in the outer isles.

Jhee stalked to the closet and threw on her cloak. She looked off into the distance. She saw the nearby veteran services center. It was as good a place as any for her to go.

When she arrived, Jhee sat there with a lump in her stomach. She had dealt with her service in her own way. She was just about to turn around to leave when a voice asked, "May we help you?"

Jhee faced the person who addressed her. It was a woman in a simple proctor's uniform. "It's late. I can come back when you're fully staffed."

"We are always open for our service members. Are you a service member?"

"No, not really. Intelligence pool."

"Some of the intelligence pool were right in the thick of it too, right beside our shock troops."

"Not me."

"Well, why don't you come inside, and we'll talk about it anyway? I mean, you are already here. And I was looking for company on my rounds."

The proctor made a gesture that invited Jhee further into the building. Jhee bit her lip, then crossed the next threshold. She and the proctor journeyed farther into the building. "I'm sorry to impose," Jhee said.

"No imposition. Are you a religious woman?"

"Somewhat. Mechanist. I believe in the First Makers and the Divine Plan."

"It is not a requirement for our help. Simply idle curiosity. We can speak before the shrines or the night gardens if you prefer. Wherever you would be most comfortable."

"The sea gardens," Jhee said, then thought about her sisters. "No, the shrine hall."

"As you wish."

The proctor led her to the shrine hall. Jhee had come empty-handed before the First Makers and would give of herself. She breathed on the ever-burning candle of the Sky Pillar, gave the sweat of her brow to the moss-covered Earth pillar. For the Unknown Maker's hollow, she clasped her hands briefly to honor this Maker but not draw Their notice. To her surprise, the shrine hall housed a Mechanist metronome. Jhee activated it before speaking with the Proctor.

"People are like mechanisms," the proctor said. "Even the most well-constructed ones need maintenance from time to time."

That sounded like something Jhee might have said. "I know that intellectually but rarely put it into practice."

"If you were to speak with a counselor here, do you have an idea what sort might appeal to you?"

"None of those flitty, flowery, wisp whisperer types."

The proctor gave her a credential card for one of the veteran's outreach counselors: Medea. "You're under no obligation to talk to her. The counselor keeps odd hours. I don't think the woman sleeps. She may be available now."

They found the counselor's sparse but inviting office empty. A framed image of the counselor holding up a giant, freshly caught tuna sat on the neatly arranged desk. In the background was the berserker bar. Was this Shep's counselor friend?

"When was the last time you saw her?" Jhee asked.

"I'm not sure. Days."

Jhee tapped her nose. "Is that unusual?"

"Not really. As I said, her hours are eccentric. Shall I leave a note?"

"That won't be necessary."

At the veteran's center entrance, she hesitated again.

"Was there something else?" the proctor asked.

"Thank you. For everything. For taking the time. I hope to visit more in the future."

The proctor inclined her head.

~

The Storm's Wish

In the intervening days, Kanto refused to talk to Jhee. She tried a few ruses to corner him so they could speak. He was not even the least bit interested. She staked out his room, yet he seemed to always somehow slip by her. Shep and Bax often ran interference for him, providing a crucial distraction at just the right time.

Perhaps it was all for the good. Jhee had no idea what she would say to him. She had been lying to him for years. He had every right to be as upset with her as she was with Shep. She was not even sure why she had done it—not beyond what she had tried to explain to him that first night.

Jhee thought about going to the volunteer center. Somehow that felt like a violation to confront him somewhere that meant so much to him, and he could not rightly walk out of it. It was a refuge, and he deserved a safe space.

She spent a lot of her time at home in the sitting room, waiting for the door. Shep also magically avoided her too. Bax's hand in all this rather perturbed her, but she could not fault him. He had served them for many years, and he could not help but have conflicted loyalties about the matter.

Shep had been understandably distant and secretive. When she could get him to talk to her and tell her where he was going, he always said the gym. Yet his gym bag was usually there all night. She had no right to complain, but still, she wondered. Where was he going? Why would he lie about it? What did it mean? Then there was the case. All those missing men and women, murdered, beaten to death. After having a dead frog left on their transports, at their homes, or place of work. It was definitely a mystery for her to ponder. Before she could finish considering these questions, the front door opened.

Jhee was sitting in the study reading when Kanto stepped into the room. She looked up from her conch. He stood, posture straight and proud, hair trimmed short and neat, in a naval cadet uniform. Jhee blinked. She slowly put down her conch. They never broke eye contact as she went to his side.

"I thought you should know," he said.

Jhee took Kanto's hand. "Are you sure?"

"Yes."

"Then fine."

The tension drained out of his stance.

"Don't get too excited," Kanto said. "I joined the auxiliaries' spirit corps.

After some basic training, it's off to the adjunct services and administration division."

Jhee expelled a relieved breath. "Logistics. Quartermasters."

"Apparently, between my marital status, who I'm married to, and a youthful incident which resulted in my both having an injury and criminal record, I got parked in the bureaucracy. There will be some weekend training so we can better understand what the troops go through."

"I'm positive you'll do well wherever you end up, and know that I respected your wishes and didn't interfere."

"The Turquoise Typhoon had the last laugh. Grandmere had me blacklisted from service. I wouldn't have put it past grandmamere to have a hand in this. She's still getting her way, even from beneath the waves."

"If you want, I can undo whatever she's done."

"Don't. I think I'll honor her last wish. Only because I found another way to be of service. She wanted to die knowing I was relatively safe. I'll let her have it. Assuming it was her design intent, not yours."

"I played no part in it. I swear."

"You do understand why I have to ask, though?"

"Yes."

"You lied to me for years. There was nothing I think I wanted so much as to be a father or a sire doubly if it was for you and Shep."

"You rarely said anything."

"I was trying not to make trouble. I wanted to learn as my denbe and denme saw fit, especially given your ambivalence about keeping me on as a spouse. I had assumed childbearing was why you had married me. Certainly not to dive and fish for you."

"I convinced myself I was doing everyone a favor. I suppose I was only doing myself one."

"Do you even know why?"

Jhee shook her head. "It had been only Shep and me for so long. I had resigned myself to a life without children so long ago. It simply wasn't an option. It wasn't who I was or compatible with the choices I had made. Then you came along, and Mirrei, I panicked. I'm sorry."

Kanto put his soft top in his hand. "And now?"

"When I saw you at the center with those children, I imagined what it would be like if they were ours."

"And?"

"I didn't dislike the idea."

Kanto cocked his head at her.

"I liked the idea. I saw you and thought you deserved to be a father. And if I was the mother, it wouldn't be a terrible thing."

Kanto furrowed his brow. "It's progress, I suppose. Grandmere gave me everything I needed to have my gentleman's surgery reversed years ago. If I chose, I could have decided the matter for you. If we are to have children, I don't want you to do so to make me happy. I don't want you to even consider it if it's not what will make you happy. Our children, if we have them, deserve parents who both love them. No ambivalence. Don't answer now. Think on it. I don't want us to live a lie. I don't want our children growing up with a mother who resents them. Agree, if and only if, the answer is an enthusiastic 'yes.'"

"That I can promise. We'll schedule another sit down with Shep. During the day, before the remote meeting with Mirrei. This time I swear I'll be there."

Kanto and Jhee touched their esca together.

"Nice uniform," Jhee said.

Kanto raised his eyebrows. "Are you trying to flirt with me, dear wife?"

"Am I succeeding?"

"Whose day is this?"

"Mirrei's. Before my error caused our present turn, Shep and I agreed until such time as she decides to come back, or we all agree otherwise, they'll be yours. If you want them."

"I do."

"When do you have to report back?"

"I think I can squeeze in some time for my dear wife."

Kanto giggled. Jhee joined him. She had a vague thought in the back of her mind about Shep until Kanto swept her up in his arms and carried her to her room.

As they lay cuddling in each other's arm later, they talked. Kanto traced his fingers along her arm sigil and tattoos, coming to rest on the command sigil.

"Jhee, how did Shep get his scar? Does it have anything to with your arm decor? I thought a sigil like yours was how they controlled all berserkers. That's not how to shut down any berserker. It's how to shut down Shep."

"I gave him the scar. I awoke one night to his hands around my throat. He was in a berserker fugue. It was like he did not even see me. I didn't want to bring this up previously for fear it would seem I was attempting to distract from my behavior."

"Would he pose a danger to our children?"

"I don't believe he would. Nothing like that has ever happened since."

10

———————

~

The Suit

Jhee used the digi-tip on her fingernail claws to write out the derivation for determining the angle and direction of blood splatter. Behind her in the lecture hall, rustling and whispering announced her students' arrival. However, as she continued to write, it grew louder instead of quieted when the more outspoken students settled. At last, she turned around. Many of the students had their conchs out. They glanced from her to their screens in wild-eyed disbelief.

Jhee narrowed her eyes, trying to get a read of the room. Her conch buzzed in her valise. A news alert displayed about the death of the island senator her legal clinic had referred to the Empire for prosecution.

Jhee sighed, sometimes it could not be helped. "All right, students, let's return to forensic cyphers."

The next day students remained abuzz. Her conch buzzed again. Senator vindicated. Within a day of his suicide, the prosecution uncovered shocking new evidence that exonerated him. Island Senator cleared of all charges. The prosecutor's office could not be reached for comment.

Jhee finished her lecture, then read the details of the story as she returned to her office. The senator's family released a statement against her.

"The Justicar who targeted my husband was reckless and had a vendetta. She

109

railroaded him, accused him of a murder he didn't commit, and he killed himself. If anyone needs to be investigated and locked up, it's her for incompetence, malpractice, and malicious prosecution. Someone needs to stop her before she destroys more poor innocent folk. Our family is hereby announcing our intent to sue her for everything she's worth."

Jhee plopped down in her office chair. She received a notice of appeal. One of the people she sentenced in one of her earliest cases was challenging her ruling. She sighed. That was fine. It happened from time to time. It was expected.

What distressed her most was being wrong about the Senator's case. She always did her due diligence. Even then, mistakes can happen. She read through the news stories trying to find out what she can about this exonerating evidence. Finding none, she called up Nevis, her judicial colleague.

"We can't be speaking."

"I know. I just wanted to know. What was this additional evidence?"

"I can't tell you that."

"Please. If I am responsible for an innocent man's death, I want to know. I want to make sure it never happens again."

Nevis lowered her voice, "A surprise new witness came forward, and it turns out he had an alibi."

"What witness? Why didn't they come forward before?"

"An Imperial one. It turns out he was having an affair with an imperial concubine."

"We investigated that possibility."

"Apparently not good enough. Even though he was exonerated, his career was over, and he had an imperial target inked on his back. That's why he must have thought the only way out was to kill himself. Unfortunately, his alibi didn't come forward until they saw his death on the news. He must have been trying to protect them. I'm disconnecting now. Lose my number for the foreseeable future."

Nevis hung up. An imperial alibi made sense, Jhee supposed. But given the severity of the charges facing the man, one would think he would have mentioned having an alibi sooner. Jhee puzzled over it all the way home. Once there, she pulled out the case file and went over every piece of evidence again. She could not see where she went wrong.

The senator had been the mastermind of a benefits scam. He was about to be exposed and had killed an underling who had found out. Or so she had thought. Jhee thought they had invented soldiers so they could defraud the victims' relief funds. The soldiers Jhee thought were fake turned out to be real.

There had been reliable witnesses. With this new alibi, the senator would have had to be in two places at once. Jhee remembered how smug the senator had been when he barged into her office. *"I have imperial favor."* His alibi may have been concocted, but she could not gainsay an imperial without substantial evidence.

Jhee awoke to Kanto gently taking the conch from her hand. She looked around, a little confused.

"You shouldn't be reading that."

"I know. His family intends to sue."

"You'll beat them. Nobody knows the law better than you. Nobody."

"I used to think so. Maybe I erred. I've been so distracted lately. Was there something I missed? He was an abusive ass. I had wanted nothing more than for him to be guilty. Did I get ahead of the evidence? Did I lead the evidence instead of letting the evidence lead me?"

"I don't know, Jhee. That doesn't sound like you at all."

"Ms. Hethyr," she said.

"From the abbey case?"

"Yes. It's like Ms. Hethyr. When I saw the bruises on Mr. Zane, a part of me shut down. I fixated on her. I got tunnel vision. It almost compromised the case and cost folk their lives. Was that what this was all over again?"

"But in that case, the guilty party received justice."

"Perhaps. I wished I could have found a more civilized solution to that. I still hear the screams and the snarls sometimes."

"The abbey killer was a brute and a beast, and the world is well rid of them."

"Was that my call to make? I love the law. I live for the law as much as I do my family, and the law says capital cases must be handled by the full judiciary. It can't be frontier justice. It can't be like it was in the Far Reaches with families bumping off troublesome and meddlesome people as they saw fit."

"I know how much you admire the law. But it's not perfect. How many murders did the abbey killer get away with? Or the well-to-do families in our home district? All because they could pay the right people or choose the right victims. You care about more than the law. You care about folk."

Her conch blinked again. She took it from Kanto. Another notice of appeal. She sighed.

Over the next few days, Jhee received a dozen more notices of appeal. Then on the long-tide, the golden seal of the Justicar council appeared in her inbox. She opened the message and braced herself. Because of the recent events, the Justicar council had no option but to initiate a judicial audit. Her credentials were suspended until further notice. She sat in her office, staring at the note.

Soon came a knock at the door.

"Come in." The dean walked in, unable to meet her eyes. "Dean," Jhee acknowledged.

"I presume you have caught the dispatches," xe said.

"Everyone has by now. I suppose I should expect a visit from investigative services."

"At least. We've received notice of your suspended credentials. I've been asked to encourage you to take a leave of absence. I've also been asked by the board of trustees to scale back the legal clinic. At least for the time being."

"My classes and lesson plans? The legal clinic?"

The dean tugged at hir sleeves. "Another professor will handle it."

"But the tribunal cases."

"Will be turned back over to the imperial commission. It's only temporary. At least until we get this whole situation sorted out."

Jhee wanted to grab the dean and shake hir. "The Academy's support overwhelms me, truly."

"The Academy can't afford the liability, especially with the incident involving the senator being done under the auspices of our legal clinic. You would do the same."

After Jhee snatched up her valise, she smirked. "You're correct, I would. I'm not sure if that makes it right, though."

Jhee stalked out.

Another Invitation

Jhee accompanied Kanto as he reported for his first day at the quartermaster's office. She could not help but run her hand through the short, spiky hairstyle he now sported.

While the receptionist connected Kanto with his mentor, Jhee said, "I would have never thought to see you on this path back in the Reaches."

"Back in the reaches, I may never have taken it."

"I always misjudged you, didn't I?"

"And I, you. It happens. We were both feeling each other out. We might never have moved passed that stage if we had stayed in the isles. I would have been too scared to step a foot out of place. I couldn't stand the Far Reaches when I was there, but I do miss it. A little. Still, leaving the Reaches allowed me and Mirrei to live our Make."

"Once we left the Reaches, is when everyone became in danger."

"Danger is sometimes the Maker geld needed to find one's path."

An efficient and well-groomed post-jubilant arrived to collect Kanto, "I'll be your onboarding guide your first week or so. There's some paperwork for you to sign at the service registrar before we can proceed."

Kanto turned to Jhee before he left. "Live your Make, denbe. Always."

To return to the townhouse now, meant Jhee had the place all to herself. She might rather wrestle a spine shark or throw herself off a bridge. The morbid thought stopped her cold. Jhee refused to have another house she inhabited turn into a mausoleum. She treated herself to a shopping trip in the market district where she sourced parts for her roster of Mechanist devotional fabrications. Most of her purchases, Jhee sent along to the townhouse. She still carried a few finds as the transport passed by the veteran's services center.

"Let me off here," she said.

Inside she found an open discussion session about to start. She kept to herself for most of it. At the end, she re-encountered the proctor. Jhee discussed her mental and legal and career woes with her obliquely. Afterward, she enjoyed watching the breeze play through the sea roses of the garden, then performed Maker devotions at the shrine hall.

The proctor caught her on the way out. "Pleasant news. I just spotted Counselor Medea. We can head over and schedule you an appointment. Perhaps you will feel more comfortable opening up to her."

Jhee's curiosity piqued, she followed the proctor to meet the oft mentioned counselor. She was a simply dressed woman, very much like Jhee with eyes more auburn in hue.

The proctor had barely finished the introductions before the counselor shoved a digital slate in her hands. "Here. Fill this out to confirm your eligibility. You can do it in my office."

The counselor ushered Jhee into her office. Her ordinary looks came as a surprising relief to Jhee. Though her curt, brusque manner was unexpected. As Jhee finished the form under the woman's watchful gaze, Jhee second-guessed this course more and more. She handed over the completed slate, convinced this wasn't going to work.

"Wait here while I talk to scheduling," the counselor said.

To ease her anxiety while she waited, Jhee analyzed the office. Jhee found the address of a slaughterhouse in the counselor's open contacts book on her desk. Jhee recognized Ursula's maye trail mark on a slip of parchment. Ursula's inquiries into the Albatross dossiers had dead-ended here. Why? With Counselor Medea still talking to the scheduling department, Jhee slipped out her conch and captured several images. She slipped away before the counselor returned.

When Jhee returned home, a transport, bearing the Imperial dual wave insignia of the Sea Throne on the doors and identifying tags, had parked in her semi-circular driveway. An Imperial messenger waited on her doorstep.

"Is it for me?" Jhee asked. "I'll receive it."

"Unfortunately, my Lady Justicar, it's for another. I have been instructed to deliver it to him directly."

Jhee quirked an eyebrow. "Which gentleman are you awaiting?"

The Imperial messenger inclined his head slightly. "Begging your pardon, my lady. I am not at liberty."

"I could refuse to receive you."

"You could, my lady."

"So, you are just going to remain there tail dusting my porch until the correct one arrives?"

The messenger's mouth twitched with amusement. "If it pleases, my lady."

Jhee had problems enough without slighting an Imperial messenger, or more dangerously for her, whomever he acted on behalf of. "Best come inside then."

She allowed the Imperial messenger entry into her home and seated him on the servants' bench in the foyer.

The door opened, and Shep entered. He spared Jhee a cool acknowledgment before noting the Imperial messenger. The messenger gave a respectful head dip but made no attempt to present his message to Shep. Shep grunted and went upstairs.

Soon after, Kanto arrived.

"Sir." The messenger rose and held out a black lacquer invitation tray bearing a bio-film invitation folded into a bear. "On behalf of the Gathering of Companions, you are hereby invited to the Imperial spouses' luncheon. The luncheon shall be held tomorrow at the Saltwater Bay Yacht Club. You are further invited should you wish it to play with the courtiers' orchestra. Should you accept, an instrument will be provided for you."

~

The Luncheon

Kanto sat down on one chaise with a carefully chosen selection of delicacies arranged artfully on his plate. His choice of chaise had been calculated. Not too close to the higher born, but near the excellent lighting of the windows. As the first mover of his rank, his peers had adjusted and positioned themselves near him. When no one showed any reluctance to do so, he breathed a sigh of relief.

He always had harbored a secret fear of making a subtle political gaffe and not knowing about it until it was too late. It had been the risk of moving first in this unfamiliar environment. This one had worked out to his benefit.

He hoped he projected an air of confidence and self-assuredness. He had talked a strong gale to Jhee and Shep about how much savvier he was than them. While it was true, amongst this crowd, he was every bit the provincial from the shallows, at least in terms of politics. The Outer Reaches had been closer to the deep sea in real terms. In the social and political terms, it was the shallowest of child's wading pools. This was the deep political waters, and here he swam with the sharks, barracudas, shell drakes, and leviathans.

The crowd was a mix of male and female, thankfully. Kanto should have expected as much off the Imperial Isles. Travel and mobility were heavily gender-restricted there so that people were not sneaking about with the Imperial consorts and concubines. Not so much here on the capital isle. A few faces from the sojourn had returned. He examined the rank and clothing of each individual. He had to be strategic about who he spoke to and when.

Foremost, Kanto must approach no one of lower rank than him. They had to be made to come to him, but only after being invited via social cues or introduction through a peer of his rank. The same applied to him when speaking to those of higher status. His safest shores for his first social landings were his peers.

Kanto noted the number of pips on people's various insignia and the specific shades of color on their robes and sashes. Most of them did not wear robes exclusively. Once they had moved to the capital, Kanto had adopted the style of the capital of combining lighter and shorter robes with slacks or suits, and he had encouraged Jhee and Shep to do the same. He wanted to keep some of their home styles, but not so much they looked backward.

As others made the same social assessments Kanto had, they clumped into their peer groups. Not quite talking yet, but feeling each other out and positioning themselves. None of the high Imperials had arrived yet. A calculated move, no doubt, to give the lesser families time to sort themselves out.

Kanto sampled one of the delicacies, a crab puff made with rare truffle and fresh arctic sea crab. Even here in the capital, getting fresh sea crab at this time of year was a tremendous expense with the seaways as congested as they were by all the immigration. The crab had to be flash-frozen, likely by an artificer and flown in. Only a handful of isles were in precisely the right climate zone to grow truffles, isles that could only be found in a few latitudes. Less now that the wall had radically changed the ecosystems of some.

The pastry on the crab puff practically melted in his mouth. He wished the rest of his household were here to enjoy it with him. Shep would point out some nuance of cooking techniques while tasting it with admiration. Jhee would politely scarf it down and maybe note some obscure fact about sea crabs or truffle location. Mirrei would try it for the experience, then likely move back on to simpler fare.

Kanto tried more of the delicacies. He bit into something tart and moving, Dundarian lampreys. He kept his face implacable, then discretely spit it out into a napkin. That was a delicacy he never needed to try again.

"Well done," the sandy-hair male on the chaise beside him said. Kanto sized up his robes and insignia, a peer maybe slightly above Kanto's rank. It might not have been polite of him to say he noticed, but it was still a compliment coming from someone who, by all rights, did not have to speak to him at all. They exchanged quick gestures to signal introductions were fine. "Aiaku of Taelos."

"Aiaku" was likely a public name, Kanto gave his in kind, "Bright Harmony of the Far Reaches."

"Grabbing the sea worms was probably the only misstep I've seen you make. Most of us have been around long enough to know to avoid them. They are served at all these functions because they are the favorite of the former Emperor's niece and her spouse. When I saw you take them, I wondered if you would actually eat them."

"Lesson learned. However, knowing what to expect should I ever meet the niece and spouse, I'll be less likely to embarrass myself if called upon to eat them."

"True." Aiaku scooped up the sea worms and ate them down with a pleasant smile. "You didn't embarrass yourself at all."

Kanto re-examined the robes, stately, single-colored. His assessment of rank had been spot on, but he was also sure that was Aiaku's way of outing himself as someone of higher rank. Could it be a trap or test? If Aiaku were higher rank, he had signaled they could speak. The only shame came if Aiaku ranked beneath him. Anyone pretending a higher rank than they were would likely be severely dealt with. "A relief for which I am truly grateful."

"Pardon the ruse. You won't tell anyone, will you?"

"Of course not, your..." Kanto paused at a loss for how to address Aiaku without knowing his true rank.

"Aiaku. We're peers, remember?"

"Of course, Aiaku."

A group of four men muscled into the solar, amongst them twins. They made a shark-shot for where Kanto and Aiaku sat. These men wore their rank proudly and brashly.

"Move," one man, a boulder with a head, ordered Aiaku. An *azunate*, hyper-male, build if ever there was one.

Aiaku took his time leaving while Kanto rose to follow.

The slimmer, lead male, no less imposing in his bearing for merely being traditional-sized, pointed at Kanto. "No. You stay. Sit."

The azunate male moved between Aiaku and Kanto. Kanto retook his seat politely. The lead male openly leered at him while the rest pretended as if he weren't there. The four gossiped but made no attempt to include Kanto.

"Zaria's been in a mood," one twin said. "She's split her time the past long-tide between my barge and my brother's."

Kanto put on his best disaffected air. Not metaphorical brother-grooms, but literal ones. Even more scandalous and disgusting, identical twins. The only rationale he could come up with for that made him blush. The Imperials were a breed apart. Aiaku hovered in the background with an anxious look on his face. He talked to a few attendees, then slipped away.

With Aiaku's departure, Kanto's hope for a dignified out dissipated, too. He cast his gaze about. There was no graceful way for him to exit their company. The slimmer lead male, whose outside or veiled name was Zazu, had moved closer to Kanto. Kanto weighed the clumsy gambit versus the wilting weed routine to affect an escape.

When Zazu thought the time was right, he slipped an arm on the chair back behind Kanto's shoulders. Zazu's eyes turned a sultrier molten gold. "You're new."

The wilting weed routine would make Kanto's predicament worse. The twins and the boulder had formed a circle around them to block Kanto from getting away. This spawn of piranha would swarm on any weakness.

"I was at the sojourn," Kanto responded.

Zazu gently rubbed his lip as he talked to Kanto, "We're having an exclusive mixer in our wing later. By invitation only. You should come."

Over Zazu's shoulder, a dark-skinned, teal-eyed High Imperial woman shook her head and mouthed 'no.' An unnecessary warning. Kanto gleaned what their parties might entail and why only certain folk merited invites.

Zazu moved closer. Kanto allowed the saucer he held to slip. The uneaten lampreys wriggled everywhere.

"I'm sorry. How clumsy of me. Allow me to fetch a servant."

Zazu recoiled. "I hate these drench creatures."

Kanto extricated himself from the circle just as Aiaku returned with several friends in tow.

"There you are, Bright Harmony." Aiaku slipped his arm in Kanto's and guided him away, "I have some friends I wish you to meet."

The azunate boulder of a man blocked their path. Zazu reached for them, but a walking stick batted aside hand.

"Go prey on someone else, Zazu," Captain Odo said. Zazu turned, ready to assert his authority against whoever had dared challenge him. Captain Odo loomed over him and raised an eyebrow. The smugness left Zazu's face. "Yes?"

Zazu tried to smile while also gritting his teeth. "Consort Regent."

"Pups."

Zazu's eyes flashed with red. "The Regent isn't Empress yet, Odo. She's practically cut you loose, anyway. The clock's ticking on you, regardless."

Zazu, the azunate boulder, and the twins slunk away. Captain Odo followed, to be sure.

"Zaria's pets," one of Aiaku's male friends said. "Zaria keeps them caged up like prison inmates. I think this is the only time she lets them leave Emperor's Isle. It's a wonder they don't know how to act in polite society and act so predatory on the few grounds where they are allowed to hunt."

"These used to be such nice gatherings," another member of the group said. "They used to serve so many functions. We used to mingle and catch up. Entertain and feel out prospective companions and *denyes*. Upon occasion, conduct business. Thanks to the likes of them, most of the decent companions never attend anymore."

A very sporty male sipped some lemonade, "I guess I lucked out with the Duke. He's gentle, generous, and doesn't have a wandering eye."

"Also, isn't he well into his third jubilee?"

"That just makes him very practiced."

The gathering also held a smattering of part-Fire Folk and part-Findari folk. Findari were sometimes called the Water Nomads. It was rare to find them this far inland. His cousins used to tell stories in the Reaches of how Water Nomads died if they were separated from their ships for more than a long-moon.

"Scoping all the Fin and Fire folk," one of Aiaku's friends said. "The imperials will bed anything."

The green-eyed Lady who warned Kanto away from the mixer invitation joined their group. "Better that than inbreeding."

Blue-black skin but green-eyed with a water drop-shaped esca: she was part Fire Folk.

"It was an observation, not an accusation, my dear."

Captain Odo returned. Aiaku pulled him and Kanto aside.

"Thank you, Captain Odo," Kanto said.

"Yes, thank you, Consort Regent," Aaiku agreed.

"'Aiaku.' Slumming it again, are we? Dress like a plebe. Get treated like a plebe." Captain Odo faced Kanto. He appeared to have several questions but settled on, "Bright Harmony, would you like me to see you back to your denbe?"

Kanto sized up Aiaku and his friends. He had yet to make any allies, and this seemed as good a group as any. "No, thank you, Captain."

The captain whispered to him on the way out, "Those were Zaria's toys. Just like that poor cad Sniffer accused of murder. I hope you know what you're doing in these shark-infested waters."

Me, too, Kanto thought.

11

—————

∼

The Bloody Shirt

A brilliant, vermilion-spotted butterflyfish splashed the surface of the carp pond to retrieve the treat Jhee had thrown in. Kanto had insisted they install the pond and a water feature during the landscaping. Jhee and Shep had decided on their new home before he signed the marriage contracts. A fact Kanto never tired of lamenting, as he would have shown them the absolute perfect house for them. To make up for it, they had to let him furnish their townhouse and put his stamp on the renovations, construction, and decor.

Jhee spooned more flakes into the pond before she returned to the townhouse porch to watch the mid sunrise. The pond was a pleasant touch, and she was glad both Mirrei and Kanto had insisted on it. She was perfectly fine to view the fish from the comfort of her porch. Without her teaching job, she had plenty of time on her hands to contemplate and think about her choices, time to appreciate blessings she did not before. Shep had not come home yet. He still refused to speak to her.

While Jhee contemplated the dawn, furious barking traveled from the kennels. When it did not calm down after a moment, she went to investigate. She crept into the enclosures only to discover a shirtless Shep treating and tenderly

121

probing bruises. At her approach, he turned. He snatched up a shirt and hastily threw it on.

"Shep?"

He started for the door to the house. She intercepted him. He refused to face her. "Please, move," he said.

"Please, talk to me. Shep, please, look at me."

He faced her. She saw where his scarred eye now was also bruised. The corner of his mouth was swollen and still had a trace of blood. The end of claw marks peeked out from his partially opened shirt. His fists had abrasions. His fingernail claws were discolored. One was broken and another missing entirely.

Jhee brought her hand to his damaged eye. "You're hurt. Let me."

He backed away. "Don't. Leave it be."

"But."

"I said leave it, Jhee."

"Shep, what's going on? Where were you?"

"The gym."

"Without your gym equipment? You've left it home every night since the first."

"Do you ever stop detecting even for one moment?"

"You stay out to all hours. You lie about it, and now I find you like this. What am I supposed to think? What's going on with you? Tell me what's going on."

"I told you I'm working through some stuff. The least of which is why you would lie to both Kanto and me for so long. You don't think you know me anymore. Well, I don't think I know you either. Now would you just back off and give me some time to get myself sorted out. Kanto needed to find his new equilibrium. Mirrei needed to find hers. Leave me alone to find mine."

"Except you're not. Shep, I need you to get yourself sorted because I stumbled on to something. Our household may need you at your best soon. Get counseling. Maybe go somewhere to find yourself like Mirrei did. Or else, I'll need you to find somewhere else to stay until you do."

Shep turned before he left. "I recognize this Jhee. This is the Jhee that showed up right after our newlyweds' holiday. The Jhee who treated me as much as her cold, deep secret as Mai did."

He pushed passed her up the stairs and into the house. Jhee walked over to where Shep had been when she came in. She found a torn and bloody shirt. She picked it up and examined it. Without testing, she could not be certain, but she didn't think the blood traces were his. A crystal kalacha poked out from beneath the torn cloth.

Jhee held the shirt, uncertain of if she wanted to know more. She needed to trust him. Yet, somehow, she couldn't with his recent secretiveness and bursts of anger. His reactions during the tribunal broadcasts had been full of hatred, hatred so fierce it had burned her through their sigil bond. That meant nothing. Her ire had been no less scalding.

~

Before the Bench

"You may be wondering why we asked you here," Justice One said.

"I presume it has something to do with the claims against me."

"In the course of going over your record, we noticed some irregularities," Justice Two said.

"A matter I'm sure can be quickly resolved. I'm a very fastidious and thorough record keeper."

"We know, which is why these anomalies concern us," Justice Three said.

"We noticed some gaps in your record of the case at Tranquility Bridge," Justice One said.

"Also, your account of the death of the retired official Bathsheba of Toho strikes us as odd."

"Lady Bathsheba died in an unfortunate accident while wandering around the cloister during a storm."

"An accident? Are you sure that's the account you want to go with?" Justice Two asked. "That's almost verbatim what this report says. Allow us to read what you wrote, 'Lady Bathsheba died in an unfortunate accident while wandering around the cloister. She ventured out too soon, having thought the storm ended and took a wrong turn in the waning storm and wandered into the courtyard where one of the visiting actors had their pet bullhound housed. The frightened creature on edge because of the storm mauled her to death.' You fined the actor for improper housing and failure to secure a dangerous animal, suspended due to financial hardship."

"I believe I also noted that the abbey, the only other party with clear standing, concurred and accepted the punishment. Did they file a challenge?"

"No. It did not strike you as odd, the vizier would go wandering about in a storm, especially after," Judge one paused and looked through the file, "not one, but two, attempts on her life?"

"Justice, the vizier had been doing her best to aid me in my inquiries. She even helped save my poor dear husband when he got lost in the abbey then trapped in its torture chamber."

"And the anomalous deaths which made you stop there? Still unsolved?" Justice Three said.

"Not unsolved. I'm sure you should also see there the account of the suicide of the individual I believe to be responsible."

Justice Two chewed on her finger quill. "Ah yes, the suicides. They certainly do seem to proliferate around you and your family."

Jhee shoved her hand in her robes and calmed herself with finger cyphering exercises. "I suspect there may have been an emotional relationship between the wrongdoer and the vizier, which may have led to a falling out or an excess of grief on the vizier's part."

"With you?"

Jhee adjusted her tabard. "Most certainly not, your honors."

"So, not an unfortunate accident then, but suicide?"

"I could not say for sure and why upset any family with the speculation?"

"A first for you, Sixteen," Justice One said. "Normally, you don't seem to mind what waterfalls you chase or waves you make."

The Justice had addressed her by her district number instead of name. Not a wonderful sign.

"I've found my recent marriages have adjusted my priorities," Jhee responded.

"Speaking of your recent marriages. I might like to inquire about your recent adventures in Galleon City, working with Investigator Paij. A private company accused you of stealing their intellectual property. One of your spouses was arrested for disorderly conduct and trespassing. You were arrested for vandalizing the city jail. Your funds were used to bail out agitators engaged in acts of violence against the empire."

"As you know, justices, many riots and protests were happening at that time."

"And you and your household decided to join in?" Justice Two asked.

"It was largely a misunderstanding. I'm sure you justices understand when enormous events happen, it's sometimes impossible not to get swept up in them."

"There were also some troubling allegations of how you handled a legal matter regarding your anchor spouse at the Tranquility Bridge abbey. Play the recording."

Jhee's hand twitched upon recognizing the voice of one the abbey's deacons, Sister Elkanah. She gave the worst possible account of Shep's raw meat-induced frenzy in the refectory, the dining hall. The bitter, disgraced cleric also framed Jhee's resolution of the matter as nepotistic in the extreme.

The three justices gathered their records and rose.

"You are free to leave, for now, Sixteen. Don't go far."

A Music Lesson

A servant escorted Kanto to the imperial conservatory. He sat on the bench and waited for his prospective student to arrive. After a few moments, Kanto set up for some pieces. He needed to assess the prospective students' skill levels. That would determine if these lessons would be teaching sessions or just an indulgence for the lessons' sponsor. As he was setting up, the door to the conservatory opened. Aiaku wheeled in a young male in a mobility chair.

"Aiaku. What are you doing here?"

"We were just taking in the lovely weather."

"We?"

"There's someone I want you to meet." Aiaku turned around the young male in the mobility chair. A large patch of hair was missing over a curious depression in his skull. Aiaku reached over and wiped some saliva off his chin. "This is Aeolus, my brother-groom. Aeolus, this is the friend I've been telling you about, Bright Harmony."

Kanto squatted down and looked askance at Aiaku before touching Aeolus's arm. "Hello, Aeolus. I'm Bright Harmony. I'm very pleased to meet you."

The relief showed in Aiaku's posture. Kanto spent the rest of the afternoon with Aiaku and Aeolus, sketching and playing for the pair.

"I'm guessing that noble never was interested in hiring me as a music tutor for their children," Kanto said.

"Pardon the deception. It was necessary with the current state of imperial infighting."

"All right, then why am I here?"

"Aeolus. A procurer plucked he and I off the straits to play in the water fountains during Imperial Sojourns," Aiaku said. "Aeolus and I were commoners. We came up together. We didn't have to worry about each other and had each other's back. Once I gained Imperial favor, I'd convinced my denbe to take him on as well. No minor feat as she could have married two high-borns instead. She loved us that much."

"May I ask what happened to him?"

"Aeolus attended one of the Zariinae cohort's exclusive events. The rest, we're not supposed to talk about. I've been hearing about your denbe in dispatches."

"You invited me to the luncheon."

"I recognized your denbe from the sojourn and the senator from other events. When I saw the Justicar on the viewer, I knew Zaria would come after her. A lesson for you, young Bright Harmony. Don't touch Zaria's toys, ever. Even when she's done with them. I wanted direct interaction with your household before I decided if I should entangle myself in the matter."

"What was your verdict?"

"You're folk worth helping." Aiaku held out a hand to Kanto. Kanto thought about it a moment, then took it. Aiaku rose and kissed him tenderly on the cheek. He smiled. "May I introduce you to my denbe? In case the seas turn for the worse, she can see that you are protected."

"Only if my family approves."

Aiaku nodded. "I think that's enough for the day. Zaria won't come at your denbe alone or directly. Just keep an eye on the shadows behind all these officials looming overhead."

~

The Sailor Reappears

"Do you remember me from a few tides back? Outside your office, at the school. I went there first. They said you was at home. I saw where you was asking around about your friend, the one who reckon I speak with you."

"Do you have information on her?"

"Well, I'm not sure see. It's just… I have another friend. He's missing too. I think he was like her." The woman leaned in and lowered her voice, "You know, a berserker."

"Oh, I see."

"I'm sore worried. I was hoping that you could, you know, help me find him. What with that tribunal being blasted on every screen, he hasn't been himself lately. We walked by a display, playing it this one time. He upped and smashed it. I won't honest with you before. It weren't me what suspected the neighbor, it were him. He had me give report, 'cuz he had a reputation with the Imps, and they'd just dismiss him."

"What's your friend's name?"

"Hammad… the Hammerhead."

Jhee raised an eyebrow but let it go. "Where was your friend last seen?"

"The warehouse club over on Packer's Pier."

"Okay, I'll look into it."

The woman bobbed her head up and down excitedly. She held out her hand. They clasped forearms, and the woman gave a good firm shake. "Oh, thank you, Magistrate. All the Makers' blessings to you. Thank you. Thank you."

Packer's Pier again. The cryptic message Jhee found with Ursula's trail marker in the counselor's office contained today's date and an address for a slaughterhouse near the docks there. Jhee rounded up Bax and Dari to accompany her. A quick change and confirmation from Odo later, Jhee found herself back at Packer's Pier One. As berserkers, surely this place with its ever-present blood smell would be some sort of trigger. What were her dear friends into?

Their arrival there coincided with a few others. A trickle of various Folk, from Fire to Water and all others in between, arrived. She had worn a sea coat and cap to make herself less obtrusive, but she needn't have bothered. Their class likewise was a social cross-section. They chatted in excited but hushed tones. There were high society types and motorcycle toughs; farmers, divers, and fisherfolk. She also noted the stance, swagger, and tattoos of military veterans. Bruised and scarred common folk commingled with the smooth and unblemished elites.

Dari whined and pulled on the leash. "She's got the scent of something, Justicar," Bax said.

"Check it out, quickly," Jhee said. "I'm going to give this a few more minutes, then pack it in."

"Aye, Justicar." Bax barely got the confirmation out before Dari nearly yanked him off his feet to follow the scent.

Jhee entered the building. It was a large converted abattoir with a cage in the center. She smelled the blood instantly, years of caked-on decayed foulness which would never go away and had soaked into the very pores of the metal and polyorganic materials used to construct the building. She wrinkled her nose. The overwhelming urge to pull out a napkin and cover her mouth and nose seized her, but she resisted.

The part glamor, part gutter crowd flowed in around the cage. A man in simple diving skirt and shirt used his conch to amplify or transmit his voice so it echoed throughout the building.

"Next up, we have two prime specimens of fighting power. One hails from the Far Isles. The other from Graydale. Give your best battle stomp for the vicious Daggerfin and the terrifying Seacrawler."

Two combatants waited by the cage steps. The announcer quickly exited. Folk whom Jhee presumed to be the combatants' match attendants sprayed a red-brown substance in their mouths. Their demeanor changed.

The Daggerfin braced and shook her head. Her back arched. She stepped into the cage, and the cage guard quickly locked it. Each combatant went into the jumping and flexing Jhee associated with berserker slipping. The Daggerfin's body hairs became thicker and wirier. Her golden eyes had begun a dangerous smolder matched only by her opponent's. They huffed, puffed, and flared their nostrils. The Daggerfin and her opponent circled each other in the ring warily. The Seacrawler made a dash at the Daggerfin, who backed off. They feinted at each other a moment, growling and posturing. They burst into a flurry of action. The two combatants tore at each other. It had none of the technical assessment or counters and strikes of traditional martial arts or fisticuffs; no carefully orchestrated feints or testing for weaknesses; no timing and setup. This was raw animal savagery.

The flurry of rage quieted. One combatant, hard to tell who, given how much blood they were covered in, staggered to her feet. She spit out blood. It was the Daggerfin. Her opponent lay barely moving on the ground.

The smell of the fresh blood had commingled with the old. Jhee felt a shift in the crowd's mood. They chanted, cheered, and stamped their feet. It was not the random enthusiasm of a typical sporting event. This was a synchronized effort to shift their mental state. One which might lead to a frenzy. From among them, she picked out the telltale signs of blood arousal. Glittering eyes sought any sign of movement or hesitation. Tongues licked lips. And there was the odd, eager snorts and chuffs. She imagined somewhere in there the stamping of feet or pawing the ground from those who had already slipped their Water Folk skin.

Many of the attendees had to be berserkers themselves. Jhee spared a moment to think of her safety should a mass fervor overtake them. Could her siren module affect this many? She had found one berserker hard enough to deal with, let alone a room full.

That had extenuating circumstances. She had not wanted to hurt Shep, and on some level, Shep had not wanted to hurt her. Still, though, Shep bore the scar across his eye to this day from where she had been forced to cut him.

The chanting and stomping continued while the two combatants were let out. The announcer counter chanted and eased the crowd down to a less fevered pitch. Attendants hosed off the ring. A layer of fabric was stripped from the ring. A bloodstain remained, but not a slippery one which posed a hazard.

The announcer named the next two combatants, and another furious match of clawing and biting ensued. *Ursula, what had you gotten yourself into?* Jhee thought. She shook her head. Is this what their old friend had come to? Jhee had seen enough.

Jhee caught her breath outside the building after the match for a bit. She savored the smell of air that did not reek of rage, bodies, and blood. Why would berserkers willingly do this? Why would they risk being a danger to themselves and those around them like this? She saw how hard Shep struggled not to let the fervor overtake him. Jhee could not fathom it.

For all they had been through, for all their experiences in the war together, this was an aspect of Shep's life she could never understand. She had hoped his work with the veteran's service center and being around other berserkers would help him cope better. For a while, it had, but now he was just as distant and keeled as he was when his service was first up. They got through it together once. They would again. Jhee had faith in Shep. She must. She wanted him to be around for himself and for their family. Jhee wished for him to have the solace and peace of children. Jhee may have looked at it the wrong way all along. Had he not brought in Kanto as a signal she should have children, but about a desire of his own for them?

The revelation knocked Jhee back on her heels. She had resisted Kanto's advances partially because she had still held the hope of her and Shep having children of their own. Then she had convinced herself she wanted to be respectful of Shep and wondered how he would feel if she had children with Kanto. She had thought to spare his feelings. Had she gotten it wrong all this time?

Ursula's bruises made sense now if this was the kind of activity she had been into. If Ursula was engaged in such a brutal pastime, it lent credence to the notion of her pregnancy not being real, unless there was more to this. More had to be going on here. Perhaps Ursula had left Jhee another trail marker. Jhee pulled out a smoke root and lit it as she casually scouted the area around the slaughterhouse.

A noise around the corner drew Jhee to investigate. Jhee tossed her smoke root and ground it under her heel. At the building's dockside, she saw folk in cages being loaded onto a freighter. More human trafficking?

A cloth with strong-salts clamped over her mouth.

"More meat for the beasties," a voice said.

12

~

Fog and Frenzy

Snarling awoke Jhee. A gag and muzzle had been fitted around her head. She glanced about her quickly. Above her, the moons shone. Earthen walls met her grasping hands. She was in some kind of pit.

The snarling changed timbre. Jhee caught the sight of reddened eyes. She engaged her siren module in animal mode, but it would do her no good if she could not give commands. She felt about her head for some means to release her silencer.

The growling was almost on Jhee. The creature leaped at Jhee. She abandoned her attempts to undo her gag and muzzle. She scrambled up the enclosure's side. The memory of the abbey and the mauling in its gated courtyard, fresh in her mind, fueled her climb to just short of the edge of the pit.

A snarl preceded the beast's bite. The teeth grazed her calf but gained a fast hold to her hem. Her mind was too chaotic to artifice. She reached out via Earth drawing, her weakest element, to the soil. Manipulation of the fine soil eluded her, and she could not get a purchase on the edge of the pit. She gambled on a blind boost with a jet of air.

Her hand breached the top of the pit. She sank her fingernail claws into the dirt. She scrabbled and clambered against the wall of the hole. Clods of dirt fell down. She used her other hand to push herself just up over the edge. The rapidly crumbling side resisted her. A cascade of dirt slipped into the pit. Jhee fought valiantly not go with it. She clawed more and more at the edge of the cavity. Any attempt at artifice abandoned in a desperate bid to escape the pit and make sure her purchase on the edge. Her footing slipped. She started to slide down into the hole, the snarling, biting animal still prizing at her robe.

Jhee became calm and gave her mind over to the First Makers' design.

A hand grabbed Jhee's wrist. Then another one caught her other wrist just as she slid back down into the pit with the monster. Her Maker within gifted her an ounce more fight. She climbed up the crumbling pit side as someone helped haul her up from the edge. At last, she lay face down on the earth.

Blessed are the Makers, she prayed to them silently.

"Justicar, are you okay?" Bax said.

Jhee nodded.

"We have to move. We have to get out of here now. Frenzies catch on like wildfire. Their blood is up, and they will be coming for you with the way you're bleeding."

The berserker from the pit had gotten her a good bite on the ankle. Bax tied up her wounds and removed her gag.

"Can you walk, Justicar?"

"I'll drench well walk out of here," Jhee said and hopped to her feet. The frenzied howls of the berserkers echoed closer than before. If she risked a field healing, they might overtake them. She threw her arm over Bax's shoulder, and they limped away as fast as they could.

They made a good clip, but Jhee's ankle cried out in agony with every step. She was slowing them down. "We have to stop," she said.

"Justicar, we can't. They're gaining on us."

"We must." Jhee dug deep inside of herself and fixed the divine clockwork in her mind. She found her cog in the giant machine and focused inward on her disturbance and imbalance not allowing the device to work as it willed. She turned, wound, and cranked the Divine Mechanism until the pain in her ankle subsided. She flexed her foot, then tested her weight on her ankle. Still sore, but bearable. "It'll have to do. Quickly."

If they had any chance to get away, she needed to slow down their pursuers. A light, low-clinging mist had rolled in from the sea. This far inland, it only carried a trace of the Storm Wall's power. However, she might use it to her advantage.

Her experiments with the templarite dust and her siren module flooded back to her. She fished around her robes for the small packet of templarite powder she kept in her devotion pouch—a minor sacrilege that may now save their lives.

Jhee tossed the dust into the air and used wind and water, drawing to seed the mist with the particulates. She activated the area effect mode of her siren module. A robust exhale dispersed her siren module's silver cloud of inspiration into the fog. With the templarite dust suspended in it, the fog amplified the effect instead of diffused it.

Jolts fed back through the Divine Mechanism, letting her know her compulsion effect found targets: a squad's worth of berserkers, at least. "Flee back the way you came," she commanded.

Her yell reverberated on the winds. The berserker unit fled. They traveled far enough away she felt their connection snap. However, yelping and howling had gained on them. How had it worn off so soon?

Jhee and Bax double-timed it. The cries and howls were almost on them. They echoed from every tree and shadow in the fog.

"Run," Jhee said and picked up her pace. It seemed an unnecessary instruction, but she had gone beyond reason in the now. Bax had already taken off at his top speed.

Jhee retained some clarity of my mind lest they lose their way in the fog. She reached out to the air and water vapor to divine a path through it. The mist reacted as a wild, alive creature in her mental grasp. Even if Far Reach lore said inland fog did not have enough breath of the deeps to capture the dead, this mist did not want to be handled.

With her will joined to the fog, Jhee gained an accurate reading on the number and proximity of their pursuers. Twenty. Thirty. Makers' Mercy, at least a platoon's worth howled for their blood. Far too many for her siren module, even with a templarite boost.

This mist now fought her as if it had a will of its own. She switched to narrow targeting with her siren module and commandeered two new berserkers. Berserkers were more susceptible to siren modules than regular folk, by design. She would also not have to worry about the three-use limit of effectiveness with them. Though, this fog, this drenchable mist, muffled her control. Jhee's hold over those she captured remained fuzzy and tenuous. The fog, the mist, something about it dampened her commands.

The berserkers were closing fast. At their frenzy enhanced speed, they would overtake Bax and Jhee soon. She thought she sensed a narrow corridor through their ranks. "This way."

Jhee veered suddenly towards the clear path she sensed. Bax followed her. His labored breathed sounded thunderously loud in the disconcerting fog. His breathing was ragged. The older man was having trouble keeping up. She heard him grunt. He was no longer at her side. She turned to see him tumble to a stop. She ran to help him.

"No, Justicar, run," he said.

"No! You don't get to leave my service until I say so."

"We will answer for our crimes before the First Makers together then, Justicar."

"Let it be an answer given loudly then." Jhee readied to form artifices, windings, and sequences. At this stage of frenzy, she'd only be able to direct a cell's worth, but she could set them to fight the others. If she took complete control of one, she could have them defend her and Bax while she cyphered and drew. To do that, she would also have to wait until one was practically on top of them. She conveyed the plan to Bax.

"As good as any," he said.

A single guttural howl cut through the snarls, a piercing cry which silenced all the others. Then another. A dark shape jumped into the clearing with them. Jhee prepared to unleash her cypher.

Dari stood before them. She turned back towards the fog. She gave a mighty howl. Then another commanding and louder. She growled way back in her throat when the other howls did not instantly cease. Dari charged off into the fog. The cries from the fog cut themselves off. Jhee heard a few whimpers and yelps, then only silence.

Jhee waited. At last, she tentatively reached out to the fog. Most of the berserkers had gone or were rapidly retreating.

Dari staggered out of the fog and collapsed before them. Her form slowly returned to her folk state, a state Dari had not been able to achieve in years. Bax leaned over her and cried. Jhee used her cyphering skills to listen for the inner workings of Dari's system. She lived, but barely.

Jhee pulled together wisps of whatever arcane reserves she had left in her. Dari's condition was rapidly deteriorating. "Bax."

He continued to cry.

"Bax! I need you. She needs you."

Bax looked up at her. "Do whatever you must, Justicar."

"Roll her onto her back. Gently."

Jhee placed her hand over Dari's heart while touching Bax's chest. She began a prayer to the First Makers and found a strength within from the father-daughter bond Bax and Dari shared. She found the interconnection where their two parts of the divine clockworks intersected and put them together, one turning the other to make the great machine move. Bax slumped over, and Dari opened her eyes.

~

The Diving Boy

"Do you want to talk about your relapse at the abbey?" Counselor Medea asked.

The sanctuary boasted a dormitory made from a converted farmhouse. Counselor Medea kept a small office on the first-floor front. Shep tried to remain seated but reverted to pacing every few minutes.

Shep retook his seat and shrugged. "I'm embarrassed by it if that's what you mean."

"That was the first time you relapsed in how long?"

"Years."

"Tell me what else was going on at the time."

"Jhee had finally needed my help with an investigation again. I had sweet-talked the abbey's mortician into letting me re-examine the bodies of some residents who had died suspiciously. No small feat. The female clergy distrusted males. I felt like more than staff again. It seemed like all I did lately was babysit the new spouses, even more so once we arrived at the abbey. The sheltered, male novitiates were being preyed upon. We wanted to keep Mirrei, and especially Kanto, safe."

Shep tugged at the hairs on his arm. Discomfort in the brand on his neck made him adjust his collar.

"Kanto," Shep said. "His help only made things worse. Then there were his efforts to undermine me."

"Yet you put up with it," Counselor Medea said.

"Our household needs Kanto. I'm beneath her. Kanto's fit and rich, a husband more befitting her rank. He belongs at court amongst royalty, on Imperial Sojourns, amongst polite society. He is not a geyser who can blow at any moment. If I lose myself at court like I did at the abbey, she will be shamed, ruined."

"Didn't you tell me you were fed raw land meat?"

"Normally, I'm fine. I don't have such an extreme reaction."

"Is it possible you may have already been close to crisis? A lot's happened in a short time. Were you troubled or stressed already by the recent upheaval to life?"

"I didn't mention the worst part. How good it felt to let go. There's also a more critical concern. Kanto has been pushing harder for children. What if I lose control around them? I want to make sure my family is safe around me."

"You admitted except for the refectory incident you felt calm and at peace there. Here at the sanctuary, you're unlikely to encounter anyone trying to sabotage your recovery and reintegration into society."

"I wouldn't be so sure about that," Shep said. An acute itching flared in his neck brand. "Gah!"

Shep leaped up.

Counselor Medea eyed him with caution. "What is it?" she asked.

"Jhee!"

The enthused, sharp cries of berserkers in a frenzy reverberated throughout the sanctuary's dormitory. He fought back the red haze that threatened to cloud his vision. The man or the beast? The sensation in his neck usually meant Jhee had found herself in danger again. The sigil had a range of many meters, but much less than the distance from the sanctuary to the capital.

The Kniver

The stables Jhee and Bax holed up in with Dari smelled of animal manure. Hay crackled with their every move. It sounded loud as thunder as they listened for the berserker gang. The kennels were next to the stables, and both were a respectable distance from the lake. The animals housed there already been worked into a lather by the heavy berserker presence in the air.

She eyed the lake warily for berserkers lurking in its depths. Despite the wide berth they gave it on the way in, her heart had still raced by the time they reached the stables. Wherever the berserkers had gone, it did not appear to be the lake. Thank the First Makers for small favors.

Bax sat vigil by Dari's side. Jhee's leg had mostly healed. She used a branch to give herself more support. She would refrain from any further healing on it, so she could save all her energy for Dari.

Just as first dawn lightened the skies, they heard voices. Normal Folk voices.

"Over here! Those were pack tactics. They had to be hunting," a voice yelled.

Jhee struggled to her feet. "In here."

"Hello?" The stable doors opened, revealing a woman in clinical dress. It was Counselor Medea from the veteran's service center.

"Counselor Medea?" Jhee asked.

"Yes. Have we met?"

"At the veteran's service center? A few nights back."

"I don't believe so." Counselor Medea eyed Jhee and Bax's bedraggled appearance. "Do you require assistance?"

"Over here, our friend."

The woman examined Jhee's clothing. "You're Dawn Wolf's wife, the Justicar. What are you doing here?"

"Tracking down some missing folk, berserkers. You know my husband? How?"

"We walk hounds together in the park."

"I was under the impression you were missing."

"Who gave you that idea?"

Shep ran into view. "Did you find them?"

He stopped dead when he saw them. His gaze took in Bax, then Jhee, and finally the now Folk Dari.

Bax clutched at Shep's arm. "Mr. Shep, help her."

Shep stood transfixed, but Counselor Medea stepped forward. Bax placed himself between her and Dari.

"Your friend is a full-skin shifter or berserker?" Counselor Medea asked.

"Yes," Jhee said. "She lost her way."

"How long had she been stuck?"

"Years," Jhee said. "Since I was a jubilant."

"Years. That may predate the berserker program. Remarkable. May I examine her? I might be able to help anyway."

"Bax?"

Bax stepped aside allowed them access. He held his hat and worried the brim in his hands.

Counselor Medea touched Dari's skin, and her hand came away covered in sweat. "How long has she been unconscious?" she asked.

"Ever since we escaped the berserkers, ma'am," Bax answered.

Medea shook her head. "Not good. No other injuries I see. Her high temperature indicates this may be a healing sleep, which is good. Some shifters I've treated have experienced this. Her vitals are otherwise strong. No tremors or twitches indicative of deep brain damage. Has she said anything or indicated any other cognitive activity?"

"I think she came out of it once or twice."

"Good. Good."

The sigil on Jhee's arm had grown hotter as Medea worked on Dari. When she sought Shep, she saw him by the door arms folded an intense glare fixed on Medea's life-saving efforts. Their gazes met.

Shep moved to Jhee's side and pointed at the inflamed brand on his neck. "What about you?"

Jhee grimaced. "I'll manage."

Shep worked his jaw, then said, "Jhee, how did this happen? What the Trench are you doing here?"

"One moment I was on the pier, the next I woke up here in a pit with a berserker."

"In a pit with a berserker, where?" Counselor Medea asked.

Jhee shrugged. "The other side of the lake."

"Hm, Hammad," Counselor Medea said.

"Jhee, you're here. He isn't," Shep said. "Does his state require a doctor... or mortician?"

Jhee grimaced, but a found a grudging logic to his premise. "Doctor. Bax and Dari found me before it came to more."

"Is he still there?"

"He may have got out."

"I've done everything I can for your friend," Counselor Medea said. "You two talk. I'll go check on him."

Shep motioned with his head for them to move to a barn stall away from Bax and Dari.

"We had kept Hammad calm. He was getting better until you arrived and set him off. What are you doing here, Jhee? This is a berserkers' sanctuary."

"Shep, the question is, what are you doing here? This is not the gym."

"Look who's worried about secret-keeping now?"

"I never lied to you. Not to you. Not in all the sundances we've been together. You, on the other hand..."

Shep snarled. He bared his fangs but otherwise kept his cool. "You told me to go find myself. I needed time without you. You always do this. Always the puzzle, no matter who gets hurt. Dari had decided to live out her days as a shark hound. Now, she may die."

"It wasn't my choice. I was tossed in a pit here by some folk in this sanctuary while investigating a lead in the case of our missing friend, or have you forgotten about her? If you had told me about this place, I could have been further along."

"Did it occur to you I might not have wanted you to know?"

"That precise thought has crossed my mind, but this is about more than us right now. It's about Ursula and Odo. I would not have disrupted your meditations, and I would have found out what I needed to know quickly and moved on. Instead, I had to go sneaking about and learn about things from the servants. I would have done my best to respect your privacy."

"Fish rot. Jhee, you can never let a mystery go, or crime go unpunished. Well, for some crimes, there is no justice, except one. You understood that back at the abbey. What has changed now? Where did this sudden attack of conscience come from?"

"It was never sudden. In war, it's different. Don't you know how much I agonized over the abbey? Or Galleon City? Don't you know how much I wished I had found another solution in both those cases? I carry it with me every day. Shep, what is it you would have me do? You don't want me inquiring into your affairs. Yet there is still a job that needs doing. I've followed other paths to give you your space. But this is an aspect of myself I can't change. I have to follow where the evidence leads me. I did not mean to intrude or put myself in harm's way."

"Jhee, I'm trying. I really am. But the whole situation with Ursula and Odo has me thinking. Maybe you and our family would be better off without me. I'm a mess. What good am I to my friends and my family? My job is to care for this family, and you are not letting me do it. I can't protect you if you don't trust me."

"How am I supposed to trust you after what you told me?"

"I don't know."

"I don't know either. I don't know how to be a good official and denbe who keeps her nose clean and doesn't keel people off."

"And I don't know how to be some dutiful house pet or kept man. The capital moves wrong. I don't know if I'll ever get used to it."

"Me either. What I know is we can't keep doing this. Shep, you can't fly off the handle every time I get into a minor scrape."

Shep rubbed his knuckles up and down his forearm. "And you need to do a better job of keeping me informed when you are about to go and do something stupid."

"The problem is I don't always know they're stupid at the time."

"I do."

"Do you want me to be the Jhee you know or a cowed, incurious academic?"

"I'd never wish that on you. We have to find Hammad before he hurts himself or someone else."

"Too late for that."

"Let me see." Shep bent down to examine Jhee's leg. Shep grunted his approval.

"I'm sorry I lied."

"I'm sorry I did, too. This isn't about that anymore. I need time, Jhee. I just need time."

Counselor Medea knocked on the entrance to the stall, "Hammad's gone."

"Take it. I also have some questions for your Counselor here."

"I'm at your disposal," Counselor Medea said.

"Is this your service record? And do you recognize this?"

Jhee showed them an image of an amphibian stabbed with a needle talon.

"Not long ago, Ursula said she found one on her doorstep. I offered to hide her for a few days."

"A stabbed amphibian?" Shep asked. "When berserkers leave this for someone, it's like an obituary. If it's stabbed with a regiment pin or crystal kalacha, it's to honor the fallen."

"If it's stabbed with a needle talon like this one?"

Counselor Medea answered, "It let the weak—meat—know they had been targeted."

"Who cares about a stabbed toad out here?" Shep asked.

"A former member of the Medical Protectorate does. Ursula didn't receive the stabbed amphibian. You did."

Counselor Medea went wide-eyed. "The warning frog was Ursula's. It's just sometimes I let her stay with me."

"Ursula found out you had once been a member of the Medical Protectorate. She confronted you at the rough and tumble bar, threatened to expose you."

"No, you have this all wrong. Let me explain." Counselor Medea's whole body sagged. Shep's eyes narrowed and turned burnt umber. "I wanted to tell you. I didn't know how you'd react."

"There's nothing to explain," Shep yelled. "You were a kniver."

"I wasn't. Not truly."

Jhee interposed herself between Medea and Shep. "When Ursula confronted you, she threatened to expose or kill you unless you paid her?"

"With what money? All I have is my Counselor's stipend and a Protectorate pension I refuse to touch. I can't even afford my own place to stay. I agreed to work night rounds at the center, so they let me stay there. As for exposure, the center knew. For center patients, it's my policy to disclose that to them during our intake meeting. For other referrals, the less we knew about each other, the better.

"Yes, I worked *briefly* for the Medical Protectorate, and it's haunted me ever since. Ever since I left their service, I've dedicated my skills to helping its victims. I try to use everything I learned there to help the people I once harmed. I tried to help Ursula. I was her backup. I wasn't the one she confronted. She'd tracked down another of the architects."

"In that case, you can't stay here," Jhee said. "Come with us. I want to take you into protective custody."

"I think I'm safer here. You've experienced the berserkers' defensive capacity."

"If that's the case, what were you doing when I visited your office not three days ago at the veteran's service center?"

Counselor Medea appeared shocked. "Three days ago? I've been here since Ursula came for me. You can ask anyone staying at the sanctuary. I stayed on after she left. She said I'd be safe here and not to leave until she came back. There was something she had to go bring back. That's the last contact I had with anyone until Hammad, and then Dawn Wolf sought sanctuary."

Jhee pursed her lips. She wasn't entirely sure if she trusted the woman. It could be some half-drowned attempt at protecting patient confidentiality. Or, Jhee thought back to the imperial sojourn and the talk of mimicry.

Counselor Medea suddenly looked about her uneasily. "Maybe I would be safer with you."

13

———

~

The Sandwich and the Nondescript Constable

Counselor Medea agreed to be taken into Jhee's custody while Shep stayed behind with Dari until she was fit to travel. They put her up in the room where they had also kept Ursula. Barely a long-tide had passed before her legal team contacted her to discuss the full extent of the professional and financial peril facing her. While they conferenced, a priority message arrived on her conch from one of her old intelligence contacts. After she read it, she put her legal team on hold. Jhee cleared and centered then walked into the kitchen to make some tea and a sandwich before she had to leave.

The construction of a sandwich was not unlike the process of formulating a cypher. It required a particular order to the faculties. Jhee inhaled the sage and coriander aroma of the artisan bread Shep bought yesterday. The one made with just a hint of spinach and hard cheese and some herbs and spices. Less than a half a loaf remained, and it had just begun to go stale and harden. It was good for sandwiches for a day or so before one either had to drown it in soup or make croutons with it.

She laid out the package of slow-roasted, thinly sliced to perfection maye slices. Once Jhee unwrapped the inner sleeve, she took a deep whiff of the hearty scent containing just a hint of the sea and garlic. Shep and Kanto loved the imported brands. She, however, was a sucker for domestic like she used to have as a child. Jhee took out a butcher knife and sliced off two thick slices of bread. She piled it high with meat, eating almost as much as she put on the bread. She topped it off with mild, white cheese. A few leaves of *kato* and a slice of water cuke and tomato together with a little sea salt and pepper, then a smathering of emulsified egg and oil became the finishing touches. She grabbed a nice cup of tea, then retired to the study with her magnificent creation.

Jhee sat in her comfy chair and made herself as comfortable as possible. She took a bite of her sandwich, then closed her eyes and savored the delicious blending of flavors. She chewed delicately and allowed each morsel to dance on her tongue, taking the time to appreciate the flavors as Shep had taught her. Jhee swallowed the bite, then took a sip of tea. She sighed in contentment.

Jhee closed the message on her conch, which had prompted her to fix a sandwich and make herself comfortable. Her intelligence contact had sent her a warning that constables were on their way to interview her. After she allowed herself another moment of peace, she resumed her conference with her legal team. Their usefulness during her imminent interview would be limited. Both her advocate and her solicitor stared at her with astonishment when she took them off hold.

"Justicar, I don't think you realize how serious this is," her advocate said.

"With your prolific case history, case files," her solicitor said, "the fines and appeals fees you're looking at are considerable."

They must not have received the notice yet. Jhee took another sip of tea. "This could bankrupt us."

"Yes. Even if the review board finds in your favor."

"Jhee?" Kanto stood in the doorway of her study. "Is that true?"

She laid her finger against her nose. "Possibly. Yes. Don't worry. I have some contingency funds and assets I can move around."

"And grandmamere's resources too. Don't forget those. I have a small trust she left me."

Jhee gave Kanto a reassuring smile. "See? That predicament has a finite solution."

"Justicar?" her solicitor queried.

Jhee bit into her delicious sandwich again. She daubed the corners of her mouth with her linen napkin. "I need to consider this. I'm afraid bankruptcy's about to be the least of my worries. I'll contact you again afterward, if I'm able."

"Afterward? Justicar, wait."

Jhee muted her legal team again. She took a few more bites of her sandwich. "Magnificent. Great, great sandwich."

The doorbell chimed, and Irina, their housekeeper, answered it.

Her advocate's conch chimed. While the advocate addressed the incoming message, her expression slipped from puzzled to grim. "I'm disconnecting now to call legates. You might want to—"

A stunned looking Irina cleared her throat. With a flustered bunching of her apron, she announced, "S-someone here to see you, Justicar."

Someone. No name. The uncharacteristic informality spoke of the woman's fear. Irina knew.

"Show them in," Jhee said.

The housekeeper kept her gaze averted as a nondescript imperial constable stepped into the study. Irina made her escape as quick as she could.

Jhee's solicitor finished the advocate's sentence for her, "… arrange for a special advocate. Justicar, we'll make arrangements and petition the Justicar's League for a legate with detention experience. They'll be at special intake before you are."

"Begging your pardon, my lady Justicar," the soft-spoken constable said. "I've been asked to escort you to etiquette review by the Style Council."

Kanto stifled a gasp. "I'll contact the Kenyattas' legates."

Jhee enjoyed another bite of her sandwich before handing Kanto her conch. "Will I need my advocate?" Jhee asked.

"I am afraid so, my lady," the constable replied. "Your good folk here can have them meet you at the inquiry office. I second the suggestion you engage the services of a special advocate."

Jhee nodded. "Do I have time to finish my sandwich?"

"If you'd like. I'm here alone as a courtesy. My force is right outside."

"Thank you." Jhee savored every bite of her sandwich as Kanto frantically made calls. She smacked her lips once she reached the end of her meal and had drained the last of the tea from her cup. She stood and accompanied the Imperial constable to the door. "May I ask what this is about?"

"It will be explained down at the offices."

Kanto helped Jhee slip on her cloak. He was practically in tears. "Legates will meet you there. I can't get hold of Shep. They can't do this, can they?"

Jhee held his face and leaned her head against his. "Shep will be home soon. I hate to interrupt Bax, but he should know how to contact him, if he's not."

"Tell me you'll be all right. Tell me you'll be back."

"I'll clear this up and be home in no time."

Kanto broke out in tears. Jhee took a deep, steady breath to prevent herself from joining him. She straightened her posture and touched her esca to his.

"My lady Justicar," the nondescript constable said.

"Yes. Wait for Shep, he'll know what to do. Comfort and occupy yourself with some reading, perhaps something you picked up while we were at the abbey."

"The Tales of Lady Cheiropthys and the Black Book."

"Precisely."

Kanto smiled and daubed his eyes. "Come back. Promise me you'll come back home to us."

Jhee faced the nondescript constable. "Shall we?"

The constable held the door for Jhee with a hint of sympathy. A group of black-clad guards surrounded the pair outside. They held back any action until she was out of sight of her front door. Once hidden from view though, they gagged her, threw the bag over her head, and forced her into their transport. Many who left with the Abyssal constabulary never returned.

The Interview I

The Abyssal Imperators' transport drove for some time. Her rank afforded her the courtesy of being seated on the bench instead of tossed on the floor like a sack of tubers. Eventually, they reached their destination, and she was escorted roughly and firmly, but not violently, down some stairs. Most of her outer clothing was stripped. After she was seated and secured to a chair, her hood was removed.

One plain table, a harsh bank of glow orbs, and a two-way mirror occupied the bare room. Cold metal pressed against the scar on the back of Jhee's neck.

A jolt of white-hot pain shot through Jhee's head. Jhee choked on her gag. The device left her dazed and drooling.

Jhee wondered if her special advocate was making any headway. She supposed if they weren't, she would already be under interrogation by now. The door opened, and a little old woman in a simple robe thrown over her skirt suit breezed in.

Perfume light and flowery accompanied the prim, grandmotherly woman. She carried a gray digital slate. She aligned it neatly on the table and set up a padded folding stool for herself. "No, no. This is much too impersonal."

The woman removed Jhee's gag. She moved aside the table, then arranged the tablet primly on her lap. She sat facing Jhee with the barest hint of a smile on her face. The woman checked the time, then folded her white-gloved hands. Aside from checking the time every so often, she did nothing else.

"Has my special advocate arrived?"

The woman touched a gloved finger to her lips for silence. The door opened. Another woman came in and whispered in her ear and left. She rechecked the time, then turned to Jhee with a pleasant smile. "I am Fire. Shall we begin? Look up here."

The woman pointed to her esca. The Makers' Mark began to shimmer and waver, but that was impossible!

"Confess," she said.

"To what? What am I being accused of?"

The woman held up one finger. "Confess."

"Please, tell me what I am being accused of."

The woman held up two fingers. "Confess."

"Please, I don't know what this is about."

The woman held up three fingers. She shook her head and tsked. With a quick gesture, a tongue of flame struck Jhee across the cheek.

Fire, as she called herself, must have flammable liquid on her. How else could she have created flames? Fire drawing could generate heat and sometimes sparks but not conjure flames. She tapped a few keys on the tablet. She turned it around to show Jhee. It was an official portrait of the vizier, Bathsheba of Toho and Wilobeia.

"An unfortunate accident." Another tongue of flame, hotter and more searing than the last, struck Jhee's cheek. Jhee pressed her mouth shut. The woman raised a hand to the glass behind her.

Again, the door opened. A beaten, bruised young man was ushered in and deposited in the chair opposite Jhee. She recognized him as the infirmarian from Tranquility Bridge Abbey.

"I shouldn't have helped you. I only did because I wanted you and that pretty male gone. You ruined everything. You killed my lady. Before you arrived with your household dripping in silks and finery, she looked out for me. Gave me fine colognes and fancy gifts. Now, look at me." The infirmarian sneered at Jhee, then spit a bit of blood and phlegm in her face. "That's her. She's the one. It was her. She killed Lady B."

The woman adjusted her shoulders after the infirmarian was led away. Jhee tried to engage her siren module. Nothing happened.

"Now you see your lies and denials will do you no good. Please, don't try any other tricks. Your command module has been disabled. Now, shall we begin again? Do you feel the heat upon your skin?"

The woman held Jhee's gaze. Jhee's hands grew warm. Warmth became searing pain. They began to smoke.

"Do you smell your flesh burning?" The smell of burnt flesh, her flesh, filled Jhee's nostrils. Jhee cried out. "Look at your hands."

Reluctantly, Jhee did as instructed. Her hands were unharmed. The man used her slate to show Jhee her face which was likewise unburnt.

"Each time you lie or refuse to answer, the flames will get hotter."

Physical pain Jhee might disassociate from. This, however, was in her mind. What could she do against that? She prayed her advocate arrived before the flames became too hot.

To Channel the Rage

"Do something, Captain," Shep said as he stalked their sitting room. A discolored streak marked his path. He had also plucked a bald patch on his arm.

"I'm trying. I've had to move carefully. With that Senator incident, you are drenched near radioactive. They are saying I put her up to it because he was my political and romantic rival."

"That's absurd."

"Don't worry, Sheepdog, aside from this little snag, your political fortunes are poised to rise. Until now, it seemed things only kept getting better for the two of you. You'll get this sorted like you always do and come out the better of it."

"I wish I could share your optimism, Cap."

"It's not optimism. It's observation. You two are practically a charmed pair. Even beyond the politics, you've survived the war and, more importantly, the peace intact." The captain gestured at Shep's eye with his cane. "More or less. The berserker process isn't ravaging your body like mine. While you do have that young pup in the stir, there's still a tenderness, an affection to how you and Sniffer regard each other."

"Don't be fooled Captain, we've had our crests and troughs but nothing on level with this. No matter how things are between us or worse they might yet become, I'd never wish this on her. I think I might give anything just to have her here with us safe."

"You still enjoy being around Sniffer, and Sniffer still enjoys being around you. I wish I still felt that way about the Regent. Do you know how often I see the Regent Sheepdog? Once a month. I used to lament that, but now even a short visit is hard for us to last through without spitting bile at each other." The captain rolled his cane agitatedly between his hands. "At the start, she only had a handful of other spouses. Now she's surrounded by young pups. She sucked them up like kreel to consolidate her power. The last time I saw her, she said I repulsed her. She felt nothing for me, yet she wouldn't let me go. All I wanted was a little happiness and affection. Ursula made me happy, and that vindictive, jealous bitch wouldn't even let me have that."

Shep paused to wonder if he could ever come to hate Jhee that much.

A loud pained grunt accompanied the captain lifting himself from the chair with the help of his cane. "There's one cardinal rule of being an imperial spouse: no bastards. You are allowed to do as you please as long as you don't violate it. The imperials though, they can have all they wish with their concubines.

"But no, not me. I'm a fourth spouse, not even a favored one at that. I barely even see my wife. Once I used to curse that, but now count it as a blessing. Yet, I followed the rules no matter how hard it was or what it cost me. All Ursula had to do was not get pregnant. That's all she had to do. My wife would look the other way as long as there were no children. Ursula had begun to insist. She wouldn't let it go.

"When Ursula got pregnant, I figured that was it. I had had enough and wanted out. Like a dutiful consort, I went to the Regent. I told her I didn't want an allowance or alimony. I only wanted a divorce, a quiet one. No scandal—I would sign anything she wanted. I was still naïve enough to think she might have been happy for me. She agreed. She was very pleasant. All smiles. That should have been my first hint. All I had to do was one thing: make a simple delivery for her. One little thing, and she would grant me what I wanted."

"Captain, I remember how smitten you two were, but I'm not sure if this is the time."

Captain Odo rolled his cane from hand to hand and chewed on his lip. "What if she did this, Sheepdog?"

Shep spun to face his old captain. "Who?"

"The Princess Regent. What if she mistook my contact with the two of you?"

The moment slowed. Shep's vision became a field of red. The captain's voice turned garbled. Shep's pulse pounded furious in his ears. A berserker fury was coming over him.

Shep locked his focus on a point on the wall beyond the captain. He filled his lungs with a deep breath of air. Then another. He took a wide stance and locked his arms. He dared not move or switch his focus.

Find your stillness. Focus in.

Shep chanted the phrase to himself over and over. He took more calming breaths. Another voice just beyond his ken joined in with a down-chant.

The captain's voice came back to the fore, "That's it. Easy now, Shep. Ease it down, soldier."

A frantic Kanto burst into the room, waving the favor list, also known as a book of boons. "Useless. As far as I can tell, none of these individuals have enough clout to help."

The interruption allowed Shep to calm himself even more. That was a fair assessment if the person who had called for Jhee's detention was the Princess Regent.

The captain grabbed his coat and hat. "I'll keep trying, Sheepdog. Plead my case to the Regent herself if I have to."

Captain Odo left.

"Should we contact Mirrei?" Kanto asked. "Maybe she's gained more influential contacts in her travels."

Shep let the tension drain from his body. He must hold himself together for his family. "Jhee wouldn't want her dragged into this."

"Does your friend have any ideas who might have done this?"

Shep considered lying, but lies helped get them into this mess. "The Princess Regent."

Kanto emitted a noise part gasp, part sob, and dropped into Jhee's chair, the spirit knocked from him.

Rage flared in Shep again. That was Jhee's chair. Jhee was coming back, and Kanto had no right.

Stay locked on their goal, retrieving Jhee relatively unharmed.

Jhee had been in custody for nearly two days, still within the window of when most detentions ended without tragedy. At three days or more, the likelihood of the detainee's safe return dropped drastically. If Jhee were here, she might quote an exact percentage. Not knowing the odds, Shep accounted a poor trade for not having Jhee safe at home.

They were running out of options. At this point, Shep would make a Dismantler's deal to see Jhee freed. The last folk he would ever want to approach popped into his mind. On the one hand, he had his sisters and on the other Jhee's mentor. Shep went through his and Jhee's contact lists.

~

The Interview II

The younger, slimmer woman leaned in to Jhee ear and whispered, "Where is the case?"

"What case?"

"Lies will not be tolerated." The woman grabbed Jhee's little finger. Jhee heard the pop first. Then the searing pain kicked. It mirrored itself across her other digits though only the one finger had been touched. She bit down to prevent crying out. "Drawing or cyphering will not be tolerated either. First, I break them. Breaks can be healed. Bones reset. You're out of the arcane circle temporarily. If your lack of cooperation continues, next, I find a more permanent way to take them away. Lose your hands, and you're out of the arcane circle. You may still be able to perform some incantations. Lose your tongue, too, though, and that's it for you, really."

Jhee focused in to distract herself from the pain. This pain was real. The Ladies' Auxiliary, also known as the Style Council, worked for several deep Empire interests such as the Abyssal Constabulary, various other clandestine police forces, and the Invokers, clerics assigned to investigate heresy. The Ladies worked in groups of four, each trained with a different elemental drawing method, to extract information from prisoners. An evaluation with them was euphemistically called an interview, but by any other name, it was torture. Time in their custody had broken many. Fire had reviewed her first with a mixture of real and phantom flames. Water and Wind had visited but had not interviewed her yet. The thin, wisp of a woman breaking her fingers was Earth.

"I've been authorized to make you an offer. My client just wants the case. You met with Ursula after she stole it. Tell me where to find it and you'll be released without delay."

Two slow, ponderous knocks on the room's window interrupted them. The woman looked at the window, then back at Jhee.

"Pardon me a moment."

The woman left. Jhee's finger throbbed, and her heart raced. She stared at the reflective window, hoping to see some sign of what lay beyond. She struggled and jiggered her chair around a bit. Jhee yelped as the motion set off a firestorm of pain in her broken finger. The door to the interrogation room opened. She flinched and let out an involuntary whimper.

Black-clad guards rushed in. They gagged Jhee, threw a bag over her head, and rushed her out. They were not cruel or overly rough, only unconcerned with her comfort. She flinched and yelled whenever one contacted her finger. They put her in a transport and drove.

The transport stopped. Jhee could not hear any city sounds. It had to be some place remote. They forced her from the transport and made her walk some ways. Was this it? No one was too high for them to make disappear. Still, she hoped her rank had at least afforded her the courtesy of her family having a body to bury if nothing else.

Jhee's hood was removed. She blinked against the dawning pinkish rays of first-sun. This made a more pleasant final sight than the inside of a hood. Gascal. Gabi. Ghele. Gram-gram. Gwyn. Gloriana. Mamere. Babere. Gamaje. Grandmamere.

How much of the story about Miramar's death had Mirrei invented? *"…she turned in time to see the towering wave bearing down on her. Defiantly, she faced it as it crashed upon our dock. That was the last I saw of her."*

Miramar. Mirrei. Kanto. Shep. Jhee took a deep breath and steeled herself.

"Jhee! First Makers' pride," Shep said. He rushed over and threw his arms around her. She winced. He drew back.

As Jhee's eyes acclimated to the light, she thought she had never seen anything as beautiful as Shep's face, scars and all. One guard removed her restraints and pushed her towards Shep. They turned away, presumably headed back to their transport. Once Jhee heard the transport's engine noise recede, Jhee cradled her hand and sagged against Shep.

"Let me see," he said. He gingerly took her hand. "We'll get you fixed right up. You're with us. You're safe."

"Thank the Makers, Sniffer," Odo said. "We thought we had lost you there."

Shep and Odo transported her home. She sat on the couch while Shep got his field kit. Kanto hovered over her. She was not sure how long she had been gone, but she could tell he had spent every moment awake and worried.

"I'm fine," she said. "This is nothing. I've had broken bones and burns before."

"Don't, Jhee. I'm fine." Kanto stopped his pacing and put on a brave face. "The Style Council *reviewed* both a cousin and childhood friend once. It's neither here nor there. Tea. I'll get you some nice hot tea. I think we might have a bit of Tranquility Bridge Gold left."

Odo sat across from her on the sitting couch. His face stern and the set of his jaw angry.

"Thank you, Captain," Jhee said.

His face softened. He hung his head. "It wasn't me, Sniffer. They laughed at me when I tried."

Jhee tried to picture the imperial family tree and where the Captain's wife was on it. It just made her head throb. She collapsed back against the cushions of the chair.

"Go. Enough. We can discuss it later." Shep, who had returned with the kit, gave Odo a stern look. At about the same time, Kanto came in with a cup of hot tea.

"I used the waver instead of the kettle. I hope you don't mind." Jhee reached to take the cup. The pain reminded her about her hand. "Allow me."

Kanto tipped the cup to Jhee's lips gently with a practiced hand. He neither tipped the container too much nor took it away before she had finished her sip. It was among the most delicious drinks she ever tasted. She sipped a few more times. She let him know with a simple nod she had had enough. How many times had he had to do this with his mother?

"Thank you," Jhee mumbled.

"You are welcome, dear wife. You sit right there and let denme fix you up." Jhee's eyes and body felt heavy, and the pain in her hand had subsided. She felt a dull burn inside her. Her burn wounds tingled. No doubt, the effect of the Tranquility Bridge's blend's proven healing benefits. It had never made her feel sleepy, though. "A mild sedative," he said as if in answer to her unspoken question.

Shep took her hand. "I have to reset it. I won't lie. This will hurt, even through whatever he's given you. Ready?"

Jhee nodded. Before she had finished the motion, Shep grabbed her hand and gave her little finger sharp pull. She roared with pain. Her hand burned then tingled. In her head, a warm feeling set in.

"See you later, Sniffer," the Captain said.

Jhee barely registered the main door closing. Each husband placed one of her arms over their shoulders and gently lifted her from the couch. Kanto trilled something sweet and melodic as they went up the stairs.

Jhee laid down in her warm, familiar, comfy bed. Shep and Kanto nestled in beside her. Kanto sang to her, every bit living up to his outside name, Bright Harmony.

"Rest. We have you."

Jhee tried to smile and drifted to sleep. The world could turn without her for tonight. Everything could wait until tomorrow. For now, she was home and loved.

A Return to Form

With Jhee returned, fury replaced fear. Shep and Kanto's thoughts had turned to vengeance. Kanto then engaged in what he did best: scheming.

"They tortured her, Shep. I want someone to bleed."

Shep did too; in his own way. What would Kanto know about vengeance and blood? It was an armchair boast at best. Worse, Kanto's machinations would take tides, moons, or Makers forbid, years to be realized. Shep wanted someone to bleed now. He did not much care who or what. Though he would prefer the real culprit, their household knew neither the culprit nor the deliverer.

Kanto did not know how to make someone bleed, but Shep did. Shep entered from the top stage left, a catwalk high and to the left of the cage. Across the slaughterhouse, on an opposite catwalk, he saw his opponent. They both descended the steps. The crowd chanted and cheered. Those closest to the catwalk chanted his name rhythmically. Dawn Wolf. Dawn Wolf. He felt the fury beginning to take hold, as the chanting put him into a deep state of trance.

At the door to the cage, a group of fighters, men and women, clapped and stamped in a slower rhythm.

"Oost. Oost. Oost."

A berserker chant meant to hype Shep up and unleash the beast within.

Already Shep could feel it inside him. That thing, that dark animal instinct, the doctors had awakened inside him. The part of him which gave lie to the fact that they had ever been civilized. Inside, no matter what, it always waited. It was there, present in them all.

The Fire Folk understood the veneer of civility to be a guise torn through like paper. They fought with a ferocity which had so caught the Water Folk off guard, it scared them into experimenting on their own people. What Shep had learned in the war, was what the Fire Folk knew, and the Water Folk forgot: the killer instinct the ordinary Folk had suppressed. Underneath the skin, underneath the surface, they were all the same. The Fire Folk fought without fear, without pretense. Some called them barbarians. The truth of it was, they all were. From the loftiest of Sky Folk to the lowest of Earth Folk delvers: they were all one.

Blessed were the Makers who had made them all the same within. Drowned be the Takers who had convinced them all to fight each other over differences of the false skin. The true skin, the true division, was that of the gang. They were all one: One waters.

Shep had never told Jhee of his sympathies, never corrected her. She thought she understood what was going on with him. He let her have the illusion. One day, though, he would try to make her see. She was already coming around. She had learned all on her own to stop calling them barbarians. The two of them would soon break through to Kanto. Mirrei was already there. And from them on to the world. One waters indivisible. Reconcile or die.

In the cage, someone would bleed. Those who hurt Jhee had better pray he never found out who they were.

"Oost. Oost. Oost."

Those fighters nearest the ring kept up the chant. Shep stamped and clapped along with them to get himself hyped. He shook his head and howled at the sky.

Medea waited nearby to tend the fighters' wounds. Hammad, his trainer and match attendant, came over. Shep bared his teeth. The match attendant hit him with the bioplasm spray. He roared at the taste of fresh blood. He saw red. His trainer flung open the cage door. Shep barreled through it. He and his opponent collided in the center.

14

———————

~

The Raid

At Jhee's insistence, the household had resolved to have the child discussion again. On the designated day, she awoke, sweating, to the memories of pain and the smell of burning once more. When she was unable to return to sleep, Jhee planted herself in the sitting room with reading materials and schematics. She would not leave for wrack or ruin. Upon Kanto's arrival, he set up his harp opposite her. All they required now was Shep's presence.

Jhee quietly read in front of the fireplace while Kanto saluted her on the harp. The interview memories went to sleep in a corner of her mind. She marked off an article about tandem cyphering and the use of the pair bond in arcana. It involved blood-based arcana. She unmarked it. Shep and Jhee never indulged in blood-based arcana. The involvement of bioplasm made it a risky proposition with Shep's condition.

Kanto gave a flourish with the harp. Jhee raised her attention from her conch to give him appreciation. Kanto smiled in acceptance.

Jhee marked the blood-arcana article again. Kanto might work as a subject. His suitability and willingness to take part in a broader range of experiments had her eager and curious. She scoured her archives for techniques she had previously dismissed. There were promising articles with respect to arcana based on blood. Though, they had other aspects that made her uncomfortable using them. Among them, their close association with the Pillarist Doombringers. She'd discuss the matter with Kanto anyway.

Another article discussed Pillarist healers or Soothbringers' work treating mental trauma with arcana. Jhee marked it. The description sounded like the reverse of what the Ladies' Auxiliary had done to Jhee. No matter what, Jhee had always been able to rely on her mind. If she learned the Pillarists' methods, she might be able to protect herself better.

Kanto began another selection on the harp. It was not as good as his lute playing, but still quite expert. He said he needed to keep up his skills on several instruments. Besides his other talents, he was a bit of a virtuoso. He had been raised to be a concubine or courtesan. When she learned all that entailed and all the skills they were expected to know, Jhee gained a newfound respect for him and them. It rivaled what she had to know as a Justicar and artificer. No wonder Kanto had nothing left to give arcane practice. She had tried to get him a proper tutor or inquire about courses at the academy once they arrived, but he was more interested in his charity work, and they mutually agreed to continue with the private, casual instruction she provided.

So much they did in their lives had been about managing Shep's condition. To converse about less weighty topics, to not have to cross-check every cypher against his triggers, sometimes came as a relief. Jhee continued to vet arcana articles.

No sooner had Jhee returned to her reading, than she received an incoming chime from Nevis, her Justicar colleague.

"I need to lose your number, but you are perfectly free to find mine," Jhee answered.

"You should come down here."

Jhee sobered at her no-nonsense tone. "Why? What's happened?"

"The corruption patrol raided a slaughterhouse on the docks. Some underground fighting society. I recognized one fighter they brought in."

Jhee thought about the bruises and the blood and the late nights where Shep did not come home at all. "Shep. Is there anything you can do?"

"They're still processing the arrested. It's big. They swept up many people. Important people. I think they intend to make an example of some to prove they are tough on corruption. Lots of scrutiny on this one. I can move him to the back of the line. If you get here with an advocate fast enough, you might be able to take him home with a minimum of scandal."

When Jhee hung up the phone, Kanto stared at her with concern. "Shep's been arrested. I don't know all the details."

Kanto stood. "Come on then."

"You don't have to go."

Kanto pfted. "It seems like every time I let a member of this family out of my sight, you get yourselves in trouble."

"As I recall, we had to come after you too."

Kanto helped her into her cloak. "Precisely. I let me out of your sight and found trouble. Besides, I know how to get folks out of jail without tearing it up. This family is three out of four on arrests. You may need someone who has not been arrested doing the talking for you."

"Without an arrest? Didn't you say something about an incident when you were young, which derailed your military enrollment?"

"Fine, a recent criminal arrest record then."

The Transmission

Shep hung up his cloak and went into the sitting room. Jhee and Kanto swept in after him. Kanto checked their missed messages. "Hi, kin. Guess you're not home. *Sas drej*. Terrible connection. Try again later."

Jhee noted the edge of sadness and disappointment in Mirrei's voice.

"Drenchit, the remote meeting with Mirrei," Kanto said. "Shep, what were you thinking?"

"May I have a few moments alone with Shep?" Jhee asked.

Kanto glared at Shep, sniffed, and then walked away. "I'll go call her back and explain to her why we weren't here."

Jhee sat down in her easy chair with a sigh. Shep grunted with pain as he took a seat in his. "Why would you take part in such a barbaric event?"

"I don't know."

"Fish flakes. You asked for space. I gave it to you. Now, I'm asking you to let me know what's going on with you."

"I don't know!"

Jhee set her lips and folded her hands. She took a deep breath. "Do you want a divorce?"

"No. I'm committed to our family."

"Are you having an affair?"

"Oh, by the Makers, Jhee. How can you even think that?"

"Then what?"

"I'm angry. I'm just so drenched angry. All the time. I don't know why."

"You don't know? Perhaps it's all the blood-sporting and immersing yourself in a world of violence and blood. Do you think that might be it?"

Shep shook his head. "I miss simple. We, all of it, used to be so simple. We were at risk in the abbey, and I couldn't even hold my weapon. Mirrei got sick, and I couldn't do anything. They came for you, Jhee, and I was powerless. All because of what the Medical Protectorate did. As berserkers, we were unstoppable. I wanted to feel that way again, Jhee. The elation, the feeling of power, that nothing could stop me or stand in my way."

Jhee held her hand out to the side. He took it. "Is there anything we can do?"

"In that ring, I had a small part of it again. Fight. Protect. Survive. The taste of my opponent's blood in my mouth felt so good. There is nothing else like it. I thought I had dealt with it. I thought I let it go after all these years. But you never forget. You never let it go. The one beneath the skin is always there, waiting. Do you ever miss it, Jhee?"

"What I experienced wasn't like what they did to you. I can't explain it. Inspiration. It's never been like that even before they enhanced it. I've felt the need to change my skin on occasion. Sometimes it's been so strong, a siren call, that's almost impossible to resist. The ability to cast helps, the mediations required to discipline the mind for artificing. I release the urge and feed it to the Divine Mechanism. I channel it there and let the First Makers do with it as they will."

"I wish I could do that."

"So, what do we do now? I've pulled what favors I can, but I'm burning through them quickly. We are low on money and influence. I can't keep bailing you out. I need you to find some other way to deal with this. We'll help you however we can. If you'll let us."

Kanto cleared his throat. "Sorry, to interrupt, denbe, denme. Mirrei left another message. I think you better watch it."

This transmission was clearer than the last but still cut out every few words. That only made the Imperial endowments seal on the letter Mirrei held up clearer. "You see this letter… 'Recent allegations against you… Recently come to our attention your involvement in certain activities.' They are calling me a terrorist. They're threatening to pull our funding."

The Dog and Pony Procession

Soon after, Jhee received an informal invitation to the Fancy Foam Equestrian and Canine Showcase to be held at the Temple Downs Race Track. *Lovely,* she thought. The informal invitation meant her attendance was optional, but that wasn't her only consideration in whether to attend.

"Are you sure you are up for this, Jhee?" Kanto asked.

"This is important to you."

"You're important to me." Kanto leaned in and whispered, "Drench this literal dog and pony parade and drench the Imperials, too if even one of them had anything to do with what happened to you."

Jhee and Kanto strolled arm-in-arm along the manicured paddock. The musky manure smell mingled with the sweet-sharpness of pollinating flowers. Proud dog and horse owners displayed their prize-winning pets both of the four- and two-legged variety. She was glad she dosed up on allergy medication.

"Technically, IES/MANTEL had me tortured."

"And they are nothing, if not wholly or partially owned, and in collusion with the Imperial family. How can you be so glib?"

Jhee gave Kanto a look down her nose. At this point, Jhee cared little about keeping knowledge of them secret. She was already on their radar. Silence and secrecy only helped them, not her. If MANTEL was the imperial families' arm, Inkerton Enforcement Services, with its hired security and labor forces, was the sword it wielded.

He sighed. "I'm sorry, it's not for me to say how you process such a traumatic experience. I'm just worried they'll come after you again."

"Isn't that why it's even more important we attend this farce? To show whoever ordered my interrogation, I am not intimidated."

Kanto gave a quick, approving nod at Jhee's correct assessment of the politics of the matter. "I saw a glimmer of the woman everyone in the Far Reaches cursed when you confronted Shep's sister at the sojourn. You know we have to hit back and hit back hard. I wasn't the only one humoring their spouse, was I?"

"I avoid politics because I know that side of me is there. It's *my* berserker essence."

Kanto shuddered. "This might backfire and provoke them. It was hard enough to get you back. It frightens and angers me to think we're at the same event as someone who would do that to you. I do suppose it's what Imperials would do. They would condemn you to a pit and then smile in your face about it later."

"Then, I leave it up to your skills to make us allies even more important than they are, and another reason we needed to attend."

"Is that all?"

"You've repeatedly expressed your faith in me, Kanto. This is my chance to express my faith in you. This is one reason we chose you to join our family above all others. You've studied all the players and what makes them tick. In this, you are the teacher and I, the student."

Kanto squared his shoulders. "Let's rile the Storm Child. We'll have to separate for maximum coverage."

"All right, who do I claver with first?"

Kanto scanned the imperial pairs. He motioned his head at the woman in the center of a cluster of red and gray uniformed men and women. "Her. The Pike branch. They are powerful, though a bit of the pariahs. Because of being highly suspected of piracy. They are heavily into military contracts and have serious military preoccupation despite most of them never serving. They publicly fought against IES outsourcing. She has served though and donates to many vet causes. Tough, no-nonsense."

"After her, who else?"

"The Wrasses. Less powerful, fascinated by all things arcane. The man in the flannel, multicolored robes off to the side, not the eldest or the inheritor but has the genuine power. If you fall into your normal arcane technobabble, he will eat it right up."

"I thought you liked my technobabble."

"He'll love it even more."

"Where will you be? In case I need help or more pointers."

"With the Mandelbrots, also known as the collectors. They like to collect unique and best in class artists, both as friends and spouses."

"And that is indeed you, dear husband. A rare beauty and talent."

Kanto raised his eyebrow. "You haven't seen anything yet. Watch me work."

Kanto sashayed away. Jhee smiled to herself and headed for the Pike matriarch. She paused a few feet from where they had gathered and took a breath. She and the matron spoke for some time. Jhee's eyebrows had drench near developed a permanent, persistent arch by the time they were done. Even those who must have been used to it still seemed taken aback at some of the outlandish and inappropriate things the woman had to say. Clearly, she had been a sailor.

"And when you mount that gorgeous sea stallion of yours tonight, give him a good one for me."

She finally released Jhee to seek other conversational prey. Jhee turned her attention to the Wrasses.

"Justicar, care for a game?" a voice called.

Jhee had not gotten halfway across the room before the voice hailed her. Lady Amani, the woman she had met in the study at the Imperial Sojourn, lounged at a gaming table with several others. She shook the dicing cup at Jhee.

Into the gathering swept the ostentatious imperial who had alibied the now dead senator. The case had discredited Jhee and set much of her current nightmare in motion. This was also the saffron eyed woman who plowed by her outside the library where Jhee had gamed with Lady Amani. The imperial, swaddled in a cream and ebony gilt-edged, crystal-inlaid wrap, bore a lightning-hot elegance, enticing if you were the type who reached out to flames; terrifying if you weren't. She zeroed in on Jhee and struck a path towards her.

Jhee abandoned her pursuit of the Wrasses and diverted to the gaming area. She made the proper gestures and bows to the women seated around the table. "My ladies."

"We were just doing some friendly wagering. Care to join?" Lady Amani asked.

"Don't mind if I do," the saffron-eyed woman answered.

"The invitation wasn't for you, Lady Zaria," Lady Amani said.

Zaria ran her tongue along the inside of her mouth.

"I believe they are serving cocktails in the turf lounge," one of the assembled ladies said.

She and several nobles hastened from the gaming area. Other lords and ladies kept playing but slyly adjusted their positions to listen in.

Lady Zaria gave a tiny fake chuckle, "As you like. See what continuing to play only with plebes nets you."

"Perhaps later," Amani said.

The two stared each other down until some signal passed between them. Lady Zaria glided from the gaming area.

Jhee thought it might be best if she left, as well. "It is most gracious of you to invite me, but I'm not much for gambling."

"Nonsense. Sit down," Lady Amani said. The high ladies rearranged themselves so that Jhee could have a seat. "This one here is simply vicious, she can be on my team."

The cards were dealt, and they began to play.

"My dear Justicar, it has been a while since the sojourn. How are you faring?" Amani asked.

"Quite well, my lady."

"Excellent. Excellent. None the worse from your interview?"

"Interview?" Jhee asked, then set her lips in a thin line once it dawned on her what the Lady had meant. "My interview, yes. It was quite unexpected. I was not quite prepared."

"Yet, you appear to have acquitted yourself well enough?"

"True. Not an experience I'd like to repeat."

"An understandable sentiment. I believe it's to you, Lady Danio."

"The stakes are a tad higher than I care to lose tonight. And with that ladies, Justicar, I shall excuse myself from the table."

Lady Danio gave the other lady the eye. "Me too. You have cleaned us out."

The third lady seemed oblivious. They played a few more rounds. Despite saying she wanted to leave, Lady Danio stuck around a few more hands. She eventually gave the other lady the eye too. She at last finally got it. "Swell playing, Justicar. You've quite cleaned us out."

Only Jhee and Amani remained at the table. "Hmm, well, with all other players eliminated, we can no longer play on the same team."

"No, we can't, my lady."

"Still, it would be a shame to stop the game now. How about we resume our match from the other night? Allow me a chance to avenge my defeat."

"I really must—"

"I insist." Jhee switched to the opposite side of the table to Amani. "Now, we have a clearer view of where the other sits. I was most saddened to hear about your interview."

"I would think such a thing would be beneath your notice. My affairs hardly rate attention from someone as powerful as yourself."

"Quite the contrary. Everyone's taken notice of your prominent role in that suicide business. In fact, I think quite highly of you and take note of much of what you do. I fear you do not fully appreciate the effect your actions have. I trust you understand now?"

"Indeed, my lady."

Amani rolled the dice and moved her pieces. "Your move."

Jhee's hands twitched. Thinking back on their meeting at the resort, the lady had addressed her as Justicar. Yet, Jhee had borne no sashes of office and never introduced herself as a Justicar to Lady Amani. Was Amani admitting to being the one who called for her interrogation? She knew much about it, regardless. Was this a warning or a challenge?

"Fold," Jhee said.

"Conceding so soon? I thought for sure you had a few more rounds in you. I was so looking forward to playing longer."

"My family needs me."

"Ah, family. Do you know where my family stands in line to the throne outside of the elective succession?"

"Rather high."

"Such imprecision and coming from you no less. Though, it is technically correct. Did I hear correctly that you stymied IES?"

"I would hardly say I stymied them. We disagreed over the ownership of a piece of medical technology. Which I thought we had resolved amicably."

"Still, you can never be too careful, especially when it comes to Imperial interests."

"I'll keep that in mind."

"Please do. Now, you may run along to your family. I'll be around if you feel the need to keep playing."

Jhee looked at the Wrasses. Amani knew why she was here and what she intended. Neither they nor the Pikes would be powerful enough to stop her. If Amani was as powerful as Jhee suspected, almost no one here was powerful enough to oppose her outside of the current immediate family of the sitting Emperor and Empress.

Jhee still had to risk it. No individual branch, perhaps. Maybe some form of collective effort on her behalf. All the families were still Imperial electors to the Imperial succession council. It could not hurt to have more allies among them.

~

To Hold Back the Sea

Jhee marched up to the Wrasses and dazzled them with technobabble as if her life depended on it, which it did. As Kanto predicted, they gushed out over cyphering and all matters arcane, even arcane forensics. Although by the end, Jhee had gently rebuffed a few offers of marriage. They did not do much halfway. She was sure they were joking, which she rather enjoyed. Most of these imperial families did not have a sense of humor. She supposed the risk of being murdered by your relations or taken away for reeducation at any moment made you act in strange ways.

Jhee handed the patriarch her credential card. "Have your wonderful niece and nephew call me, and I'll happily answer any questions they have about cyphering training."

"Well met, Justicar, well met. Here, have your man there chime us up to discuss tutoring my youngest as well? You take care. Take care of yourself now."

The patriarch's expression was concerned yet sincere. He had guessed Jhee's purpose here as well. Jhee took the personal credential card. Later she would have their servants arrange the exchange of their more formal credential cards, but this was a direct line without having to go through all the proprieties of a formal meeting. Two down, all to go.

Jhee sought out Kanto. As said, he was still with the Mandelbrot set. They were inspecting a pair of Pomeros puppies. Jhee joined them as they went down the rows of fancy dog breeds. She touched Kanto's shoulder.

"Hello everyone," Kanto said and looped his arm through Jhee's, "this is my dear wife, the esteemed Justicar of District Sixteen and renowned author of 'Dispatches from Arrow Point.'"

"Hello there, my Lady Justicar we were just discussing these magnificent animals with your man here."

"Denbe, these are my friends the Mandelbrots and Aiaku."

"Pleased to meet you, my lords and ladies."

"You as well, Justicar," Aiaku, the sandy-haired man, said.

"We met at the sojourn while Bright Harmony performed."

"Indeed we did. Small seas."

Jhee relaxed for a moment with Kanto, the Mandelbrots, and his apparent friend. Despite the stakes, Jhee's anxiety eased. She had one assurance with this crowd she usually never had: none of them viewed Jhee with an eye to trade up the way most secondaries spouses did when she was invited to functions. They had or were already married to Imperials. They could get no political or wealth gain from a simple government official with fairly distant, almost nonexistent claim to the elective succession. Every noble family had some claim. However, the most powerful families made sure the most distant were kept distant and ineligible. On the other hand, they did like to have companions. If the way many of them eyed her and Kanto was any indication, they were still sizing up their eligibility for that purpose.

Kanto whispered in Jhee's ear, "Aiaku is from Taelos."

"The ones who tried to hold back the sea."

Kanto inclined his head. "Their male population was decimated trying to stop the wall. I think he's on our side."

The young man raised his glass at Jhee and Kanto. Jhee did likewise. It seems her actions against the Storm wall had gained her one admirer instead of an enemy.

Kanto adjusted Jhee's collar. "So, how did it go?"

"I charmed the robes off both the Pikes and the Wrasses."

"Then why do you look like you just ate Dundarian lampreys washed down with a gallon of bitter beer?"

Jhee held Kanto's hand. "Please. We'll discuss it later."

Kanto pulled his hand loose, and his eyes flashed with anger. "Who?"

"Let's just enjoy the rest of the event."

"Point them out."

"It will do no good. They are too powerful."

Kanto scanned the crowd and soon gave a knowing nod. "I see. No one is too powerful. We'll just have to be slower and clandestine. And sweeten the offer of friendship. We already have something powerful to barter: my tenth share of M-corp preferred."

"You'd really give up your noble title?"

"So long as one of us has one or the shares to maintain one, it's all that matters."

"Please, no. I think I got us a truce. Can we please not push it?"

"You think? But you are not sure?"

"No."

"Was it someone you came into direct conflict with?"

"Direct contact, not direct conflict. It didn't seem personal."

Kanto sighed. "We still need to keep to the original plan. The worst thing we can do is being seen to roll over. If we can't do anything about the head of the drake, then we need to strike the tail."

"What do you mean?"

"Find whoever set you up and make an example of them. With no direct quarrel between you, it means they used a lesser branch or slab to do their dirty work."

"Won't that just escalate?"

"Perhaps, but the person who did this is savvy enough to know if you don't retaliate, it will be open season on you. Even if they do nothing, a lesser branch could take you out for their own reasons. It's probably why they so easily agreed to a truce. They will have used a cutout they don't mind losing. Now, this is important. How did they seem to react to your being here?"

"Impressed."

"Good. I think that means they expect you to eliminate the problem for them. They may have been testing you."

"Kanto, can't we just please let this go."

"No, Jhee, unfortunately not. Now think, could this person be the mysterious imperial Counselor Medea was talking about?"

"Almost certainly so."

"So, that means that to orchestrate the attack on your career, they needed someone privy to your confidences. Someone you would trust. They needed to know something about your movements. And your temperament. They needed to know the senator would set you off. Your prolific and high-profile investigative work would provide some insight, but not all. They needed more to go on, on how to get to you. If our family was in a worse place, I'd say all three of your cohort would be the obvious suspects."

Jhee raised an eyebrow. "Including you?"

"Yes, if we weren't on such excellent terms. Grandmamere said, 'always start with the spouses.' The overly ambitious ones, while obvious, often want to protect their position first and foremost. The ones to watch out for are the ones who feel slighted or harbor unspoken, minor grievances. Those fester and lead to rash action. They often want acknowledgment and to avenge their injury more than they want power. Our cohort is also small enough that we can address most issues before they can fester."

"Someone with a sense of grievance which would make them reckless." The Senator's family or his imperial lover, Lady Zaria, Jhee thought. They fit the bill perfectly. But she did not think it would be a smart idea to be seen to target the people she was in a public feud with and who had a case brought against her. All the reasons Kanto said why they should retaliate made sense. However, if she did, she was committing herself to politics and giving up on the law. She might get herself reinstated, but she would still no longer be considered credible. Her reputation as a Justicar would be tarnished. She needed for the board of Justicars to vindicate her. If she went after her accusers, even obliquely, it subverted the system.

Jhee tipped the peach cocktail to her lips. She watched Kanto work the event. This time they had gone after her. A risk she could live with. Next time, they might go after Shep, Kanto, or Mirrei. Jhee squeezed her eyes shut. She must keep them safe. No matter what it cost her. Preserve life first. Preserve her family first.

Jhee pulled Kanto aside, "If an occasion arises for you to save yourself, take it. If you find a situation that allows you to protect yourself, agree. Use your tenth share if you must. All I ask is for you to help Mirrei if you can."

~

The Flame and The Rod

When Lady Zaria headed for Jhee this time, Jhee had no obvious exit. She stood her ground at the clubhouse bar.

"Ah, Justicar, what an unexpected surprise." The woman narrowed blazing saffron eyes at Jhee. "And in such health, no less. I would have thought you would have been indisposed for longer."

"Well, you know what they say? Hard to cage a goldfish."

"Indeed. I trust you found the experience edifying."

"No doubt. Very educational. It certainly has focused my sights."

"It was impressive that a minor noble such as yourself could have managed such a brief stay."

"I find I am often underestimated." Jhee's boast was a leaky boat with nothing to keep it afloat. She still did not know how or why she had been released. Or targeted.

"We shall see. Won't we?" The woman picked up a flute of champagne from a passing waiter. "Well, how about a toast? Cheers, a drink to your continued good health?"

"And to yours, my lady."

They each drank. Although Jhee did not think the woman would be so obvious as to poison her, she was glad she had taken her poison neutralizer for today.

"Ah, Lady Zaria," Odo said. He hobbled over and took a glass of champagne himself. "Justicar. What are we drinking to?"

Captain Odo had denied credit for her release. One of her torturers promised freedom in exchange for knowledge about a case Ursula was supposed to have stolen. Had Jhee inadvertently provided them with the information they wanted?

"Our continued good health," Jhee said.

"Splendid. Splendid. Do you mind if I steal my old friend here, Lady Zaria?"

"I was just about to move on. Well, until we meet again, Justicar. And make no mistake, we will meet again." The woman inclined her head to Captain Odo. "Consort Regent."

Jhee let out a deep breath once she had gone.

"Making friends, I see, Sniffer."

"Just putting her on notice."

"About your brief vacation. You think it was her?"

"Most likely. Who else could ignore your request?"

Odo upended his champagne glass. "That was foul business. I'm sorry you had to go through it."

"The one who should be sorry is the person who set me up."

Odo cast his gaze about. "Sniffer, call it off."

"What?"

"This entire thing. The investigation into Ursula. The veteran care center. Everything."

"Ursula is gone, Captain. Our friend. Your lover."

"Would you keep your voice down?"

"Don't you want to know why?"

"I know why!" he said then cut himself off. "Someplace private, now, Sniffer."

The captain ushered her to some hedges between the paddock and clubhouse.

The captain continued once they were out of full view, "I'm sorry about what happened to her. I'm sorry about what happened to you, Sniffer. I'm sorry I ever learned about that drenched brief. You should have just told them where it was. It's over, Sniffer. Just let it be."

Odo shuffled away. The Earth drawer with the Ladies' Auxiliary had asked her where to find the case. They knew Ursula had met with her. Jhee's heart constricted. The captain, it had to be the captain. He had informed on her. But why?

Jhee took off after him. "What was in that case?"

"Leave it alone, Sniffer."

"It's you. You spawn of the trench. This is all on you. Ursula. My imprisonment."

"Please, Jhee. No one was supposed to get hurt. Not you. Not her. I didn't know what was in the case. Not until after it and Ursula went missing."

Jhee turned her back on the Captain, "I'm not interested unless you plan on going on record."

Odo snatched Jhee's arm and spun her back around, "You know I can't, Sniffer."

"I'm not interested in more lies or excuses from you, Captain. You may be willing to let the matter drop and forget about Ursula, but I'm not. She tried to mark the trail for me, but I was too full of myself to notice."

Odo's fingers bit into Jhee's arm. "You don't understand. I can't let this go any further."

With fire drawing, Jhee generated a burst of bright sparks in her hand. She averted her face. She tossed the dazzling cluster over her shoulder at the captain. He cursed and released his grip. Jhee sprinted for the paddock. Shep appeared in the exit.

"Jhee? Cap?" Shep asked. "What's going on here?"

Jhee whirled back around. Captain Odo stood, hands trembling. His walking stick poised to strike Jhee down. Odo lowered his cane.

"Jhee, are you all right? I thought you were in danger."

"I'm fine," Jhee said and began herding Shep back towards the crowds. "We'll discuss it at home. If you're here, who's looking after Medea?"

"Bax. Medea suggested I keep watch over you, and she was right. I smell burnt hair. Cap, were you attacking Jhee? Why?"

"Sheepdog, I can explain."

Jhee faced Odo. "No, you won't. We're leaving. Don't contact us again."

"Would someone tell me what's going," Shep demanded. Her arm sigil began to tingle. He refused to be moved. "I'm not going anywhere until I know why were you throwing fire and the captain is singed and looks as guilty as a Trench trawler?"

Jhee closed her eyes and whispered, "It was him."

With a roar, Shep charged Odo. Odo rolled his head from side to side, and his form took on the features of a giant walrus. They went at each other tooth and claw. Once Shep had gained enough of Odo bioplasm, he too became more walrus-like.

Jhee touched the sigil, now burning her arm and engaged her siren module. The timing was key. Incapacitate either combatant before the other, and the deactivated berserker would be defenseless against the active.

Shep was the younger and more combat-trained of the two. He quickly overtook the older man. Jhee knew what she must do, yet an ambivalence, a hesitation, paralyzed her. The captain had her tortured. Her fingers twitched, and her skin tingled in remembrance of her encounters with Fire and Earth.

"Yield!" Jhee yelled, the shutdown signal embedded in the command word. Simultaneously, she dug her nails into her arm sigil. Both berserkers dropped. They shifted back into a more Water Folk form. By now, a crowd had gathered. A few gasps went out. The Imperial guards rushed in and seized Shep.

"Let him go." Odo got to his feet. The Imperial Guard stared at Odo and took in his state of dress. "Nothing to see here, folks. Just a little roughhousing between old friends that got out of hand."

"Any assault—"

"I said, 'let him go.' There was no assault. I just asked him to demonstrate a few wrestling holds. Old and as clumsy as I am, I botched it and fell directly on my tail. No harm done."

The Imperial Guard looked at the captain's bloody and torn clothing.

"Are you refusing an order of a Consort Regent, *Lieutenant*?" Odo asked. "Or is it now corporal of the nursery squad?"

The guard lieutenant gestured. The Imperial Guard released Shep. "My apologies, Consort Regent. Sir, allow us to call a transport so that your friend might take his leave immediately?"

"No need. I'll see to it myself. You are dismissed."

The bulk of the Imperial Guard left. However, two guards remained at the periphery of the crowd even once Shep and Odo began to walk away. Odo clapped Shep on the back to seem chummy. They walked out of Jhee's earshot. Odo seemed understandably agitated and animated. Eventually, he and Shep seemed to calm down.

Shep stalked over. "Let's go."

"Thank you, but never do something that rash again."

"What?"

"You're lucky he covered for you."

"He's lucky I didn't kill him."

"Keep your voice down." Shep looked at her bewildered. Between his obliviousness of the peril and the captain's actions, she refused to hold back anymore. "You almost got yourself arrested on imperial grounds where they'd be able to hold you, put you in a hole, and do whatever they want to you!"

Shep's expression melted into a horrified one. Her equilibrium evaporated. Jhee buried her face in her hands and cried. He crushed her in his arms.

"I'm sorry, Jhee. I didn't think."

Jhee sagged against Shep too exhausted to reply. They collected Kanto and went home.

15

The Dawn Wolves Reunited

Shep gazed up at the ship docked at Packer's Pier. He had watched from the shadow of a nearby boathouse half an hour for Odo's informant to show before taking a closer look. The gangplank had been left down. He made his way on deck.

Where the Trench was the informant Odo promised? Was this wise? Why meet here? Shep had received a cryptic message from Odo to meet his contact here if he wanted to know who else played a part in Jhee's detention. After a few minutes poking about the wheelhouse and looking through the navigation maps, he was convinced this contact wasn't going to show. He had been sent on a wild wisp chase. Another negative tally to put on on the Captain's balance sheet.

A whiff of cologne made Shep pause.

"Sheepdog?"

Shep came about at the sound of Odo's voice. Whatever else had deteriorated about the captain, his light step had remained.

The captain hobbled forward. "I'm glad you contacted me. I didn't know when I might hear from you or Sniffer again."

"I thought I was meeting an informant. I may not have come otherwise."

"I'm glad you did. About the way we left things…"

"Thank you for calling off the Imperial Guard."

"It was the least I could do."

"You're right. It was."

"Please, let me explain."

Shep pushed past the captain onto the main deck. "I don't want to hear your explanations. I only want to hear who put you up to it."

"It wasn't like that. None of this was supposed to happen."

Find your stillness. Focus in. The time had begun to slow, and the captain's voice recede. Shep muttered counter chants to keep the rage in check while the captain uttered excuses.

"I even went further afield in my affection: a male. The chance of bastards virtually nil and a fellow imperial who could look after himself. I thought he would be safe. *He* was. His other lovers weren't, neither were their children. But me? Wifey never went after me. Never me. She wanted to make sure me and everyone else got the message loud and clear: hers. She made Zaria look like the founder of the Open Seas Movement. I was good for a while. I dutifully stayed on the island and waited for her to show up every few months to insult me and wave her newest conquest in my face. Then Ursula showed up, and it was like the years in between had never happened. She needed my help. I knew if Her Imperial Terror got one whiff of it, it was over."

Shep paced about the deck. He took one calming breath after another. "So, you set Jhee up?"

"I figured the Regent would assume the same thing everyone else did. I was right. The more she thought I cared, the more she wouldn't be able to resist. She knew there was someone before she came along. Someone I served with. The Regent could be quite charming when she wanted something. When she wants you, she pulls out every stop, sweeps you right away like the riptide. Sniffer came to my bunk one time. Did you know that, Sheepdog?"

Shep snarled. "Liar."

"It's true. She found messages between you and Miramar. Jhee would have never looked twice at me if you hadn't betrayed her. I was a nice shoulder to cry on, safe, comforting. I sent her away. One of the few times I ever did the right thing in my life. You remember what I was like in those days. Heart-stopping, virile. Handsome. Too handsome.

"Now, look at me, Sheepdog. Being a berserker did this to me. I'm losing coherence. I may revert completely, lose myself to my berserker skin and turn into a walrus permanently or some Unmaker's hybrid. It was all supposed to be so simple: steal the contents of the case and use it to barter our freedom from the Regent. The Regent had plans of her own, which involved Ursula being killed after we made the delivery. Luckily or unluckily for us, we had to take a peek to see what was in it. After we did, Ursula refused to make the drop and disappeared with the case. That's when I approached you. I needed to find her before the Regent did."

The red began to come over Shep's vision again. He counted and breathed. He moved toward the railing of the deck. That way, he might be able to leap off instead of attack.

"Look, Sheepdog, don't go all red-eyed on me again. I hadn't meant for Sniffer to be taken. Ursula disappeared again right after we left your place. Soon, I got a call. They said they had her and let me speak to her. They would let her go in exchange for the case. I told them I didn't have it. They didn't believe me. I pointed them at the only other person I knew she had been in contact with. I had no idea who they were or who might have sent them until the Abyssal constables grabbed Sniffer."

Shep gripped the railing and bared his teeth. "Because you showed a callous disregard for Jhee's life."

"If it were a choice between Sniffer and Ursula, you would have done the same."

"I would have made them kill me first."

"I'm not you. I'm done sacrificing what I want. It's cost me my youth, my vitality, and my essence. I'd be drenched if it would cost me Suli, too. The one person in this Sphere who still loved me and always did."

Shep tilted his head up to contemplate the thin clouds covering the moons. "You're wrong, Cap. She wasn't the only one who still loved you. I would have laid down my life for you, for any of the Dawn Wolves. Now, only for Jhee."

"So it appears you have chosen. The tribunal, M-Prot's abuses being dredged up, capsized everything."

Deep breaths, one after another, brought Shep clarity, but he did not trust himself to speak.

"Here we are, Sheepdog, the last of The Dawn Wolves. Many were rejects, buried in the deepest hole someone could find. One only wound up there if you were toxic or keeled someone off royally. The only way out: Medical Protectorate. Some voluntarily. Most because they were disposable. It turns out I was, too. I was only supposed to be your minder, not a berserker. But I know I couldn't let my squad do something I wouldn't. How did we get here, Sheepdog? Years ago, I never would have dreamed of turning my claws on you."

Shep glanced at the captain, hunched over his cane, eyes greened by melancholy. "Me neither."

Pity for the Captain came over Shep. Gone was the scheming imperial who had used him and Jhee. Now all he saw was a broken man clutching at anything that might put him back together. Shep stroked the eye scar Jhee had given him. What a hypocrite he was.

"Do you know who gave the order?" Shep asked.

"I was telling the truth when I said I thought it was the Regent. Now, I'm not so sure anymore." Captain Odo refused to meet Shep's gaze. "Please, Sheepdog, let's go for a drink like old."

"Where is Ursula now?"

"I don't know."

"So, Jhee's pain, betraying us," Shep said. "It was all for nothing. You lured me here to talk. You talked, I listened. We're done."

"What do you mean I lured you here? You asked me to meet you here."

~

The Two Theas

With her Justicial authority under review and her teaching credentials suspended, Jhee had all the time in the world now to work on her experiments and derivations. She had tried to relax with net weaving. But after the first few days around the house, she had been bored out of her senses.

After a few more days, Jhee wandered about the townhouse, so empty with only her and Kanto. Memories of doing the same growing up at Hillside while her two parents sat in darkened rooms isolated in their grief overwhelmed her. She needed something else to occupy her time. She fished out her old design for a room-scale orrery, the ultimate Mechanist devotion.

One day, as Kanto was heading out to the center, he stopped by her workshop. "We could easily hire someone to put that together for you."

Jhee climbed down off the ladder, where she had been taking synchronance measurements of the planned orrery space. "That's not the point. The point is to design and construct it yourself as a sign of devotion and adherence to Mechanist principles. Some Makers want you to do pilgrimages or missionary work. The Prime Maker wants Mechanists to construct a series of devices. I must draft the plans and source the parts myself, or else what have I learned about first principles. I've made the compass, astrolabe, sextant, and I'm almost done with the chronometer. I even constructed a few small scale telluriums without all the heavenly bodies. All that remains is a more or less full-sized orrery."

"All right. Enjoy your day."

"Off to the center? How is the fast track to joining an art or education council coming?"

"Slowly. Volunteer work only counts ten percent. Not that joining the council is why I'm doing it."

An idea struck Jhee's fancy. "Mind if I come with?"

"I would be delighted," he said.

Kanto split his time between the youth center now and work and training at the spirit corps auxiliary. He switched to homemade lunches. Instead of the usual transport, Kanto had taken to cycling to work. He had full access to their finances. Even though Kanto had not said so, she was certain he had done so because he knew the financial strain using a transport service was. They each had bicycles, even Mirrei, a gift from Shep. At the sight of the cycles, Jhee couldn't help but feel wistful. Shep still kept strange hours and still came home bruised. She was uncertain what she could do about that.

It had been some time since Jhee had ridden one of these cycle contraptions, but she got the hang of it again after a few hundred meters. She and Kanto cycled to the center together. As they secured their cycles, Kanto smiled at her fondly.

"I had wondered how long it would take for puttering around the house all day would get to you. Shep, Mirrei, and I all had a bet."

"The servants' pool included an over/under? Who won?"

Kanto harrumphed. "Mirrei. She claimed to have used some complex mathematical derivation based on how many current experiments you were running, but I think she pulled the number out of the ether."

Jhee laughed. "Ether way sounds plausible to me."

"Aw, Jhee, that was terrible. I don't see a future in comedy for you." They secured their cycles. Kanto removed his helmet and did a quick touch up of his hair, then offered the mirror to her. "One thing I can say is this haircut isn't prone to helmet head."

Jhee touched hers up. As she handed the mirror back, she ran her fingers through his short coif. Not only his hair had changed, but his stance. He had taken on the more rigid, disciplined stance of someone with training. "I don't know. I kind of like it."

"Guess what happened at the aux?"

"What?"

"You're supposed to guess."

"Work at the auxiliaries is going well." Jhee looked him over. His sketch notebook had seen a lot of recent use. It was too soon for him to be planning next season's household wardrobe. "You got a promotion or additional responsibilities. Something to do with your practiced eye and keen fashion sense."

"Almost spot on. We got the contract to redesign the navy's uniforms. I've been asked to lead a team to come up with some concept sketches. I'm in charge of one group. If they choose our designs, we'll be put in charge."

Jhee hugged Kanto. "Congratulations! You earned it."

He turned away sheepishly. "I haven't been picked yet. Just promise me, no fishiness. I want to know I can do this on my own."

Jhee gave a wry look. She was not sure if she had enough influence left to arrange her way out of a parking fine. "Of course. I wouldn't dream of it."

She and Kanto walked inside hand-in-hand. While Kanto went about his regular duties, Jhee spent most of her time completing paperwork and viewing the center's orientation and training. Towards the end of the day, she could finally assist Kanto during his lessons.

She found Kanto, and they had a late lunch in the break room. They sat and ate together quietly and contentedly. Kanto's lunch bag contained a leftover sandwich and second piece of fruit. As they ate, the quiet girl from the other day wandered over. She said nothing.

"Hello, Almathea, how are you and Ms. Muffin today?" he asked. The girl hid her face in the doll. "This is my wife. Do you remember her from the other day?"

The girl nodded.

"Pleased to meet you. Almathea, what a lovely name. My name is Galatheia. My close friends call me Jhee. Do you know why they call me Jhee?"

Almathea shook her head.

"It's a tradition where we're from to give children a forename tied to their house name. I was the youngest of seven whose name all started with a 'G.' Even my parents had a hard time keeping track of our names, so they gave us shorter ones. For the longest time, I thought my name was g-seven."

Kanto chuckled. "I never knew that. Almathea here has one of the sweetest singing voices I've ever heard. Don't you, Almathea?

The girl nodded again.

"Would you like to say hello?"

"Hello," the girl said in a tiny, hushed voice.

"And hello to you, too," Jhee said.

Kanto smacked his forehead. "Oh, would you look at that? Looks like I brought way too much lunch again. Jhee, would you like some?"

"No, thank you. I think I brought too much myself. I couldn't possibly eat any more."

"What about you, Almathea? I've got all this extra food it would be a shame for it to go to waste. You think Ms. Muffin might like some for later?"

The girl nodded slowly. She shyly and embarrassedly took the apple and sandwich from Kanto. Almathea looked both ways before squirreling the food away inside her doll. She gave a brief smile, then ran off.

Jhee gave a bittersweet smile.

"For her sister," Kanto said. "We're only allowed to give them a single breakfast and lunch. The sister can't stay here because their father insists she work."

Jhee remembered the older girl who had come to pick Almathea up. "What kind of work could a child that young possibly perform that's legal?"

"Selling lottery tickets. There's a chance and entertainment exception. She helps sell lottery tickets to the tourists and the dockworkers from her father's cart. The tourists especially are more likely to buy them from children."

Kanto pulled out a pocket full. "She's a prolific seller and rather good at it."

"Those are Imperial lottery tickets. Do they know children are being asked to sell those? That can't be legal."

"Jhee, don't make trouble for them. Her sister is practically the only means of support for their entire family. She does it so Almathea can spend the day here."

Jhee hung her head sufficiently chastened. "I'm sorry. Old habits."

"You're allowed. I want to help them all so much, too."

Jhee and Kanto finished up their day at the center and waited with Almathea for her sister to show up and collect her. They hopped on their cycles once the two girls made it home.

"I know you asked me to leave it alone," Jhee said, "but I can't stop thinking about them. I can't use my influence to help you, but maybe I can help them."

"How so?"

"Junior academy scholarships come with room and board. With her older sister's math skills and the younger's singing, they may each qualify for one."

"I'm not sure if their father would accept."

"Certain scholarships also come with a stipend which as their guardian he would be in charge of administering. He's already willing to make a living off the backs of his daughters. It should more than calm his objections."

Kanto thought about it and nodded. "I know of someone who can get them the supplies they need for free."

On their way home from the center, Kanto said, "Jhee, I wanted to run something else by you."

They cycled along. "Sure, what?"

"While at the aux, I saw a pilot program they have for the vets. I want your help to set up a mentorship program between the kids and the veterans, a summer program."

"That sounds like a marvelous idea. The veteran service center already has an agreement with both the nearby kennel and stables. Perhaps we can have the veterans help teach the children how to ride and care for the animals, and train the service animals, too."

"Exactly the thing I had in mind," he said. "Thank you, Jhee."

16

—————

∾

Guard Captain Petra

Imperial Guard Captain Petra rounded the corner of the building. The Consort Regent had given her the slip again. She held up her conch and read her tracking devices' signals. After she traced them to the water's edge, she presumed the trackers she had planted lived at the bottom of the harbor. The Consort had gotten wise to those, too. Petra did not envy returning to her superiors yet again with another report of how Lord Odo, a barely mobile blob, had gotten away from her again.

Petra could not express her utter contempt for the Imperial spouses and concubines enough. Shaking their Imperial protection details was a lark for them or a rite of passage; for Petra, it meant life or death or an etiquette training timeout with the Style Council and Ministry of Manners. It was a game to them. She had sworn to die for the Imperial family. Dying in their service meant a pension for her family and imperial honors. Dying in review or etiquette training would see her stripped of rank and her family left with nothing. She was already on notice for losing track of him at the Imperial Sojourn and for the incident at the Fancy Foam Equestrian and Canine Showcase. One more incident and she would have to perform atonement or take the black, polar protection detail.

Guard Captain Petra gave a sigh of relief when she received a signal from one of the backup trackers, the only one not with these. It was almost a game figuring out how to plant them without being found by the target. This one was a tracer she had slipped into his food. It stayed in the bloodstream for a few hours, usually the length of his daily excursions to see his mistress. And more recently, the Justicar.

Petra had not been present for when that report hit the Princess Regent. She swore she had felt the palace quake. The Princess Regent had taken it about as badly as the woman's husband seemed to. It was always something with these neglected spouses. The Justicar was a modestly attractive woman, but every much Lord Odo's type, commanding, no-nonsense, and with just enough power to make the Regent take notice. Petra had been in charge of all the pedigree checks and backgrounds on the entire household.

If Lord Odo confined his activities to commoners, they would all be the better for it. A simple bit of poison or knifework saw those dealt with. Instead, Lord Odo liked to push to see what he could get away with. The palace nearly erupted into a civil war that time Lord Odo tired of nobles and took up with another Regent.

Eliminating nobles took elaborate planning and permission. The paperwork and bureaucracy and negotiation involved meant it sometimes took years. If that was Lord Odo's plan to protect his paramours, it usually failed. Once he had moved on, the Princess Regent, having gone through the trouble of gaining the permissions often had them eliminated for spite. The Justicar had proved more resourceful than his usual lovers.

Petra was rapidly approaching the tracer's location. On top of having to deal with the Princess Regent, there were all the angry spouses, both imperial and otherwise. The Imperials were always seeking ways to advance their position. No one had yet unseated the Regent's current senior spouse, though many had tried. Lord Odo's place was square in the middle—not much to be gained or lost taking him on. The senior spouse's guards practically lived like nobles themselves off of their tips. Petra admitted the monetary tips from the other Imperial spouses had more than covered two of her children's Imperial academy fees. She almost had enough to put her youngest twins through until secondary.

Perhaps the Justicar's spouse did not think what Lord Odo had offered for his silence was enough. Which had happened oft enough, too. Most spousal objections were monetary. They saw Imperial, and they pictured wealth and influence, regardless of which branch had taken up with their spouse. They imagined themselves set for life.

The spouses of the lovers often did well for themselves too. They had various sweetheart deals and arrangements with the Imperial harem. Occasionally, they were jealous, but mostly they objected to the fees being too low. Especially if one of the blood had come after them. Petra assumed something similar had taken place between Lord Odo and the Justicar's husband. Likely a monetary dispute as he had either been present or at least knew of the meetings between the lord and the Justicar.

Petra had read the report on Shepard, a berserker who had served with the Consort Regent. He had been keeling off the well to do for years. One would think his time as a Medical Protectorate plaything would have taught him better, the only fate comparable to an interview with the Style Council. Petra needed to monitor him. She had doubled the guards. His background as a berserker made him very dangerous. The standard imperial detail would not be enough, which was why Petra was even more keeled at Lord Odo. Her approval for extra guards had come in, and if the incident at the dog show was any sign, even the lord's background as a berserker was not enough protection. The other man was the better fighter.

Petra, at last, arrived within a few meters of the tracers. They were at the fighting society's slaughterhouse where the Justicar's husband had recently been arrested. Petra sighed and called for backup. This could not end well.

Petra surveyed the slaughterhouse. She wished she could stride in and grab the lord by the ear. But that was another part of the game: Petra had to remain hidden to at least give the spouses the illusion of privacy. She muffled the light and sound of her conch as she grew closer. She would not feel right until she had eyes on him.

The slaughterhouse was exposed and open. Petra made her way to the center of the slaughterhouse where the cage was. Two figures were in it. One knelt on his knees over the other, who was not moving. Petra rushed the cage and threw open the door. The Justicar's husband knelt over the beaten dead body of Lord Odo. Visions of Petra's modest home, two husbands, her two other children already in the academy, and of the twins' scholarships—they were going to sit for the boards—flashed through her mind. She would end up in review at the Women's Auxiliary for this. Petra dropped to her knees and wept.

JHEE'S CONCH chimed with Shep's sequence. She answered. "What's wrong?"

"It's not your husband, Justicar," a voice Jhee didn't recognize said. "He's in trouble. You better get down to Imperator's headquarters with advocates of the highest order. Your lover's dead. Shep was found bruised and covered in his blood."

"My lover? Who is this?"

"No one of consequence anymore. I'm getting my family to safety. You should do the same with yours."

The conch clicked. Jhee removed a digitally sanitized conch from its hiding place in the book *The Harvest Home Tales*. She messaged Kanto on her way to the imperator's station.

Worth Knowing

"I hear your denbe is going after IES," Aiaku said and grabbed a glass of champagne from a passing waiter. "It's a bit of a risk. Do you know how many imperials have their hands in that pie?"

Kanto sipped at his champagne and took a gander around at the attendees at the garden party. "I imagine quite a few. Still, they keep coming for us, and well, we need to reach some accommodation with them. It's not our first encounter with them."

"And it won't be your last," Aiaku stated. "How close is your denbe to the elective succession? Why is she doing this? As far as I can tell, she is so far outside the line of Imperial succession, she would have to eliminate most of the court to even be considered."

The garden party was being held at some ghastly ultramodern mansion on a folk-made jetty built to prevent erosion. Rounded, marble lawn fountains clashed with the angular polyglass and chrome house. Whatever decorator had approved this travesty should have been banished. The affair's attendees were many of the same crowd as the sojourn and Fancy Foam Showcase. While it was better if Jhee were here with him, Kanto understood why she had passed.

"My denbe is a woman of principle," Kanto said. "A rare thing around here, it seems. She will do anything to protect us."

Aiaku nodded. "Rare indeed. It's good you're here. You can't be seen to be backing down. What with your denbe's visit to etiquette school, I wasn't sure if you'd be here. How is she doing? How are you holding up?"

"We're doing fine. The attendees are acting differently than I expected. Why are they acting so solicitous? I'd think they'd be scared to associate with her. Or me."

"Quite the contrary. Someone important wanted your denbe taught etiquette, and yet here you are. More importantly, she found a way for that not to happen. In which case, you might be someone good to know."

Kanto still could not believe that Captain Odo had a hand in Jhee's detention. He had eaten their food and enjoyed their hospitality. Then betrayed denbe and denme in the worst way imaginable. Captain Odo was an imperial. Kanto should never have let his guard down. Being around Jhee and Shep had blocked his nose for these matters.

"Any consensus on who?" Kanto asked, hoping to tease out what Aiaku might know.

"You haven't already worked that out?" Aiaku asked.

Kanto chose to play coy. "We have our suspicions and made our moves. It helps to know who else we might have to look out for."

From what Kanto understood, the Captain had pointed the finger at Jhee but not ordered the detention. If he or a Regent had ordered Jhee schooled, Jhee would still be detained. If Captain Odo and the Regent were unlikely to have freed Jhee, that begged the question who got her released. All Kanto and Shep knew was they had received a call where to pick up Jhee shortly after Kanto had made a pass through the vizier's favor book.

Aiaku passed off his empty champagne glass to another member of the wait staff. "The obvious money is on Zaria. She had practically cut the senator loose when he was arrested. Doesn't mean she wanted him dead, at least until she chose. Least of all because of some upstart Justicar from the shoals."

"What of Lady Amani?"

Aiaku lost a step. "She is powerful enough, true. I think there is another player at work."

"Such as?"

Aiaku picked up a crab puff and popped it in his mouth. "Can't expect me to do all the legwork for you."

"Of course not. And what of you, Aiaku? Are you here because you think my household is worth knowing?"

"I'm here because I thought we were friends."

By Kanto's research into those listed on the vizier's books, none of them were powerful enough to challenge Zaria either. Kanto gave 'Aiaku' another examination. His robes and sashes still denoted him as Kanto's peer even though he knew that to be a lie. Maybe a name or two on the vizier's list similarly hid their true rank.

"I suppose we are," Kanto said. "Still, I wouldn't mind knowing more about what you are getting out of all this."

"Aeolus. You remind me so much of him like he was before. He was so handsome, and he had the voice of a siren. We thought he would be the next Nishadahl. We gave him the best instructors and music tutors from all over the empire. Your skills in music and performance are a rare light in this world. I don't like to see such lights snuffed."

"You sound like a Mandelbrot."

"Perhaps."

The crowd at the garden party had begun to murmur. Kanto watched the assembled lord and ladies, concubines, and consorts for clues as to what had happened. The last time it had been a fight between the captain and Shep.

A notable amount of the servants of those who distrusted conchs had arrived to whisper into their employers' ears. Those with conchs had made surreptitious moves to check theirs. Kanto chanced a quick glance at his, as did Aiaku. The assembly's attention slowly turned Kanto's way. A plainly stated message from Jhee advised him to exit the event quickly and quietly. She'd have a transport pick him up dockside near the water taxis.

"Bold move," Aiaku said with a touch of admiration, "eliminating the Princess Regent's consort. And risky. And so publicly no less. The question everyone's wondering: now is your denbe crazy or so sure of herself she feels she can get away with such a very disruptive play? Now they're calculating if it's recklessness or a demonstration of power. I pray it's the latter."

"It's better for them to wonder." Kanto noted the Imperial Guard positioning themselves near the exits. "A bold enough move to back Zaria off?"

"I'd say there is an excellent chance. She can be petty, but not stupid. If it is recklessness, then it's in her best interest to let the Princess Regent do the hard work of finishing your denbe off. If it's not, it means your denbe may be more powerful than she expected, and she should call it even."

Kanto picked up his drink and began to casually stroll around the fountain, looking for other viable exits. There might be a way out through the stables. "That alone would be worth it."

"Which side of your building did you arrange for your transport to pick you up? You wouldn't show up with this news about to break without an exit plan."

Kanto eyed Aiaku skeptically.

"You can trust me."

"North," Kanto said. The water taxi pick-up was actually to the northeast, yet easily reachable from the north side should he need to give Aiaku the slip. This way should Aiaku prove to be false, his exit route would still be protected. If Aiaku were leading him into a trap, there was not much he could do about it now. As they moved, Kanto assessed what had happened. Odo, the Princess Regent's consort, had been killed in a way that made everyone suspect Jhee. Not good. Aiaku had laid it out pretty accurately. It was reckless on Jhee's part. Maybe her imprisonment had upset her more than she let on. He wouldn't put it past her. But she did not act this rashly or angrily. Something else had to have happened. True, they had stumbled upon someone from the vizier's list or a contact powerful enough to get Jhee released from etiquette school, but undoubtedly not powerful enough to provide cover for an Imperial assassination. Jhee would not put them at risk that way.

Kanto's suspicions there was an exit through the stables proved correct. Rather than a route through the stables, Aiaku brought him through the kitchens. A small door and docks waited for fresh sea meat delivery from smaller fishing vessels. "Here, this should provide you with easy access to wherever your transport actually is. Keep along the waterline, and you can reach any side of the building relatively undetected."

"Thank you, Aiaku."

"This is the most fun and excitement I've had in some time. Hopefully, Zaria takes the hint and whoever else she's working with too."

Whoever else she's working with is the genuine threat.

Two-Way Glass

"You should talk to your advocate or solicitor about this, not me," Nevis, Jhee's Justicar colleague, said.

Nevis and Jhee met at the drinking establishment down the street from the Justicar's Annex. They faced away from each other while seated on the perpendicular sides of the bar's corner.

"I'm talking to you," Jhee replied.

"I can't do anything about this. It's a capital case. Imperial security. A royal assassination. This may even rise to the level of treason. I can't go anywhere near this. Unless you want me to wind up in the same black hole you were in."

Jhee flinched, and her hand twitched. Nevis's posture relaxed.

"Sorry. That was uncalled for, but this case and you are toxic. I didn't believe this situation could become even more radioactive than it was before."

"May I at least see him?"

"Imperial Intelligence has him. They're making plans to transfer him to State for," Nevis lowered her voice, "special detention."

"If that happens, I may never see him again. It has to be now."

"Then I advise you to tap one of your other contacts. My hands are rightly and thoroughly tied."

"May I at least know what he is being charged with?"

"For the moment, Imperial assassination. Even if Shep wasn't, Jhee, that's not the only thing."

"What else could there be? What else are you going to charge him with?"

"Jhee, maybe you should back off this one. You've lost your job, you've been detained, and now your husband's in jail."

"Please, tell me."

"The lord consort was beaten to death. They found his blood all over Shep. And Shep looked like he had just been in a mighty fight."

"There must be a mistake."

"No mistake. There's more. The Consort Regent wasn't the only one."

"Wasn't the only one what?"

"Those names you asked me to run."

"The ones who all turned out to be dead?"

"They were all beaten to death."

"Surely, you can't suspect Shep?"

"His berserker bioplasm was found all over the scene."

Jhee touched a hand to her mouth. "Please, I have to see him."

Nevis looked about her. "I can take you to where he's being detained, but that is about as close as I can get you."

"Thank you." Jhee looked at Shep through the two-way glass. Shep sat in a medical gown as they had taken his clothes for evidence. He stared at the wall. "Has he said anything?"

"No. This is bad. The Consort Regent had no defensive wounds, so we suspect he knew his attacker. Shep was found by the Imperial Guard kneeling over the body and covered in the Consort Regent's blood."

"The Imperial Guard. They could have been bribed. What of his protection detail? Where were they? I want to question them."

"LAS or fleeing with their families. At the time, he was only assigned one bodyguard, and he had apparently given her the slip. No one's seen her after she called it in."

"Has it occurred to you they might be the guilty party? Or else why would they disappear?"

Nevis pursed her lips. The expression confirmed what Jhee's worry had caused her to ignore. Involved or not, the Imperial bodyguard expected a Style Council interrogation. "Nevertheless, I have to wait for Imperial Intelligence. They will take over this case. If you have any favors left, I suggest you use them now."

Shep could not have done this. He couldn't. Even after Odo's hand in her imprisonment and torture, he and Shep were still friends. Shep was all about protecting those he loved. That used to be Odo at one time. True, he had lost his temper at the Fancy Foam Showcase, but he had had time to calm down since then.

Yet Shep had been so angry lately. Jhee's gaze lingered on the scar across Shep's eye. Her hand went to her neck. His unyielding dedication to those dear to him had not always held true. Once she had to resort to the knife she kept in the bed stand. He let go but still came after her. It wasn't until she slashed his eye had she been able to talk him out of it.

Shep had been so repentant. Until then, he had been reluctant to get help. He had insisted he was fine and did not need any help. He could handle it on his own. It was after that they had a Fire Folk artificer who owed her a debt outfit them with the control sigil set.

Her hackles raised at the sight of Shep, disheveled and bloody. "Help me, Jhee. I swear it was an accident. It had to be. I just woke up covered in blood beside the Captain's body."

Shep stared at the two-way mirror. He knew Jhee was there. Between the link created between them by the control sigil set implanted in them and his sensitization so she could use arcana on him, he might always know when she was near. Jhee stroked the sigil to calm him. She still could not find the right levers to push to get his protection protocols turned over to her command. The Empire might still have need of their weapon. A looming threat all the berserkers faced: they could be recalled by The Empire to duty at any moment. So could she, for that matter. If the berserkers were imperial property, so was the siren module tied to her central nervous system.

While a siren module did not give the handler complete control over a berserker, it allowed a handler to shut them down. It was an off switch rather than a remote control. Berserkers were at their "best" undirected—a countermeasure to the use of diviners and prognosticators. It kept the Fire Folk and Water Folk diviners and prognosticators from uncovering their true intent.

"May I talk to him?" Jhee asked.

"I'm not even supposed to be letting you see him. You better let your legal team handle this."

"You and I both know once they take him into custody, the chance of that happening will be next to nothing."

"May I suggest you need to concentrate on your own woes and the rest of your household? Given the history between you and all the recent events."

"They'll think he was acting on my orders. My entire family could be charged with crimes against the thrones."

Jhee must think more practically now. Pragmatism required she view Shep as a starfish arm, to be used as a sacrificial limb. The best path, the pragmatic path, forward was to divest herself of him to broker peace with Lady Amani and the Princess Regent. Whether they wanted vengeance or for her to back off, letting him take the fall would be a sign of her good faith and perhaps her only way to salvage her name, reputations, and fortunes and keep Kanto and Mirrei safe. The law had let her down, and so had Shep. She would have to cut him loose. Spending resources to protecting Shep had been a costly mistake.

And yet, the thought of doing so left Jhee's stomach feeling sour. She needed to return to first principles.

First Principles

"And that's pretty much the way it happened." Jeja of Marpele, Jhee's mentor and the woman who sparked her love of the law, concluded her talk to the small bookstore gathering.

"Except for the big hats," Jhee yelled out.

Jeja and her aforementioned wide feather-topped hat turned Jhee's way. Her mentor smiled. "Quite right, my dear. Your descriptions failed to capture the scale and grandeur of my hats, which at one point shaded an entire battalion. Distinguished members of the Southern Stars Reading Club. May I present to you the renowned author of 'Dispatches from Arrow Point' herself."

Jhee walked forward to take Jeja's outstretched hand. They embraced. Those assembled applauded. While the indefatigable Jeja autographed copies of her memoirs, Jhee waited patiently. Now and again, someone asked Jhee to sign a copy, too, as she featured in them. Even less frequently, Jhee was presented with one of her own "Dispatches from Arrow Point" novels to sign.

At last, Jeja and Jhee found a nook in the bookstore to talk in private. "I expected to hear from you much sooner than this. Especially once that cad you married messaged me. I'm glad to be able to see you again. Know I pulled out my favor books as soon as I heard."

"That may have made all the difference with my release." Jhee's fingers twitched, and the memory of the flames made her face tick. Not all of the fire had been real, but she still remembered the searing sensation and cooked flesh smell.

"I hope so." Jeja squeezed her hand and slid a hot cup of kolal and cinnamon roll in front of her. The sweet, delightful scents overwhelmed the remembered ones. "Sorry to bring that up. I also heard about whats-his-name's arrest. I assume that's why you're here."

"Partially."

"While I've never been his biggest supporter, I'll do whatever I can to help. What do you need from me?"

"Tethering. Should I help him?"

"Remember, first principles. Motive? Why would he have supposedly murdered the Consort Regent? I don't believe this nonsense about romantic rivalry."

"My detainment. The Consort Regent was involved."

Jeja's eyes widened, and she swallowed hard. "That would certainly do it. While I don't doubt he might kill for you, I doubt he would risk this sort of peril to you or your family."

Jhee pushed away the half-eaten pastry. "He hasn't been himself lately. Fights. Violence. He joined some underground berserker fighting society."

Jeja polished of the cinnamon roll for Jhee. "He has some sense, if not a lot. He contacted me after all, knowing how I feel about him."

"I'm tired of this, Jeja. I also have two other spouses to consider."

"Dear, I say this with love: get your head out of your Trench and stop the self-pity. *Justicar*, your duty is to your constituents. He's one of your constituents. If he came to you as a stranger and asked for help, what would you do?"

Jhee hated Sharlet for years over the decision to feed Shep to the political leviathans of the Reaches. Was this the choice Sharlet had to make? Cut Shep loose or see her entire family dragged down as well? Yet, should Shep receive a lesser measure of justice than she would afford anyone else because he disappointed her?

The gears began to turn in Jhee's head.

This had to be a setup, Jhee thought. It just had to be. Shep would never beat someone to death, least of all the Captain. Jhee understood traditional law enforcement's logic, flawed as it was. They knew Shep killed the Consort Regent because he killed the others. And they knew he killed the others because he killed the Consort Regent. If Jhee found evidence to break the link between the two, then it would surely exonerate Shep of the other. Since she would be allowed nowhere near Odo's case, she had to start with the others.

Shep's bioplasm being at any of the crime scenes could easily be explained away. From attendee and fight staff to any constable present for the raid, anyone could have gotten a sample after one of his bare-knuckle brawls.

Jeja grinned. "There she is. That's the woman I know."

17

~

Dead End Trail

Jhee took out her notes on the case so far. She needed to go back to the beginning. All these other matters had been distractions. These attacks on her family and her career had been designed to keep her away from something. She needed to go back to square one, Ursula. They had not seen hide nor hair of her since she left with Odo from the townhouse ahead of the Abyssal constables. Ursula had led a double life, not just as the down-on-her luck soldier, but as a spy. What was she investigating that led to this entire mess?

The key must be in the attaché case Odo asked her to deliver. If the killer had found it, he or she wouldn't be out to get Jhee. They must think she had it or knew where it is. Why else would they turn her life upside down like this? Then the question remained where Ursula would hide something like that. Jhee and Bax had turned Ursula's life inside out. They had even found her secret apartment. Or had they?

Ursula was a soldier and thought like a soldier. Where would a soldier hide things?

Jhee palmed her esca. Of course. The answer had been staring her in the face the whole time. The last time she had seen Ursula before this entire fiasco started, Ursula had just been her usual obsessed self. But what if…? What if she was hiding something? Jhee and Ursula had fallen out of touch long ago. Jhee's home would have been the last place they would have looked. It had not even occurred to Jhee until now.

Jhee should not go alone. She went to Bax and Dari's room, where Bax was keeping vigil over Dari. She knocked gently and was given leave to enter. "I'm sorry to intrude."

"What do you need, Justicar?"

"Shep has been arrested for murder. Several murders. They say he killed his friend, the Consort Regent."

"Imperial assassination. The whole house is at stake." Bax drew a shaky breath that caught in his throat. "What do you need from me?"

"Backup and your thief's mindset. I have an idea of where to look for something that may exonerate him, or if it doesn't, gives me the leverage I need to flush out the actual killer."

"Give me a moment." Bax touched Dari's hair, then kissed her on the forehead. "I'd forgotten how beautiful she was. Justicar, did Mr. Shep do it?"

"I wish I could be sure."

"She'd want us to help him no matter what."

Jhee nodded. She and Bax went to her academy office. "She was standing somewhere over here when I came into the room. I came in, she stood up suddenly, and drew me away from the area."

Bax walked over to the trophy case. This was the same mirrored case where Jhee had had an encounter with her mist mimic the other night. The dream still had her shaken. It felt so real. He scanned it. "Aye, here," Bax said.

Bax pointed at damaged plaster next to the trophy case. One of Ursula's trail markers had been carved into it. Jhee pulled out the hardwood disc. She compared it to the marker on the wall then to the image she captured of the marker left in the counselor's office. Three markers Ursula had left at least. Three points made a data set.

With them together, Jhee saw the elements of a rough cypher in the symbols indicating direction and sequence. She reeled back through her conch's image history. At last, she found her record of cacography from Ursula's leather-bound notebook.

The three markers formed the starting sequence. She unlocked the coordinates to a walking trail near the lakebed. The leather-bound book was an investigator's logbook that contained a series of coordinates. From there, each marker they found allowed Jhee to progress further. They followed markers and coordinates through unused walking trails throughout the capital to a mostly ignored section of shoreline.

"Aye, here," Bax said. He pointed at a slab amongst a series of rock forma-tions. It bore the final trail marker.

Jhee and Bax pushed aside the slab. Instead of a case, they found Ursula's twisted and broken body. Jhee clasped her palms together at angles for the First Makers' blessing and touched her hands to her esca.

May Ursula be remade magnificent.

Jhee took out her conch and called the imperators immediately. She had found Ursula's body, but there was no sign of the attaché case. She had thought for sure it would be there. If it wasn't there and the killer didn't have it, where was it?

At the imperator station, Jhee sat pondering. Shep remained in custody. Odo and Ursula both dead. That left Shep as the last of the Dawn Wolves, a berserker orcinus alone without pod or gang. With decent proof or reasonable cause to doubt he killed the Consort Regent, she could free him. Jhee convinced Nevis to meet her at a nearby, busy lunch counter while Bax kept watch outside.

"Did the coroner's report come back in on my friend?" Jhee asked. The way the patrons, she, and Nevis were packed in amongst the bustling meal crowd reminded Jhee of sardines in a packet.

Nevis kept her eyes forward and trained on her conch as she spoke, "Broken neck, multiple fractures of the fifth and sixth cervical vertebrae. Consistent with a slip and fall and with her blood alcohol level, I would agree."

"A slip and fall? Then who stuffed her in the hiding hole?"

Nevis shrugged. "They estimate she's been dead between ten and twelve days."

"Ten to twelve days. That's impossible. Ursula was at our townhouse, not a long-tide ago."

"I'm just telling you what the report said."

"Ridiculous. Let me see that."

Nevis yanked her conch out of Jhee's reach, then gave her a light touch on the forearm. "Take a break. Go home and get some rest. You will need it. I suspect the Imperial Intelligence will want to question you soon. And this time, I bet they are going make sure they can hold you for much longer this time."

Without Shep here to examine the body or access to the autopsy images, Jhee was reliant on the local constabulary who it seems were incompetent or part of the obfuscation. Ursula did not slip and fall, and she certainly did not put herself under that slab. Jhee thought about it more. Some environmental factors may have been at work, which confused the time of death. She accompanied Bax back to Dari's bedside.

The last person her household had seen Ursula with had been the Captain.

Could he have killed her? If he found out Ursula lied about being pregnant, perhaps. That made a better motive for Shep to have attacked the Captain than any the imperators had furnished—after the Captain's betrayal and if, and only if, Shep learned Odo killed Ursula. Then and only then would Jhee believe Shep had murdered the captain. That was a ridiculous number of qualifiers.

The question remained, where was the attaché case, the one the Captain had lied about saying they contained love letters and mementos? Jhee had thought for sure she would find it on the shoreline. Ursula wasn't just a soldier, she had been their scout. What if it had been a ploy? Ursula knew someone was after her. She was laying a false trail. But from where to where?

The point farthest away from Jhee. If Jhee was the false trail, she represented the point farthest away from the genuine one: the captain himself. Jhee got Kanto to do some digging in the records. "Look for anything tied to Captain Odo."

Kanto's face went slack with concentration, and she heard furious typing. "Here. Try this address. Marina Place. Apartment sixteen-oh-three."

Jhee gave a wry laugh. The apartment above Ursula's. Rather than under her nose, the solution had been above it. Hidden in the closet, she found the attaché case in a lockbox with Ursula's trail marker scratched on it.

The case contained a series of dossiers on everyone who had worked on the berserker project from janitor to division head. Jhee also found a black sharkskin bound diary, the companion to the Triptych of the Creed, and a copy of *Imperial Births and Lineages, Volume Ten*.

"The Eclipse Chest, or effects and paperwork collection Lot Number Fifty-one. Lot Number Fifty-one was a strongbox containing various papers, relics, and a dodecaptych, twelve-part arcane manual, gifted to the abbey."

The Triptych of the Creed was a partial cyphering manual all the clerics had tried to read at the abbey. So much in this investigation kept coming back to that one: the accursed abyssal bible of arcana, the merry little band of smugglers and traffickers. What she wouldn't have given for another sip of that black orchid tea. Why couldn't that have been the item from the abbey that still plagued her?

Jhee tapped a finger aside her nose. While this was all interesting, she had come no closer to breaking the causal link between the cases. Her Maker within pinched her. They were trying to link her beating victims to Shep. Did she still have a copy of her clinic files?

Jhee pulled up her consultation copies. She pored over the trace evidence found. The victims had traces of their attacker's bioplasm on them, which were sent off for bio-typing. Jhee switched to the bio-typing reports. These grouping factors did not match Shep's. How could someone have called these a match?

This time Jhee marched proudly into the Justicar's Annex. She placed her conch with the consultation files on Nevis's desk.

"Nevis, here have a look at this."

Nevis sighed. Her brow furrowed, and she shook her head. "This is hardly conclusive. Records on your conch cannot be taken at face value."

"I'm not asking you to do so. But if these reports are correct, it means yours have been tampered with. Please, check the access logs."

"Fine." Nevis's dubious expression turned to a scowl. "There are some anomalies here, but I don't think it's enough to clear him."

"Is it enough to see him free of special detention?"

"That depends on your legal team."

A Dismantler in the Making

The confirmation notice from the flower service arrived. Once Shep had been released to Jhee's custody, she had bought her legal team the biggest floral arrangement she could find. She planned to throw them an enormous celebration if her household came out the other side of this mostly intact.

Counselor Medea and Kanto met Jhee and Shep as they arrived home. Kanto regarded Shep with coolness and uncharacteristic silence.

"Welcome home," Counselor Medea said and fidgeted. The four of them stood about trying to figure out where to look and what to say until Medea broke the silence again, "Dari's doing better. Would you like to see her?"

Shep nodded. He and Counselor Medea left the foyer. Jhee and Kanto had a long hug. He guided her into the study, where they seated themselves in their favorite spots. "What's the situation? Is he released pending trial?"

Jhee rubbed the bridge of her nose. "He's been cleared for now. They found someone had tampered with the test results. There's also some question about the witness accounts as they put him in multiple places at once."

"So, he was set up? Zaria again?"

"Very likely."

Counselor Medea appeared in the sitting room doorway and cleared her throat. She held one of the valises she brought with her from the sanctuary clutched to her chest. "Excuse me, may I speak with you privately?"

Kanto frowned. Jhee motioned for him to stay and got to her feet.

"Let's go to my study," Jhee said.

In the study, Counselor Medea cast her gaze about them.

"Forgive me for not sharing these with you before now." Counselor Medea squared her shoulders then pressed the valise into Jhee's hands. "I managed to get these files for Ursula before I was forced to go underground. They contain personnel records for many of the scientists and doctors at the Medical Protectorate. I thought the duplicate and dummy files were for a benefits' scam, just as you did. Veterans double-dipping, claiming full benefits while working on the side. It turned out to be more than that."

Jhee flipped through the records Medea provided. This was precisely what she had discovered before. Soldiers with no or practically non-existent histories kept showing up to claim veteran's benefits. Jhee dug out Paij's data shell and the one Ursula slipped her.

Counselor Medea straightened a stack of records that had threatened to topple. "I've got dozens and dozens of records of veterans drawing a pension while also being on the IES payroll. Maybe even hundreds. You know what this means? Someone might actually bring down IES once and for all."

Now that Jhee could cross-check the files, the calibrations and alignments of the Divine Mechanism began to lay bear this puzzle's solution to her. This solution linked IES with the Medical Protectorate's abuses. "We'll need witnesses. If we can track some of these veterans down and get them to testify, we could hurl IES on the Unmaker's discard pile."

"Exactly what I was thinking."

The idea of being Inkerton Enforcement Services' Dismantler sent a secret thrill through her. Their involvement in the Galleon City mess, from worker and refugee exploitation, throwing her into a hole to be interrogated, to last but not least, their role in nearly getting Mirrei killed, had her itching to take them apart. Doing anything about their handlers at MANTEL would take more patience and planning.

Medea stared at Jhee a moment, then leaned in and kissed her. Jhee pulled away. Medea's eyes pinked with embarrassment. "I'm sorry. I thought—"

Kanto burst into the room excitedly. "It's time," he said.

"Time? For what?" Jhee asked and put distance between her, Medea, and the stack of bio-parchments.

Kanto folded his arms and glared at them. "The remote meeting."

Jhee touched the heel of her hand to her esca. "Oh! I had completely forgotten."

"So, I gathered. I'll expect you promptly." Kanto gave Medea a contemptuous glare. "Family only."

He jaunted off.

"Remote meeting?" Medea asked.

"My youngest," Jhee said. "She's traveling somewhere remote. She can't always check in. Would you mind continuing to work without me for a while?"

"Not at all. Nothing is more important than family. And yours is quite lovely."

Jhee nodded. "I think I'd do just about anything for them."

"Family is indeed a treasure. About my forward behavior…"

"Never mind. Go to bed, and we'll get an early start on tracking these people down in the morning."

"You do not understand how lucky you are. Now, go tell them how much you love them."

"Thank you."

Jhee pushed away from the table and joined Kanto in the sitting room. Shep arrived shortly thereafter. Kanto flipped on the wall viewer. A generic message said there was no signal and to please wait 'while we connect your other party.' They waited a few minutes, then Mirrei's image popped on screen.

"Hey, kin." Mirrei excitedly waved her hands at them. The background behind her was dark and storm ridden. "Finally."

"Mirrei, it's so good to see you," Jhee said.

"You'll have to speak a little louder. It's hard to hear where I am."

"I said, 'It's good to see you.'"

"You too. Keeping things calm and boring as always, I hear."

"You know us," Kanto said. Her image showed artifacts. The screen blipped in and out and sometimes doubled and dropped frames. Kanto banged on the receiver a few times as if that might do something. "This darn thing."

"What was that?" Mirrei asked.

"I said, 'we missed you.'"

"Me too. Denme, how are you doing? You keeping out of trouble?"

Jhee and Kanto shot Shep a look. "Never," he said.

"What about you, denye?"

"Somebody has to," Kanto said.

"Good, good," Mirrei yelled.

"How's the work going?"

"Awesome. I think we've helped hundreds, thousands even. Finally, I'm glad I got you all here. I wanted to let you know." Her image cut out again, then popped back in. "The clinic. Continue on. Rim isles."

The background behind Mirrei had gotten worse. Water spotted the lens. The background bobbed up and down as larger waves rocked the boat. The image dropped out and in.

"Star, what was that again?" Kanto shouted. "I told her to install a signal booster, first thing. But does she ever listen to me? No."

"They'll be taking the clinic to Far Surdale. With retrofits. Polar."

"When are you coming home?"

Mirrei waved excitedly at the camera and blew them kisses. The image dropped out, but they still had audio, "I have to go now. Looks like we've encountered a squall. These tropical storms are the worst. That's all for now. Bye-e. Love you muchlies."

"Wait!" Kanto yelled when the call dropped. "Did either of you catch what did she said about the polar regions? Does that mean she's not coming home?"

"I'm not sure. It was garbled."

"Has she said anything to you? Asked for divorce parchments?"

"I don't know. In the confusion, I'm not sure if I sent them or if I did, if she received them. There's been so much going on. Pestering her about divorce was the least of our problems."

"But?" Kanto started.

"She's safe and relatively protected where she is," Shep said.

Jhee nodded. "He's right. If she's halfway around the world on a floating clinic, it's probably the best place for her. She's out of harm's way, and it will be hard for any of the blowback we are experiencing to hit her there."

Kanto sighed. "I get what you're saying."

Jhee and Shep both put their arms around Kanto. Shep covered Jhee's hand with his. "We miss her too."

"I know, I know. Well, I had just thought. I had hoped. Well, you know."

When Mirrei decided to go off with the Boundless Healers Alliance, Kanto had hoped it was only temporary. He had expected her to spend a few months out on the rough seas without their luxuries and come running back to them. To be honest, Jhee had hoped so too. Apparently, Mirrei had a different arrangement with the Maker of Paths. "If helping people permanently is what she wants to do, then we should celebrate it and not hold her back. We've always known this was a possibility."

"But the ice caps? I didn't make her any clothes warm enough for that region."

"She'll find a way. But that doesn't mean you still can't. I trust you could whip up a polar jacket and footwear combination, which would make her the envy of every seal and walrus for thousands of miles around."

"You bet I could."

Jhee laid her head against Kanto's. Shep met her gaze and smiled.

A faint shuffle came from the doorway. Medea stood hesitantly outside of the sitting room. "I'm sorry to interrupt, but I think I found something."

"No interruption," Jhee said. She dabbed at her eyes. She had not expected to take the news so hard. Jhee had known, she had known for some time. She had thought she had prepared for this. Still, the reality of not knowing when or if they might even see Mirrei again had hit her harder than she expected.

Jhee would leave whether to divorce in Mirrei's hands. She would respect Mirrei's wishes either way. If she needed it, Jhee might give her a generous settlement. Jhee had made sure not to entangle those funds and properties she received as Mirrei's dowry too closely with her own for just such an occasion. It should not take much to sign them back over to her so she could found a house of her own. Even if the homes and most of the lands were underwater, the sea rights and mineral shares were still worth much.

If Jhee was being honest with herself, she felt a bit of relief. She had speculated about Shep's affair with Miramar, Mirrei's mother, for many years. It had been another matter to have it confirmed. It helped that she did not have to look at Mirrei day after day and wonder. Or be reminded of Miramar and her family's treachery.

"We should really get back to work," Medea said.

"Why don't I help you go through these?" Kanto offered. "More company and hands to make the work go faster."

Kanto placed his chair between Jhee and Medea and grabbed a file folder. Eventually, Shep joined them.

"I found another one," Kanto said. He tagged and flagged another case record. "How many does that make?"

"Almost two hundred," Jhee sighed.

"Two hundred? That almost the size of a whole civilian auxiliary."

"IES had its tentacles in a lot of lairs, and there are many veterans who'd allow their identities to be used, eager to keep working and making a difference."

Jhee hazarded a glance at Shep. He appeared to be studiously avoiding looking at her. That was fine. He was allowed. They would have to hash this out eventually, though.

Jhee picked up the conch to contact Nevis, her friend at the local Justicar's office. She'd have her run down these names, and then maybe they could get some answers. Was this too reckless? If she was on the verge of bringing IES down, they had to proceed carefully. She was not about to risk her family.

The puzzle was important. They knew this was something Jhee had to do.

They supported her no matter what, and she must honor that. To move against IES, she must be absolutely certain their evidence held water.

There was another precaution Jhee should take. She composed a simple note to Mirrei, slipped in with the divorce parchments, and prayed it reached her. "Don't come home," it read.

18

~

Protect the Matriarch

"It surprises me you and the Justicar don't have children," Medea said.

Medea made her play and set down her tile. An excellent move, Shep thought. She must have been going for a reverse snake snare.

"You know, with our careers and her duties. It was never in the Mundane Design. Shep countered with a contrasting tile, which would force her to divert.

"Still, a virile man should see his bloodline propagated."

"Ha." It escaped without him meaning it too. Virile—something, if he were honest, he had not been in many years. Not that he couldn't, it was just that it was not consistent. Even when it was, the remotest thought of passing on whatever this was inside him on to a child made him want to vomit his guts out.

"Even with that strapping young pup in the picture?" Medea placed a tile. Suddenly his stronghold was threatened.

"He's rich and fit, and his lineage can bring her legitimacy mine can't. I handpicked him myself. Jhee's line will have strong offspring." Shep had to bring in a Lancer to cover, a play he had not wanted to make so soon. He had thought to solve the heirs problem by bringing in Kanto. Jhee, as always, had her own ideas. His shame had known no bounds when Jhee came home with Mirrei in tow, a proxy inheritor should she have no heirs. What Mirrei became after that was a constant reminder of all the ways Shep had failed his family.

"You could have gone with a more traditional sire arrangement. Why did you get her a second husband?"

"I didn't want her to be alone."

"Alone?"

"After I killed myself."

Medea used her tile to execute a handmaiden gambit. "What of yours?"

"What of my what?"

"Your family line."

"The Stargazers were the lowest rungs of nobility who still lived on the wrong side of the channel in Briny Town. My family got our title from rescuing someone important from drowning." Shep placed his tile. Medea immediately set down her handmaiden to neutralize his Lancer again. She was as cutthroat a player as Mirrei. Mirrei always thought he held back when playing her. She had consistently underestimated her skill. "My sisters have heirs more than covered."

"Your family line will be carried on by your sister. Jhee's will carry on through her and Kanto. Then it appears you've served your purpose."

Shep surveyed the board. Her tiles were in no position to breach. He placed a tile to set up for a matriarch formation. "I have other uses."

"How many resources has Jhee had to spend? How many times has Jhee had to bail you out? It appears you've been more of a drain than a help."

"Jhee knows my worth."

"Does she? I know your worth too. You were one of the best fighters in that cage. I wanted to thank you for not telling her."

"Jhee has a lot on her mind right now."

"I think I located another med divisioner."

Shep gripped the tile he held so tightly his knuckles went white. "Where?"

"Are you sure you want to do this? You don't have to be the one."

"You are convinced someone from IES, one of them killed Ursula."

"Yes. I think they might come after your wife. Protect your family."

"This is at least something I can do. End this before anyone else in my family gets hurt."

"One fell swoop. Cut off the head of the drake." Medea placed a tile. "Breach."

"What?" Shep examined the board. His stronghold appeared fine. Then he saw the contrasting tile. Medea had slipped her Lancer through the side to neutralize his matriarch. A risky move as she had to leave a clear path through her own stronghold and leave her matriarch undefended. He could have seized on it if he hadn't been so focused on protecting his position and gone in for the kill. He even had a tile in perfect position for it.

"Your matriarch fell because you weren't paying attention and did not do what needed to be done to protect her. Are you in?"

"Yes."

Shep had been so scared that night he went to Jhee. He had just found out he had lost the lottery. Not only would he be drafted, but his family also did not have the resources to keep him out of the thick of the fighting. He had confessed to her his cowardice and how much he had not wanted to die. One was not supposed to admit that. The war with the Other Folk was stupid and pointless. Yet, everyone was supposed to march off and die with a smile on their face for Imperials who thought you beneath their notice. Armchair tough guls who saw them as pieces on a board just like these tiles.

He had confessed his love to Jhee. They had spent the night in each other's arms. The next day, she summoned a parish priestess and had them married. It had been such an edifying reversal: Jhee tongue-tied and flustered by him. In those days, if he looked at her for longer than two seconds, she'd blush and look away. He enjoyed that it wasn't him for a change. It might have gone to his head. He had taken that adoration and used it.

Shep had been a weakling and a coward. It was only fitting when they put him in a berserker unit and subjected him to experiments, which ensured he knew no fear and would not run away again. Then there was Jhee coming to his rescue like she always did. Yet, time and time again, he failed her. Shep could not give her children. He could not advance her career. He could not prevent her detainment and torture.

Shep swore and banged the table. The tiles flew up and the air. Many scattered and fell to the ground.

"You were distracted," Medea said. "Your mind was on other things. I took advantage of that. I'm sorry."

Shep sighed. He started gathering up the tiles. "No apologies. I'm usually a much better sportsman than this. It's not like it's the first time I lost."

"Still, it can't do much for your state of mind right now. You were making tyro mistakes. You were too focused on protecting your position. Several times you had a clear shot at my matriarch. You could have ended the game there and saved your entire stronghold. You lost sight of the bigger picture. Save the stronghold. Protect the matriarch."

Shep harrumphed. He had lost sight of the larger image. Perhaps he had at that. Fight. Protect. Survive. "I've already screwed this up once before. Jeopardized my house. Made things worse for her."

"This time, you've got me to help."

The Geas

Jhee sat and looked over the records Medea had brought her again. Then she pulled out the files she had consulted on with the imperators and compared them. Her missing persons were homicide victims. Only two had not been killed, Medea and Hammad. They had survived because they fled to the berserker sanctuary. On the other side, though, were those involved with the Albatross files. Everyone who stumbled upon them or was mentioned in them had died or gone missing. It appears someone was tying up loose ends.

Was this like the Eclipse Chest, she wondered? At the abbey, the search for it and its content turned out to be a wild wisp chase. The ill-fated attempt to use the arcane knowledge it possessed had resulted in a cascade of unfortunate events, which led to the deaths of three novices and the previous abbess. Most of that had been from the vizier covering up her tracks.

Perhaps it was the same here. Jhee had gotten to Counselor Medea before the killer could. Who else was left? Jhee brought out Ursula's data shell and her copies of the Albatross files. One by one, she compiled the credentials of those who had signed off on various stages of the identity swaps and benefits approval. Within Ursula's records, which included some Jhee had not found, she uncovered the island senator, the Vizier of Finance, and another name she recognized: Sharlet Stargazer. Jhee wrinkled her mouth.

Sharlet had been involved in this all along. Why should that have surprised her? Over the years, Jhee had murderous thoughts about Shep's sister more times than she could count, yet she deserved better than to be beaten to death by a squad of berserk killers.

Jhee must have faith in the law.

At the end of the Making, though, the berserker squad was the only justice many of these villains would ever see. Jhee could not think about that now. She had skirted the law before and look at how that had turned out and all the unintended consequences that had befallen her. Sharlet and everyone involved in every facet of these schemes had to be brought to the judgment bench.

Jhee left the townhouse and shark-shot to Sharlet's office.

"Why, sister-in-law, what an unexpected surprise."

"Clam it, Sharlet. Tell me about Project Albatross."

"I'm sure I don't know what you are talking about."

"Scores of former Medical Protectorate workers, all given false identities supplied by you."

"Sister-in-law, I don't really think you want to do this."

"Enough, Sharlet. I'm tired. Your fellow schemers have had me arrested, interrogated. I've seen your brother accused of being a sequential murderer. Two of my oldest friends are dead. All because of something you've had a hand in. I'm tired of all these games. Your brother's life and that of his family may be at stake. If you care for him as you claim and you want to make up for what has passed between us, come clean about this now."

"You don't understand. I can't," Sharlet said. Jhee rolled up her sleeves and performed a winding designed to get to the truth. "No. Please. Don't."

"I'm getting the truth out of you one way or the other." Jhee waved her hands and seized the handles of one of the great gears of the Divine Mechanism. This was one of the most compulsive weapons in her magical arsenal, reserved only for Justicars and only to be used under the most extreme of circumstances. She was one of only a handful to whom it had been taught. Not even the Invokers were allowed to use it.

Jhee reached out through the Divine Mechanism and found the connection between her and Sharlet. Jhee examined it and brought order to it and went to the pathways that would unlock the truth from the woman's own lips.

"Tell me about Project Albatross," Jhee ordered.

Sharlet opened her mouth to speak. She made a choking noise and grasped at her throat. Jhee leaned into her cypher and felt resistance. Another force worked against her. The more she tried to loosen Sharlet's tongue, the more the counter force tightened. Sharlet started turning purple and clawing at her throat. With her other hand, Sharlet had grabbed a letter opener. The woman's hand shook as she pointed the letter opener at her throat. Jhee released the cypher and grabbed Sharlet's wrist.

Sharlet dropped the letter opener, coughing and gulping for air. Jhee rendered her aid. Sharlet shoved her away, then flung the letter opener away. "If ever there were a time for you to once listen to me in your whole stubborn life, it's now. No, quite literally, I can't," she rasped.

"An Imperial Silence Geas."

"Worse, an Imperial Compulsion Geas. I can't speak about it even if I wanted to. Anyone tries to force the information out of me, and it triggers a suicide protocol."

"You agreed to that?"

"I didn't have much choice."

Jhee grabbed Sharlet's upper arm. "Fine. I'm taking you into custody."

"What for? You have no proof. It will all just get swept under the rug of Imperial security. Do what I did. Just take the money and agree to keep your mouth shut."

"This explains your sudden rise to the surface."

"There was nothing I could do for Shep. I could, however, try to claw our family out of the trench he had cast it into, though. I figured what harm could it do? The Mitsus, your family, my family all agreed."

"No one asked me."

"Of course, we didn't. You thought we would? You were so snout over flippers for my brother you wouldn't have agreed."

"I wouldn't. You're right."

Sharlet pursed her lips. "We cut that anchor loose because he almost took our family down with him. You should follow my lead and do so, too. Sooner rather than later. He'll only drag you down with him. I always liked you, sister-in-law."

"It didn't feel that way when you and the likes of Kaisonia were taunting me on the fields of play or insulting my clothes."

"Youngsters can be cruel, especially when they're trying to fit in. The unlikely heiress and the diving boy from the wrong side of the channel. Sounds like something from one of your stories. The noble, good-hearted Shep? Or the womanizer with an island-sized chip on his shoulder? Shep had something to prove. He would live in one of those enormous mansions. He would be lusted after by those girls who treated him like a servant. Puberty hit, and he filled out. Shep, the diving boy from the wrong side of the channel, almost did it, too, until he became a proxy in a feud between two powerful families."

~

The Hunt

Far Reach lore said the restless dead turned into wisps or mist wights and became part of a region's fog. Folk's essences belonged under the waves with the ancestors and the First Ones, or in the Spheres with the Makers. To be trapped as part of the fog, bound to the land of the living unable to pass on or help and only able to mislead, must be the worst fate imaginable. One might prefer Unmaking or the Discard Pile.

Mist, the last breaths of the dead, had rolled in. Shep and his gang did not mind. It would be their ally. They smelled their prey's fear on the fog. They heard his heavy, ragged breathing and tasted the sour, rancid brume of his fear. The ground sent tiny tremors of his panicked flight. It would do him no good. The gang was faster. They gained on him.

They hunted together as one unit: a gang of hes, shes, and even a few xes led by their anchors, Medea and the Hammerhead. Protect the stronghold. Save the matriarch. He remembered now. They must do this.

Fight. Protect. Survive. They had to eliminate the threat, the threat to his she and all his future pups. Protect the matriarch. Protect his she. He did not matter. All that mattered was the survival of his gang, his pod.

Their prey faltered. An excited howl went up from the Hammerhead. Soon they would be their prey. Soon they would eliminate the threat. Through his red-eyed vision, the whole of the fog had become blood-red mist. Only a dark, amorphous shape in the center that represented their prey stood out. Shep stopped and took a good sniff of the air and the ground.

This felt right, more right than anything had felt in ages. Fight. Protect. Survive. This is what he was meant to do. This is what he had denied himself for so long. Shep had tried to be the man for so long. He had tried to deny how good it felt to dive, to hunt, to kill. No more. Kill the man and let the beast be reborn.

In the back of Shep's mind, he had the vague idea of his life as a man or the older she, Dari, whom he had lived with, who had killed the woman and let the beast take over. He had spent many years staring into her eyes, wondering why she had made that choice. He had understood it on some level, but not like he had now. He had stared into Dari's shark hound eyes. The eyes always had a glimmer of something more than he saw in other hounds' eyes. It was why all the other dogs gave her deference. They knew she was different, something more, something they must fear and obey.

Their prey fell, and the Hammerhead was on him. The scent of blood filled the air, driving all other thoughts from his mind. A howl escaped him. Fight. Protect. Survive. He rushed forward to join in on the kill. Another berserker cut across his path.

Shep looked down at the victim, and a faint flicker of recognition flitted through him. They weren't just chasing some dock rat of the two-legged variety. He had seen this man before at the sojourn: the vizier of finance.

With the delay, an image of the Lady of the Isles appeared before Shep. Her face seemed familiar, a remnant of the man's memories. The vision faded away.

Shep sought to rush forward again to join the rest of the gang. The image appeared before him again. Not his gang. A false gang.

The she, the anchor, she was barking howling insistently that he join the fray. An itch, a tingle in his neck brand brought him to a halt. He shook his head, a man's head, a Water Folk head.

Water Folk. Folk. Beings capable of operating by more than their base skin's needs. Shep peered down at his hands. Hands, not talons. They had claws and paw-like attributes, but they were still hands. He stared at the surrounding berserkers. They stood upright as he did. His companions were Water Folk, not sea wolves or whale crushers. They never were wholly wild animals. They never were. That was the lie. They were Water Folk. They could choose.

Other members of the gang had stopped. They regarded each other and him. They had realized what he had. This was not real. Their false inner essence as mere animals never was real. It was a suggestion the doctor had put in their heads to get them to act like killers triggered by the smell and taste of blood.

Shep realized the deed had been done. Their prey lay dead and unmoving on the ground. His throat ripped out, the stink of death rising from him. Which one of them had done the deed, Shep did not know. He was splattered with the man's blood. Yet others were drenched in it.

The she-anchor came over. "You did it. You saved the pod and protected the matriarch."

Shep and Medea returned to the mansion. They cleaned themselves off in the stable amidst the snorts and whinnies of the animals housed there. They knew there were predators in their midst. As she changed her clothes, he glimpsed her soft, sleek skin and the pale underbelly with two primary teats, four smaller ones. Teats which might someday nurse a full litter. He thought about his she and the young pup with whom she mated more frequently than she did with him. She constantly smelled of his stink. Shep took the all too familiar side path up to his room. Medea had followed. Something stirred inside him, which hadn't in a long time. He moved up behind Medea. The she turned to face him and smiled. He brought her down on the bed.

~

All Cried Out

While Jhee puttered about her orrery space, she pondered the implications of an all-out war with IES and eventually MANTEL. She found herself headed to Shep's room, as this affected him too, she wanted his input. Kanto might readily agree, but Shep had become more and more of a closed-door to her. She could no longer assume he would just back her up.

Jhee knocked and heard a grunt of acknowledgment. She opened the door to Shep's room and strode in. She found Shep and Medea locked in an embrace, naked. Jhee gasped.

Shep glanced her way. His expression bore surprise as if he had just awoken from a spell. "Jhee!"

Jhee quickly turned around and pulled the door shut behind her. Shep scrambled to follow. Kanto stepped out into the hallway. The entrance to Shep's room flung open, and he came out half-naked, Medea in tow. Kanto's mouth dropped open. Jhee hitched up her robes and ran for the stairs.

"Jhee, wait!"

Tears of humiliation stung her eyes. Shep seized her arm. A blur struck him. He and Kanto crashed into the wall. They fell into a heap on the floor. Kanto scrabbled to the top. He gripped Shep's shoulders and slammed him repeatedly against the ground. Shep did not resist.

"Kanto, enough," Jhee uttered.

The younger husband continued to wale on her older husband. Beyond them, Medea only watched, her clothing clutched to her body in some half-drowned attempt at modesty. Jhee leaned hard into the siren module. "Kanto, stop!"

Kanto sprang to his feet without taking his eyes off of Shep. He came to Jhee's side and held her. She took a step towards Shep. He still lay on the floor. Her gaze went from him to Medea. "Get out! Both of you!"

Jhee squared her shoulders. She straightened her posture, strode passed them into her room, and slammed the door. Inside, she collapsed against the door. She put her entire essence into a soul-yell and slid to the floor, cried out.

19

~

Unerasable

Jhee stood at the top of the stairs when Shep came by a few days later to pick up some belongings. Bax, Kanto, and the servants kept him in the foyer. He gave them a list of items, and they retrieved them for him. She felt nothing when she looked at him. Not anger, not contempt. Nothing. She had tried so many years. So many years balancing his feelings with her duties. So many years wanting him to look at her with even a fraction of the desire he had shown for Miramar.

She had believed once that Shep would come to love her the way she always wanted. What she had to admit was that she was more adept at lying to herself than he was to her.

Shep approached the bottom of the steps. "Please, Jhee, may we talk in private?"

Kanto blocked his path. "She has nothing to say to you, *denme.*"

Shep grabbed him by the robes. The servants unsheathed short knives. Bax brandished his blade at him. "Mr. Shep, please."

Shep released Kanto. He smoothed out his robes. Jhee descended the stairs. She stopped a step or two above him and waved away the servants.

"I suggest you engage a solicitor," Jhee said. "No divorce because I can't deal with another scandal right now. But I'm withdrawing my financial support."

Kanto took Jhee's hand. "We're starting procedures to have your name taken off the marriage charter."

"To be replaced with yours, I suppose," Shep snapped.

"Why not? You've done nothing but shame us since we got here. I've done everything, given everything, to save our family. You've done everything you can to ruin it."

"Why not, indeed? Looks like you are getting what you always wanted."

"You think this is what I want? I admired you. I used to lament the fact that I was not more like you. You're a coward. You have no honor." Kanto stepped closer to Shep. "Don't be another problem she has to manage. You broke her heart, and for that alone, I will never forgive you."

Shep redirected his attention to Jhee. "Jhee, please, if we could just talk."

"I'm done talking to you," Jhee said. "Done. I can't do this anymore. I can't go through this anymore. If you want someone other than me, I release you from your obligation to pretend otherwise. You're allowed to keep my name, but you will get nothing else from me. I have nothing left for you. I'll hold you to the same rules as other noble spouses. Take concubines and whores as you wish, but no bastards."

Kanto returned to her side and placed an arm around her shoulders.

"Now, the servants will oversee the rest of your visit. Kanto, see he takes nothing that is not rightfully his."

"Please, Jhee," Shep said.

Jhee stormed up the stairs.

Once in the comfort of her room, Jhee took out her schematics and parts tables. She arranged them carefully and precisely on her desk. After ensuring each was properly aligned with the corners and in proper relation to each other, she took out a finger quill and a blank sheet of bio-film. She wanted the visceral feel, which could only come from working the derivations out by hand. The precise designs and specifications could be relied upon unlike much in this world. The derivations were challenging but straightforward and elegant. Unlike people.

A rhythmic knock came at her door.

"Enter," she said.

Kanto came in and sat in the chair beside her worktable. He covered her hand. "He's gone."

Jhee wiped a tear from her eye and patted his hand, then went back to her derivations. "Thank you for seeing to it."

"It's the least I can do."

Kanto paused and looked about the room.

"Was there anything else?" Jhee asked.

"No, I suppose not."

Jhee continued with her derivations. Kanto picked up the lute he kept there and played. His sketchbook sat on the bedside table now, and he had moved a few of his toiletries into her bathroom. With Shep's ouster and Mirrei unlikely to return, she felt little point in separate rooms anymore to maintain household unity. She turned her chair to listen to him. It was just vibrations of a string projected through a resonance chamber. Yet, the music it produced was so divine, like the First Makers' Design.

This all had to be the First Makers' Design. Jhee had to believe that. But what lesson did they want her to learn? What device were they trying to construct from the ruins of her life? She must have some greater role to play in Their Design. Had she been too prideful of her intellect? Had she been too lustful of Kanto's beauty?

Kanto finished his pieces. Jhee would have applauded except for the tears running down her cheeks. It was impolite of her, she knew. He wanted to please so much. She should have shown her appreciation, yet she couldn't. "I'm sorry," she said.

Kanto kissed her. They made love slowly and tenderly on the rug in a tangle of half removed robes. He nuzzled her chin afterward.

"And so, the line continues," he said. Her bloodline. Besides him moving into her suite, they had dispensed with all pregnancy precautions. "You loved him while he loved only Miramar. I love you while you still love him."

Jhee opened her mouth to deny it.

"Please, Jhee. Our family has had enough lies. At least respect me enough to admit it. Never lie to me again, and I'll never lie to you."

"I swear."

"I swear, too."

"May I sensitize you so we can practice artificing together?"

"If that is your wish."

"We need to work on a common code. I must look into blood rites and rituals. I always avoided them before for fear of triggering…" Jhee trailed off.

"It's all right, you can say his name. No lies, remember. I know it will take time. I am devoted to you, Jhee, our house, our family. You don't have to pretend you don't still feel anything for him. He's been an enormous part of your life since long before I got here."

Jhee wrapped her arms about him and held him close. "Thank you. Thank you for everything. Your strength, your courage."

"Jhee, I know you said you're not worried Shep would be a danger to our children… With his erratic behavior…. What if I am?"

She took his hands in hers. Kanto had that right. Yet Jhee had no answer to his fears. He nestled against her.

"I don't expect you to forget about him overnight. You can't erase him from your thoughts or your heart so quickly, and I wouldn't want you to."

Can't erase? Jhee thought about Kanto's complaint he could not erase the copy of the judicial archives she put on his conch at the abbey. She sat up suddenly. "Kanto, may I see your conch?"

He raised up on his elbow. "What is it?"

"The copy of the judicial archives. Is it still on there?"

"Yes, unfortunately. It says I don't have permission to delete it, and it's encrypted, so I can't even see what's in it taking all the space."

Kanto handed her the conch. She kissed him. "Brilliant. Thank you."

"If that's the thanks I will get, I should let you borrow my conch more often."

Jhee used her old access credential and opened the judicial archives. It was out of date and was not connected to the primary system, so her old credentials still worked. The hack they had done had preserved it and kept in roughly the shape it was when they set it up at that night on the yacht. She did not need the latest codes and records, all she needed was basic access.

$$\sim$$

Of Uniform Design

"What is it, Jhee? What have you figured out?" Kanto asked.

"Medea," Jhee said.

Kanto wrinkled his snout. "That viper. I can't believe what they did after all you've done for them."

Jhee shook her head. "I can't think about that right now. I think I know what the mastermind behind all this is after."

"Seriously? You are thinking about the case at a time like this."

"I can't help it. I can't explain it. Everything that's happened to us. I feel it's all connected."

"And you have to see it through. It's in your nature." Kanto sighed, hopped to his feet, and helped her up. "Come on then. Let's help you figure out this puzzle. Left side of the closet."

Jhee cocked her head at him quizzically.

"I know you, Jhee. You should find something sufficiently functional and stealthy there." He went over to the wardrobe and brought out black garments. "Sufficiently stealthy and functional. Whatever you propose to do probably is not best done in full daylight. So, I whipped these up, complete with my handy hidden pockets. Form-fitting with an ear towards minimizing sound. These are yours. This one is mine."

"Yours?"

"I always fancied going along with you on one of your ill-advised nighttime sleuthing jaunts. I knew though that others were more suited for it, like Bax and he who will not be named. You always had a tendency to rush out there unprepared. Well, this time, I intend to make sure that does not happen. I'm the only backup you have right now. Bax's out of commission, and denme's not here. I'm not letting you go anywhere alone right now."

Jhee opened her mouth to protest, then shut it. "Yes. Yes. Of course. Although I prefer social engineering. We won't be needing the night suits."

"Dang, I'd been looking forward to putting all my lessons with Bax to excellent use, at last."

The social engineering Jhee had in mind involved Captain Odo's almost forgotten writ and bluffing their way past the archive company's security. Their search for the right company would be made more complicated by the fact some had gone out of business since the archives first started. Jhee sat and thought it through. "We need to check older company records. We needed an older archive service, one likely to have gone out of business and that either sold or warehoused their assets."

"Doesn't that also mean there is a chance they destroyed them? A merged company is what you want. We need to look for one where the aim of the sale was to get their hands on the struggling companies' assets…. Like the uniform archives."

"The what?"

"The record of the old uniform designs. I have access to those records. Legal bureaucracy. They kept a record of the old designs along with some old personnel files. We had to get them unsealed because they had stored them along with the operational data. They weren't very good about curating their data. There was an old company that had archives of many of the records. Personnel records, etc. One of the old archival companies which had a record of the old uniform design reqs also had hard copies of other data."

"Kanto, that's brilliant."

"I know."

While Kanto changed, Jhee noted the hard archives building's location. She tapped the underside of her desk to reveal the compartment where she had stowed the open writ Odo had given her, along with the key to Ursula's apartment. The captain had said it was good only once, the likely consequence if its notarization came from a stolen seal. The moment she used it, it was burnt, and they would catch on to what he had done. She had to make it count.

The Hard Archives

As the guard at the hard archives building processed Jhee's writ, sweat began to make her scalp itch. She recited statutes in her head to keep herself calm. She glanced at Kanto to see how he was faring. He had dressed in the tans of a low-level civil servant. With his hair mussed, he affected the harried demeanor of a junior official quite well.

"All set, Justicar Rasbora. Sign in," the guard said.

Jhee tapped her credential card to the register.

"Your assistant too."

"Ah, of course," Kanto said.

Kanto strode confidently forward and tapped his credential card to the register.

"All set," the guard replied.

The guard waved them by. Jhee queried Kanto via her expression. "Mirrei's wild side had its advantages."

Jhee and Kanto made their way to the records room. She went over to the shelves and started pulling out boxes.

"Now, Jhee, what exactly are we looking for?"

"Hard storage. Cards, acrylics, crystals, etc. from approximately the time of the Flower Wars. Anything that would not be automatically updated along with the central systems. I think main records were tampered with."

"A-ha, I get it," Kanto said and rushed over to a nearby shelf. "Anything connected would be automatically updated with the false information. Hard storage wouldn't as it's kept offline specifically, so should something happen to the primary system, there is an independent record. A backup."

"The question is, though, I'm not sure when the change was made or how many redundant copies of hard storage they keep. I don't know what their turnover regimen for hard storage is. Eventually, the altered data will make it into the hard records. If the alteration is relatively recent, we might get to the hard storage before it's replaced."

"Understood."

Jhee and Kanto tore through storage boxes. They could not conduct a systematic search of each of the archives, because she was not sure how long it would be before they were found out. Jhee and Kanto proceeded through the archives box by box. At last, Jhee found what she wanted. "Kanto, I think I got it. We must check these out and get them to an old crystal reader. We can't view them here."

"There's an old crystal reader at home. It used to belong to grandmamere. I use it to listen to recordings of Grand Mere singing." Kanto paused.

Jhee squeezed Kanto shoulder. "All right, let's go."

After they arrived home, Kanto said, "I'll go get the crystal reader."

"Good. I'll work on wiring it to the viewer."

Jhee examined the face associated with bioprint via the crystal reader. It wasn't the real surgeon general who committed suicide and whose likeness had been splattered all over the tribunal coverage as the Architect of Sorrows. This face belonged to the women they knew as Counselor Medea.

They had found the original bioplasmic records of the actual Architect of Sorrows, the head of the Medical Protectorate. The bioprint confirmations of her remains had to have been faked.

Jhee heard a sound behind her. She turned Medea stood there bearing the provenance and dodecaptych from the Eclipse Chest. "Hello, Medea. Or should I call you the Haddondeep's Butcher?"

"Oh, so you figured it out, did you?"

"It took a while, but yes."

"As one of my former participants, I rather prefer you call me Architect."

"Never again."

Jhee flipped on the light. Medea replaced the dodecaptych in the Eclipse Chest but kept the provenance. Jhee jutted her chin at the Eclipse Chest beside Medea.

"Is that what all this fuss has been about?" Jhee asked. "Is that what you detonated my life over?"

Medea sat down in the chair opposite Jhee and stared at the uncleared game of tiles on the kolal table. "It was you or me. Simple choice."

"What in that chest is worth all this?"

"Proof pointing to the location of the last remaining record of my identity and heritage."

"And that is?"

"Vivyan-Rin Shodan."

Jhee gripped the armrests. "The butcher of Haddondeep."

20

―――――――

～

The Last Scion

"The butcher of Haddondeep," Jhee repeated.

Medea folded her hands, then started resetting the tile board. "The last scion of Haddondeep. The residents of Haddondeep killed themselves."

"Would you prefer the Doctor of Death?"

"Actually, I think I would. I rather like that one. It includes the title to which I am more than entitled. I fancy I feel about Doctor the way you feel about Justicar."

"You and I are nothing alike," Jhee said.

"Aren't we? If only in our taste in men?"

Jhee cleared and centered and did not rise to the bait. "So, you didn't commit suicide?"

"Afraid not."

"And the poor unfortunate they found in your cell?"

Medea rotated the tile board, deciding which color to play, blue or green. "No one of consequence. Are the rest of the Eclipse Chest's content still here?"

"What are my chances of living if I were to reveal that?"

"I don't want to kill you. I've done my best to avoid it, though you have given me cause."

"Sorry to disappoint you," Jhee said.

"Not at all. I understand you and what drives you. I spent time under your roof with you and your family. Such a lovely family. I envy you, you know that?"

"Is that why you seduced Shep?"

"I would have preferred to have seduced you. Go right to the source. You're something of a frigid bitch, you know that? No offense."

"None taken."

Having decided on green, Medea doled out the tiles. "It's a compliment. I am myself. Shep was already vulnerable and close to crisis. Add in some pheromones, and all it took was a nudge. In the throes of passion, though, your name was on his lips. He's so wracked with guilt. Now, Kanto, his attraction to powerful, older women is fascinating, if obvious. I'm sure with time, I might have swayed him, too. Even your do-gooding junior wife if she were here. You are all so predictable. It was quite disappointing. I would have thought you had better taste. Speaking of tastes, that blood of Shep's. Had you and he really never sensitized him?"

"Enough!" Jhee said. She placed her hand in the center of the tile board. "What will it take to get you to back off? You want Shep. You can have him with my blessing."

Medea lifted Jhee's hand from the board, then laid her first tile right-center. A standard opener. Jhee capped it with her blue tile.

"Hmm, feeling me out, are you? Try this."

Medea put a green tile at parallel to Jhee's. This did not just limit Jhee's moves, but hers. A more likely move would have been to cap so she could work towards a stronghold. Jhee placed her tile to block Medea's in.

"Going for early aggression. Don't get too far ahead of yourself."

Medea's counter tile placement blocked her in. Jhee swore. She needed to keep her head in the game. Jhee went back to Medea's original tile and placed to expand.

"Good. Good. Now, you're thinking more clearly. Shep wanted nothing more than to protect you."

Medea placed a tile to lure Jhee in. Jhee opted to continue expansion and said, "Protection is his instinct. You and the doctors saw to that."

"Quite the contrary. The berserkers were shock troops. Their tendency to coordinate and work in packs was born of some instinct within the Water Folk nature. It was almost uncanny really how they could position themselves across immense distances with little overt communication. Pack is less appropriate. Makes us sound like Earth Folk. Perhaps more accurate is a flock, a swarm, or school."

As if to illustrate her point, Medea placed a tile in formation. She had enveloped Jhee's expansion line.

"Would you like to ask me questions? I'm sure you must have many."

"How far are you from the succession?"

"Closer than you, further than the likes of Zaria and Adama. The Princess Regent is in her own league. Why? Are you looking to move up? For now, those three are playing nice with each other. When they go at it for real, you could use some protection. I can make that happen. But to do so, I need everything from that chest."

"What for? A cyphering manual can't be worth all this," Jhee said.

"No, no, no, the Eclipse Chest contains several items far more valuable than arcane polyptychs. One of those compendiums contains a family tree and other pseudo journal entries made by one of Thaedra's pupils while she mused on formulas. It gives insight into a certain love child."

"The Halfmoon Cove Compact. You didn't want the dodecaptych or the Eclipse Chest. You wanted the chest's provenance."

Medea smiled. "I see you know your history."

"I know my law. It set an obscure legal precedent about inheritance. Half the claimants for the Sea Throne invalidated."

"Just so. What's revealed through those relics could upend the succession hierarchy amongst other things."

Jhee kept one eye on the board and the other on Medea, who had almost forgotten they were playing. "More importantly, it could redistribute the Imperial company shares in MANTEL. With the proper resources and stock interests, one branch could acquire a plurality of electors. Blood order succession can be neutralized. A major bargaining stone no matter where you are on the chain."

"Even without a chance at the Sea Throne, one could become a sovereign appointer."

"No Empress Vivyan-Rin, then?"

Medea folded her arms. "No, that's just how I secured Zaria's help. I have use for all the knowledge in the Eclipse Chest. I'm a simple woman with simple pleasures, much like yourself. This whole tribunal business has forced me to amend my activities. All I want is to be left to do my work in peace."

"The veteran's center and berserker 'wellness' sanctuary."

"Among other interests."

"You've been recruiting new candidates via the veteran's center and street fights. You're trying to start another Haddondeep research facility."

"Biotech is such a fascinating field. My fellow imperials were content to profit off my work so far as no one knew. They didn't care what I was doing as long as their shell investments went up. The hypocrisy. They were war profiteers charging exorbitant fees for substandard equipment and transport. My work improved the fortunes of our warriors."

"By turning them into mindless killers."

"By giving them a chance against the stronger, faster Fire Folk warriors. Our troops weren't prepared to face them. The previous dynasty should account themselves lucky they could escape with their lives after losing all the Sacred Monuments to the Fire Folk. Barbarians, indeed. Their dismissal and condescension of the Fire Folk's capabilities made them send our soldiers out there unprepared. Medical Protectorate was tasked with finding some way to turn the tide. The upper echelons didn't care how. We gave them a fighting chance.

"The Sky Folk can fly. Fly. Luckily for us, they crack like eggs. It's only by the Makers' graces have the ground pounders proved so inept at interplanetary travel, or no doubt they would have defeated us too. Between their toughness and their shielding, the Earth Folk shrug off enormous amounts of damage. The Storm Folk can full shift and are the most powerful artificers I've ever seen. What can we do? Hold our breath and hide under the water? Our grace is our navy; fortunately, the Fire Folk navy is utter trash."

Storm Folk? There was no consensus on if the term referred to the Fire Folk or the Water Nomads, also known as the Makers' Failed Prototypes. The consensus, though, was whoever they were all Folk acquired their ability to skin slip from them.

"With our standard military options dwindling, we had to be more creative and go farther and farther afield for soldiers. When the throne had to step into your feud in the Reaches, we discovered the treasure trove of Folk who inhabited the Rim island groupings. We barely noticed those from the Rim—a snobbery which saw us looking primarily among the populace on the main isles. Short-sightedness on our parts, as your region seemed to be teeming with the perfect candidates for our experiments. Your isles were a treasure trove of those with slipping and arcane abilities. Probably the result of your more frequent interaction with the open sea and interbreeding with other kinds who also have extraordinary aptitude in those areas. It's a shame really that our prejudice has prevented us from studying those whose abilities stretch the boundaries of physical, mental, and mystical limits."

Jhee tapped her nose and positioned another tile. "The berserker program started with full-slippers like Shep."

Minor changes came over all Folk, all the time. A great change total and complete had been reserved for the few, like Shep and Dari, until the Medical Protectorate intervened. Jhee always felt Shep's losing the lottery was no accident of chance, and his subsequent assignment to Medical Protectorate no retaliatory act of a capricious family. Both Jhee had attributed to family politics. What if it was more? A deliberate harvest of those from Rim island groupings such as the Reaches?

"Poor, guilt-ridden creature," Medea said. "Are you looking to me to absolve you? No such luck. Shep and those like him had been beneath our notice until your families' silly games brought them to our attention. Your feud put the Far Reaches on the board, and once on the board, you all became game pieces."

"Parley."

Medea squinted at Jhee, then studied the board. While she had ranted, Jhee had continued her aggressive expansion. Jhee had foregone reinforcing a stronghold to go straight for her opponent, as had Medea. Jhee could breach in two if Medea chose not to divert her.

~

No Parley

Medea's mouth twitched. "Clever. No parley. Let's just see how this plays out."

The woman placed a tile on Jhee's flank. If Jhee did not forcibly divert to address it, she would forfeit her lead tile and be in no position to breach. It had been the downside of such an aggressive approach.

Medea regained her composure. "The downside to such an aggressive approach. I should have been more subtle, wooed you, lured you in more. I must admit I underestimated you. It was a mistake to go after your family. The side effect of dealing with the high born—their family members are disposable. I had expected you to cut Shep loose sooner. I also hadn't counted on the Consort Regent to be such a romantic. He used his own beloved mistress as a tile. I had thought she was another of his side pieces. I didn't realize he had actual feelings for Ursula. It was an unexpected bonus that he brought you in. You played the game well."

Jhee sneered and moved another tile towards Medea's makeshift stronghold. "Breach in two. Parley."

"Not yet. You impressed me. You struck a blow for every bookish nerd against the Zaria's and Princess Regents of the world who think we are beneath their notice and who view our fascination with learning as banal. Overwhelm in three."

Jhee examined the tile board. Medea had lured out and isolated her tiles. If she made a move to breach with any of them, she left the others vulnerable. Jhee placed a tile to consolidate. They might break through and have them reinforce each other.

"Diversion forfeit." Because Jhee had failed to close in for the breach, Medea got to claim one of her tiles as her own. Medea picked up one of Jhee's blue tiles and replaced it with a green. "Looks as though you are running out of moves and tiles. Perhaps you should realize this is not a negotiation. Play. It's the only way out. You can't disengage. You can't detach. No negotiation. Those are the laws, and you always follow the law."

Jhee continued with the consolidation play and lost two more tiles. The only pieces she had left was a rough spearhead formation, which in no way threatened Medea's measly one tile stronghold.

"See, it's not always the size and strength of one's fortifications that count or the ability to aggressively take the fight to the enemy. Sometimes, it's simply the willingness to die on the smallest of hills. Fight for such small stakes that it confuses your opponent. Sad, lonely little Justicar. Always the one left waiting behind on the shore."

Roaring and the sounds of struggle carried from upstairs. Medea smiled and placed the lute pick on the table.

"I suspect that's your oldest husband reclaiming his rightful place as your First. Or maybe it's your Second confirming his Naming Rights status. It doesn't really matter to me. A shame, really. Both beautiful and talented in their own ways. I wonder how much it matters to you?"

Jhee rose.

"Sit down, please," Medea said. Her voice bore no hint of anger or it being a command, but Jhee complied. "Jhee, I need that Chest. I'm prepared to be generous."

"I don't want or need your blood money."

"Don't you? Defending yourself against all those lawsuits must have taken a toll. I know funding them was."

"So, the litigants were all cut-outs, proxies, funded by you?"

"Guilty as charged. You know a little something about that, don't you? Just ask the Mitsus." Medea held up a lute pick, one of Kanto's favorites. "This might make for an interesting Lancer. What I am offering isn't money. I'm offering to return your loved ones to you in more or less the condition I found them. Now that we have completed the preliminary round, how about we move on to the final?"

Jhee kept her face still as she picked up her conch and tried to contact Kanto. Kanto's distinctive chime for her communications emanated from Medea's pocket. She pulled out Kanto's conch and answered it. "Kanto can't answer right now. I've got him under lock and key."

Medea disconnected.

"How?" Jhee asked.

"The same way I got in here."

Jhee tucked away her conch and left her hands within her sleeves. Instead of practicing finger cyphers, she prepared a stunning grasp cypher. "Shep."

"Partially. You should have changed the security codes. Shep was more than eager for a little payback on your poor, untrained weekend warrior. Can you imagine the gall of Shep to be jealous? He brought him in, practically forced him on you, then complains he's felt shut out. No one enjoys being cast aside. Imagine what he might do once he finds out the junior spouse is in the early stages of pouching. You didn't waste time, did you?"

A rustle behind Jhee caused her to turn with her cypher at the ready. The Gray Lady of the Deeps stood there bearing Jhee's face. Jhee hesitated. A blow struck Jhee across the head. She slumped over, scattering the tiles.

The Needle Talon

Jhee awoke strapped to a med table. She struggled.

"Please, don't bother," Medea said.

Jhee turned her head what little her restraints allowed. Medea sat on a stool beside the med table. Shep stood beside her, eyes half-focused, staring off into space. He had taken on more of the appearance of a sea wolf with its sleeker shark-like form rather than an orcinus like he did when he was in the middle of a full berserker rage.

"Shep?"

"He can't hear you now. I have him in standby. That is unless you activate your authority chords. Then you may get through to him."

"Shep, please."

Medea picked up her conch and tapped it a few times. "I'm finding the deep encryptions on his berserker conditioning hard to crack. They've been rewritten. I can get him to act in a limited fashion for a certain amount of time. Somehow, he keeps resisting. You must have buried an override deep within his psyche with your siren module. It activated whenever we tried to take complete control of him, then broke our hold over the others. Perhaps, if I can unlock your siren song..." Medea seized Jhee's arm, turning it, so her sigil was in full view. "All right now. Here we go. Berserkers are imprinted to obey and protect the Architect via pheromone coding and conditioning. It seems you found a means to disrupt it. Is this how you did it? Why the sigil when you have a siren module?"

"He's immune to my module. A security precaution because we were married." What game was Medea playing? She knew why. Did she want Jhee to confess to treason? Perhaps, if Jhee kept her talking, she might find a way out of this, or Shep might break free from his berserker fugue. "The knowledge on how to make my module work on him was classified. To reveal it would be to betray the Empire. It would be treason to share it with anyone else. If I wanted to talk him down, I needed to use another means."

"You opted for a foreign Arcano-tech implant. Such loyalty to the empire. You wouldn't have to tell me. I could reprogram your siren module for you. I wanted you for the berserkers. Intelligence wanted you, too. In the end, we compromised. That Fire Folk device in your arm now makes me want you all the more. I have so many ideas how I want to play with it and you. What I need are exemplars from someone with the original, unencrypted copy of the siren code and uncorrupted bioplasm from a berserker who isn't losing coherence. Which I could get by merely dissecting you. Or, we can avoid making a mess of your flesh. Just tell me what I want to know, and you can all walk out of here."

"In exchange for my silence."

"That would be a necessary part of our arrangement. I've seen from your case files you have used inspiration to get a confession out of several witnesses as recent as a few moons ago. Why isn't your module failing? Why isn't he degenerating? I also have these."

Medea showed Jhee her conch.

"Your original Medical Protectorate records. Before you had them expunged. What is it you don't want people to know, I wonder? It can't be the siren module. Those were small fish as far as state secrets went. Why are you two fine?" Jhee looked defiantly at Medea. Medea tilted her head to one side, "As expected. Asset Sheepdog, there are three wheels in the sky. The third wheel controls the yaw."

Shep's head rose, and he blinked. Jhee struggled. That had to be a code phrase to deactivate standby mode.

"This spy has vital documents hidden within her somewhere," Medea said. "Help me find them. Hold her down."

Shep pinned Jhee to the med table. Medea took out a long wicked sharp looking piece of biometal, a talon needle. Jhee's eyes grew wide. As Medea pierced Jhee's side with it, Jhee screamed. Medea withdrew the talon needle from Jhee's flank and glanced at Shep for a reaction.

"Use your command codes. Tell him to release you," Medea said.

Jhee's side burned. Her breathing was heavy. She huffed and puffed to calm herself. Medea pierced her side again. Jhee screamed again.

"Don't scream. Command, Magistrate. You sees, I be knowed all about you, the secret thirteenth member of their gang. All the berserker regiments had 'em like. They'd have given you the command codes and whatnot to shut down any of the berserkers in your unit or call 'em to ya aid. I know this hurts. Now, cry out to him for help."

Jhee only had a moment to register an oddness to the way Medea spoke, before the woman stabbed her again. Jhee felt the spittle flecking her mouth. Her chest heaved. "I don't have them," she yelled.

Medea cocked her head at her. "I don't have time for these games. You were their intelligence liaison. Of course, you had them. I take no pleasure in this. Not like some did. I find it all rather vile."

Jhee squeezed her eyes shut. "Conflict of interest."

"I need those codes if me and or those like me are ever to be free of this thing, this whatever it is they did to us."

"They wouldn't give me his codes because we were married. Yes, I could pull strings to get myself assigned to his unit. But they drew the line at giving me everyone's code except his. They gave that code to someone else."

"I don't believe you."

"It's true. Captain had his shutdown code. He was the only other person in the unit with the clearance. The regular troops weren't supposed to know, or else they might do exactly what you are doing now. It was too big a risk if they found out."

Medea looked confused. Jhee might have been breaking through. She looked at Shep. He had cocked his head and stared at her. "Shep, please. I know you don't want to hurt me."

Medea snapped out of it. She placed a gag over Jhee's face. "If what you say is true, then you are of no use to me, and this has just been a waste of time. She lied to me. She must have known you would not have the codes. So why did she—"

Shep fell upon Medea before she finished securing the gag. The two squared off. Medea changed into an ocean lynx with its feline snout but webbed, taloned almost Folk-like hands. Unlike a normal skin slip, Medea's form melted and undulated in a way that made the bile rise in Jhee's throat. Medea's face melded into a facsimile of Ursula's then the sea dog sailor's before settling into its feline appearance. They went at it tooth and claw.

Medea, a berserker.

The thought drifted through Jhee's mind. Medea? The way Medea spoke clicked into place, a sea dog accent. Jhee rocked her head to dislodge the gag. Pain lanced through her stab wounds. She took heavy, panicked breaths to cope with the pain. With gritted teeth, Jhee engaged her siren module.

"Yield!" Jhee yelled the shutdown command, imbuing it with every dram of power that remained in her.

"Medea" dropped. Shep's claw caught her across the belly. Shep's focus snapped in Jhee's direction. He growled, but his brow furrowed. "Medea" lay dead on the ground. A victorious Shep stumbled over to Jhee and rubbed his head against her and lapped at her wounds. Jhee winced. His eyes changed first, then the rest of him.

"Pity," Medea's voice came over an intercom seemingly from every corner of the room. "She was one of my favorites, you know? When the shifting process started breaking down for her, it granted her a certain elasticity, the ability to mold and shape her form in remarkable ways. I have new favorites to play with now."

A hissing emanated from the vents and gas filled the room.

~

Hammers and Bars

Shep awoke slumped against metal bars. He pulled himself upright and looked around. The floor swung underneath his feet as he rose. He saw a familiar hulking form standing on a nearby platform.

"Hammad. I suppose I have you to thank for this cage?"

"The work isn't done. There's still more of them out there," Hammad the Hammerhead answered.

"This was a setup, from the moment they paid you to pick a fight with me."

"You got it backward, *Dawn Wolf*. The payment flowed up to Hammad the Hammerhead, not down." Hammad slapped his chest with his palm. "Those recruiters worked for the Hammerhead. It was my gym, my training facilities, my slaughterhouse. I started this because something needed to be done about those bastards. The Counselor and the Hammerhead needed the strongest, Toril's finest. Someone had to do something, or else those bastards would get away with it again. I helped turned those like Ursula around, gave them purpose, like the Counselor did with me.

"Who wants reconciliation? Meat. Another excuse for them to get away with it. I wanted blood. They needed to pay the ultimate geld, their lives to Toril. The Empire owes us blood, their blood."

Shep tensed at the mention of Toril the War Maker, a controversial Maker many berserkers worshiped. They weren't supposed to because he had been stricken from the Maker canon. That hadn't stopped them. When he stayed on at the abbey on Torilsisle, even he took the rare opportunity to perform devotions to the chiseled-out effigies that remained there.

"Warriors fight in the arena. Meat is brought to the slaughterhouse. Are you a warrior, Dawn Wolf, skin brother, or meat?"

"Open this cage, and you'll see which I am."

"Your brand and sigil are an invisible leash. Free yourself. Leave their world behind, stay with us. Complete the work. Makers make it so, for the War Maker."

"My family needs me."

"Do they? They can join, too. More geld for the Merry Maker. All they have to do is accept the gift and gain the ability to full slip. And survive the ring. We will welcome them with outstretched limbs."

Hammad the Hammerhead flexed his now clawed hands and slipped partially into his shark form. Shep resisted his desire to snarl and bare fangs. He stared Hammad down as the man, not the beast. Hammad pushed his cage away from the platform to hang over a pool.

"Meat it is," Hammad said and activated the crane controls on the platform behind him.

Once Shep's cage lurched to a stop, he climbed to his feet again. Another occupied cage hung across from his.

21

~

The Moon Pool

Jhee awoke she was not sure how much later in a strange room.

"Good. Good. You're awake now. Pardon the violence. I was unsure of how else to get you here."

Two transparent enclosures hung suspended above a gigantic pool of water. Someone moved inside each. Jhee squinted to clear her vision. Shep and Kanto waited, restrained in an enclosure. Jhee yelled, but a gag muffled any sound. She struggled and found she was likewise secured to a high-backed chair. A strap across her forehead prevented her from turning her head either to the left or the right.

Jhee tried her hands against her bonds. She could not see her hands and thus could not correctly work a silent cast. She had not done it frequently herself. Her mentor had taught it to her for situations where you found yourself in a jam.

Jeja had taught her a few other things. Don't use artificing as a crutch. Her restraints were entirely secure. Had she been awake when they secured her, she might have been able to use Jeja's old stage tricks to ensure the bonds had been loose.

Medea walked over behind her and tightened the straps. "Excuse me. It appears someone has loosened these. We can't have that now."

She sat in a chair diagonally from Jhee just inside her range of vision but left a clear sight line to the enclosures. She pulled out a conch. "Let's see here. Galatheia-Jaide Gombessa. Jhee to her friends and intimates. May I call you Jhee? After having slept under your roof and partaken of you and your husband's hospitality, I feel I've earned."

Jhee struggled against her restraints.

"I'll take that as a 'yes.' Youngest and only known surviving daughter of House Gombessa. Infamous pirates and squelch-runners turned right-side up. Long before your time. Money can buy you a nice pedigree, as you earlier surmised. Your treatises on the legal ramifications of magical experimentation, brilliant. You have a fascinating mind, Jhee. Much like my own. How I would love to crack open that skull and unravel its secrets. What sort of person volunteers not to join Medical Protectorate, but to be a subject? I suspect that had something to do with Shep. You ran chasing after him into the infantry like the seastruck jubilant you were. After all this, was it worth it? The berserker procedure is breaking down in most of the subjects. Those implanted with siren modules aren't faring much better. All except you two. Maybe it's your support network. Maybe it's those illicit Fire Folk implants. I will enjoy cutting you open to find out.

"You failed the water and ocean fitness proficiencies. The Mitsus got hold of it and spread the rumor you failed deliberately because you were a coward. Miramar knew the truth, yet didn't speak up. Did it hurt to have her help her family use that knowledge against you? That she stayed silent as it spread throughout the Far Reaches you were a coward? The friend you trusted, the one who knew you better than anyone else, and the friend you betrayed."

Jhee yelled and tried to scream despite her gag. Perhaps she had always hated Miramar. Perhaps that made it so easy to ruin her after she had seduced Shep. Beautiful, popular Mai. Hunky, athletic Shep. Plain, but rich Jhee. In contests between them, Miramar won. She always won. It hurt no one believed that even for a moment Jhee had seduced Shep. Not this time, though. And Miramar couldn't stand it.

That night Shep arrived at the Academy was like a fantasy come true. So much of a fantasy, Jhee never stopped to question why then. What had changed with Shep? The clues were there. Jhee should have figured it out.

Shep had taken off Jhee's lenses, let down her hair. It was slow with none of the previous awkwardness of the night Jhee's sister died. He whispered against her skin repeatedly how beautiful she was, how he had always wanted her secretly for years. Jhee did the same. She poured out the unrequited feelings she had for him. They awoke before dawn and went in search of an officiant to marry them. She found out when they returned to her family and declared how much they were in love, Shep had lost the lottery.

"Tell me, Jhee, did it feel good to bankrupt those who tried to take advantage of your family in their time of need? Don't answer just yet. I will allow you to prove it. I'm proposing another game.

"Oh, sorry about all the precautions. We can't have you artificing your way out of this. This is to be a pure contest of wills and desires. Shep seems to think you have cast him aside, and he has no value to you anymore. Meanwhile, Kanto believes he has now claimed the foremost spousal position for himself. How about it, Jhee? Are they right? If given the choice between them, who would you pick? Mind you, you only get to choose one."

Medea set out the tile board again.

"Now, let's try this again, shall we. I'll control Shep, and you'll control Kanto. I was impressed with the efficiency with which you ran your household. It was a frequent tactic when I was growing up to pit the spouses against each other as much as it was the various branches. It minimized the number of spouses looking to trade up, especially when you were a consort confined to the isles. Confinement to the isles minimized the chances of base-born bastards, but it also put your consorts within easy reach of other Imperials. Zaria made an art of it. Her pack of consorts was especially good at convincing spouses to seek her favor. You were confined to the isles without very much anywhere else to go. Their parties were much anticipated. Perhaps, too much. They lured many an Imperial consort and concubine into a compromising position which she would then use to pressure them to provide information on their fellow cohorts or spouses."

The Perfect Play

Medea undid the restraints on one of Jhee's hands. "You will need a hand free to play. I'm not an artificer myself. I've studied it as a theoretical matter. While there are some single-handed casts, I will risk it. It says here your particular specialties are Wind and Fire. At the berserker sanctuary, even though you had full use of both hands, it didn't help you much."

Jhee struggled.

"The rules are simple: each husband pleads his case, and you decide which one to release. The first move is mine."

Medea moved her piece forward, and Kanto's cage lowered towards the moon pool. Jhee countered. Kanto's pen rose, but then Shep's dropped a foot towards the water.

"Careful now, Jhee. We don't want orcinus fricassee. Have you learned your lesson? Or are you still just as blinded by love as you were then? Maybe you might be fonder of seal chowder."

Jhee made her next move. Kanto dropped a few feet.

"Very sloppy, Jhee. Concentrate or else they both die," Medea said.

Jhee swore, but the gag made it only come out as an angry muffle. She squeezed her eyes shut. She needed to concentrate. There had to be a way out of this. It appeared Medea had thought of everything. If she played too aggressively, Kanto would die. If she played too defensively, Shep would. If she didn't play at all or didn't beat Medea, they both died.

She made her move, and Kanto's enclosure got further away from the hazard. Shep's cage dropped precipitously closer. He placed his head against the glass. "Save Kanto, Jhee. I'm ready for this all to be over."

You don't get to decide that for any of us.

Jhee screamed silently at him. With all the wreckage and broken lives they left in their path, she would not have his death on her conscience, as well. He did not get to walk away. None of them did.

Jhee examined the board. Her pieces were scattered all over. She had not formed a cohesive strategy. Jhee had played solely to keep their cages above water. She had played to not lose instead of win. The board reflected that reality.

Medea had been brilliant, cunning indeed. She knew Jhee's inherent curiosity would keep her engaged. She would want to uncover the secret as much as Medea would.

"You're like me, Jhee, you will see the game through to the end no matter what. We are both driven by knowledge. We both have to know. It's a curse, really. I have to push the limits of science to know what it's capable of. Just like you have to push the limits of the law. There is another way out of this, Jhee. You could kill me, then have to face another judicial review. Given all that has happened, they would probably excuse your conduct. However, you'd never be able to practice law again. Killing a court official and an heir elective: I can't think of an even more blatant way to flout the law. Your career would be even more over than it is now. There would be no chance you ever get your credentials back. Ever."

If Medea died, there would be no proof of her crimes, like Jhee had thought with the vizier. Medea would be a martyr. She had made a mistake with the vizier. But it had been the only play she could make, yet to this day, she still regretted it, and it had come back to bite her. Had there been another way out of that? Or had her outrage at what the vizier had done, kidnapping Kanto and perhaps more egregiously outsmarting her, blinded her? Had her decision to kill the vizier been a just one or a vengeful one? The revelation of the copy of her records on Kanto's conch proved had she left the vizier alive, she might have been able to bring her to justice. All she had needed to do was be patient and have faith in the First Makers' Design. But she had acted as if she were above the law. She took the law into her own hands and look what it had wrought.

Medea was right. Jhee and Medea had much in common. She was every bit as arrogant as Medea. It was always about the game, the puzzle, and when the vizier beat Jhee at it, she could not cope and accept the loss gracefully. If Jhee had, there was a slim chance she could have brought the vizier to justice someday. The right way. In the meantime, though, how many other youthful men would have fallen into her clutches? The vizier had vowed not to stop, and Jhee had believed her. Could the vizier have gotten another puppet abbess installed? Another bureaucrat disdainful of men and refugees who viewed them as vermin no better than crab-rats? Who would look the other way? Or worse, see the vizier as performing a valuable service? View it as justified because, what were they, just men and refugees? A burden on society better off eliminated.

"Of course, if you'd rather not play against me, you can slip the skin with this and get out of those bindings." Medea held out a vial of bioplasm. She placed it on the edge of the table, within reach of Jhee's free hand. "I've been working on a new serum."

Jhee surveyed the scene of Medea's game. All the pieces were positioned precisely as Medea wanted. No matter what Jhee did, Medea would win. She would have her proof Jhee was no better than her. What was it Medea had said? Accept her as her master, accept her teaching. She viewed herself as another Thaedra. She wanted another disciple. Not one like the vizier or the berserkers, but one in her own image, who thought as she thought, did as she did. One who understood that science and knowledge came first. People were just a means to an end. They were all secondary to the law or to science or to whatever other philosophy or academic pursuit. Knowledge first.

The vizier: pleasure first.

The Imperium: power first.

The vicar: identity first.

Medea: science first.

Herself: the law first.

Something else always came first, except for what truly mattered. Jhee had lost sight of why the law had mattered to her. On her isles, growing up, the lords had acted as a law unto themselves. They had ground the common folk in their gears. There was no fairness, only arbitrary whims, as if on the sea and subject to the moods of the Storm Child. Jhee had hated that. She had wanted circumstances to be better. To be fair. So that those with little power like Shep's family would not be subject to the whims of the rich and powerful. Her family had power by the time she had been born, but they had come up almost by accident. In the meantime, other families had fallen. It was all subject to the whirlpool of fate. The law, on the other hand, the law, like the Divine Mechanism, was governed by knowable rules. You could learn them and manipulate them. You could bind them to your will to bring order out of chaos. Jhee had naïvely thought at the time it was so egalitarian. Everyone was protected by the law or could use arcana to better themselves. Unfortunately, it did not work that way. Some gatekeepers controlled it all.

Folk were always only pieces in someone else's game. Jhee was no different. On the cosmic scale, what was the Divine Design then? A cosmic game in which Jhee was just another piece. Like a tile, it was arbitrary which one became the matriarch based on which moves the player made. Initially, no piece was more important than the others.

Jhee struggled, and her chair moved. Medea looked over at her. "Jhee, what are you doing?"

She jumped her chair a few more inches backward. It teetered but did not fall.

"Jhee, stop!" Shep called.

Jhee hopped her chair once more. She fancied trying to smile as her chair tipped over the edge, and she hit the icy water.

$\sim$

Storm Child, Storm Child, Today

When you know it's the end, think of pleasant events, of what you most wanted to see, of all the loved ones you miss, and let them take you away.

Frigid water enfolded Jhee in a long-awaited embrace. Her Maker within guided her back in time to the day her sister, Ghele, died. Jhee could not swim. She had never learned how. Ghele had barely finished the proficiencies, but that had not stopped her from jumping in to save Jhee and others.

Jhee's mind went into a panic. There was nothing she could do tied as she was to a chair and with only one hand but not the arm free. Even if she could clear and center, she had little control over water. Everything beneath her fell away. Down and ever down, she sank.

That was what disconcerted Jhee most about water. A body could seldom tell where they were. Up could be down, and down could be up. One never knew unless they reached the bottom. A person could sink forever. To her, that always represented the greatest horror of the Unmaker's Trench, to fall forever.

Jhee tried to hold her breath. Eventually, her lungs burned.

What Jhee needed to do now was not panic and think through calmly and rationally what was happening to her. Still, Jhee tried to keep her mouth shut, to keep the water out. She had felt dizzy. Her lungs screamed for mercy. Her flesh burned as her body changed and reconfigured itself to the watery environment. There were limits, though. She could become a seal or an otter or some other sea mammal. Their lung capacity was limited too. Even if she had not gone into the water with only her Water Folk skin's lungful, what she could not become was a fish. Shifting did not allow you to change your skin that much. That was a change that went way beyond the skin to the essence. It always worked with what you were.

Her chair struck the bottom with her attached. She had gone in the water as a Water Folk with only a lungful of air. Despite the changes to her body, she must surface or else run out of oxygen. Her body reconfigured itself to a skin more extreme, a maye then a shark. Closer. Her fuel reserves were running low, not just from lack of air, but the rapid shifting. But tied to the chair she could not pass enough water over her gills.

Emissary. Until all are one.

The sigil on her arm, her esca, and the siren module at the base of her skull throbbed.

At last, she could not take it anymore. She opened her mouth, and the water forced its way into her lungs. She closed her eyes and let go.

Beneath the Waves

Far Reach lore said the restless dead turned into wisps or mist wights and became part of the region's fog. Many times since the tour boat accident, Jhee had dreamed her family and the sea folk beckoned her from beneath the waves.

Jhee was underwater again. She felt the eye of the drake upon her, bathing her in light.

Jhee sank under the ocean again, drowning. She couldn't touch the bottom. The waves battered her about. Now and then, they slammed her against hard, sharp rocks. The wind forced from her lungs by the impact. Her limbs were so heavy. She could not fight anymore. Mouth clamped shut, lungs burning, she contemplated the briny depths below.

As she let go, an enormous, brilliant, scaly eye opened, bathing her in light. She opened her mouth to scream. Ocean poured in. A hand grabbed her collar.

She had visions of the deep, of being welcomed by Gwyn and Gloriana and her parents. Gascal and Gabi were there too. They all welcomed her.

Stay beneath the waves with us.

Gascal and Gabi knocked an air bladder about with their snouts while Gwyn, Gloriana, and Ghele swam around a warm volcanic vent. Every one of them appeared as mayes, but her Maker within recognized their essence. They frolicked and batted about an air bladder in the waves as the Sea Kings and Queens of old they were. Her family had not drowned. They had been remade magnificent and taken their rightful place beneath the waves.

Stay with us. Stay and play forever. We are not dead.

Yes, Jhee thought. They had not died; they were only awaiting her arrival. Her kin and skinfolk waited for her to shed the skin of land and take on the true form of her spirit and theirs, the maye. None of them were dead, only where they belonged under the waves with the sea children. It was where she belonged too, where she could stay if she so chose. Disappointment that Miramar was not there cast a pall over the scene, though she thought she might have glimpsed some of her old friend's drowned kin. Jhee had hoped that somehow in the Makers' Sphere, they had sealed the breach between their families, their two pods joined as they should have been in life.

An ethereal, billowing woman appeared, gliding towards her. At first, Jhee thought it to be the White and Gray Lady of the Deeps come to bear her to the Trench. As if in answer to her silent wish, the figure became Miramar. Miramar greeted her bright and shining like the Lady of the Isles Jhee sometimes fancied herself to be. Turtles and sea folk, the Lady of the Isles spectral companions, surrounded them. Miramar seized her and headed for the surface. No, they should head down to be with her family. If Miramar sought to take Jhee away from her family, she was the Lady of the Deeps. Jhee struggled until her limbs widened into maye wings.

Miramar released her. Jhee strained to swim toward her family, but they receded farther and farther away. She heard their muffled voices calling her name.

"Stay with us, Jhee."

Seaweed wrapped itself around Jhee's limbs and prevented her from following. The more she struggled, the more it bound her. Her form had become as heavy and solid as quick cement, holding her where she was, preventing her from joining her family and friends in the depths. Jhee belonged with them now.

The voices calling Jhee's name had become clearer. Though they still sounded far away. They, however, came not from below. They came from beside and above her. The First Makers calling her to the Spheres and the sea in the sky, perhaps.

Jhee came to in a shallow canvas hammock with water running past her. Life-giving oxygen made its way over her gills, deep into her core. Her gills gradually returned to lungs.

"Jhee! You're going to be fine."

Jhee's lungs suddenly ached and felt heavy. She gagged. Water forced its way past her lips. Her lungs seized. They spasmed to rid themselves of excess water. She coughed, and more seawater forced its way out of her. Jhee wanted to tell the voice to go away. She had found her true home. She wanted to stay beneath the waves. Instead, her current skin rejected the water.

"She's Folk again. Bring the oxygen." Her head pounded. Jhee reluctantly opened her eyes. A paramedic leaned over her. A bright light swept across her vision. She squeezed her eyes shut. "Good, we've got pupillary response."

"Jhee! blessed be the Makers!" the words, this skin's name, sounded so strange to be coming through the air instead of the water. The words were spoken by her family above the waves: Shep, Kanto, Mirrei.

Jhee shook her head. She tried to tell them to let her go back. All she managed was a series of gagging coughs. The arms of her family above the waves enfolded her. Kanto rocked her back and forth. Shep and Mirrei wrapped their arms around them both. Jhee stared out through the haze.

"Don't talk. Go back to sleep if you need to," Shep said.

Imperators led Medea by her gathering. Her hands were secured behind her. She smiled with relief when she saw Jhee awake. "You won, Jhee. Drench it all if you didn't win. You're a worthy adversary. I underestimated you again. I won't next time. Be warned. I never lose twice."

Medea's grin grew impossibly wide. The imperators carted her off.

"Don't you ever do something so foolish again, denbe," Mirrei said.

"Star," Jhee began, but it unraveled into a cough as the air and foam tickled her tonsils. "Dreaming?"

"No, I tried to tell you during the remote meeting. I was coming home. I tried to reach you again, and there was no answer. Looks like you all were having quite the adventure without me. You can tell me all about it at the hospital. The irony I'd be the one looking after you."

The paramedics placed Jhee on a gurney and transported her away.

22

———

⌇

A Fish Tale

At the hospital over the next few days, Jhee's throat remained so raw she could barely speak. Mirrei turned the tale of how she found them on the Medical Protectorate's deep-sea platform into a performance using traditional academy cyphers combined with ones learned in her travels.

Mirrei narrated as she used light and shadow to re-enact coming home to find the empty house. Bax informed her of some of what had happened. She had found Kanto's discarded conch and notebook. She knew something had to be wrong then. The youthful spouse went nowhere without one or both.

"I tried contacting folks via conch to let them know I had arrived. My conch was inundated with messages and alerts once I got in range. It died, but not before I had caught up with some of what had happened. I tried the townhouse first and found the tracking program on Kanto's conch. I remember from Galleon City he threatened to put a tracker on me if I didn't report in more. It only stood to reason after everything he'd put a tracker on one or all of you. I opened it up, and sure enough, he had multiple trackers going."

The young woman waved a hand. Several pinpoints of light faded in. She mimed throwing away the extras lights.

"I picked the signals I thought would likely be you, and on the off chance followed it. Turns out I was right. A friend of his called while I was tracking you down, an Alexi, Aiaki, or someone. I told them I suspected you were in trouble. By the time I got here, the Imps had also arrived. I'd never seen a law enforcement response like it. This gul got the Imps here so fast including gyros, I didn't even know what was up. The tracker, though, was pointing out to sea."

A bird-like shadow flew into Mirrei's mystical frame over sailing ships.

"The Imps gyro'd me to some Findari ships near the tracker location. I had made friends with the Water Nomads during my healing work. They gave me passage back inland. I contacted them before they headed back out. I used the tracker to trace you to the rig in the middle of the ocean. The Findari refused to take their ships too close. According to them, and I concur, it was a foul accursed place, the House of Knives. The perimeter was guarded by lesser drakes, likely berserkers, and patrol boats. So, a small dive team and I went in alone in a small submersible."

With a gesture, Mirrei reconfigured the shadows into fish and whales approaching a rock formation.

"They still spotted us. The Findari engaged them in underwater combat while I went on ahead. I reached the moon pool not long after your chair hit the water and sank. I grabbed the chair and tried to swim up with you. But we started to get dragged down until the fascist lady helped. Though, I didn't know who she was. You had adapted some, but as we pulled you up, you full skin slipped into an otter and escaped your bonds. Then you became a maye and tried to swim for the depths. We barely caught you and got you back on the rig. Once we were back on the rig, Shep and Kanto called out just as the fascist lady tried to brain me. I punched her out and freed my brother grooms. Shep and I kept you watered until the paramedics arrived, while Kanto made sure she didn't get away. We almost lost you, Jhee."

Mirrei ended with a maye silhouette turning into a woman's silhouette.

"Fascist lady got you out of the water," Kanto said, "but Shep and Mirrei, they saved your life, Jhee. Though, if it hadn't been for him, your life wouldn't have been in danger in the first place."

Jhee stared at Shep and tried to feel grateful. All she felt was anger and loss. Shep refused to meet their gaze.

"Never forgive you," Kanto mouthed at him.

As grateful as Jhee was to Mirrei, a sliver of disappointment undercut it. Miramar had not appeared to welcome her. There had been no posthumous reconciliation. In her oxygen-deprived state, she had mistaken Mirrei for her mother, Miramar.

The doctor came in. "You should all go. The patient needs her rest. Come back tomorrow."

Kanto and Mirrei kept her company the next few days as she recovered. She developed a mild case of pneumonia and had to remain in the hospital. She did not see Shep. However, when she awoke in the morning, she always had the sense that someone had been there, a trace of musky cologne. She, also, sometimes found a shark's tooth or shell carved with the Lady of the Isles' likeness.

A small cask of Tranquility Gold healing wine arrived from the abbey with a note from their new permanent abbess: Umeala.

"The prioress has taken the name Umeala, and she wanted you to have this as a token of thanks for all the help you've given her with the refugees."

"Aw, wasn't that sweet of her?"

At last, Jhee was released. Mirrei and Kanto wheeled her out to the waiting transport. She thought she glimpsed Shep, but when she looked again, there was no one there. She must have been mistaken.

~

An Enthusiastic "Yes"

Jhee rested on the porch and watched Kanto and Mirrei play with the butterfly-fish in the carp pond and water feature. A dispatch from the estate of the Lady Kaydence, the Turquoise Typhoon and Kanto's formidable grandmamere, had arrived recently. Jhee reread it.

I had my doubts about you, Jhee, but you've done well enough by him I feel confident enough to leave the most important part of my legacy aside from him: a full share of MANTEL preferred stock. Use it and him wisely.

Jhee's attention returned to the younger spouses. How different and more vibrant Mirrei appeared because the skin underneath her fur had taken on a deeper, more golden color. She had the deeper blush of health to her, whereas before, she often looked deathly pale. Together with her sun-lightened brown fur, she glowed like a star. She had also filled out enjoyably. Mirrei had acquired much healthier proportions, which no longer filled Jhee with the compulsive desire to feed her. She had all but abandoned the robes in favor of loose pullover shirt and wide-legged pants. Necklaces and bracelets of shells and beads hung in layers from her neck and wrists. Her hair had gotten long. She now sported several braids adorned with beads and shells and a feather or two. Kanto had given her a critical eye at first but had kept his own counsel about it.

The three of them sat on the porch, taking in the mid-dusk sunset. They had ordered food from a restaurant yet again. Although Jhee made an impressive sandwich and Mirrei had learned how to cook a host of more straightforward provincial dishes, none of them was an adept cook. They tried together last week to put some molecular gastronomy equipment to use. After the fire service left, they had to dine at a local eatery while the house aired out. No one said it, but without Shep, they would soon have to decide whether to hire a cook and cooking staff.

Jhee and Mirrei went through a series of finger casting exercises. Mirrei demonstrated some unorthodox methods she had learned on her journeys. Jhee favored her stiff fingers, the ones the Ladies Auxiliary had broken. She had regained most of her physical dexterity, and the wounds had been healed in short order. The psychological sensation, though, lingered.

Kanto paid them little to no mind. He perched on the steps of the porch, conch balanced on one knee and his sketchbook on the other. He bobbed his head up and down and chewed on his finger quill.

"I've got it," he said. "Look at this. Tell me what you think."

He displayed his sketchbook to them, which contained a series of new robe designs. Kanto projected images from his conch, copies of those Mirrei had taken during her journey. He pointed to the various robes and the elements from the images that had influenced the design.

"Inspired by your travels," he said. "I wanted to incorporate your new style."

"Drej," Mirrei said. Drej was slang she had picked up on her voyage. "I love it."

She and Kanto hugged.

"It's so good to have my denye back."

"It's good to be back."

Jhee touched them both. "What made you come home? We had thought you would continue to the arctic. My note, it said for you not to come back."

"Correction. It said: *don't come home*."

Jhee laughed uproariously. "I guess I gave myself away."

"Yeah, you did."

"You staked much on one word."

"Besides, I missed my family," Mirrei said and shrugged. "That floating clinic was very uncomfortable. I'm not crazy. Why would I continue if the choice is between going to the frozen southland with nothing but snow-mist bears and waddle birds or coming to stay with my family in a fabulous townhouse? I know which one I'd pick. If it's a choice between you guls and the waddle birds and the snow-mist bears, I'd choose you guls every time."

"Thank you. I think," Jhee said. "Does this mean I should tear up the divorce papers?"

Mirrei's smile faded. "Not quite yet, not until I come clean about all the lies I've told you."

A glimpse of movement in the tree line caught Jhee's eye. She saw a quick image of glowing eyes in the darkness. A bird flew out of the underbrush. The tree branches shook for a bit, then went still.

Kanto's hackles raised. "Do you want me to get Bax?"

"No," Jhee said. "Let Bax and Dari enjoy their time together."

Kanto stood up. "I'll deal with it myself."

"Leave him be," Mirrei said. "He's not harming anyone. You know what? Let's just go inside."

"He can't keep doing this." Kanto turned to the trees. "If you want to see us, you need to horn up and do it to our face. We have a front door. Use it. Coward."

In the sitting room, Mirrei told sea stories in the proud tradition of the Reaches to lighten the mood. "In the proud tradition of the Reaches" meant gargantuan-sized embellishment and color. Despite Mirrei's efforts, they slipped back into picking at their food listlessly.

"If this is going to be the new way of things," Mirrei said, "we need to reach a new understanding."

Jhee glared at Mirrei, then expelled a slow breath. The youthful woman was right. "I'll leave it to you and Kanto to manage. My days are free now. I'm fine with only one day completely to myself, however else you want to balance it with your various activities."

"I think I might want to volunteer at the nearby veteran's center. Don't want to horn in on Kanto's work."

"No, seriously. More help equals more geld for the Merry Maker. I could see you with a little children's health clinic across the way."

"The youth center's your path. I think I want to do a little something different. Veterans and refugees. A series of nursing or teaching schools for the Fire Folk, though there aren't as many Fire Folk here. I think I definitely want to do something more about those state schools. If you have the proof of wrongdoing by IES, I say we go for it."

"Have you spoken to the Academy about reinstating your teaching credentials?" Kanto asked.

"Not yet," Jhee answered.

"Why not? You love to teach. You love to learn. Bouncing all your ideas and exchanging notes with all those students and other colleagues. I couldn't have thought of a more natural environment for you."

"I think I need more time."

"Well, you can't just sit around the house all day. That's not the woman I married," Mirrei said.

Jhee nodded. "I'll think about it."

"Promise?"

"Promise. Now, tell me about you. I saw some recurring faces in those images. Any special face I need to note?"

"Perhaps. We'll see after I've been home a little longer and the lack of close quarters has given the ardor a chance to cool."

Kanto gave Mirrei a droll look. "You are lucky you came home when you did. We were five seconds away from turning your room into a nursery."

Mirrei's face lit up. "Really?"

Kanto gave a smug smile. "Really. We're still considering options right now. We wanted to discuss it with you first."

"I'm in. Whatever you want me to do. I can be Auntie Mirrei. I can be co-mother Mirrei. Dame Mirrei."

"I think I want to pouch. I want your name on the birth charter with ours, though. But you have to teach me how to put on one of those shadow shows first."

Mirrei left her seat and threw her arms around them. "I'm so happy for you."

"For us." Jhee held them tight. As excited as she was about children, her thoughts went to Shep somewhere outside, stalking the grounds trying to get her notice.

"Us," Mirrei amended.

A New Make

Jhee and Mirrei watched from the front row as Kanto and his team unveiled his new uniform designs to the public. A Kanto with a very swollen belly pouch came forward to take a bow with his team. Jhee and Mirrei stood and cheered when each of them came forward to take a bow.

Kanto walked them through the showcase for each design.

"A new Make for a new age," the solemn, theatrical voice-over said. "These new suits and uniforms feature the latest in concealment science with light- and sound-absorbing materials. Made of lightweight, self-wicking fabric, the marine models sport the latest in waterproofing technologies for conditions on the open seas where excess water can mean life and death. The polar editions are designed to insulate and capture body heat to prevent hypothermia. They are rated for temperatures as extreme as fifty degrees below. These desert skins can withstand and keep the troops relatively cool at some of the most extreme heat conditions. The tropical model also features some marine model waterproofing and features an antimicrobial lining specially designed to resist mildew and rot."

Kanto further regaled them with why his team had made individual design choices and the various cutting techniques they used to make the uniforms easy to mass produce with minimal waste, yet still maintaining maximum functionality.

"Now, these are my personal contributions and the ones I'm most proud of: the dress uniforms. Because when they are parading around for us civvies, they must look top line. Nothing says that while they are keeping us safe, they can't also look good."

"Amazing," Mirrei said. "My denye helped make all these. Who would have thought it?"

"You did amazing work," Jhee said. "I'm sorry I ever doubted you."

Kanto smiled and blushed. "No worries."

The three of them walked hand in hand through the exhibit.

"Ah, Justicar," an authoritative voice said.

"Chief Justicar," Jhee said. "Justicar no longer. I am merely a regular citizen now."

"Hm? I was given to believe you were reinstated."

"Not that I know of."

"Odd. I viewed the registers this morning, and your name was clearly listed. Perhaps it was an error."

"Must be."

"Have you tried recently? Why not check now?"

Jhee pulled out her conch and tried to access the judicial archives. The "Welcome Back Justicar" screen displayed as if she had never left. "Well, quench me in the quiet."

"You see. Right as rain. Now, if your lovely household doesn't mind, I'd like to speak to you a bit about a new training program we are starting at the Academy."

Jhee and Chief Justicar Elver walked on further. "How can I be of service, Chief Justicar?"

"Allow me to first apologize about that business with the review. We had to do our due diligence, what with the seriousness of the allegations against you and your family."

Jhee put on her official-at-court face. It no longer felt as natural as it once did. It had been so long since she had to don it. "Of course, Chief Justicar."

The Chief Justicar lowered her voice, "Given the way this 'Medea' business turned out, you were definitely in the right of matters at Tranquility Bridge. This upcoming trial will be a disaster."

Jhee could not believe what she was hearing. Was the Chief Justicar praising her for the killing of Lady Bathsheba? She set her mouth in a thin line. She clenched her teeth together, knowing she was only mere moments away from telling the Chief Justicar exactly what she could do with her credentials.

"Our extra thanks for the discreet way you handled the abbey matter. We had not understood the choice until we received your full record. You were right to be concerned about the scandal and give the vizier a choice. We see now that offering her a choice was the only proper action to take under the circumstances."

"Choice?"

"Of a messy trial or quiet suicide. It was best for everybody. We got to avoid an imperial scandal, and the abbey could keep her Imperial pension. When that member of the Imperial family came to me and explained to me the situation, I realized it was the only course you could have taken. The debt of gratitude we owe you."

"The Imperial Family?"

"Yes, and your mentor, the honorable Jeja Marpele. They both backed up your full account entirely and said that you had been sworn to secrecy. You had asked her advice. How you simply wanted to spare the Empire a messy trial. For which, you have my eternal thanks and that of the entire judiciary. Between the mistaken prisoner and the many Imperials implicated, this Architect trial has already been a profound embarrassment to law enforcement and threatened to tear the entire palace apart. Again, my gratitude; however, if you ever tamper with judicial records again, there will be no more second chances and no quarter."

The capital's lone Justicar save herself, Nevis, approached Jhee after Jhee and the Chief Justicar finished their chat. Her colleague briefly flashed a six-pointed Star Chamber emblem pinned to the inside of her robe. "Delicate work with Vivyan-Rin. How would you like a chance at calling all the Architects to account? She was only one, the Architect of Knives. We believe scientists on both sides were secretly in contact and working together. They seem intent on taking up where the Doombringer nihilists left off. Think about it. Get back to me."

Nevis slipped away, leaving Jhee with her consternation. At the far edge of the crowd, she saw Shep clearly, as did Kanto and Mirrei. They quickly came over to her and took her arms. Shep raised his hand in a tentative greeting.

"We've got to talk to him some time," Mirrei said.

"No," Kanto said.

"Why is there forgiveness for me but not for him? Was what we both did really so different?"

Jhee turned her attention to Mirrei.

"Of course, we know why you would want to forgive him," Kanto retorted.

"Hey, keep it nice, would you? I'm on your side, remember. I had a foolish crush. It's long over now. We still need to have a serious talk, Jhee, about him and about me. I'm all about our family now. And until we divorce him, so is he. We have to decide one way or the other because this right here is not working. If you don't want him around, cut him off. If not, we need to come up with a better arrangement than this nightmare."

~

A Wanderer Returns

Jhee, Kanto, and Mirrei gathered in the sitting room, going over the backgrounds of prospective birthing helpers for the baby. Kanto examined swatches and furniture for the nursery. Jhee projected one profile for a pair of caregivers in front of Mirrei.

"How about these two?"

Mirrei gestured through their background, then threw out their file. "No."

"What was wrong with those two?"

"Nothing if you are a fan of human trafficking." Jhee stared at her with consternation. "See here. Doublefire Caregivers has a history of ethical and labor violations as well as hiring and exploiting refugees and undocumented Fire Folk."

"I hadn't realized that. Are all the employment and birthing helper agencies corrupt?"

"Not entirely. Be more careful about which agencies you are getting the nannies from. Look, really look into their backgrounds."

"I thought I was."

"Let me see this list. No. No. No. You have to be better at checking out the agencies they come from."

"Is there a list?"

"Yes. The Blue Waters Foundation and the Forging Forgiveness Project put out a list of ethical labor agencies, including nanny services. They rate various employment agencies on their human rights record."

"See. Therefore I left it to you," Kanto said.

"I can't save every starfish. I can only ensure our servants are sourced from a reputable and ethical agency."

Mirrei winked. Jhee could not have believed how much she had changed and grown in such a brief time. She must admit it was very attractive. Mirrei had also filled out nicely, her figure now more on the traditional side than dainty. She no longer felt as if you might break her if you held her too close. Jhee leaned over and gave her a kiss. Kanto cleared his throat.

"What do you guls think of this layout?" He placed his conch flat for them to see. "I'm thinking one of these two color schemes."

"We want the crib over here so we can get the positive energy from the western wind and waves."

Jhee browsed at the layout and moved the crib. "No, we want the crib over here so we can watch the water feature and the sunrises while we are nursing."

"You are both wrong. We want the crib precisely where I put it, or else everyone who goes into or out of the room will trip over it and wake up the pouchlings. You want to nurse while looking at the sun or getting positive vibes? Move the drench nursing chair. What's wrong with you two? I thought you two were supposed to be the practical ones?"

"What about these two?" Mirrei brought up another caregiver profile.

Kanto grimaced. "Blessed Makers, what are they wearing?"

"We are not hiring them for their sense of fashion."

"You're not. I suppose I could put a detailed outfit list for them to follow."

"Are you telling me you don't already have a series of drej baby jumpers already planned?"

Kanto plopped his sketchbook on the table and opened it to pages of baby onesies. "Plenty. I'd be constructing them now if you two would let me."

The alarm on all their conchs went off. "Nutrient up."

Kanto sighed and made a face. "Do I have to?"

"Yes," Mirrei said. "We put you on a strict dietetic regimen with a strict supplement schedule."

"I forgot once. Once."

"You forgot 'once' a day for two tides and nearly passed out."

Jhee pulled out the chart. And looked at the nutrient schedule. "Your turn."

"Done." Mirrei leaped to her feet. "You've got two choices. Kelp or seaweed?"

"I'm just on bed rest. I'm not an invalid. I can make my own snacks," Kanto said. Mirrei folded her arms. "Kelp."

"One nutrient blend and kelp salad coming up."

Jhee pulled out the pill organizer and lined up the proper dose of prenatal vitamins for her and Kanto to take. "It will be over soon. The appointment's all made at the breaching center. They have a lovely water breaching room where you can pass on the sac to Mirrei."

"Then she gets to be the one everyone's hovering over."

"I remember there was a time you would have relished being the center of my attention."

"I still do."

The water chimes sounded. They heard the servants go to answer it. A moment later, Mirrei came to the door of the room, bearing Kanto's snacks. She seemed dazed.

"Who was at the door?"

Mirrei looked at the floor. "Don't be mad."

The sitting room door opened wider. Shep stepped inside. He gave a sheepish smile.

Kanto rose from his chair. "What is he doing here?"

"Kanto, no." Jhee made him sit down. "You can't have any stress right now."

Shep tugged at his arm hairs. "You look well. I expect you will breach soon."

"What do you want?" Jhee asked.

Shep eyes were wet with tears. "I want to come home, Jhee."

23

A Case Argued

"You've got some nerve." Kanto tried to rise from his chair again. Jhee stopped him.

Jhee stalked over to the door and forced Shep out into the foyer. Mirrei went inside with the snacks and closed the door.

"Is this your home now? Or just a place for you to breeze into between bouts of getting your head bashed in and rutting with deviants?"

"I deserved that."

"First Makers' blood, you did. Do you need money?"

"Your allowance has been more than generous."

"Then what?"

"I miss my family, Jhee."

"Or do you just have nowhere to go with no one else willing to take your raggedy tail in?"

"I've been staying at the veteran's hostel at first. Then Sharlet's been letting me stay with her and her family. I've been going to counseling."

"Good for you." Jhee turned away, then turned back. "I begged you to confide in me. I begged you to get counseling. You threw your family away for a fight and a fling with a woman who turned out to be a psychopath. If she hadn't, would you even be here right now?"

"She meant nothing to me. I know I messed up, Jhee. I'm sorry."

"Sorry? You're sorry. Fine. Apology accepted. I'll double your allowance. So long as you never come here again."

"I don't want more money. I want my family back."

"You don't deserve your family back."

"What a world this would be if we all got what we deserved."

Jhee yelled in frustration. She stalked to the veranda entrance. He followed and placed a hand on her shoulder.

"Why?" she whispered.

"I don't know why."

"Bilge and cockle drivel. Was she that irresistible? Did you love her?"

"I love *you*, Jhee."

"What do you want me to do with that? Loving me wasn't enough to keep you faithful. Loving me is never enough. Loving me, raising me, wasn't enough to keep mamere and babere from drowning themselves. And it wasn't enough to make Jay stay around once they were gone."

"She meant nothing to me."

"Then, why? I have a way to get the truth out of you." Jhee rolled up her sleeves. She formed the gesture for the first sequence of a compulsion cypher. "They haven't geased you. I'll have the truth out of you one way or the other. You know I can."

Shep dropped his hands to his sides. "To know if I could. It was precisely because she meant nothing to me. I would know, and then I could walk away. It was after the raid, I felt pumped, on top of the world. I wanted nothing more than to be with you, but you were with Kanto *again*."

"So, this is my fault?"

"It's our fault. She was like a viper in my ear. It's no secret our sex life has been less than satisfying for years. When I met Kanto, I thought I had found the perfect solution for everybody. It turned out to be the perfect solution for everyone but me."

"I didn't want a second husband. I was fine with our marriage as it was."

"Were you, Jhee? Could you have been once we got to court and the Imperials' intrigues and scrutiny abounded? A place full of the conniving who all wanted to know about the status of your house."

"I would have dealt with it."

"You would have done what you've always done, sublimate your needs to mine or your duty. No matter what you wanted."

"You brought him in. Insisted."

"And you did what you usually did, your duty. Until you didn't. I'm not sure if I thought it all the way through how it would truly make me feel. When I got jealous, I thought I could plow through it. At first, you were so standoffish to him. I thought it would be a few months, maybe a year. You constantly announced your commitment to offloading him once we reached the capital. I thought that would be it. You'd have your needs met, and we might get children out of it. Then once we got to the capital, it would just be the two of us again, possibly plus pristine children. Except it wasn't. It backfired. You grew fond of him, of both of them. You came in with Mirrei in tow, and then it became clear neither one was going away."

When Jhee refused to do her duty, she nearly broke the Far Reaches. Her duty had been to marry a Crag Hall heir; instead, she eloped with Shep.

"You should have said something," Jhee whispered.

"What? I owed you, Jhee. You don't think I know that. You saved my life. Gave me a loving home. I should have been grateful. You deserved to have your needs met."

"'What a world this would be if we all got what we deserved?'" Jhee quoted. "This whole arrangement was your idea."

"I know. It wasn't supposed to be like this. I wasn't supposed to be here!"

"What?"

"I chose him because I didn't want you to be alone after I…"

"After you what? Left me?" Jhee finished. Shep's deflated posture and inability to meet her eyes seemed to confirm the assumption. Then she looked closer at his trembling hands. Memories from when he first brought Kanto around came to the fore. In preparation for their relocation to the capital, he had given away many of his war souvenirs and keepsakes from his sisters. He had been preparing to leave her, but not by walking out. "After you killed yourself."

"Yes," he sobbed.

Emotion seized up Jhee's throat. She rocked back on her heels. Despite her near-obsessive inability to let a mystery go, to forgo the chance to solve a puzzle, if Shep had gone through with killing himself, she would have failed to solve the one puzzle that meant the most to her. He had needed her, and she had been so absorbed in her job and her duty she almost missed it before it was too late. Had she been too quick to lay the blame solely at his feet? "You—How—"

"Throw myself into the sea for one last dive."

Drowning. Like Jhee's parents who had filled their pockets with rocks and swam out to Wailing Point. Like Ghele. Like Gwyn and Gloriana. Jhee wanted to flee, then spun back to face him. "The sea," she whispered.

"I know. You understand the lure of the Storm Child and the ones beneath the waves. I've seen you gaze over the vast waters of the sea folk's domain. I've known what was in your mind. To be one with the sea, to rejoin your family under the ocean. I tried more than once. I adapted. Gills. That's when I realized how extreme the changes were, what they did to me could bring about. Ursula talked me back from the brink."

The Unlikely Heiress and The Diving Boy

Jhee reeled, grasping at the veranda's balustrade for equilibrium. She scraped her hands against the gritty stone. The painful abrasions and the solidity of the material grounded her.

Shep took her hands and performed a minor arcane field dressing.

"When I met with the Captain the night he died, he was so bitter, resentful. He railed against his wife, his situation. He was a Consort Regent, and he hated the woman he married. I remember how much he had adored her in the beginning. He thought he would be fine with it. In the end, he resented her. They were full of nothing but venom for each other. She found him disgusting, and he found her vile. I didn't want that for us, Jhee. I wasn't sure how to stop it."

Jhee pulled her hands away. "And you thought Medea would fix us, is that it?"

"Not us, me maybe. I don't know. She tricked me. I came home from the raid that night. She had filled my ears with venom before that. How I was a burden, unneeded surplus. I had no role in the family anymore. I had been replaced by a younger, more handsome man. Then afterward, she was full of compliments. But it was what I wanted to hear. How useful and great I was. I alone had protected my family."

"Lobster drivel. I want to believe you. I might believe you if you hadn't already betrayed me with Miramar. What was your excuse then?"

"I was dumb, cocky, seastruck. I had gone to Mai, where I proposed and confessed my love. She laughed in my face. When I lost the lottery, I had thought it might change things. She rebuffed me again. You think I would have learned. Years later, when you and I seemed to have some semblance of happiness, Mai visited me. Some part of me still loved her then. I thought she realized she felt the same. It turned out what she cared about was that she lost. To you. When I realized that, it killed whatever feelings I had left over for her."

Miramar's mention snapped Jhee back into hostility. She clapped her hands slowly. "Are you done? You've had your say. Now what?"

"Please, Jhee."

The sting in her hands paled compared to the one in her heart. "Was Mirrei's crush only one way?"

"I already told you so, Jhee."

"Once a cheater. Always a cheater. I don't think I can ever trust you again."

"You can. I love you, Jhee. You believe you know about secret longing. For as long as you have loved me, I've loved you longer."

"A love so deep and abiding when Mai crooked her finger, you went running right back to her bed."

"Do you remember what you were like back then, Jhee? Once we came back from our newlyweds' holiday, you changed. You started treating me as she had, like a drench servant, a dirty little secret to be hidden away. If I wanted to be treated like that, I might as well have stayed with her. That's what she offered at first. She had to marry Crag Hall, but that was no reason for us to stop our relationship. She'd set me up some place nice and come visit me when she could. Sound familiar? I was her grimy secret, too. The hugs and the smiles and affections went away the moment we got anywhere near her family or anyone who 'mattered.' I think I was five minutes away from being sneaked in the servants' entrance when her parents weren't looking. Her family may have had lower social status than yours, but they were ambitious. Their daughter, the pride of their family, would not marry some diver boy who still stunk of the Brine. When her family refused suit, I knew it was only a matter of time before I lost her. My losing the lottery wasn't the whirlpool of fate. It was the Mitsus getting rid of an unwanted suitor."

"You two deserved each other."

"No, you two deserved each other. You're right. Miramar was passionate and funny and all about living life to its fullest. But she wasn't you. It could get fatiguing, keeping up with the Mai show. She was always on."

"Don't I know it." Jhee faced out into the night and focused on the water feature. "Once we returned from our holiday, several people almost gleefully informed me you'd been conscripted. After proudly declaring our marriage, I was berated for my stupidity at being taken in by an ambitious schemer who had only married me to get himself out of military service. In my insecurity, I believed them."

Shep moved close enough she felt his warmth behind her. "On some level, they were right. My plan was to hop a smuggler's boat out of the isles. I hadn't gone to the academy to woo you, but to say goodbye. Though, I may have had some vague notion of you coming with me. When I gazed longingly at your home, my sisters thought it was envy. It was you. I always wondered about the pretty girl who took a stick and chased away the bullies with me and then needed someone to sit with her while the search team looked for her family."

Some youths from the Bracken family had decided to filch the catch a puny boy had been set to watch. Jhee had come upon the outnumbered boy trying to fend them off. Later, after the ferry accident, when everyone else was preoccupied, he made sure she wasn't alone. She used to think him a mute until he started appearing every time she and Miramar turned around during their early adventures.

Jhee faced Shep with a sharp turn then touched his jaw lightly. "You were Pip Shark, the gangly kid with the dirty skin always shadowing me and Mai?"

"Long after the rescue parties had stopped, I went out to the site of the wreck. I dove and dove until I recovered a turtle-shell locket. It was your sister's, and you used to wear it when she let you. I left it on your window."

"That was you?" Jhee's words hitched as she remembered finding the locket and presenting it to her parents. The only other trace of Ghele they found was a shoe. Having the necklace for Ghele's memorial had brought her family such peace. She clasped Shep's forearm for support without thinking.

Shep steadied her, then placed his hands on her shoulders. "They didn't start calling me Pip Shark, Patchy the Pip Shark actually, until after that. Because of those dives, I caught pneumonia and reef rash. I was sickly, a runt, for a while, barely able to help my family, a burden. Then my glandular bloom happened. Our first meeting was you chasing away my bullies with a stick. Yes, we met while I was bringing in the family nets, right before those bullies jumped me. The story you like to tell of our first meeting with me laying bounty at your feet wasn't. That was a carefully staged meet to get your attention.

"You never noticed me until I filled out. I mooned over you for years as the skinny diver boy with the temporary skin condition. Then I got sleek and thought you'd notice me. You didn't. She did. I tried to wait for you. Finally, I got tired. Miramar was as fun as she was unapologetic in her interest. It felt nice to be the one pursued for a switch. When I won that swim meet, my social currency went up. When I dated Miramar, my social currency went up. At last you noticed, but by then, we were Miramar and Shep. I became as much a prize for her as she was for me. If we broke up, that went away."

"I noticed. Mai noticed you too. I decided to step aside. I thought I was being noble. The last thing I wanted to do was quarrel with my friend over a boy. She usually won anyway. She wanted it more. Miramar always wanted it more. No matter what it was. It meant more to her, and with her demanding family, why not step aside and allow her something she clearly wanted more than I did? My ambivalence made me doubt if I'd be a satisfying partner or show you the affection you'd want. No, she would make the better romantic partner for you in every measure, so why risk our friendship."

"Did it ever occur to you to get my input? Or declare an interest and let me decide?"

"You would have never chosen me over her unless you had no other choice."

"How do you know? You never asked. Jhee, I didn't think you cared until a jealous Miramar is accusing me of flirting with you and exploiting your crush."

"I thought I had hidden it. I didn't want the situation to be awkward."

Shep roared with laughter. "It was nothing but awkward!"

A mixture of laughter and sobs overtook Jhee.

"Thank you," she whispered once the reaction passed.

"We can't keep doing this." While Jhee had raised her voice, she tempered her tone with humility and compassion, "I have nothing more to give you. I've got two spouses, a brace of pouchlings on the way, and a new judicial division to set up. Shep, I can't manage you too."

"It doesn't have to be permanent," Shep said. "I'm asking for a chance to earn my way back as a member of this family. Besides counseling, I've been taking child-rearing courses and household management and jealousy exercises. I've looked into trust breach services and infidelity reconciliation. I've been doing the work. Jhee, I screwed up. I know you've been looking into caregivers. Well, I've been working on getting a caregiver certificate—from a reputable and ethical agency, of course. I'll work part-time and maintain the same living situation. I'll stay with Sharlet for now. And if at some point—after I've earned it, if you let me, if you want me too, I'll move back in. Whatever it is you need me to do. I'll do it."

"Of course. Sharlet always lands on her feet, doesn't she?" Jhee shook her head, then continued, "It's not my decision alone. You didn't just hurt me or breach my trust. We are a family unit. I'll discuss it with Mirrei and Kanto. It's them you need to convince. I'll abide by whatever they decide. Plead your case to them, not me, but after the breach. Kanto can't have any stress right now."

Jhee withdrew inside with as much dignity as she could muster. In the foyer, she fled to her bedchamber. Her door creaked, and she realized Shep had followed. He waited beyond the threshold. As she went to close the door, he blocked her with a firm, gentle hand on the main paneling. Shep brought his hand down to cover hers and stroked the back of her hand.

"Don't. I barely remember a time when I wasn't in love with you. My feelings for you unmoor me in a way nothing else does. You know it, and that's why I can't have you around."

Jhee freed her hand and sought to close the door by pushing higher on the edge. Shep rubbed his head against her hand. Despite herself, she brushed her knuckle along his facial scar.

"Love unmoors us all, my Lady," Shep said and cupped her face. They kissed. He pressed against her, letting her feel his desire.

This was the Shep she hated, the one she never got enough of, the one to whom she was always vulnerable. Jhee wanted to push him away and scream for him to leave the bedchamber. The action though between her mind and the execution, turned into them removing each other's robes.

She dreamed of that night, of them meeting alone. Of him telling her, she was the one he truly loved, of them making love, and finding a priest the next morning.

Jhee awoke before Shep did and went to work on her orrery. A minor noble and divers' son not far removed from Briny Town had married the plain daughter of a wealthy family never meant to inherit. This had been the opposite of how Jhee thought this would work out so many years ago. Kanto would be her First and the career man, while Shep would be the stay-at-home caregiver. Mirrei was a world traveler, bolder than them all, while Jhee nested.

New Rules

Shep awoke to an empty bed. Mirrei's day. He had to leave soon. With a slow sweep, he took in the extra room details. It showed the younger spouses' influence everywhere, now. From lacy window treatments to lilacs, the room contained little flourishes and decorative touches Jhee never considered. Whatever room she designated as hers had always been laid out functionally and pragmatically. A little chair next to her desk held Kanto's lute. The two Findari green and gold polyglass mosaics and a seashell doll were likely Mirrei's contribution.

After morning push-ups and sit-ups, Shep meditated for a few minutes. He had stopped frequenting the berserker gyms and the arena. His calm had to come from other means. He had so much work to do on himself and on regaining the household's trust. There was still also stamping out the last of Medea and Hammad's operation. Even if Shep had wanted to with Hammad gone and Medea in jail, the entire operation was in disarray.

The thought of Hammad still out there wound Shep up, so he meditated again before he slipped from Jhee's room.

Kanto caught Shep sneaking out. "Let's tame that mane of yours."

Shep helped Kanto down to the salon where two green blended concoctions awaited with a note from Mirrei, which read, "Pick one."

With a disgusted face, Kanto downed one bottle. He pushed the other toward Shep. "Breakfast with me."

Once Shep choked it down, he asked, "What is this we're eating?"

"Mirrei's green drinks. Don't ask for more specifics than that. I've got some maye steaks we can throw on the grill once Mirrei goes to work." Kanto paused, then straightened his posture. "So, she's taken you back in?"

"Subject to your and Mirrei's approval."

"You brought me in as a second for when your tail screws up. I'm fulfilling my role. Guess what? You screwed up imperially. You and I need to work something out."

"I know I need to do right by her and by you. Is there anything I do to make up for what I did?"

"Yes." Kanto moved into his space. He raised his gaze to Shep and stood there in challenge. "Unbreak her heart."

"I wish I could."

Kanto lowered himself and his swollen belly into the barber's chair. "You coward."

Shep rested his hands on the countertop and hung his head. "That I am. I never claimed to be otherwise. When I mocked you being a soldier, I had no right. I jeered those principled refusers—those who objected to serving—as loudly as anyone; meanwhile, I prayed I'd never have to join."

The young man rubbed his hand over his pouch in a circle. "Medea tried to get to me too while you were in custody. 'Surely, it must have occurred to you, Bright Harmony, that maybe, you had not won her over. She was simply biding her time until your grandmamere died. That, of course, was the deal she made with your grandmere. Marry you and become her heir. Now that she has inherited, she can return to her original plan of seeing you married off to another.'"

"I don't know what else I can say."

"Shep, the pouchlings are moving. Do you want to feel?" Kanto asked.

Shep's breath caught. "May I?"

Kanto placed Shep's hand on his breach pouch. The pouchlings undulated under Shep's hand like a wave. A fresh life wave on waters made indivisible. A smile twitched on Shep's lips.

"Do you feel that?" Kanto asked.

"I do," Shep said, tears welling up in him.

"It's not just the movement. It's the fear that comes with the knowledge you're ushering another of the Makers' creations into the world. That they're depending on you."

"Yes," Shep said, unable to hold back the tears.

"You feel that, too, don't you? The protective instinct?"

"Yes."

"The certainty you'd destroy anyone who dared harm them?"

Shep nodded. "Fight. Protect. Survive. But more than anything, protect."

Kanto removed Shep's hand from his breach pouch. "These pouchlings matter more than any of us. I won't let Jhee's weakness for you jeopardize them. Hurt this family again, there will be no reprieves or pleading your case to her. There won't even be a body. Do we understand each other?"

"If I hurt this family again, I'll do it myself," Shep paused, then added, "denme."

"Denye," Kanto replied.

Kanto held out his hands to Shep. They clasped forearms, then lightly touched their foreheads together enough for their esca to brush. Then Kanto seated him for a shave and haircut.

~

After the breach and once they were certain Mirrei's pouching had taken, Jhee allowed Shep to return and speak with the rest of the household. Shep made his case plain. Mirrei and Kanto did likewise. They were civil, and Jhee contented herself to a limited role as scribe and arbiter.

Shep would be taken off the marriage charter. His name would not be on the birth charter either. They would revisit the issue if they had more children. He had no legal standing regarding the children. Not co-father, sire, or father of record. They would be allowed to call him uncle. In the case of any calamity befalling Jhee, Kanto, and Mirrei, only then would Shep be named guardian. Shep did not like it at first, but he thought it was fair and more than he deserved. She wrote up the new agreement which their advocates made official later. They still brought in another nanny to complete the pair.

24

———

∼

A Friendly Game

They received an Imperial lunch invite from Kanto's friend Aiaku. It had a hand-written note. "Not one of those luncheons. Please, come. Whole family welcome."

The invite named them all. Jhee wanted to refuse anyway. She had had enough of the Imperials, their invites, and their intrigues.

"He did save our lives," Kanto said in the transport on the way to the yacht.

Aiaku had mobilized an amphibious rescue operation for them at the House of Knives when Mirrei told him Kanto was in trouble. Her husbands may not have escaped Medea's clutches without it. That counted for much with Jhee. What she feared was the hidden cost attached.

"To which he will expect no end of gratitude," Jhee replied.

"He's not like that."

"We'll see." Jhee patted Kanto's hand at his sad face. "If you say it, I take you at your word. I trust you. If he is your friend, he is my friend."

"Given how you treat your friends, Jhee. Perhaps it's best if you treat him like he's a royal."

Once the Imperial yacht docked, Kanto's friend Aiaku greeted them along with the same porter from the Summer Sojourn.

Aiaku held out his hands to Kanto, and they clasped forearms. "I'm glad you accepted."

"How could I not, Lord Aiaku?"

"Please, call me Aiaku-xan."

While this still meant they were on an external name basis, "xan" was a diminutive which denoted friendship and informality. Aiaku greeted the rest of their family in a similar, warm manner. They walked slowly and leisurely from the dock to the atrium, a suitably covered place for them to dine more or less privately.

"As you wish, Aiaku-xan. I hear we have you to thank for our timely rescue."

"Think nothing of it. I account you, Kanto, as a good and true friend of mine."

"Is that to which we owe some of our other wonderful fortunes?" Jhee asked.

"Not entirely." They reached the atrium doors. Aiaku paused with his hands on the handles. "My denbe would like to meet you both."

Kanto gave a sad smile. "Our family needs us. My situation has changed. I have other responsibilities now."

"I gathered." Aiaku inclined his head towards Mirrei's swollen belly pouch and smiled. "Please, I would still like our *denbes* to meet."

Jhee nodded to Kanto.

"All right," he whispered.

Aiaku pushed open the doors. A male in a mobility-assistance chair sat beside a stuffed high-back chair. Jhee heard the rattling of a dice cup. A moment later, a dark, smooth-skinned hand appeared from behind the high-backed chair and slammed it on the table to reveal the results of the throw.

"Amazing, you win again, Aeolus." Lady Amani peered from behind the chair at the newcomers. She raised the dicing cup and shook it. "Would you care for a game, Justicar?"

Jhee stopped dead in her tracks. Lady Amani set aside the cup and approached her. Jhee regained her wits and made a traditional bow. "High lady."

Lady Amani gave Jhee the polite acknowledgment of an equal. Jhee stayed in the bow, dumbfounded. "It's customary for you to rise now."

"Of course," Jhee stammered. "High Lady."

"Amani. And I may call you Jhee?"

"Yes. Yes."

"This must be your lovely family. Star Mirror, Bright Harmony, and Dawn Wolf. Did I get it right?"

"Yes."

"Aiaku, have the servants get the Justicar's household some refreshments.

They must be tired after their lengthy journey. I have things I wish to discuss with the Justicar."

"Yes, dear wife."

Aiaku escorted Jhee's household to the table. Amani had already started walking. Jhee hurried to catch up.

"Have you seen the hedge maze yet?" Amani asked.

"Not in full light."

"Then that shall be our first stop." Amani slipped her arm in Jhee's. They entered the hedge maze. "I will show you right to my favorite spot. At various times, one or the other of the Imperial branch's job is to see to the upkeep or make their own additions to the maze. This one was my contribution. Do you like it?"

"It's very lovely."

"Do you know what I love so much about it? One feature of this part of the hedge maze is a charm against eavesdropping."

"I hadn't known that."

"Now, you do. Mauled to death by a wild animal. I imagine with delight it was a rather painful way to go. Please, tell me she suffered."

"High Lady?"

"You're supposed to be calling me Amani. You have my sincerest gratitude. Lady Bathsheba was a rabid dog who needed to be put down. I see you are too polite to take such pleasure in such things. I had tried to see the deed done myself, but my hands were tied. We shall speak no more of it. Now that I know who had protected her, I can openly express my thanks. I tried to declare my support at the Fancy Foam Showcase. It wasn't until much later I learned you thought I was declaring myself the architect of your misery, not your ally. Didn't you wonder how you got released so quickly?"

"Yes, but I thought perhaps my mentor or the captain...." Jhee trailed off thinking about Captain Odo and Ursula. The Captain had outright said he hadn't.

"I thought I was wrong about backing you when you capitulated. Nice to know I wasn't. I know value when I see it. I must thank your man and Aiaku for helping me realize my mistake. Finding out who saved Bathsheba from me was a delightful bonus. As you learned, her support had a long tail. It needed to be to protect her from me. Also, don't worry about Zaria and her brutes. Without the Architect to back her up, you seem more than capable of dealing with her. She'll slink off. I'll take care of it if you want me to, but it will be best if you do so yourself."

Jhee glanced back towards the atrium and Aeolus, the man in the mobility chair. "Lady Bathsheba's handiwork?"

"Because she supplied exotic mood adjusters, Lady Bathsheba could always finagle an invitation to events, especially those teeming with younger spouses. While there, she socialized with the imperials and indulged in her favorite pastime, corrupting youths. We're not sure what she gave him. Something to calm his nerves? Something to make him play better? It took days to find Aeolus. After so long, there was only so much even the best healers could do."

"Amani, I don't know what to say."

"Thank you would be a start."

"Thank you." Jhee thought about it a moment, then added, "I don't know how I can repay you."

"Consider this a gift. Also, the offer Aiaku extended to your husband does not just apply to him. I could see a place for you here. I'm much more selective than others. My spouses number only two: Aeolus and Aiaku."

"I am honored, truly."

"Ah, 'no' then. I get it. However, would you be willing to be my partner for cards and gammancala? I would like to continue where our last game left off. I'm willing to stipulate that you folded in error. If you would be amenable, I would like to extend an offer to join my dicing club. We meet twice a week on different imperial isles."

"That would be acceptable."

"Lovely. Now let's return to the atrium and get some of those refreshments I promised. You fancy mango punch if I remember correctly. No Dundarian sea worms, thank the Makers. I ate them as a gag once, and everyone became convinced they were my favorite dish. I have them put out now as a prank to see who is actually foolish enough to eat them."

Jhee and Amani returned to the atrium and ate lunch with their spouses. Afterward, Amani and Jhee retired to play cards. "Jhee, where do you stand on the wall?"

"Nowhere anymore."

Amani took a long sip of punch and dealt their cards. "It's an unworkable mess. Those of us who oppose it must play the long game. The wall folks may have won for now, but we have planted the seeds which will grow. It starts with reaching out to them and the Fire Folk, knowing them, knowing what they want. For when the day comes to reconcile with them."

"You're a One Waters reformist?" Jhee said, wondering if she should have stated it so bluntly. Jhee picked up her cards and arranged her hand.

"Nothing so extreme." Amani looked at her cards, "But, perhaps with the little shakeup your little discovery caused, we might make a little forward progress."

"Instead of fifty serious candidates for the throne," Jhee said after she drew a card, "you are one of thirty, forty."

Lady Amani discarded. "Likely twenty-five or even twenty when it's all said and done. And lest you think me thoroughly altruistic, I did a thorough audit of your holdings before making my household offer."

"Why give the provenance back to the Halfmoons of Haddondeep? Why not use it yourself?"

"To blackmail Zaria? I've poked that bear enough for now." Amani laid down her cards, having made her trick. "They need my support. She and the Princess Regent leave me alone as long as I don't interfere or make a play for the throne myself."

Jhee made her matches as well. "But the Halfmoons are now back in the eligibility for the Sea Throne. How does that help you?"

Lady Amani smiled and took another sip of punch. "The Halfmoons have nowhere near enough support to be genuine contenders. They are just another vote."

This hand Jhee dealt. "Voters who owe you a debt of gratitude."

Amani arched an eyebrow and discarded a card.

Jhee surveyed her hand. It was workable at best. "Like me."

"No." Lady Amani laid her hand on Jhee's wrist when she reached for another playing card. "You owe me nothing. I still feel it is I who owe you."

Jhee nodded.

Amani returned to a more relaxed posture. "The Princess Regent doesn't quite have the electors needed to win the vote. Any scandal can derail her negotiations or cost her the votes she needs to ascend to the throne proper. Had she kept her temper in check, perhaps she would have won you over."

"I've heard she's quite charming when she wants to be."

"She is." Lady Amani took another sip of mango punch and studied Jhee. "From the runt of the litter to the inheritor of three, or is it four houses."

Jhee gazed up at the Maker Sphere. "I'd trade each to have my brothers and sisters back."

"Just so. All military?"

"Only two," Jhee replied.

"I must have been misinformed. Thank you and your family for your sacrifices on behalf of the Empire, regardless."

A cog clicked into place in Jhee's mind. Her mouth dropped open once she puzzled out with whom she had been dicing and playing cards. "Amani? General Amaneri Adama Arie. Amani, the ever-victorious."

"If only."

"Gwyn, one of my sisters, served with you on the Blue Sword. She was there when you…"

"Mutinied."

"Saved the ship and its crew from a captain who had lost her nerve mid-battle. Gwyn admired you greatly."

Next Move

Mirrei blocked the sitting room's closed double-doors. "Now, remember, you said you would keep an open mind?" she said.

Jhee, Kanto, and Shep passed looks between each other as they waited in the foyer to be allowed back into the sitting room.

"Just let us see it already," Jhee said.

"Okay," Mirrei said. She threw wide the sitting room doors and stepped aside.

Their full household, Jhee, Kanto, Mirrei, and Shep, surveyed the new arrangement of chairs and furniture in the sitting room. Mirrei waited, lips parted for them to speak. Irina placed a fluffed throw pillow on the relocated couch. Off to the side, Bax stood cap in hand while Dari supported herself with a standing roller.

Kanto entered the rearranged sitting room first. He inspected every relocated bit of furniture and new addition with much ceremony. Findari wall hangings replaced several military souvenirs. Cords and plugs had been secured or concealed. His performing seat had been positioned in between Shep and Jhee's two cushioned chairs with hers now facing the fireplace while Shep's remained off to the side. At last, he walked to the rocker chair that occupied the performing seat's former location.

"No," Kanto declared.

"You said you'd keep an open mind," Mirrei cried.

"I did," Kanto said.

Jhee and Shep gazed Sphere-ward. She sighed, knowing this just meant longer before she might be able to sit down for a relaxing read and some tea. Kanto strode to the performance seat and started dragging it. They rushed forward to stop him.

"You shouldn't be moving furniture so soon after pouching," Shep said.

"Neither should Mirrei, but you didn't stop her," Kanto replied.

Mirrei rubbed her stomach, now swollen even more by the nearly due birthing sac. "Correction: Bax and Irina moved the furniture. Dari and I supervised."

Speaking of the servants and other vital parts of their home, Bax, Dari, and Irina had hustled from the sitting room, closing the door behind them.

"There," Kanto declared again. While they had been distracted, he had swapped Shep's chair for the performing seat. The cushioned chairs faced the fireplace. Now, though, each husband's designated seat flanked hers.

Mirrei nodded, then Shep, and finally, Jhee. They guided Mirrei to the rocker. Everyone else took their seats engaged in their favorite relaxing activities: Jhee reading, Kanto playing, Mirrei embroidering, and Shep watching cooking videos. Once everyone was settled and comfortable, Jhee sent for tea.

After tea, Jhee retired to her study. She shut the door, leaving her spouses to entertain each other. She went over to the corner and pulled out a gaming table. On it, she had replicated the tile board as it had been in her showdown with Medea. Jhee had examined the crime scene images and had a simulation of the scenario Medea had enacted recreated in exacting detail. She had ended the game on her turn by taking herself off the game board. Deep inside, though, she wondered. One more move, and it had meant death for one or other of her husbands.

Sharlet had sacrificed Shep. Kaisonia had discarded Kanto.

Jhee seated herself at the tile board, where she lifted the piece she had been holding. The game had ended on her turn because she had chosen not to choose. If she hadn't, could she have sacrificed one of her husbands as their families had? She stared at the board and contemplated her next move. She held the piece over the board.

The End

Leave a review!

WANT MORE JUSTICAR JHEE?

EXCERPT: JUSTICAR JHEE BOOK 4

Please enjoy this excerpt from Justicar Jhee Book 4…

Death sails the high seas… Only Justicar Jhee, the Empire's foremost magic-wielding sleuth, can stop it making landfall.

Justicar Jhee and her spouses continue to cope with the capital and its challenges to their unconventional family. When a body is discovered in the ruins of her wife's ancestral manor, they must return to their home district to confront ghosts of the past.

Chapter 1

The jailer beside Jhee signaled to the one in the booth. She tipped her hat, and then the gate in front of Jhee slid open.

"Sign in, please."

Jhee tapped her credentials against the visitor's log.

"All personal effects and small items in the box, please." Jhee emptied her pockets, even those Kanto hid in the robe linings, and put them in the box. An instant manifest was generated that she had to sign off on. "Here's your claim ticket. You get them back at the end of the visit."

Another jailer gave her a quick pat down and sweep with a detection wand, then nodded to the other to show she didn't have any deadly items secretly hidden on her person. She wondered if Kanto's signature pockets would have gotten by them.

"You are an artificer, yes?" the warden asked.

"Yes," Jhee said.

"I'm not legally allowed to bind you, but I must ask that you refrain from any aggressive actions which might resemble cyphering or drawing. I'd also like you to wear this tag. It will change color in the presence of arcana. The guards are under strict instructions should any cyphering happen, both you and the prisoner will be subdued immediately. No exceptions. Do you understand these terms as I have given them to you?"

"Yes."

"Do you agree to abide by them?"

"I do."

"Good. Thank you for doing this, Justicar."

"I don't understand. She asked for me?"

"Ayup, that she did. You understand the position the throne is in. We would like to avoid a long drawn out messy trial. She offered to confess only if you were the one she could allocute to. Otherwise, she threatened to summon an army of advocates and solicitors which would have the crown tied up in courts and tribunals for years to come. She also threatened to name and shame the Imperial family. I've been asked to reiterate how much the Prince Regent prefers to avoid that and would take it as a personal favor if you could get her to confess."

If choosing the successor to the previous Empress had turned into a chill, bitter war, the Emperor's succession had been a hot and bloody one. A boy barely beyond his first jubilee had emerged as the winner.

The fallout from the IES and Medical Protectorate experiments still had yet to settle throughout the Blessed Isles. A great number of Imperials had died suddenly or took sudden retirements. Not everyone's involvement in IES business had come to light, but enough had that the rest ran scared. Jhee had half expected some mishap to have befallen Lady Vivyan-Rin Shodan before this. The heightened security was as much to keep her safe as to protect the public from her. Vivyan-Rin still must have some leverage.

Jhee entered the gray visitors' room. Vivyan-Rin was already there, shackled to the table. Vivyan-Rin wore the traditional prisoner's wrap robe. She leaned back and crossed her legs when the jailers shut the door behind Jhee. Jhee pulled out the chair opposite her and sat down.

"I'm glad you came. You should see the food. Nothing like even the simplest dish Shep could whip up. How is he doing, by the way? Has he swam his way back into the house or your bed yet?"

"What do you want?"

"I just wanted to see you again. How's your head feeling?"

Jhee regarded her with an ice-hard expression.

"You full slipped with a siren module in your head. We specifically screened against that when choosing siren module candidates. Wouldn't want it tearing its way through their brain and spinal column if they shifted. I'm so glad that didn't happen to you or that your head didn't explode back in Galleon City."

Jhee fought not to touch the surgery scar for her siren module. She had long since surmised the danger a templarite chain reaction might cause. The effect of an ill-advised skin slip, on the other hand. "I asked what you wanted."

"There is no need to be so unpleasant. How is your family? I meant it before when I said you had a lovely family. In another life, I could have seen myself with a family like that."

"They say you've offered to confess."

"Yes, that. They seemed keen on it." Vivyan-Rin held up her mangled hand. "They even had some very polite ladies ask me nicely."

Jhee swallowed. She felt a twinge in her fingers.

"But I don't want to talk about that. I saw you on the viewers the other day. read about you, too. I hear you will be a proud mama soon."

Jhee adjusted her robes and blanked her face to not give anything away.

"Don't be like that. It's so boring here. They won't let me near anything remotely sciencey. I guess they are afraid of what I can do with a little knowledge and ingenuity. And you know what? They're right."

Vivyan-Rin leaned forward and her eyes went dark umber. Jhee fixed Vivyan-Rin with a frigid stare while assessing the rooms' exits and objects either might use as weapons. The jailers faced them. One's hand hovered over a giant red button.

The madwoman tone faded from Vivyan-Rin's eyes. She grinned, leaned back, and held up her hands again. "As if I could artifice. I was never fantastic at cyphering or drawing in the first place. It's the practitioners like you who give us an awful name. They think we are all some mini goddess of arcana. Most of us can barely generate a spark. But then there are those like you. You have a thirst for it. Like I do for science."

"I understand the fear of magic. I understand why people distrust it. Yet, so far, the Empire's worst abuses were often done without it."

"Too true, Jhee. Too true. But if you believe it is Their design for us to know all and master all, you must also concede that I am also a part of it. My lack of conscience, a counter action, a correction to those who would never dare. I am the balancer of the equation."

Vivyan-Rin had been a brush with evil such as she had never experienced before in her entire career. Jhee recited statutes and cyphers in her head lest she forget herself. Her hands she kept still. Her normal habit of doing finger cyphering exercises might see the jailers rush the interview room.

"If you want to confess, confess. Why ask me here?" Jhee asked.

Vivyan-Rin feigned hurt. "I thought we had gotten close. That we understood each other. You should have killed me, Jhee."

"You belonged to the law."

"Drivel. Do you know why you couldn't? Because although you refused to admit it, we're the same. You had wanted to see the game play out. You wanted to know just like I did how the game would turn out. Which one of us would prevail. Who's will and wits and were stronger. Given the option of whether or not to play, you will always choose play. You will want to see it out to the bitter end. Even now you are still wondering how it would have turned out if we weren't interrupted. You can lie to yourself, and you can lie to everyone else, but you can't lie to me. I see through you."

"We're done here."

"Hardly, Jhee. We've only just begun."

"You murdered a pregnant woman."

"A pregnant woman, yes. Not the children inside her."

Jhee's lurched forward. "What?"

The jailers tapped on the glass. Jhee smoothed her robes.

"I figured that would get your attention," Vivyan-Rin said. "The Regent was always so short sighted in romantic matters. Two of my creations had bred. Most of you opted not to, or the procedures left you fallow. The Regent was fixed to wage war. She had determined to kill Ursula no matter what. Ursula went to her friendly, sympathetic counselor and confessed her fear for herself and her unbreached children. I hid her and took care of her. I made sure she and her offspring were safe until she gave birth. Of course, I had to protect the fruits of my experiments."

"Where are they?"

"I'll tell you, eventually. You just have to keep coming to visit me. Have them bring a recorder. I'm ready to give my confession now."

Jhee paused before fulfilling the request. "The face shifter mentioned something about my M-Prot records being expunged? I never did that."

"In due time. Now, you sit right down there and listen to me and take down everything I say."

Jhee sent for a recording device and a finger quill. "Shall we begin?"

Vivyan-Rin smiled. "It started back in the years before the Flower Wars."

Coming Soon

Thank You
Join the Swiftnesse Patreon community!

Thank you for reading this Book 4 excerpt! If you would like to read more, consider joining the Swiftnesse Patreon community – a tiered rewards program for avid readers and superfans. There you can get exclusive flash fiction and early access to scenes from my upcoming novels.

ACKNOWLEDGMENTS

Adam C., Anne K., Elizabeth Frenette, Joe H., Melissa V., Michael S., Molly K., Tina P., Val A.

ABOUT THE AUTHOR

TREVOL SWIFT is a sometimes-sassy author of fantasy who grew up in Connecticut. She graduated from WIT with a BS in Computer Engineering Technology and now lives in Eastern Massachusetts. In her spare time Trevol enjoys gaming of all styles, cosplay, reading, writing and dancing. She also likes to relax by getting creative, with drawing and storytelling among her favorite pastimes.

Follow her on BookBub to get notifications of new book releases and sales:
bookbub.com/authors/trevol-swift

You can also contact Trevol Swift at:

Website: swiftnesse.com

facebook.com/swiftnesse

pinterest.com/swiftnesse

twitter.com/Swiftnesse

instagram.com/swiftnesseauthor